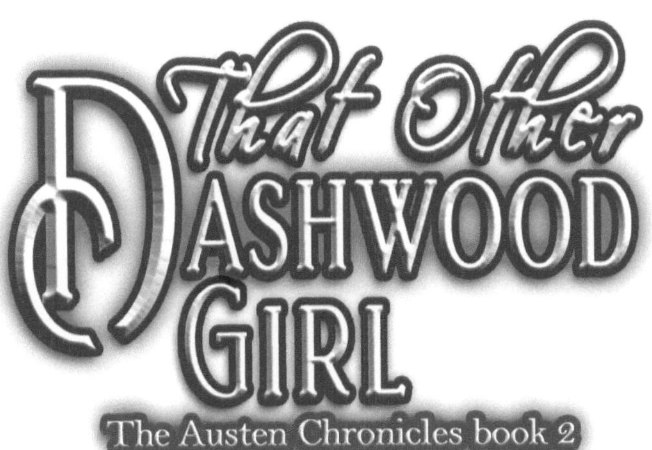

That Other
DASHWOOD
GIRL
The Austen Chronicles book 2

I0770287

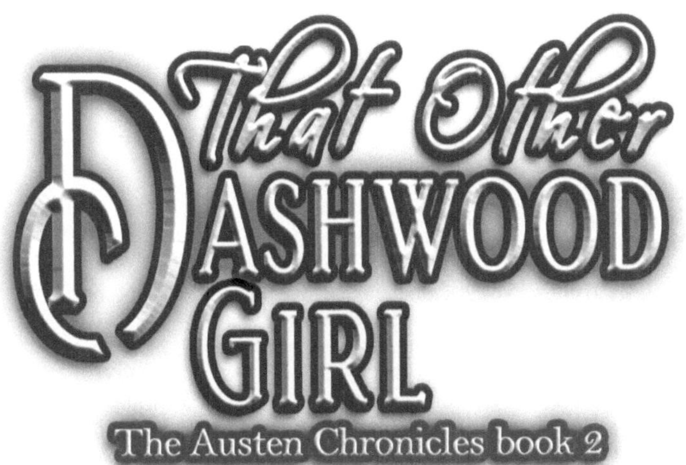

That Other Dashwood Girl

The Austen Chronicles book 2

4 Horsemen
Publications, Inc.

A.R. Farina

For Lea,
Thank you for going on this journey with me.
It's always better with you.

"Kinks Shirt" by Matt Nathanson.
Lyrics used with permission.
Thank you, Matt!
Maggie and I are eternally grateful.

Table of Contents

ACKNOWLEDGMENTS

When I started *Welcome To Mansfield,* I wrote it without thinking it would be a series. I made Maggie British because I wanted someone in my shared Austenverse to be British. When I decided to turn this into a series and when 4 Horsemen in general, and Beau Lake in particular, liked what I was doing here, I opted to leave Maggie as she was because I liked her that way, and it just added some fun to the universe.

Well, I am an American who writes in American English. This book is written in American English, but the characters speak using English terminology, and they attend school following the UK rules, and they drive on the other side of the road, but my knowledge base is limited. I am an American who does American things like weigh myself in pounds, not stones. I also know that American muffins look like and sometimes taste like cupcakes, and they are roughly seven million calories of deliciousness, whereas English muffins, which are my preferred muffins, by the way, are flat-ish, round-ish foods that one puts butter and jam on and are around 130 calories.

So, in order to thread the needle between American English and British lingo, I enlisted some folks from the UK to help me out. I've peppered them with questions about a lot of things to make sure I'm calling things the right thing. In fact, these folks agreed to give this book a first read to make sure I had it all locked down. However, I want to acknowledge that any mistakes that made it through are all my fault, and they were just really trying to help, and they did.

Thank you to James Carroll, Ria Carrogan, Mike Burton, Megan Gritti, Paul McGuigan, Emma Price, and Spider-Dan for being so supportive and patient when I asked stupid questions like, "What do you call the members of a village government?" or "What is sixth form?" or "Do you know what the chicken dance is over there?" If you are interested, there will be a note from the author section at the end of the book where I go over the terms and why I changed some things based on the brilliant feedback of these folks. Please make sure you don't peek ahead.

Finally, and I promise the book is about to start, I wanted to make a note about the music in this book as well. Maggie listens to a lot of music, and there is a running soundtrack through this book. If you haven't heard the songs, please go to my website www.arfarina.com/music and you will be able to see the playlist for this book. The songs are in the order they first appear in the book. Some of them come back around more than once, but I didn't include them twice.

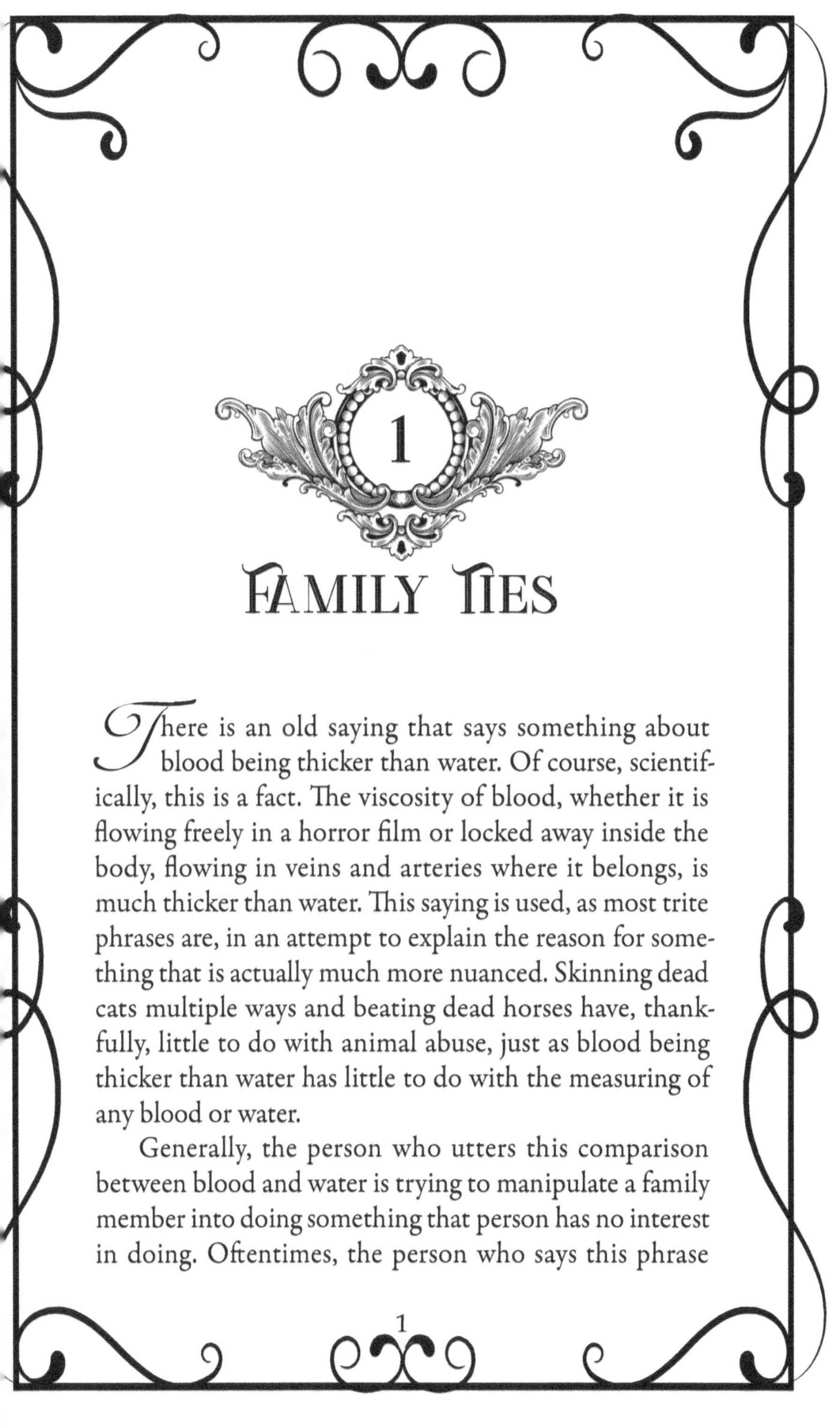

1

FAMILY TIES

*T*here is an old saying that says something about blood being thicker than water. Of course, scientifically, this is a fact. The viscosity of blood, whether it is flowing freely in a horror film or locked away inside the body, flowing in veins and arteries where it belongs, is much thicker than water. This saying is used, as most trite phrases are, in an attempt to explain the reason for something that is actually much more nuanced. Skinning dead cats multiple ways and beating dead horses have, thankfully, little to do with animal abuse, just as blood being thicker than water has little to do with the measuring of any blood or water.

Generally, the person who utters this comparison between blood and water is trying to manipulate a family member into doing something that person has no interest in doing. Oftentimes, the person who says this phrase wants his children not to bicker during a holiday meal. Other times, someone is asked to skip her best friend's birthday party to attend the wedding of a first cousin, once removed. These favors are mundane, and they often lead to the persuaded person having a fine enough time, and when that person looks back on the event, the person will feel some fondness without any rancor.

However, there are times when the "blood is thicker than water" card is played, and the ask is so big that the person being asked simply can't abide by the wishes of the asker. It may be that a car breaks down three hours away in the middle of the night, or worse yet, a crime might need to be covered up, and/or bail money is required. In these cases, most reasonable people agree that blood thickness is irrelevant, and the person in need of the favor should call a tow truck, a lawyer, or a bail bondsman. When things like this occur, family strife often follows, yet it is rarely long-lasting and becomes the fodder for an excellent story at the next family function.

There is still one more instance that is much rarer; just as the person is preparing to shuffle off this mortal coil, the person asks that extended family come together and live in harmony in an attempt to heal some long-standing rift. In some tales, the family dynamics are so broken that this is simply impossible. The person asking knows this but is just trying to leave this existence on a positive note. In other cases, the person's final wishes go unheard for a variety of tragic or petty reasons. More often still, the person who is tasked with doing one final favor for the rest of the family is simply not up to the task. Oftentimes, the person asked is the oldest, or was born male, or both. Science has yet to prove that being born oldest, or male, or both makes one more competent than younger siblings of any gender, yet cultures all around the globe hang onto this myth. It could be that the person is not very capable or that this person is easily manipulated. In extremely rare instances, the failure is the result of someone both being inept and gullible.

Rarities do happen from time to time, and thus, our tale begins with a gullible, inept firstborn who also happens to be a man asked to fulfill his father's final wishes. Being an easily led nincompoop, he sets in motion a series of events that will find one of his sisters near death, one caught up in an absurd love triangle even though she loathes love triangles and finds them tiresome in fiction and in real life, and one, who will ultimately be the heroine of this tale, packing her bags to attend a university in an entirely different country.

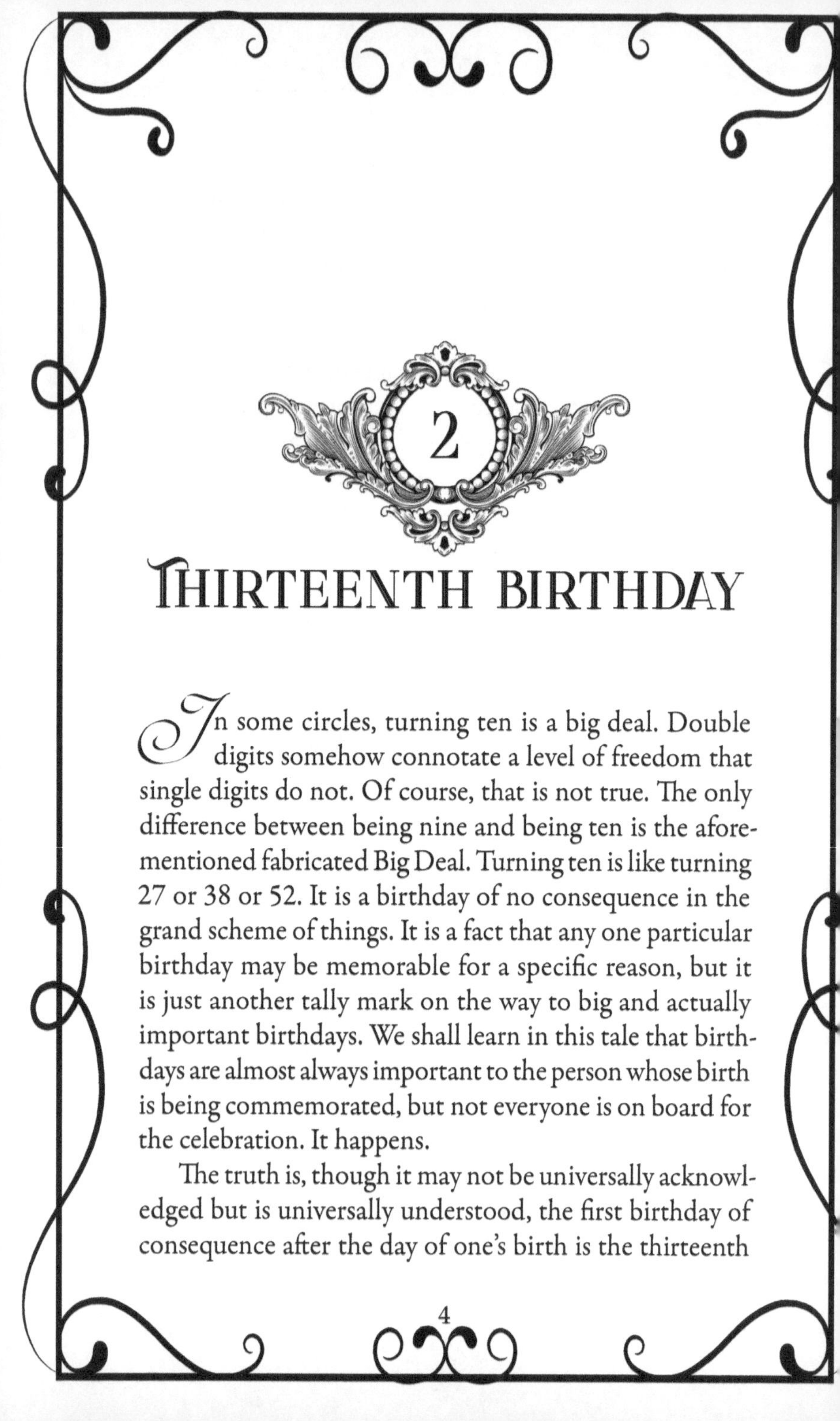

2

Thirteenth Birthday

In some circles, turning ten is a big deal. Double digits somehow connotate a level of freedom that single digits do not. Of course, that is not true. The only difference between being nine and being ten is the aforementioned fabricated Big Deal. Turning ten is like turning 27 or 38 or 52. It is a birthday of no consequence in the grand scheme of things. It is a fact that any one particular birthday may be memorable for a specific reason, but it is just another tally mark on the way to big and actually important birthdays. We shall learn in this tale that birthdays are almost always important to the person whose birth is being commemorated, but not everyone is on board for the celebration. It happens.

The truth is, though it may not be universally acknowledged but is universally understood, the first birthday of consequence after the day of one's birth is the thirteenth birthday. It is from that moment on that one is part of an official group. Teenagers are, for the most part, reviled by everyone who is not a teenager. Children long for the day they can join the exclusive club as they think it will bring them status and freedom, which of course it will, but not right away. They don't know that there are three tiers to being a teenager and that older teenagers dislike younger teenagers. Those who aged out of the club dislike those still in the club for a variety of reasons. Sometimes it is jealousy. Sometimes it is due to a lack of trust. Mostly, it is due to the fact that very few of them would ever go back to being a teenager if given a chance. Being a teenager is a six-year emotional trainwreck. While the reasons are varied, the fact is that when adults of any age utter the phrase "kids these days" in a disparaging way, they are almost always talking about teenagers.

So, it was that with all that hope and longing mixed with a lack of knowledge, our heroine, Maggie Dashwood, sat on her bed with her sketch pad on her knees, waiting for the clock to turn over to midnight. She had actually set a countdown timer at midnight the night before, so she watched the numbers click down on the screen of her phone. She positioned a standing mirror at the foot of her bed to capture what she looked like in the final moments of what she considered her childhood. The yet-to-be-completed sketch featured a self-portrait of the back of Maggie's head looking into the mirror. The face in the mirror was blank. The picture featured the back of her head with her messy bun on top, pencils sticking out of it in several directions to represent the 12-year-old Maggie. The faceless young woman in the picture wore a Frida Kahlo self-portrait tee that Maggie had worn for the weeks leading up to this day as she worked on her sketch. It should have been laundered as the smell of 12-year-old girl was starting to soak into the shirt, but as the rest of her family rarely walked up to the attic room, and she only wore the shirt in her room for the past week, no one told her.

When the clock struck midnight, she wanted to have the face of a newly minted teenager with her hair down, instead of up in the bun, framed around her face staring back at her. In her best photo-realistic style, she included her print of Magritte's *Time Transfixed* prominently behind her head, just as the poster hung above her bed. She showed the clock as a mirrored image while having her own mirror above the mantle in the print. It took her several attempts to get it just how she wanted it to look. The floor in her actual room and the bed in the drawing had crumpled up attempts strewn about. She cheekily changed the time in Magritte's masterpiece from 12:43 to midnight. She didn't think he would mind, as surrealists don't mind subversion, but she silently said a prayer of apology and thanks to him just in case.

When the countdown timer hit one minute, she reached over to her tablet, where she had her streaming playlist ready to go, and pressed "play" on Matt Nathanson's "Birthday Girl." She wanted it playing at the right moment, and she didn't want to be distracted by hitting "play." The song started, and the drums and the "ohs" built up to a crescendo. By the time his crooning voice came through her Bluetooth speakers, she was positioned just where she wanted to be. She looked into her own eyes, trying to get a sense of this new person she was about to become. Had she spent her summers in Europe like most of the kids at her private school, she would already be 13, but she waited for the time to click down where she was in her ancestral home of Norland.

With 20 seconds to go, she took a deep breath and held it. She counted down in her head, not wanting to look away. She leaned forward to see if a wrinkle might appear around her eye or if a pimple would sprout suddenly on her cheek. The alarm sounded when she was only at three in her head. She gasped and whispered, "Two-One-Zero" quickly before she turned to silence the alarm. She picked up her pencil and turned back to finish her first work of art as a teenager.

As she looked up in the mirror, she saw her bedroom door swing open. The reflection of her mother faced her there. Maggie prepared to see her mother's angry face, annoyed that Maggie was awake at midnight. She had been moved up to the attic for this very reason. She made lots of noise at night, and her father's office was just below the attic space; thus, there was no one to hear her make all the noise or be bugged by the lights pouring under the crack in her door as she stayed up drawing, and dancing, and doing what she did. It took a few seconds for Maggie to realize that her mother wasn't angry; she was in agony.

"It's your dad."

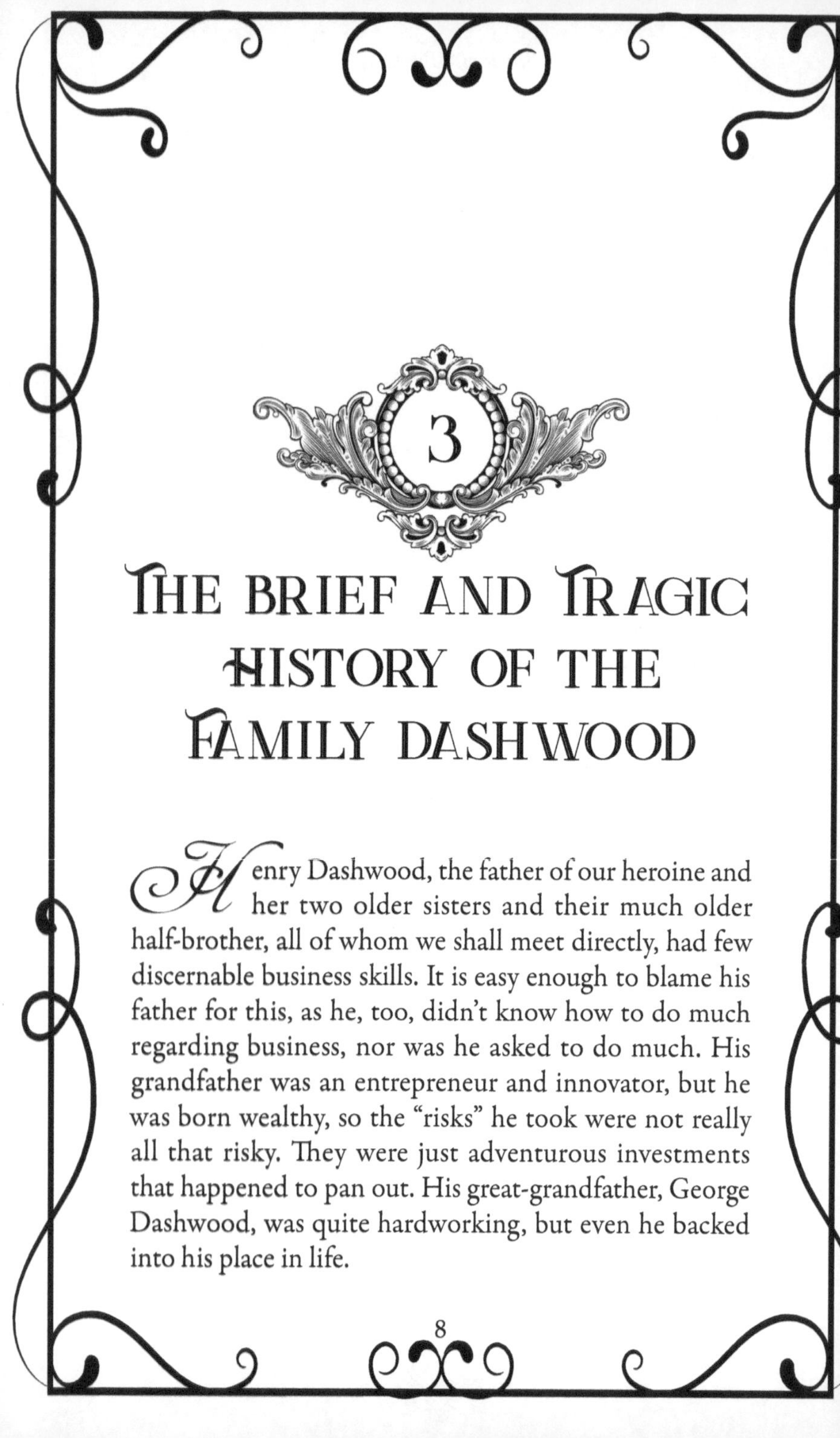

3

The Brief and Tragic History of the Family Dashwood

enry Dashwood, the father of our heroine and her two older sisters and their much older half-brother, all of whom we shall meet directly, had few discernable business skills. It is easy enough to blame his father for this, as he, too, didn't know how to do much regarding business, nor was he asked to do much. His grandfather was an entrepreneur and innovator, but he was born wealthy, so the "risks" he took were not really all that risky. They were just adventurous investments that happened to pan out. His great-grandfather, George Dashwood, was quite hardworking, but even he backed into his place in life.

George Dashwood did not start from the bottom of the heap. His wife was a minor member of a northern European royal family. She was minor enough that had there been royal watchers at the time, she wouldn't have been on their radar. Still, even the minor members of such families got a nest egg for simply being born. She met her husband while he was on a three-day leave during his time serving in the British Armed Forces. It was a whirlwind romance that culminated in what would be called a shotgun wedding in some parts of the world. Others would say she was in "trouble," and others would say she was "in the family way." Whichever term one used was irrelevant as they moved to England, where he promptly resigned his commission. They constructed a country home called Norland and formed Dashwood Holdings Corporation. Both the home and the business would be the foundation upon which the rest of the family and this tale are built.

They focused on real estate in those early days. They bought up defaulted mortgages and business loans all around Europe, capitalizing on collapsing economies after the Great War. Homeowners became renters on long-term leases, and businesses gave up ownership percentages in addition to paying reasonable rents on the buildings owned by Dashwood Holdings Corporation. By the time George Dashwood's son Richard was born, Dashwood Holdings Corporation had passive control of a variety of businesses while owning tens of millions of pounds worth of real estate. This afforded Richard the opportunity, upon his graduation from the University of Leeds with a business degree, to invest in manufacturing. The post-WWII boom was a boon for the Dashwoods, which led to the Dashwood Holding Corporation becoming a publicly traded company, affording the next several generations of Dashwood men the opportunity to do very little. Richard worked hard and focused on the business until the "will they or won't they" speculation about him and his long-time secretary resolved itself, and they married and had Paul Dashwood.

Paul Dashwood, whose mother never went back to work after she had her son, was determined that he wouldn't have to work as hard as she and her husband did. His mother doted on him and promised him that the name Dashwood was all that mattered. She came firmly down on the nature side of the eternal nature v. nurture debate, and so she assumed Paul would turn out just fine. As long as he went to Leeds and found a suitable woman to tolerate and procreate with him, all would be well, just as it was for all of the men in the Dashwood line.

Paul did go to Leeds. He did find a suitable woman called Linda. She, too, was a well-to-do woman from a well-to-do family whose job was seemingly to have a child who would be born well-to-do. Paul took his place at the family business but didn't really have a head for it. Had he been allowed to branch out, he would have been an excellent visual artist, but that simply wasn't anything other than "a fanciful hobby." And thus, that talent lay latent until the heroine of our tale unearthed it. Paul and Linda eventually had one son, Henry Dashwood, who, as we already know, wasn't very good at business and who, like the majority of the Dashwood men, won't feature prominently in person in this tale after this chapter, although his choices are the combustion engine that pulls the train along.

It is easy to speak of the men of the Dashwood family because, until Henry Dashwood, each generation featured one male progeny. That boy was tasked with going to the University of Leeds to earn a business degree so he could return to Dashwood Holdings Corporation to work as a minor board member until the day his father died, and he would be promoted to president. The job of the president was to stay out of the way of the CFO and to stay out of the tabloids.

So it was that Henry Dashwood married a woman, Billie, whom he met at the University of Leeds. She, like him and his parents, was the only offspring of a wealthy family. They graduated, and he was installed as a minor board member at his family company. There is an undeniable fact that 95 percent of all heterosexual men, to borrow a boxing parlance, punch above their weight. They almost all marry a woman who is either better-looking or smarter than her husband. In the case of Henry Dashwood, it was both.

Unlike her husband, Billie Dashwood took an active role in her family's business. They owned a media empire with worldwide reach. Even after their only son John was born, she continued to work. She majored in journalism. As a child, her heroes were Rosalind Russell's Hildy Johnson in *His Girl Friday* and Lois Lane. Eventually, she learned about real journalists, and she owed them all a debt of gratitude, but in her heart, she always aspired to be as amazing as Hildy and Lois. She loved the work so much that she often traveled the world to act as a producer, as her family didn't think putting the namesake of the organization on camera was a good look. It was during one trip to a warzone that she tragically met her end. We know that her last thoughts were about John, and she hoped that he would grow up to be a good man who understood the choices she made. We can report that neither of those things happened.

We can never know if John's mother had lived whether he would have grown up to be as kind and clever as she was. Instead, he spent two years being raised by the servants at Norland, who treated him like a spoiled little prince, something his mother would never have allowed. Eventually, his father sent him to a boarding school in Scotland. While there, John's last name and wealth made him incredibly popular, even though he was incredibly dull and dimwitted. He eventually ended up at the University of Edinburgh, breaking the family tradition of going to Leeds. He found his footing in his mother's media company, where he met and eventually married Sissy Ferrars, an executive producer with big ideas for how to use the media. While Sissy is not technically the villain of this piece, as there are several terrible people in the forthcoming pages who do their best to make things hard for the Dashwoods, it is a safe bet that no one will be lining up to buy "Team Sissy" shirts any time soon.

Henry Dashwood did go on to re-marry a woman who brought both him and Norland back to life. Samantha Chamberlain, a junior executive who had a skill for marketing and a passion for music, but alas, no talent when it came to its creation, who couldn't find her way into the music industry to promote the art she loved most, and who didn't have the heart for selling the junk she was selling, met Henry Dashwood during a mix-up. She was on a blind date, back when people still did that sort of thing. She thought he was the man she was supposed to meet, whose name was also Henry. She walked into the pub where she was supposed to meet her date and saw a handsome enough man with premature grey at his temples at the bar, nursing a drink. She sat down next to him, confirmed his name was Henry, got light-headed when they made eye contact, and smiled big, thus making him smile for the first time in years.

She realized pretty quickly that he was the wrong Henry, and while it was clear he was the wrong one for the date, he was the right Henry for her. It turns out the other Henry fell asleep on the tube and had a totally different adventure. We don't have time for that here. His life worked out fine, and he still tells the story of the time he fell asleep on the tube on his way to a blind date. It was a real *Sliding Doors* moment for him.

The day of the botched blind date began a lovely friendship that became a real, beautiful, love-filled marriage that produced three girls, one of whom we have already met. It was a marriage full of much more joy than sorrow, regardless of the sudden, shocking ending. So it was that while Maggie Dashwood was preparing to finish her first teenage piece of visual art, her father, who was as far as anyone could tell at the pinnacle of health, had a brain aneurysm, fell, and hit his head, never to wake again.

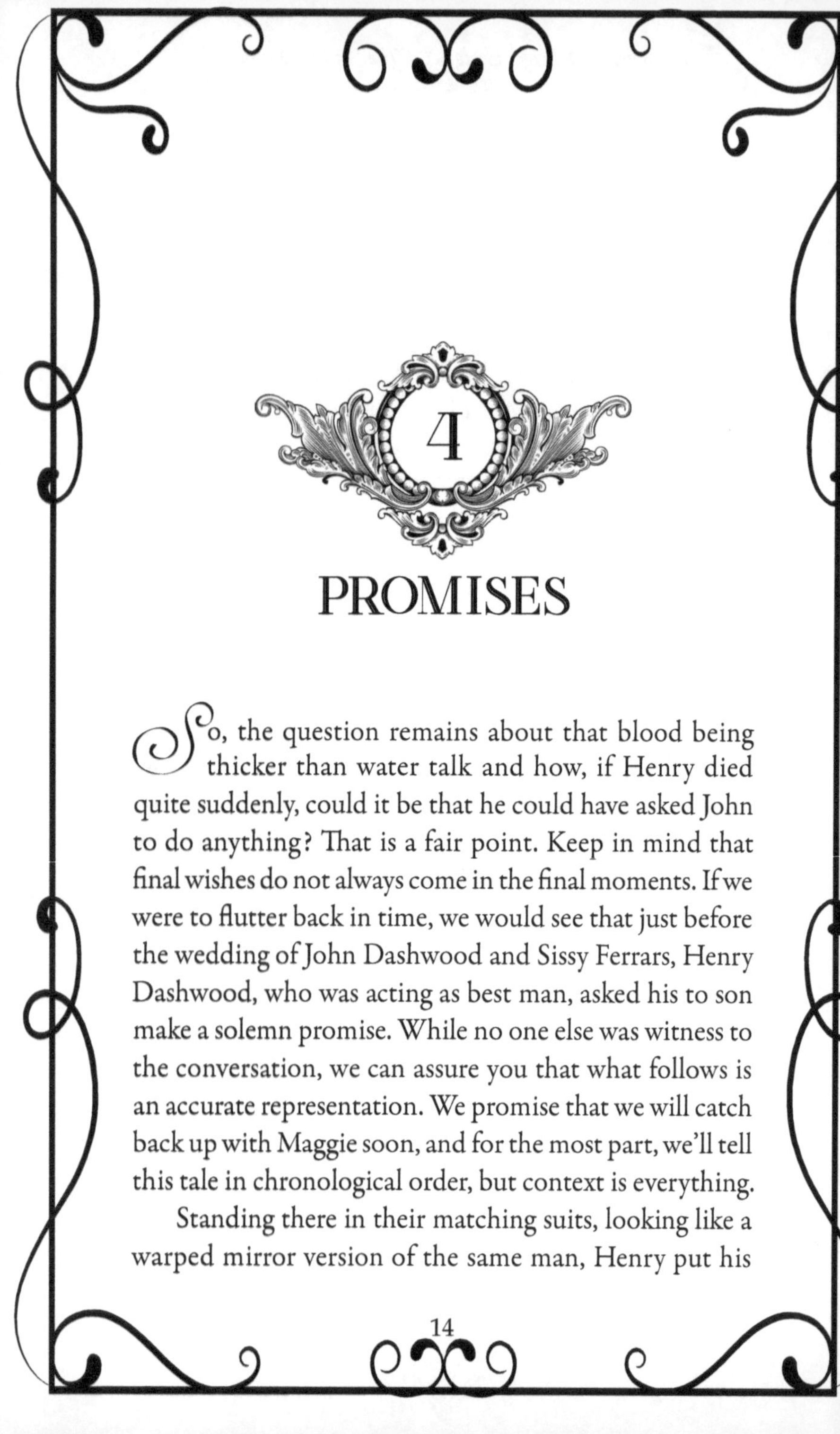

4

PROMISES

So, the question remains about that blood being thicker than water talk and how, if Henry died quite suddenly, could it be that he could have asked John to do anything? That is a fair point. Keep in mind that final wishes do not always come in the final moments. If we were to flutter back in time, we would see that just before the wedding of John Dashwood and Sissy Ferrars, Henry Dashwood, who was acting as best man, asked his to son make a solemn promise. While no one else was witness to the conversation, we can assure you that what follows is an accurate representation. We promise that we will catch back up with Maggie soon, and for the most part, we'll tell this tale in chronological order, but context is everything.

Standing there in their matching suits, looking like a warped mirror version of the same man, Henry put his right hand on his mirrored younger self's shoulder. "Son, before we go out, I need to say a few things."

John, who was not accustomed to any kind of affection from his father as a rule, felt a sudden tightening in his chest. Even people with emotionally vacant parents long for the day when their parents put their hands on their shoulders and look them in the eye to make an apology. John Dashwood never believed he would see the day, but he wished mightily for it to happen.

John reached out and put his right hand on his father's left shoulder. If anyone had walked in at that moment, it might have looked as though the elder Dashwood was teaching the younger how to dance. There would have been no need as John Dashwood took ballroom dancing courses at Sissy's insistence. Their first dance was quite lovely actually.

"Yes, what is it, Father?" John Dashwood never called his father dad, pop, or any colloquialism. The squeezing in his chest forced him to take a deep breath here, making his father think he was going to say more.

"First, I want to apologize to you…"

The vice in John Dashwood's chest released, and tears began to flow. He used the back of his left sleeve to wipe his face, but he refused to look away.

"…I was never a very good father to you. I was a miserable man whose heart was never fully mended until I met Sam. I know that isn't fair to you. You should have been enough. Your mother would be so disappointed in me."

"No, Father…"

"Don't. It's true. I know it. You know it. Everyone who knows me knows it. Your sisters know it. Your soon-to-be bride most assuredly knows it. I see how she looks at me.

I deserve those looks. It is fine, Son. Don't argue with me. Let me apologize properly as I should have done years ago."

John sniffed, wiped his face again, and nodded for his father to continue. Crying is a Dashwood trait, as we shall see, and being first born or last born or male has nothing to do with it.

"I want you to know that it is truly an honor that you've chosen me to be your best man. I don't deserve this, but when you called and asked, my heart swelled. I am incredibly proud of you for being a better man than I am."

"You are a fine man, Father. You just..." John trailed off.

"Don't make excuses. Yes. I just had a rough go, but so did you. I just assumed that your mother's money would make it better. I thought sending you to a school where people could care for you and give you the structure I couldn't would be good for you. I want you to be your own man, living in no one's shadow. I know your mother would be pleased that her money did give you a chance to stand on your own, even though it was no replacement for having parents to care for you. I am so pleased that you found your place within your mother's company and that you have found a way to honor her legacy."

We would be remiss not to jump in during this tender moment to say that John Dashwood did no such thing. His mother would have disliked the direction he and Sissy took the company. They moved away from real journalism and into political punditry under the guise of news. One can't know for sure how responsible John and Sissy were for Brexit because no one can see into the hearts and minds of all voters, but we can say that they certainly helped fuel a narrative.

"I just want you to know, Son, that while you don't need it, your place at Dashwood Holdings is secure should you wish to have it."

"Thank you, Father. I just thought once the girls were born that..."

"Well, Son, that is the other thing I wanted to discuss with you. Now that you are about to get married, and I am sure you will be a father yourself one day, I want to honor the tradition of the Dashwood family and pass the company down through you. I promised my father when you were born that I would do that."

"I ... don't know... What about the girls?"

"Well, Son, that is just it; we Dashwoods pride ourselves on being men of our word. It is why it is important to me that you know how sorry I am for how I treated you as a child and that I wanted to ask you to give me your word, here and now, that while you will own Dashwood Holdings, you will always look out for your sisters. I want you to have this as a testament to how sincere I am about my apology. I owe you this, Son. I trust you to be the man I wasn't. I know you will take care of my girls. You are so much better than I could ever hope to be."

John Dashwood, fully crying without reservation, nodded and hugged his father tight. "Of course, Father." He spoke into his father's ear. "Of course. I promise you here and now that I will make sure that Sam and my sisters are well cared for, just as you wish."

So it was that Henry Dashwood broke down crying himself, and it took some time for both of them to compose themselves enough to walk out and take their places at the front of the church. When they did finally emerge from the rectory, blotchy-faced and puffy-eyed, they were both smiling, leaving the guests to assume they had shared tears of joy, which is essentially true.

So it was that from that moment forward, Henry Dashwood never worried about a thing regarding the fate of his wife and daughters. His son was a Dashwood man, and Dashwood men were, as far as he knew, men of their word, and that word, once given, was clad in iron forever and ever, Amen. Of course, if that were true, this would be a short story. The heft of the tome makes it obvious that the word of Dashwood men was made of tissue paper, not iron.

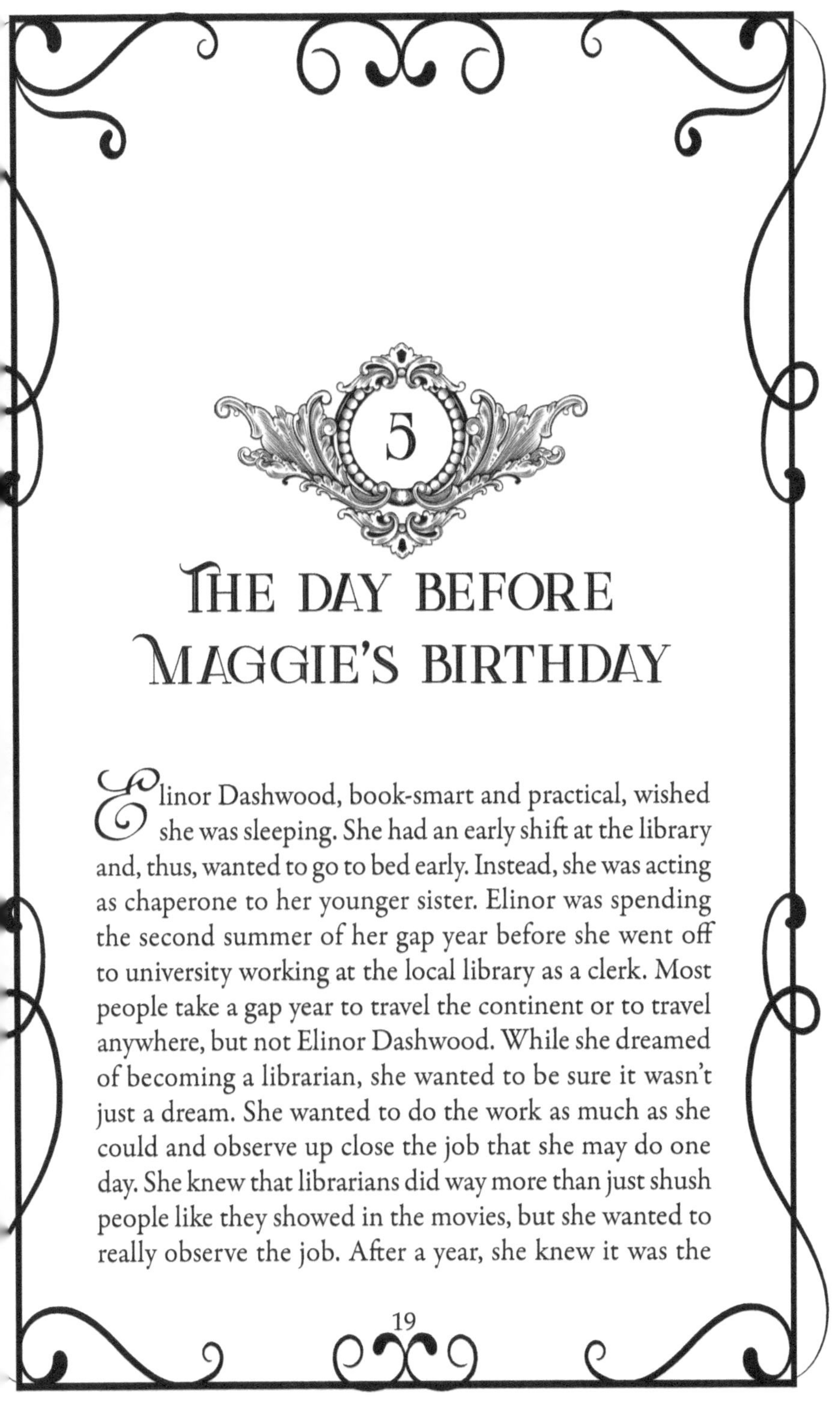

5

THE DAY BEFORE MAGGIE'S BIRTHDAY

Elinor Dashwood, book-smart and practical, wished she was sleeping. She had an early shift at the library and, thus, wanted to go to bed early. Instead, she was acting as chaperone to her younger sister. Elinor was spending the second summer of her gap year before she went off to university working at the local library as a clerk. Most people take a gap year to travel the continent or to travel anywhere, but not Elinor Dashwood. While she dreamed of becoming a librarian, she wanted to be sure it wasn't just a dream. She wanted to do the work as much as she could and observe up close the job that she may do one day. She knew that librarians did way more than just shush people like they showed in the movies, but she wanted to really observe the job. After a year, she knew it was the perfect profession for her, and she was ready to head off to Aberystwyth University in Wales to earn her B.Sc. in Information and Library Studies with a plan of going to City, University of London for her graduate degree. The one-year delay was worth coming up with an excellent plan. She loved a good plan.

Marianne Dashwood, prone to melodrama and lovesickness, was coming in just before curfew, much to Elinor's chagrin, from a night out with a boy she thought she liked. She was trying to make sure he liked her back enough that they would "make their relationship last" once they each went to different colleges the following year. Marianne, having finished up her GCSEs, earned A levels in Performing Arts and so she was off to college to study that. The boy, whose name is irrelevant here as he will never again appear in the pages, was going to study Economics. He would be very successful for a short time. Marianne would cyberstalk him occasionally until she discovered he ended up in jail for securities fraud.

She didn't see her father collapse and hit his head, but she found him lying in the front hall. She tried to scream but couldn't. Her legs folded in on themselves. She wept and gasped for breath. She couldn't find the power to pull herself up, so she sent a text to her mother, knowing that Sam Dashwood slept with her phone on full volume at all times. It read "HELP."

As her younger sister tried to catch her breath and do anything remotely human, Elinor knelt down next to their father and began chest compressions. She wasn't sure if it was the right thing to do, but it was a thing to do, and doing things was Elinor's forte. It turned out that it was neither right nor wrong, but it didn't do any further harm.

Sam Dashwood, a light sleeper, wasn't asleep because her husband wasn't in bed, and her two eldest children were not home. She heard him get up 20 minutes prior. This happened often. Henry couldn't sleep, which meant Sam couldn't sleep. They discussed having separate bedrooms, but they thought it sent the wrong message to the girls. The girls were all capable of understanding this quirk, as they knew of their father's insomnia and their mother's propensity to wake up at the slightest noise. She heard the front door open and close when Elinor and Marianne arrived. Seconds later, her phone made the water drop sound, which was Marianne's specific text sound. Sam, who was on her phone at the time, reading an article in *The Guardian* about some of the things her stepson and daughter-in-law were up to at their media empire, saw the text appear just as the water drop sounded. She was on her feet and out the door throwing the phone down on the floor, cracking the screen.

She sprinted down the hallway and to the grand stairs that emptied into the front hall. From the top of the stairs, she could see her husband lying motionless on the ground with Elinor pushing frantically on his chest and Marianne curled into a fetal position, clutching her phone, shaking and in shock. Sam's insides turned to liquid. She dropped to her knees on the landing. Afraid she would fall down the stairs and leave her children with two dead parents, she slid down on her backside.

When she arrived at the bottom, she crawled over to Henry's body. There was a trickle, not a river, of blood coming from his head. He was still warm. She assumed, wrongly as we know, that it meant he would be okay. She pried Marianne's phone from her hands and held it up in front of her daughter's terror-filled face to unlock it. Due to the movement of the convulsing and the tears and snot on her face, it took several tries. She didn't need to go through this process as emergency calls work on an unlocked phone, but Sam wasn't thinking particularly clearly. Sam dialed 999 and did her best to explain exactly what was happening.

The dispatcher asked questions that Sam tried her best to answer, but no one actually knew anything. After they determined that Henry had a head wound, they instructed Elinor to stop compressions. Unsure of what to do, she slid across the floor to her middle sister, who was still shaking and sobbing. Elinor positioned Marianne's head onto her lap and stroked her hair, trying to be calming. The ambulance took many minutes still as they were quite far out in the country. Sam looked at the grandfather clock in the front hall and realized what time it was and what it meant.

"I'll get Maggie," she said to Elinor, who also realized what day it almost was.

"Oh..." She couldn't finish. There was no word that could really follow it that could express the anguish she felt for her sister who was about to turn 13 and who would have this mark on her birthday for the rest of her life, for her other sister, who would surely need medical attention herself considering how hard she was shaking, and for her mother who had to still be a mother instead of a distraught wife.

Sam waved her hand. "I know, honey. Just..." She gestured at what she was doing trying to comfort Marianne. She and her eldest locked eyes for seconds, and they nodded. Sam touched her heart and her lips, which was her standard action for goodbye. Elinor repeated the gesture with the hand that was not rubbing Marianne's head.

Sam looked down at her husband's unmoving body. She pulled a long breath in through her nose and touched her heart and touched her lips. She started walking up the great stairs. With each step, the adrenaline faded, and the reality set in. The weight of it tried to hold her down, to stop her from climbing the stairs. If she didn't get to the attic, she wouldn't have to tell Maggie, and if she didn't tell Maggie, then her family wasn't entirely changed. Still, as is the way of a determined mother, she pushed through the added gravity of grief, and she climbed the flights of stairs. The tears finally started, but she wasn't aware; thus, when she finally opened Maggie's door, when we first saw her in this tale, her face was streaked with tears and twisted with anguish. She opened the door, heard a song with a kick-drum and a rhythm guitar, and saw her daughter looking at herself in the mirror, pencil in her hand, sketch pad on her lap. They made eye contact in the mirror. She could tell that Maggie thought she was in trouble. She spun her head, ready to defend herself but in that second realized that this was not an angry visit. Sam had practiced all the words she might say on the way as she walked up the miserable steps to the attic. She could only croak, "It's your dad."

6

JOHN AND SISSY

It was Sissy who answered her husband's ringing phone. It rang through once, went to voicemail, and immediately started ringing again. Like his father, he had terrible insomnia, and thus, he was not in the room when the call came in. Unlike her mother-in-law, Sissy could sleep through John's late-night wanderings. When their son Harry was born, his insomnia allowed John the opportunity to bond with his son at all hours of the night, a connection that would, as we shall see soon enough, be used to manipulate him. On the night in question, Harry and John were crawling around on the floor of Harry's nursery playing with farm animals. Harry loved the cow so much that "moo" was his first word.

Sissy rolled over to John's side of the bed, noticed he shut the baby monitor off, which meant he was in Harry's room, and picked up his phone. She almost didn't answer when she looked at the screen and saw that the call was coming from his half-sister; she was always sure to add that moniker to her father-in-law's other progeny. It was the middle one, the one she found silly and troublesome. Sissy assumed Marianne had gotten herself into some kind of trouble and she wanted John to get her out of it using his money and influence without letting their father know. Sissy prided herself on having never once been a stupid teenager who did stupid teenage things and, so, she was annoyed at the mere thought of anything to do with teenagers, especially at one in the morning.

The ringing ended and, once again, started back up. Sissy assumed it was big, big trouble if she wouldn't leave a voicemail or if she was unwilling to text as kids these days always did. She thought of the possibility of having something to lord over her half-sister-in-law for years to come, so she answered. "Hello?" she asked as though she had been pulled from a deep sleep.

"Where's John?" The clearly adult voice came through the phone. It wasn't as much of a request as a demand. There was the sound of wailing children in the background.

"Sam?" Sissy sat up, dropping all pretense that she was going to get something out of her half-sister-in-law.

"I need John. Sissy, where is he?"

"I..." She looked around the room and held the phone away from her ear, trying to get a sense of things. She crawled over and turned up the baby monitor and heard her son saying, "Moo, moo, moo" and her husband saying, "Baa, baa, baa" over and over with far too much energy for one in the morning. "...he's in with Harry."

"Get him."

"What is..."

"Now." One couldn't say that Sam raised her voice necessarily, but there was a tonal shift that made it seem louder.

"Fine." Sissy could forgive one demand from her stepmother-in-law, another moniker she always used, but two moved her from worry to perturbed. She dropped the phone on the bed and went down the hall, into the other wing of the house, and into her son's room. She found her husband on his stomach with a toy sheep in one hand and a toy horse in the other making them dance around the cows her son had in his. "Phone," she said without preamble.

"What?" John asked in the way that people who clearly heard what the other person had said but didn't quite understand the context.

"Sam calling from Marianne's phone. Sounds like someone is crying. Marianne probably broke a nail or something."

"Oh. Well... uh..." he said as he stood up. He handed the sheep and the horse to his wife, expecting her to hand him a phone in return.

"I left it on the bed."

"Oh, well, can you..." He nodded his head down at Harry, who was looking up at his parents with the head of a cow in his mouth so that the business end was facing them.

She sighed in exasperation. "I will not crawl around on the floor with him. I am his mother, not his playmate. I will read him a story. Put him back in his bed, and I will find something calming."

"Oh, well... yes, dear." He scooped his son up, kissed him on the head, and placed him back in his crib. "Mummy will read to you now. Be good and get some sleep. Daddy needs to go talk to Granny Sam."

"Step-grandmother Sam," Sissy corrected.

"Yes, well..." John trailed off. He kissed his wife on the cheek and said, "Thank you, dear." He went out of the nursery and hustled down the hall to get his phone.

He wiped his hands on his pajama bottoms before he picked up his phone. While almost everyone who ever met Sam found her delightful, she made John nervous. It could be argued that he also found her charming and delightful much to the chagrin of his wife, and thus, his conflicting emotions caused the flop sweats. He picked up the phone. "Sam?"

"It's your dad."

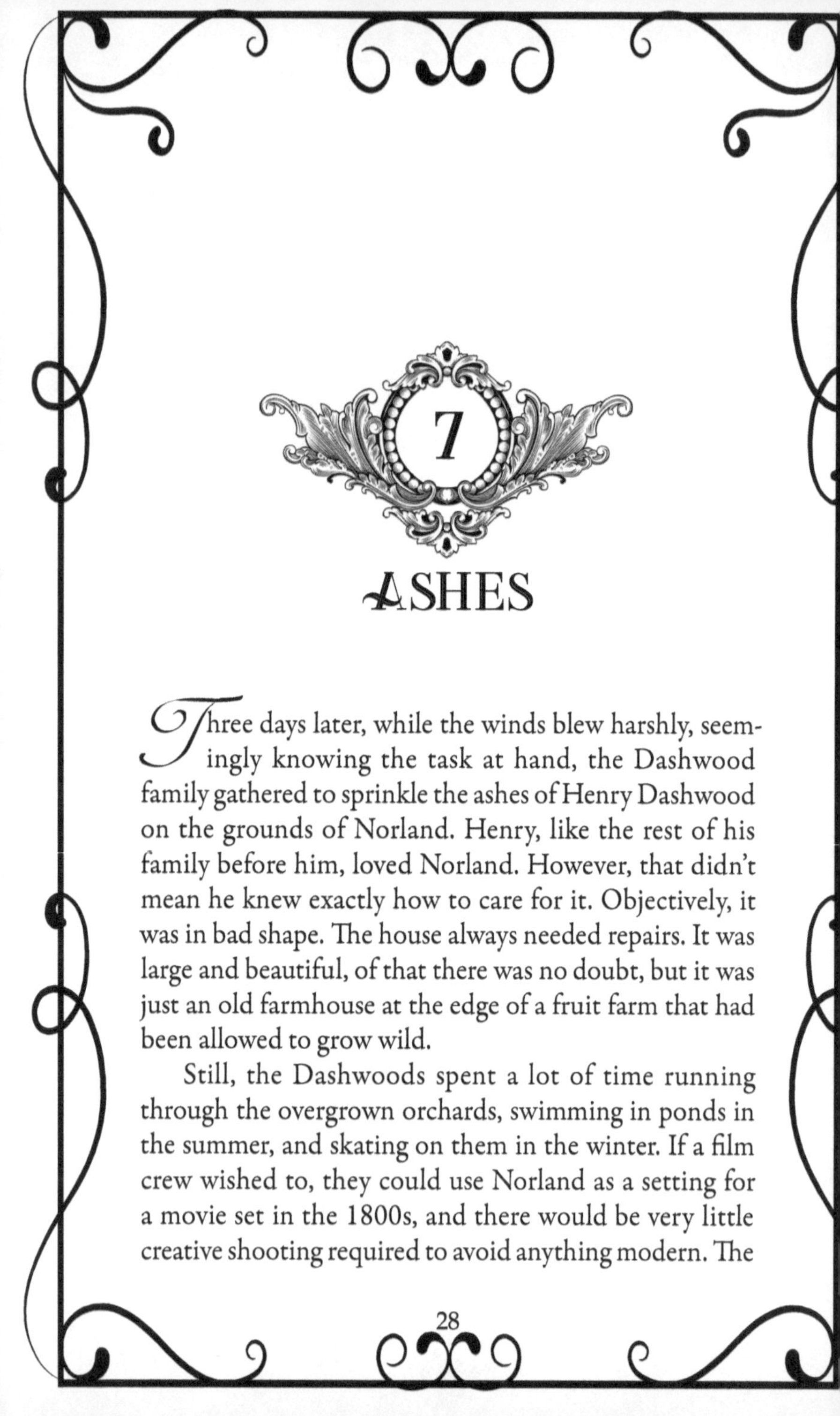

7

ASHES

*T*hree days later, while the winds blew harshly, seemingly knowing the task at hand, the Dashwood family gathered to sprinkle the ashes of Henry Dashwood on the grounds of Norland. Henry, like the rest of his family before him, loved Norland. However, that didn't mean he knew exactly how to care for it. Objectively, it was in bad shape. The house always needed repairs. It was large and beautiful, of that there was no doubt, but it was just an old farmhouse at the edge of a fruit farm that had been allowed to grow wild.

Still, the Dashwoods spent a lot of time running through the overgrown orchards, swimming in ponds in the summer, and skating on them in the winter. If a film crew wished to, they could use Norland as a setting for a movie set in the 1800s, and there would be very little creative shooting required to avoid anything modern. The drive was dirt. The lawn was often overgrown. There was even a working hand pump next to the back door.

After the service at the funeral home for all the people who wanted to pay their respects, and after the post-service gathering where people the Dashwood girls had never met came up to them and touched their faces and hugged them while sobbing uncontrollably, and after Marianne cried so hard she had to rush to the bathroom to revisit her breakfast, and after Elinor explained for the 20th time that she was not Sam, but Elinor, and after Harry had a meltdown so epic that Maggie took him into an unused showing room, put him in a casket and let him fall asleep, the Dashwood family came home to Norland with the ashes of their patriarch.

They stood under the treehouse Henry built, with full electricity connectivity. It would be better said that he had it built under his "strict supervision" when Elinor was born. He always wanted a treehouse, and his father wouldn't oblige. He said, "Why would we clutter up this majestic land with garbage? We don't run a scrapyard do we, Son?" While Henry nodded in agreement, he crossed his heart's fingers. He originally planned on building it together with John when he turned ten, but we all know now that did not happen.

The treehouse cost thousands of pounds so that it could hold thousands of pounds. Henry, Sam, and the girls spent many an afternoon up there fighting pirates, or being pirates, or fairies, or lost girls, or some variation thereof. Eventually, as Elinor and Marianne grew, they spent less and less time in the treehouse, and when they stopped going up there, Sam and Henry stopped going up there too, as is often the way of families. The older sibling leads the way, and the younger sibling is forced to keep up or be left behind. Left behind or not, Maggie was determined to never grow out of her love for the treehouse. If one were to climb up there on that particular day, one would think that it was a special place built just for her. She built a desk into the wall. She had an easel set up. There were paint stains on the floor and pencil shavings stuck into the paint splatters, making it look like a multimedia canvas.

Below the mess that Maggie made, dressed in mourning, the Dashwoods stood, heads bowed, not in prayer necessarily, as they were not a particularly religious family, but in contemplation, as anyone would be in a moment like that. John held his son in his arms, holding him tight so that he wouldn't drop him. Sissy looked up at the underside of the treehouse and calculated how hard it would be to remove. Elinor stood between Maggie, whose tears were streaming down her face in silence, and Marianne, who was wailing and sobbing. She held Maggie's left hand and Marianne's right. She remained silent, teeth clenched, head tall, back straight. While the British stiff upper lip wasn't invented by Elinor Dashwood, it could easily be said that she perfected it. Sam stood, clutching the urn to her body with her back to the tree, looking out at her family. Her eyes were puffy; her body was heavy. She felt ready to be done with the day, and she felt guilty about that.

"I'm not sure what to say," Sam began, "that would do justice to the man we all loved, so I want you all to say whatever your heart tells you to say." She turned to her stepson. "John, will you go first?" She removed the lid and held the urn out to him.

John turned and tried to hand Harry to his wife, who wasn't ready for the exchange, and so Harry slid down her body like it was a fireman's pole until he plopped on the ground, which was where he really wanted to be anyway as his father's grip was getting to be a bit too much even for a two-year-old. John reached into the urn and removed a handful of ashes. "Father and I didn't have the life together either of us thought we would, but I understand. I've long since forgiven him. Grief is..." His lower lip started to quiver. He took a moment to steady himself, opened his mouth to speak again, and realized he couldn't. He looked down at his son who was putting a stick in his mouth, oblivious to the proceedings but seemingly happy. John threw the ashes into the air and let them blow away. He bent down and scooped up his son, hoping to find comfort there.

Sam looked to Sissy who had no intention of touching the burnt remains of her father-in-law. "No, this isn't about me." To one who didn't know her, it might have almost sounded sincere.

Elinor brought her two hands together and allowed her sisters to let her go and grip each other instead. She stepped back and walked around Marianne, letting her hand rub on her back as she did so. She took a fistful of ashes and said, "Thanks for being my dad." She threw the ashes in the air and blew a kiss after them.

Marianne couldn't speak. She was racked with sobs. She rubbed her handful of ashes together so that they slipped through her fingers agonizingly slowly. When her hand was empty, she touched it to the trunk of the tree. Elinor wrapped her in a hug and let her snot all over her top.

Maggie, whose right hand had been clenched in a fist, opened it to produce a small bag. She placed her handful of ashes into it, zipped it closed, put it between her teeth, and climbed the ladder of the treehouse. When she came down empty-handed, she nodded to her mother, who bent over and kissed her on the cheek.

Sam looked down at the urn and back to her family. "Henry, thank you for giving me the best life a girl could ever have. I regret nothing." She kissed the urn and then spilled it out. The wind took it. She put her arm around Maggie as they stood silently watching the ashes until they disappeared. "Right. Who wants whiskey?"

Everyone's hands shot up, including Maggie, who at that point had never tried whiskey but had some wine on special occasions. Sam came from an extended family that adhered to a "kids drink at home policy." It was legal in most of the UK for kids as young as 5 to drink on private property with the consent of their parents and so they did just that. They didn't let their children drink until they were at least 12, nor did they allow it every day or all the time. They felt by letting them do it in small amounts, under supervision, they made it less of a big deal. Let the record show that no member of Sam's extended family was ever arrested for public drunkenness or for drunk driving. Sissy may have disapproved, but she disapproved of everything, and she wasn't the girls' mother, was she? They went into the house, and everyone, excluding Harry, because he was not even five and Sissy was his mother, raised one final glass to Henry Dashwood.

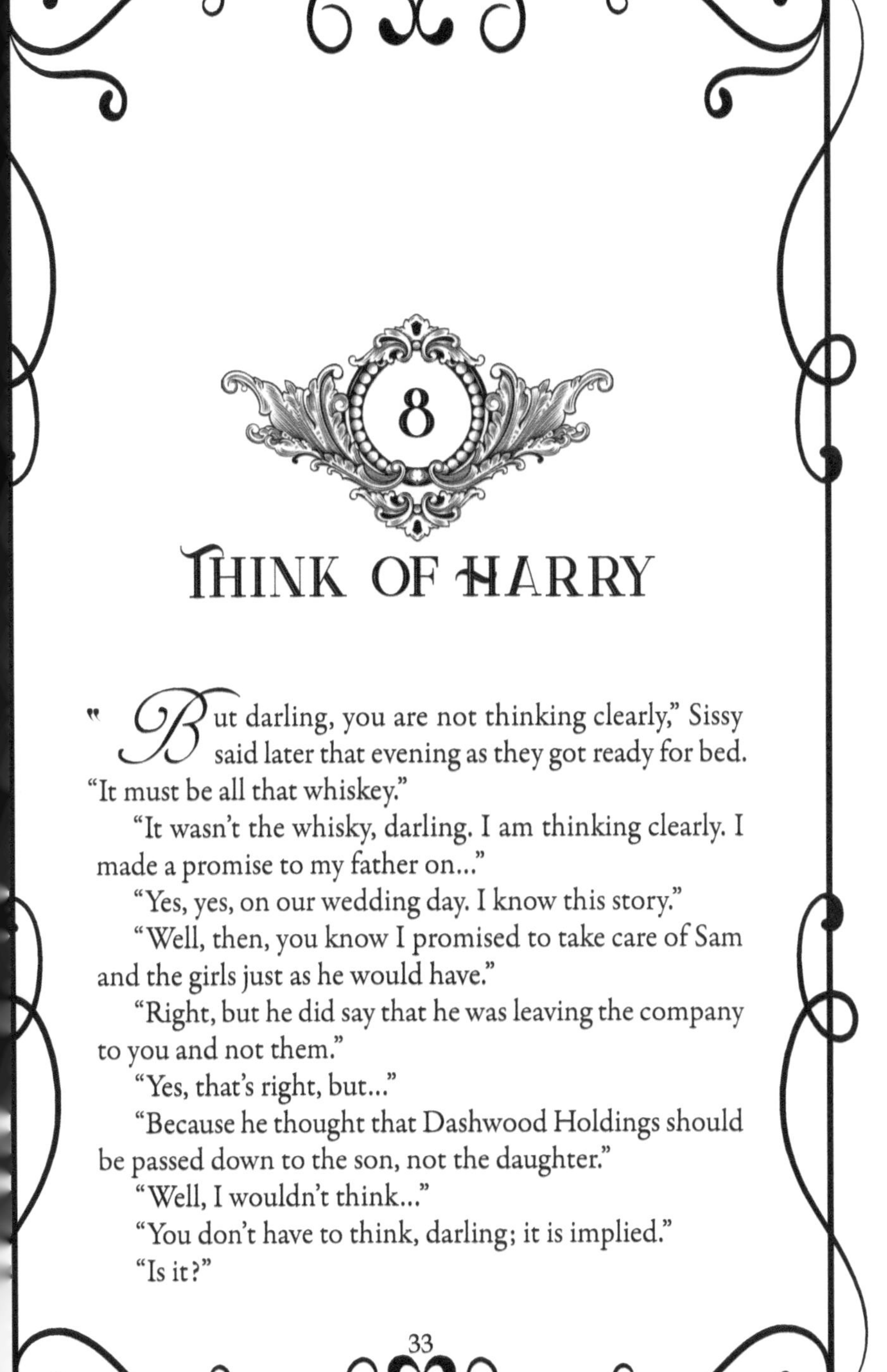

8

THINK OF HARRY

"*But* darling, you are not thinking clearly," Sissy said later that evening as they got ready for bed. "It must be all that whiskey."

"It wasn't the whisky, darling. I am thinking clearly. I made a promise to my father on…"

"Yes, yes, on our wedding day. I know this story."

"Well, then, you know I promised to take care of Sam and the girls just as he would have."

"Right, but he did say that he was leaving the company to you and not them."

"Yes, that's right, but…"

"Because he thought that Dashwood Holdings should be passed down to the son, not the daughter."

"Well, I wouldn't think…"

"You don't have to think, darling; it is implied."

"Is it?"

"Of course, dear. If he wanted to give the girls the company, he would have split it four ways, but he didn't. He left it to you, so you could pass it down to your future son."

Dear Reader, we may look back a few pages to determine if Henry did, in fact, imply this. Semantically, one would argue it was inferred, not implied. Add to that the fact that Sissy wasn't even there, so all she can do is infer. While John worked in journalism, he was not his mother, and thus he often confused the two words. However, he knew that he misused them, so he did his best not to use either of them if he could avoid it. Did Sissy know this? Of course.

"Well," John paused and looked out of the window of the guest room onto the darkened silhouette of his ancestral family home, "that may be true, dear, but what's the harm with letting them stay here? We have our own place in town and…"

"The harm is that this place is barely holding on. You saw the state of it. And that is what it looked like while your father was with us. The property is a mess. It looks like one of those dreaded American trailer parks out there. If you leave it to them, how will they keep it up? Is Sam going to get a job? Is she going to hire a gardener? Is she going to tear down that dreadful treehouse that is a broken arm waiting to happen? How could she? The life insurance policy would just get swallowed up trying to maintain it. If she doesn't have this burden, the life insurance can keep them safe and sound until Marianne is out of college. Do you want her, like your father did when your mother died, to focus on the wrong things? Shouldn't all of her concern be on those girls?"

He turned to look at his wife. His eyes glistened with tears. "Yes, dear, but Sam is..."

"A grieving widow. You can't ask her to do for her three children what your father was unable to do for one, can you?"

John wiped at his cheeks. "I suppose not. It's just that Father said..."

"He said to take care of them. Yes, by all means. Take care of them. Do you think giving them a huge estate to manage on their own is taking care of them? Would your father really want you to burden them with that?"

"Well, I suppose not. I could set them up with a yearly allowance that could..."

"Yes, whatever you want, dear, but is a yearly allowance really the right thing? If you set that up for them now, would they expect it forever? Will you be required to pay for them? Are they to be kept women? Elinor is going to university. What does she really need? Marianne is almost in college. I've seen her closet; she has all the clothes she will ever need. There is really nothing more they need. Think of Harry. Would you deprive him of his inheritance? If his half-aunts and step-grandmother have a yearly allowance, what would be left for him? He is just a boy, and they are fully-grown women. He can't be expected to give his older pseudo-relatives money for the rest of his life, can he? Is he supposed to give up his birthright, that is Norland, so some old ladies can turn it into Grey Gardens?"

John paused, trying to process what she was saying. "Well, that's true, but what about Mag..."

"It is true. They will be much happier in some smaller flat somewhere else or in some cottage in the country if they really want to live out here. The girls will be gone soon enough, and Sam will be all alone. What, is she going to live here alone? That isn't realistic. Think of Harry; he is just a child and has so much of his life ahead of him. They've had their time here. They were all leaving soon. I'm sure of it."

"I suppose so, dear, but Magg…"

"Yes, something else will be better. If they rent something, then there will be a landlord who can take care of the lawn and things they clearly neglect. Sam obviously can't be asked to maintain everything in her condition."

"Her condition? She isn't infirm, is she? She's only 40."

"Well, not that we know, dear, but again, look at this place." She rubbed her finger on the dresser, which came back totally clean, but Sissy wiped her hands on the bedspread as though it was filthy. "Obviously something is wrong with her or this home would shine from top to bottom. Look at our home, dear. We both work all day, and the house is immaculate."

"Well, Gloria comes in once a…"

"And besides, we need this place so that you can be closer to the office while I work at the network out of the house in town."

"So, I'd be here by myself?"

"With Harry, of course. It is really his birthright, isn't it? He should be moved in right away to acclimate. We can pay Barbara to move out here with you. She could live right here in this room. It is perfect just the way it is. I would be here on weekends, darling. I can't be asked to quit my job and move to the country just because your father died. I loved him and everything, but just because he married a woman who wanted to stay at home doesn't mean you did."

"Yes, yes, of course, darling."

"Excellent. So, it's settled then. You can tell them in the morning, dear. They should be out by the end of the month so that Marianne has time to switch to a new college. Good night." She shut off the light, crawled into bed, and slept as soundly as though she was in her own home; which, technically, she was.

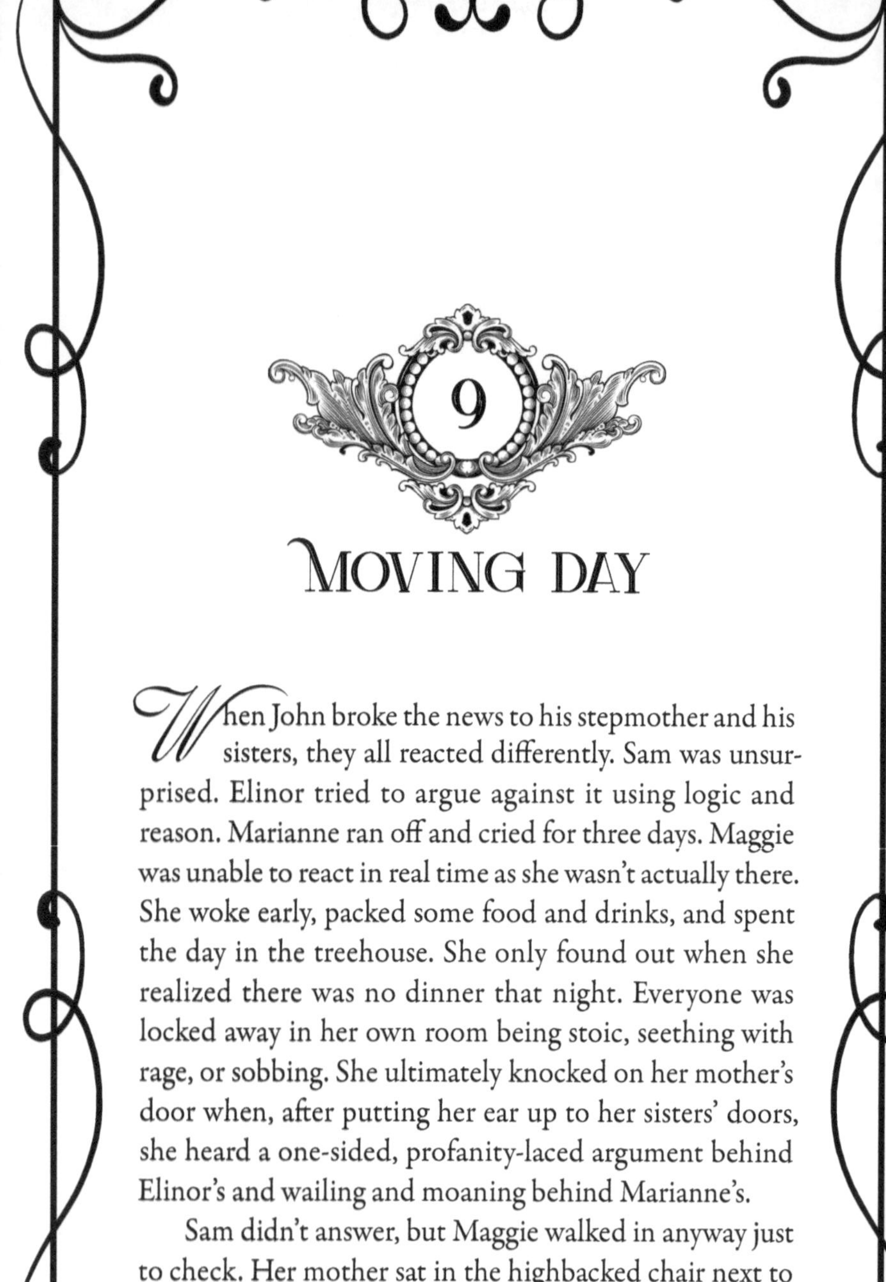

9

MOVING DAY

When John broke the news to his stepmother and his sisters, they all reacted differently. Sam was unsurprised. Elinor tried to argue against it using logic and reason. Marianne ran off and cried for three days. Maggie was unable to react in real time as she wasn't actually there. She woke early, packed some food and drinks, and spent the day in the treehouse. She only found out when she realized there was no dinner that night. Everyone was locked away in her own room being stoic, seething with rage, or sobbing. She ultimately knocked on her mother's door when, after putting her ear up to her sisters' doors, she heard a one-sided, profanity-laced argument behind Elinor's and wailing and moaning behind Marianne's.

Sam didn't answer, but Maggie walked in anyway just to check. Her mother sat in the highbacked chair next to her bed, staring at the wall. "Mum?" she asked in a tone that asked several questions at once.

"She's taking the house from us, and he's letting her do it" was Sam's only reply. She said it without turning or looking directly at her daughter.

Maggie was bright enough at 13 to fully grasp who the "she" and "he" were in that sentence, but regardless of age, and without the ability to eavesdrop on the conversation that led to the decision, as we have been lucky or unlucky enough to do, Dear Reader, no one could ever really grasp why. Although, having read it, it may still be confusing. The truth is, some people are born bad, and other people do bad things. Sissy was the former, and John was the latter.

So it was, that one month and three days after Maggie's birthday, her family was loading their possessions into a container that would be picked up by a moving company that would deliver it to their new home somewhere in the south of England, outside of a town to which none of them had ever been. John had insisted that he pay for it because he "promised" his father he would take care of "his girls."

John arrived at 6 AM with his brothers-in-law, Robert and Edward Ferrars, to help the Dashwood women load up. Edward, aged 20, self-serious and smart, was trepidatious about the day. He had gotten to know the Dashwoods better than anyone in the Ferrars family, although he wasn't, anyone would say, close to all of them. He was studying ancient history and philosophy at the University of Leeds and living in an apartment in town. He frequented the library where Elinor worked. He somehow always managed to arrive most days just in time for her break so he could sit with her and have tea while she drank her coffee. They both knew it wasn't an accident of timing, yet they were both awkward enough to be unable to address the feelings they were feeling, and so they drank their beverages and spoke of books, and art, and nature, and whatever young people think is important with the utmost sincerity and passion. He was heartbroken on her behalf that she and her family would be moving, and yet, he was simply heartbroken that his chaste and lovely romance was coming to an abrupt end before it even had a chance to begin. He was all too aware that his sister was the villain of this story and that Elinor felt this way too, but she was too good to say it directly to him. So it was that they spent a month's worth of breaks talking past the issue. He arrived knowing that there would be no getting past it that day.

His younger brother, Robert, 17 going on 8, who cemented this by demanding he be called Robbie, was blissfully unaware of any of the family drama. He had been out with his mates the night before and was so drunk that he decided not to sleep at all for fear that he wouldn't wake up, and he would be forced to deal with an angry Sissy who was, believe it or not, actually much worse than a regular Sissy. He was still a bit tipsy when he stumbled out of the backseat of his brother-in-law's car. The sun was dawning on the horizon over the overgrown orchard, and it struck him as hysterical to crow like a rooster, and so he did. John, who thought Robbie was amusing in the way men of means see younger men of means do things they wished they had done, laughed and laughed. Edward, who had never once been amused by his brother, walked toward the door with his head down, embarrassed by the scene and by the whole day.

Sam had warned the girls that they would arrive early and made them promise to be ready to go at the break of dawn. Elinor, not one to want to break a promise, fell asleep fully clothed in her "moving clothes" on her mattress on the floor, surrounded by boxes that had been filled for almost a month. When she heard the crowing of Robbie Ferrars, she was already wide awake but was lying on her bed with her hands resting on her stomach. Her eyes popped open, and she felt sick but determined not to let anyone, most of all Edward, know.

Marianne planned to stay up all night wanting to "savor every second" of the final moments in her room while it was still recognizable. She cried herself to sleep early, so when her mother knocked on her door and walked in to let her know that her brother had arrived, she saw a room that looked exactly as it did 33 days prior when they got the news; that is to say, exactly as it had since she turned 13 herself. Not one item was in a box, nor were there any boxes in the room. The room was trapped in amber while the rest of the house disassembled around it. Her middle daughter was asleep in the fetal position on top of her fully made bed. Sam released a sad sigh, crawled onto the bed, and whispered in Marianne's ear until her puffy eyes fluttered open. When they heard Robbie crow, they both groaned.

Maggie's attic room had been empty for weeks save for her furniture, which she couldn't move and was told she couldn't take. Because of the narrow stairs and the oddly placed door, her furniture had been brought up in pieces and assembled there. It was Sam's intention to leave the room as Maggie's permanent space. Until Maggie moved up there, the room was empty, and thus, it was proclaimed that it was hers to have forever and ever. There was no way to know that forever was going to be so short-lived. Upon hearing the news that she was no longer going to live in her family home and that it wasn't only she who was an afterthought in her father's eye, but both of her sisters were as well, Maggie packed every unbreakable thing she owned, willy-nilly into boxes, taped them up, and pushed them down the stairs one at a time. She slid them down the hallway toward the grand staircase, where she pushed them down again. The grand staircase was much less steep, so gravity didn't do all the work. She had to follow some of the boxes down, giving them a good and satisfying kick until they came to a rest in the front hall.

There were already boxes there full of the items Sam wanted from Henry's office. Since the girls had hardly been in his office, they had no idea what could be packed away in the boxes. They were taped up and stacked in the front hall. She stacked all her boxes in the front hall next to her father's and left them there, waiting to be collected and moved. Neither of her sisters nor her mother came out to inquire what the noise was or offered to help her in any way. Grief had deafened them all.

She packed her art supplies and personal tech in bags, rolled her canvases up and put them in tubes, and took them to the treehouse where she planned to live until moving day. Since none of them were making or having any family meals, she ate whenever she could be bothered to do so from her stash of microwaveable meals. She came in every other day to shower and to rifle through the boxes in the front hall to find clothes. She replaced and placed her dirty, unwashed clothes in a rubbish bag next to her boxes. When she needed to use the bathroom, she did. She rarely ran into anyone, and if she and one of her sisters or her mother happened to cross paths, they gave each other a silent head nod. Grief had silenced them as well.

Maggie's drawings of that time, if one could even call them drawings, would have been very telling about her mental state had anyone thought to send her to a therapist. No one thought to do that, and thus, her sketchpads told a story of a broken, sad, and confused girl who was coming to grips with the fact that she and her brother would ultimately have more in common than she could have ever imagined. In the Dashwood family, misery did not love company, much to the detriment of the children.

She was sitting on the wrap-around porch of the tree-house with her legs dangling over the side. She was drinking black tea. The Dashwoods didn't believe that caffeine stunted one's growth. Coffee and tea flowed freely. To be fair, none of them were particularly tall, but they were not unusually short either. She, like Robbie, hadn't slept. She already packed her bags and put them in the Range Rover. She drank tea and watched the sun come up and let herself cry and cry. When she saw her brother's car pull up, something inside her closed that walled herself from her tears. Maggie was, and is, a crier, so when she doesn't, that means something pretty bad is going on. When Robbie crowed, anger banged against the wall, but it couldn't get out. She felt the banging inside her but didn't know what to do. So, as has been the case for British people for centuries when faced with something painful, she made more tea.

She didn't know that most people offer tea to the distressed, not because there is some healing property in the tea but in the conversation that comes while drinking the tea. Maggie was, as we know, totally alone up there, so she drank the tea and let it burn those feelings down. Be assured this wall shall not stay up forever. Help is waiting for her in these pages. This story, much like being a teenager, is full of some painful moments that can be overcome but that feel overwhelming at the time.

John and the Ferrars brothers were joined by Elinor for an early breakfast of store-bought pastries, tea, and coffee. Sam focused on getting Marianne on her feet before they finally joined the party in the kitchen. Maggie silently ate her breakfast and had her tea on the deck of the treehouse. By seven, the food was finished and partially digested. John took over Marianne duty. It was his task to get her room packed and brought downstairs to the front hall to await the moving company, who was hired to pick up between 8 and noon. Robbie was tasked to help Sam, whose room and belongings were already packed, much like her eldest daughter. Edward and Elinor went to work on Elinor's space. We won't follow them into that space, but suffice it to say lots of tears were shed, and promises were made.

Within the hour, everything was out of Elinor and Sam's rooms. All six of them were working frantically in Marianne's room. Well, five of them were working frantically in Marianne's room while she sat wailing in the corner. It was only when they heard the rumbling of the moving van coming up the drive that reality caught up with Marianne. She understood that whatever wasn't in the back of that van by noon, she wasn't going to be able to keep. Possession is nine-tenths and all of that. She wiped her face on her sleeve and ordered everyone out. She promised that if they came back within one hour, the room would be ready. Skeptical, but ahead of schedule, they left her to it.

Sissy arrived at the same time as the van and took charge. She instructed the movers to load the furniture on the lawn and the boxes in the front hall only after she opened them all and decided the materials in them were "acceptable." Apparently, the only things Henry owned that she cared about were his house, its belongings, his money, and his business. His personal effects were not of interest, nor did she consult with John to see if there was anything in the boxes he may want. She then set her sights on Sam who had spent the last of her mental energy that morning just getting Marianne out of bed. She just stood silently and stared at Sissy as she spoke. Sissy insisted that everything except for the bedroom furniture came with the house. Sam stood mute, and thus, it was so. The rugs, the art, the tapestries, and anything that she could proclaim a "Dashwood family heirloom" was claimed and was left behind. The only thing from downstairs that Sissy didn't manage to keep was the silver settings that were actually a wedding gift and Chamberlain family artifact. She did make the argument that Sam's grandmother intended it to be at Norland, but when Sam's focus shifted from some spot in the middle distance to directly into Sissy's eyes, not liking what that look had to say, Sissy dropped it.

Marianne was true to her word, and her room was ready by 9. She, Elinor, and the Ferrars brothers brought everything down and placed it on the lawn. The movers had already packed up the meager furnishings and the boxes from the front hall, and so it was that by 10, two hours ahead of schedule, everything the Dashwoods could take with them was packed in the van or in the Range Rover. Sissy wanted to make a claim on it as well, but since Sam was listed as co-owner, she knew it would be a struggle.

However, she repeatedly said that she didn't understand why they needed a car that size as it was a car designed for a growing family, disregarding the fact that there were four people in Sam's family and three in Sissy's.

Maggie stood alone in the drive and watched the van pull away from Norland. She watched it go knowing that she would not see it for a few more days. It would be making several more collections and drop-offs on the way south from Norland, somewhere just outside of Leeds, to their new home, a guest house on the property of one of Sam's cousins that none of the girls actually remembered that they knew, somewhere outside Exeter.

Maggie, who hadn't really been anywhere that wasn't Leeds or Norland, wasn't exactly sure where she was on the map in relation to anything else. When she was little, her family mocked her when she asked if the sky up in Scotland was the same sky as they had in England. She didn't have a full grasp of the globe or how maps worked. She looked at the map of the UK and saw Scotland up above her. She understood that the floor of the treehouse blocked out the sky when she stood underneath it. It was her contention then, at age 6, that Scotland must be sitting on England's head, so it should be always dark, not just mostly dark. Her mother and Marianne laughed and laughed while not actually explaining anything. She did not think it was very funny. Elinor, who did not laugh and laugh, pulled her aside later and explained it by using an apple. The stem was Scotland and the bite was England and if Maggie turned it just so, everything had its own space, even when it was out of sight or seemingly overhead.

She had, of course, grown to understand distance and perspective in her drawings, but that sense of unease of people laughing at her for not knowing things sat on her heart. So, it was that in all of her drawings, she always envisioned what was hidden just out of sight behind the hedge or what lay just beyond the horizon. Even if no one saw it, and even if she didn't share, she knew, and it helped.

She didn't know how long the trip would take, what it would look like when she got there, or if she would like anything about it. She looked it up online, but the map said it would take five hours, but the map fit on her phone, which fit on the screen, which fit in her hand. Time and space meant very little. She had been 13 for 33 days and she felt both 3 and 83. She didn't know what was really happening, and she had lots of questions that she wanted to ask but was sure people would laugh at her. Worst of all, she couldn't see what was hidden behind any shrub, and the horizon was a long, long way off.

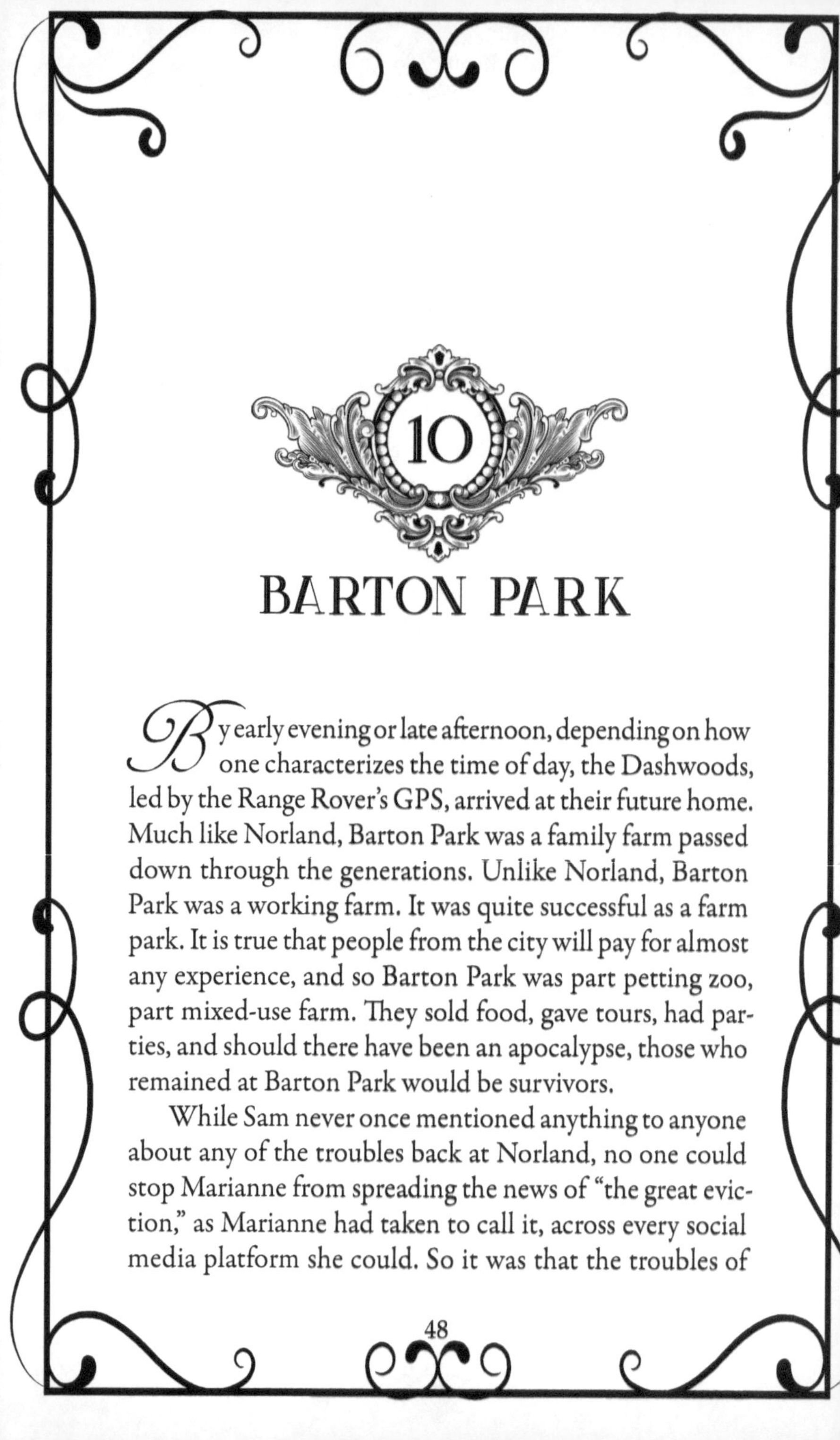

10

BARTON PARK

By early evening or late afternoon, depending on how one characterizes the time of day, the Dashwoods, led by the Range Rover's GPS, arrived at their future home. Much like Norland, Barton Park was a family farm passed down through the generations. Unlike Norland, Barton Park was a working farm. It was quite successful as a farm park. It is true that people from the city will pay for almost any experience, and so Barton Park was part petting zoo, part mixed-use farm. They sold food, gave tours, had parties, and should there have been an apocalypse, those who remained at Barton Park would be survivors.

While Sam never once mentioned anything to anyone about any of the troubles back at Norland, no one could stop Marianne from spreading the news of "the great eviction," as Marianne had taken to call it, across every social media platform she could. So it was that the troubles of the Dashwoods caught the attention of the patriarch at Barton Park. He had an empty guest house that could easily accommodate the four Dashwoods. He had fond memories of playing around Barton Park as a young man with his cousin Sam, and while they hadn't seen each other since her wedding, he held no ill will. She had, after all, lived far away with children of her own to raise. He reached out, made the offer, and was refused; he insisted, she asked about terms, and he refused to give any. It went back and forth until, ultimately, it was settled. Sam didn't have to even try to find a solution; one was made for her.

The man who would give the Dashwoods a new start was a bearded, jovial giant named Jack Middleton, who was called Middy. When he was younger, his rugby coach thought, due to his unnatural size, it would be ideal for him to play defensive midfield. Middleton the Middy eventually translated to Middy becoming his nickname. While his rugby days were well behind him, the name stuck.

His wife, Lady Jennings Middleton, whose birth name was, in fact, Lady, due to what her mother called a "drug-induced spelling error," was her husband's opposite in every way. He was large; she was petite. He was loud; she was quiet. He was jovial and quick to make a joke; she was cautious with her jokes and liked to keep them within the family. He was dark-skinned; she was so pale that her veins were visible in direct light. They were madly in love. Their four children, who at the time of this story are quite small and who do appear often to do something chaotic and/or goodhearted, would spend most of their childhood disgusted by their parent's love and affection only to desperately seek the same in their own relationships. If there was a poster couple for opposites attracting, it would be Lady and Middy.

Gran Jennings, mother to Lady, whose birth name was not Gran but who preferred to be called Gran as she enjoyed riling up children and making a quick getaway, was so frequently at Barton Park that she had her own room. She had her own home in Exeter, the nearest town to Barton Park, but it was empty and reminded her very much of her husband, who had passed several years prior. She preferred being around people. She and her son-in-law had similar senses of humor and sensibilities. If people didn't know better, they often thought he was her son and Lady her aloof daughter-in-law.

Barton Park will be the primary location of the remainder of our tale. There shall be quite a cast of characters who come and go as we move forward, but we shall meet them as they arrive. Many of them will bring drama into the lives of the Dashwoods. The Ferrars brothers will show up again, as will John and, unfortunately, Sissy. Some will be much more important than others, but believe it or not, Dear Reader, we have already met the one person who will be our heroine's saving grace. Sometimes good things are wrapped in human-shaped packages.

To reach their new home, the Dashwoods had to drive past the guest entrance of Barton Park and pull down an unmarked, unpaved drive. To help them find it, Middy had balloons staked into the ground at the edge of the road. It took them five minutes creeping along the drive before they finally pulled into the clearing where their new home sat at the bottom of the valley. The single-lane road widened as it became the final drive that led to the house. The guest house, which was called The Cottage, would never be called a cottage if it were not adjacent to a house that would rightly be called a mansion. While The Cottage was smaller than the family home at Norland, it did have three bedrooms, two full bathrooms, and a fully finished attic room with a dormer that had a built-in desk. When Middy discovered that Maggie would be arriving without any furniture, he had some of his employees move the furniture from the master bedroom up to the attic. He planned on having the other bedroom furniture moved into storage at the big house once the Dashwood's own items arrived. The main floor had a parlor and living room, which were both fully furnished. Middy had the kitchen fully stocked with everything he could imagine his cousins would need. He didn't ask them exactly what they liked, so he just got a little bit of everything.

The Dashwoods climbed out of the Range Rover. They stretched and popped their backs and joints. Sam had spoken to Middy earlier in the day, and he told them that the house would be unlocked and that once they arrived, if they needed help unpacking, they should give him a call. However, he had been watching the security cameras at the edge of the property, so he started walking down the path from the main house to The Cottage, and he came over the hill just as Maggie opened up the rear door of the Ranger Rover.

"Hello, Dashwoods!" His voice boomed. "Welcome home!" He approached the house with his arms open wide, as one does when one expects to give or receive a hug. Normally, Dear Reader, we don't condone the use of exclamation points that often when recounting these events, yet it must be clearly stated that Middy spoke in exclamations quite often, so there it is.

"Oh, Middy, you didn't need to come all the way down here," Sam said as she walked up to him to be engulfed in his hug. She tried to say, "We could have handled it," but it was muffled against his barrel chest and sounded like "Meee cldve mandled it."

"Oh, I know you are all more than capable, but I wanted to see you all and meet my young cousins and invite you all up to dinner. We've waited for you!"

Sam stepped back from his hug and turned to look at her girls to see what their reaction would be to this invitation. Maggie slammed the back door of the Range Rover and nodded. Unpacking could wait. She was hungry. She was always hungry. Puberty burns a lot of calories. Elinor, who couldn't eat while traveling as she got severe motion sickness, was quite hungry too and nodded. Marianne did not feel like eating with strangers without first making herself presentable and said so.

"Oh, you look lovely!" Middy exclaimed. While it was true Marianne almost always looked lovely, she wouldn't hear of it.

Maggie sighed and re-opened the back of the Range Rover. She knew well enough that one vote from Marianne always counted as three votes to her and Elinor's two. Elinor too knew it was true, so she opened the back door to grab some bags.

"Fine, fine! Let me help you unload, and I will give you a tour." He walked toward the house. Even though he moved slowly, he covered ground quickly. He swung his arms with each step, giving the impression that he was running in slow motion. He was at the back of the SUV, towering over Maggie. "You must be Maggie." He extended a hand to shake.

She reached out and her whole hand disappeared inside his. "Yes. Hi." She shook, hoping he wouldn't rip her arm off at the shoulder. "Thank you for letting us..."

He let go of her hand and waved her words away. "Oh, nonsense. What's family for?"

"What indeed?" she replied. He absorbed the wave of hurt that poured off her, knowing all too well to whom she was referring.

"Let me help you carry some of your things. I've got a surprise just for you." He smiled a big toothy grin down at her.

"Oh?"

"Yes! I promise you will like it. Just let me meet your sisters first. Don't head up to the attic without me."

"Sure." She felt herself smile for the first time in 33 days. She tried to stop it, but it turns out that some people are infectious with joy, and Middy Middleton was just one of those people. He managed to make Elinor laugh and Marianne giggle. It is true that she was, and still is, by nature easy to cry and easy to giggle, so a giggle isn't a huge shock, but at that time, it sure seemed like a miracle.

Middy showed them around The Cottage and explained the furniture moving situation. He had a blow-up mattress set up in Sam's room. He was one of those parents who thought that parents should put themselves out for their kids. He rightly made the assumption that Sam would be the same. Of course, those kinds of parents are often disappointed later in life when their kids don't realize, but not Middy. He was never disappointed in any of his choices when it came to the way he treated children, be they his or someone else's.

Maggie, having been thoroughly surprised by her setup in the attic, allowed some tears to slip out over her wall. There were just a few, but they were there, and they were significant. They were the first, but not the last, tears she would shed in front of Middy. After what seemed like millions of "thank yous" from Maggie and "my pleasures" from Middy, he left her to personalize her new space. She wanted to make it her own, but overwhelmed by the day, all she could do was lie down on her new bed, star-fish style, and try to soak it in. The bed was so large that even fully extended in all directions, none of her appendages hung off any part.

Meanwhile, Marianne "freshened up," and Elinor, Sam, and Middy sat around the kitchen drinking the tea that Middy insisted on making. Middy had a way of asking questions in such a way that the person felt it would be rude not only to answer in graphic detail but to add little flourishes the speaker didn't plan on including. So it was that the events of the past 33 days unfolded. We don't need to go into them again. They've been covered.

Eventually, after Marianne appeared, looking almost exactly as she had before, the Dashwoods followed Middy up the path that connected The Cottage and the big house. While the drive to The Cottage was not paved, the path was marked by actual pavers. One could, if one were so inclined, step from paver to paver along the way and never touch a blade of grass. Of course, when walking five abreast, that wasn't realistic. The grass was worn down in the way that happens when people walk over the same area for years and years. Every few meters, there was a lamp post with motion-detecting lights. Because it was summer, the lights did not flicker on during their walk. We mention them here because there will be one night in the future when those lights will quite literally play a role in saving one of their lives.

Middy phoned ahead to let his wife and mother-in-law know that he was on his way with their new residents and that they should go about getting dinner on the table. When the Dashwoods finally walked into the main house, they had a debate about taking off shoes or not but were told by Middy that everyone wore their shoes indoors in the big house all the time because of the cold stone floors. They made their way through the back door and down a narrow hallway that twisted and turned until they arrived in the informal dining room. The room was called the informal dining room because instead of one huge wooden table that was older than the combined age of everyone in the room, as one would discover in the formal dining room, there were several smaller tables that could seat small groups. When they walked in, they smelled dinner, which was set up buffet style with a variety of meats, cheeses, bread, fruits, and crips, along with all the accoutrements needed to make hot or cold sandwiches. It was only then that the Dashwoods realized just how hungry they were. It was sandwich day because, while the adults were trying to wait for their guests to eat to not seem rude, the boys were boys and couldn't, nor shouldn't, wait, regardless of manners.

Introductions were made all around. Lady was not the hugger that her husband was, but her eyes were bright and welcoming. She was genuinely pleased to have the Dashwoods in her home. Having four boys aged 10 and under will make anyone yearn for the presence of teenage girls.

As was the case with most people who met the Dashwood sisters, Lady was polite to Elinor, briefly acknowledged Maggie, but felt utterly compelled to talk to Marianne. If Marianne had been in Barton Park back during the days it was lit by candlelight, one could expect the candles would flicker and struggle to stay alight with her in the room as they would be competing with her for all the oxygen.

Sam and Middy sat together and caught up. They were really very good friends when they were children and as is the case of people who are genuinely close, they shook off the years like cobwebs. Before too long, if one would have shown up unexpectedly and figured out how to find the informal dining room through the huge halls and warrenous turns, one might see them sitting side by side and assume that they were siblings.

Elinor, who liked children more than one might expect, made her way to the end of the table with the four boys. She did something so few people thought to do; she asked them about themselves. By the end of the meal, Elinor had broken all the ice and had put in plenty of good words for the rest of the family. She had to pry the four-year-old off her leg and was only able to keep the eight-year-old from sobbing by promising to return for dinner the next day. In fact, they were all invited back to dinner; while Sam already had some concerns about seeming like a freeloader, she did want to talk in detail with Lady, who ran the business side of the farm, about the possibility of joining their team at some point down the line, even if it was only part-time and only to earn her keep.

Maggie made herself a sandwich fit for a rugby player right after practice, filled her plate with crisps and fruit, and sat alone at the empty table. She was halfway through her sandwich, with a mouth full of a bite that was much too large, when she realized she hadn't bothered to get herself anything to drink. Just as she was looking over to her right at the buffet to see what her drink choices were, a can of fizzy drink appeared on her left.

"You look like you are going to choke, dear. Maybe this will help you wash it down."

Maggie turned to see who was speaking. She needed to get a sense of how the comment was made. She was prepared to say something snarky, or she was prepared to smile. It all depended on who said it and what that person's face looked like. As is the case for children who have not yet realized they are growing as quickly as they are, she craned her neck up, expecting to see an adult towering over her. She realized she was looking far too high. Standing next to her stood an older woman who was only a few inches taller standing up than Maggie was sitting down.

She knew immediately that she wouldn't be saying anything snarky. Gran Jennings smiled radiantly. Her big brown eyes disappeared into the smile and wrinkles on the sides of her face. Her teeth, all her originals thank you very much, shone brightly. Her face, which was described as "cherubic" when she was a young girl and "angelic" when she was a young woman, could only be described as luminous.

"Mk mu," Maggie mumbled as she reached for the can. She popped it open and took a swig, felt the food soften up, chewed some more, and gulped it all down.

"You're welcome, dear."

Maggie wiped her mouth on the back of her hand and spoke clearly. "Thank you again. Lifesaver." She patted the

chair next to her. "Please, sit. I'm Maggie." She reached out her hand.

"You call me Gran. Everyone does," Gran said as she shook Maggie's hand.

"I've never had a Gran." Maggie didn't realize she was going to say it until she did. It was a big confession to a total stranger, but it was true. Maggie had no memories of any of her grandparents. She was not sure what grandparents did except in the abstract and what she gleaned from books and movies.

"Well, dear," Gran said as she sat down, still holding Maggie's hand with her right hand. She patted the top of Maggie's hand with her left, "You do now." With those words, Maggie found herself a permanent dinner companion. For the days that eventually spread out into months and years, they sat together. Maggie ate and ate while Gran talked and talked, and eventually, Maggie found she could share some of her own words too.

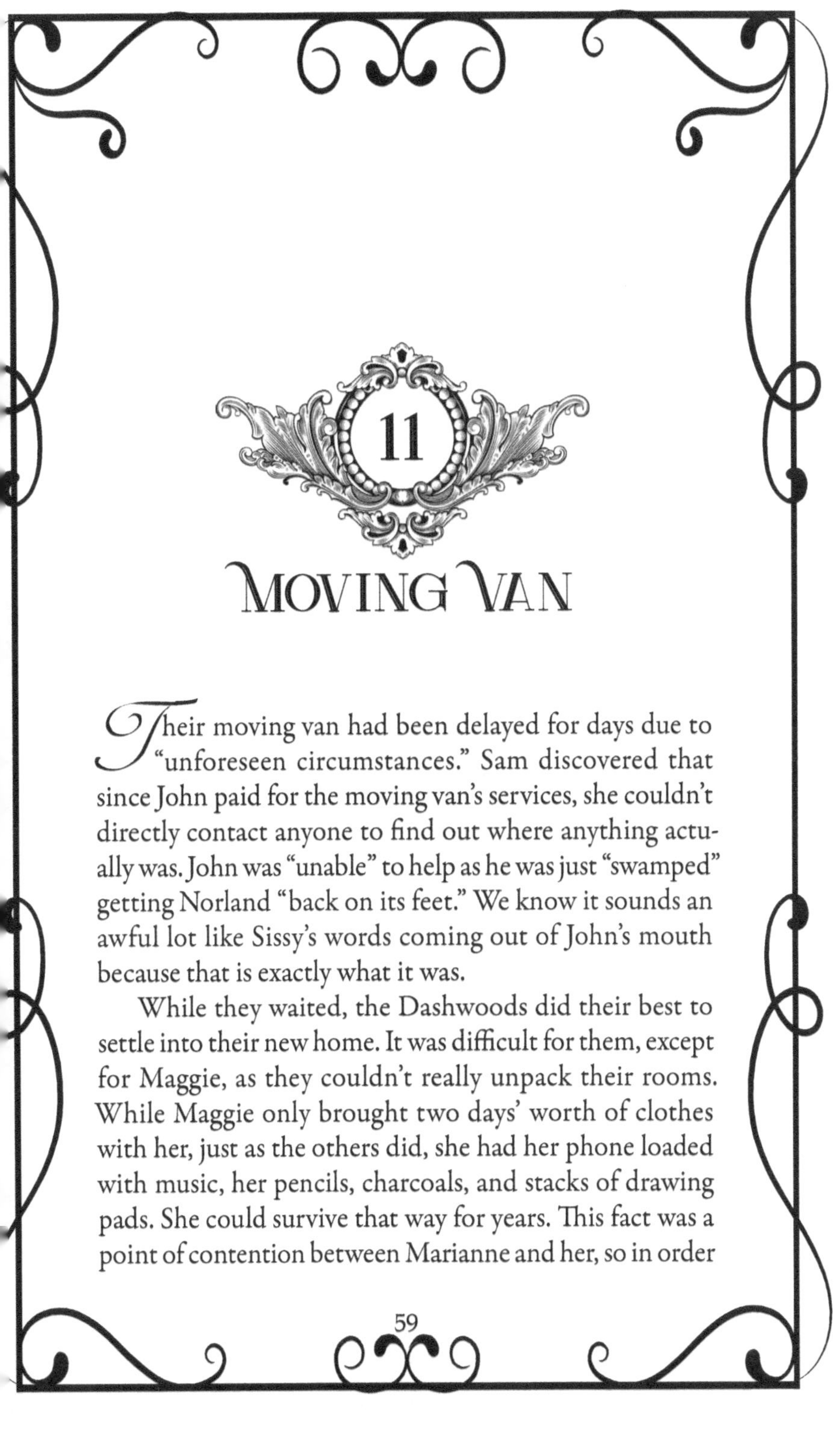

11

MOVING VAN

*T*heir moving van had been delayed for days due to "unforeseen circumstances." Sam discovered that since John paid for the moving van's services, she couldn't directly contact anyone to find out where anything actually was. John was "unable" to help as he was just "swamped" getting Norland "back on its feet." We know it sounds an awful lot like Sissy's words coming out of John's mouth because that is exactly what it was.

While they waited, the Dashwoods did their best to settle into their new home. It was difficult for them, except for Maggie, as they couldn't really unpack their rooms. While Maggie only brought two days' worth of clothes with her, just as the others did, she had her phone loaded with music, her pencils, charcoals, and stacks of drawing pads. She could survive that way for years. This fact was a point of contention between Marianne and her, so in order to alleviate the tension and avoid appearing smug and happy, Maggie spent most of her time wandering around the grounds of Barton Park. Middy had made sure to give them all uniform shirts emblazoned with the Barton Park logo to wear that allowed them the freedom to wander everywhere during the day. Because it was a working farm and a working tourist attraction, and they were new to the property, it would take time for them to be known by everyone. In the summer, the staff fluctuated, so it wasn't out of the ordinary for many of the temporary staff to go unnamed or unrecognized by the full-time staff.

Maggie spent the majority of her time on the backside of the property, away from the customers, but she made sure to wear the button-down shirt over whatever she had on that day. There were working parts of the farm that were not for everyone, yet all employees wore the same uniform. The sheep that were not being shorn for public entertainment were kept in the back. She discovered that she enjoyed watching the sheep wander around in a pack in their enclosure. They were constantly touching each other, and while she didn't think she would constantly want to be touched, she thought maybe being touched sometimes would be nice.

Maggie was sitting on the fence of the sheep pen with her sketch pad on her knee and her earbuds in her ears when the music cut out, and a notification pinged. The message from Marianne used some graphic language about which parts of Maggie she should "haul back" to The Cottage as the moving van finally arrived, and she was needed. For being such a pretty girl, Marianne used the ugliest language. We also want to interject here, that there was nothing about Elinor or Maggie that anyone would call ugly or grotesque. They were just normal-looking girls who were funny and smart. Lots of people will find them attractive. Some people in this story will find them attractive, in fact. However, as is the case in families like these, when there is one member of the family who is an 11 out of 10, that person gets called "the pretty one" even if everyone else is a 9 and a half.

When Maggie came over the hill and peered down at The Cottage, she saw the moving van was indeed there. Her mother was having an animated conversation with the driver. Marianne was looking up at someone inside the van and was making pointing gestures and trying to explain where she wanted everything. Of course, nothing could actually go where it was supposed to be until the current furniture was removed from her room. As she got closer to the house, Maggie picked up the back end of the conversation between her mother and the driver.

"...have a schedule to keep, ma'am."

"Really? A schedule to keep? That's rich. We've waited for days..."

"In a furnished home, ma'am."

"Did you know it was furnished?"

"Well, no, we didn..."

"Yet you have the gall to talk to me like that because I'm a woman in a house full of girls? If there were a man here, would you dare speak..."

"But there innit a man here, ma'am. There's jus' you and the girls, as you say. You can't tell me how I might talk to a man, cos'..."

"Fine!" she shouted and threw up her hands. "Just dump it all on the lawn. Don't do the decent thing. Don't give us 30 minutes to clean out the rooms. Don't offer to help us move anything that we could've cleaned out had we known you'd be coming today."

"As I said, ma'am, we did call and report we'd be arriving in two hours. We called the number on the slip. Ain't my fault that I didn't have your number, is it? My guess is you really mad at whoever din' call you after we called em', not me." He smirked down at her.

"Going for psychology, are you," she paused and read the name on his shirt, "Brian?"

"Yeah."

"Gonna need to work on your empathy a bit, you twit. Just dump it." She spun away from him. "In the house, girls." She ushered them all in and slammed the door behind her.

"You 'eard the lady," Brian said to his colleague in the back of the van who, along with Marianne, had stood silently watching the reality show argument that escalated quickly in front of them. "Dump it."

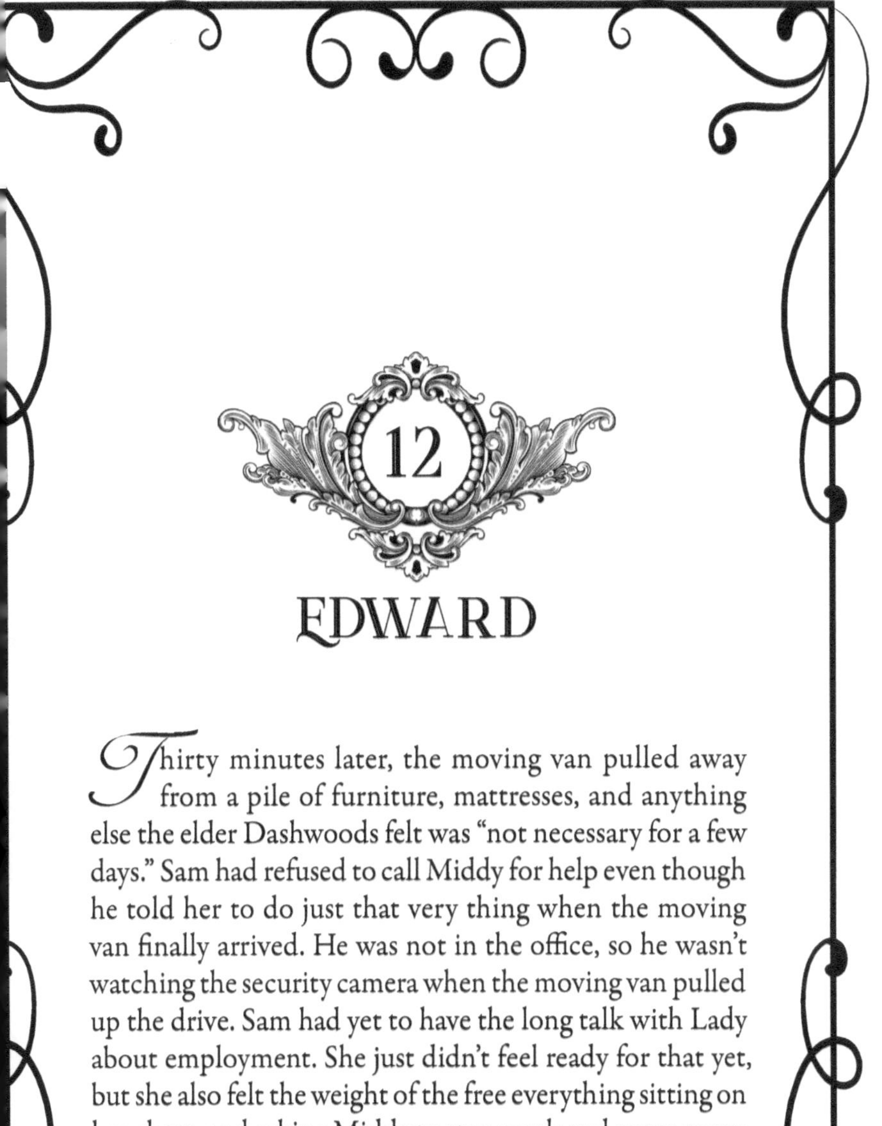

12

EDWARD

*T*hirty minutes later, the moving van pulled away from a pile of furniture, mattresses, and anything else the elder Dashwoods felt was "not necessary for a few days." Sam had refused to call Middy for help even though he told her to do just that very thing when the moving van finally arrived. He was not in the office, so he wasn't watching the security camera when the moving van pulled up the drive. Sam had yet to have the long talk with Lady about employment. She just didn't feel ready for that yet, but she also felt the weight of the free everything sitting on her chest, and asking Middy to stop work and come move things would have only added a few more stones there.

The life insurance money wouldn't be paid out for another few weeks, and while she did have quite a bit of money in the account that she had in her own name and in the account that she and Henry shared, Middy and Lady refused to take any of it for the groceries they provided. They wouldn't let her pay for the utilities as they were on the same bill as the big house because they kept the house fully operational year-round just in case any guests arrived who didn't want to stay in a guest room at the big house.

Maggie had gone up to her room and watched them dump all of their belongings. She was angry, but she wasn't totally sure why. She took off her Barton Park shirt and angrily threw it on the ground. She felt guilty, as though Middy would somehow find out and think she was mad at him. So, she picked it back up, put it on a hanger, and tried to smooth it out with her hands before she hung it up. When they were done and closed the side of the moving van, she opened her window, placed her speaker there, connected her phone to it, and cranked up The Front Bottom's second album, *Talon of the Hawk*. The opening tambourine of the first song, "Au Revoir (Adios)," jangled. The opening lines blared down at them, and Maggie screamed them out to them, reminding them how very small they were. They gazed up at her with quizzical expressions. She gave them the two-fingered salute.

Normally, Marianne hated the band. She groaned when they came on too loud. She would demand Maggie put in her earbuds. She felt that the singer, whose name also happened to be Brian, was screechy. She didn't understand the lyrics. She thought the production value was low. She thought indie rock was coded language for junk. Yet, that day, as the movers were looking up at Maggie, who was silently telling them what she thought they should do to themselves, Marianne came out and screamed along with the lyrics that she didn't know until that moment that she knew.

Maggie left the album playing as the soundtrack to moving day part two. Since Sam's room was empty save for a blow-up mattress, they started by moving her bedroom set. Marianne and Sam worked as one pair, and Elinor and Maggie worked as the other. By the time the album ended roughly 40 minutes later, they had all of the furniture in Sam's room. It was still in pieces and strewn about, but it was off the lawn.

At Sam's insistence, Marianne got to choose the next album, and they would move on to her room. She clapped and woo-hooed. She ran up to Maggie's room, and Taylor Swift's *Speak Now* live world tour album started up. It was a crowd-pleaser. There was a lot of bad karaoke sing-along. By the time that extra-long album ended and the encore played, they had the Middleton's furniture out and Marianne's furniture in.

Sam declared it time for a break. They were sweaty and tired but pleased with the progress. She made the girls sit outside and rest. She went into the kitchen where she grabbed four bottles of water and a tin of biscuits. They ate and drank like savages, not caring where the crumbs went or if they dribbled water down their fronts. Just as Elinor begrudgingly accepted a dare from Maggie to see if she could fit a full biscuit in her mouth, and how long it would take to chew it and swallow it without any water, they looked up to see the front of a silver Volkswagen Jetta pull up the drive. Three of them were quite clueless as to who was behind the wheel, but Elinor, who had spent many a break leaning on the fender of that car, knew all too well.

She tried to swear, choked on her cookie, made a sound that sounded like "ack," and ran inside. They all turned to watch her go with different expressions. Sam was amused as she figured it out right away. Marianne was confused as she didn't know who it was until he climbed out of the car. Maggie was annoyed as she wouldn't find out how long it would take for Elinor to eat the biscuit. She tried later alone in her room. It took just under two minutes.

"Edward!" Marianne shouted, genuinely surprised when she saw him. "We'd all give you a hug, but we all smell like..."

With that, the front door banged open, and Elinor appeared in a clean shirt, face washed, smelling of freshly sprayed something or other and wearing a head scarf to hold down her frizzy hair.

"Edward, what a pleasant surprise." She looked at him, trying not to let her smile break her face. "Sorry, we all look a fright. We've been uh..." She pointed at the pile of furniture.

"Moving in, yes. That's why I'm here, actually."

"Really? How did you know?" Sam asked.

"Well, I was in South Hampton picking up an antique something or other for Mum, and I was on the phone with Robbie, who was at Norland when the call came in about the movers arriving today. Since I was already in the neighborhood, I thought..."

Sam interrupted, "But South Hampton's almost three hours away."

"Two-and-half if you don't speed, and I did just a little." He smiled a smile that would be called sheepish in some circles, but after having lived on a farm with sheep, none of the Dashwoods ever would again.

"What about your mum's antique something or other?" Elinor asked. "I wouldn't want her to be upset if..."

"It isn't anything she needs right away. I'm going up to Scotland in another few weeks, so no need to worry about that."

"What is it?" Maggie asked the question they were all thinking but lacked the social restraint to ask.

"It's ummm…" He turned his whole body to her and saw her for the first time. Her hair was wild; she had somehow smudged herself with either some kind of dirt or chocolate from one of the biscuits. She had both water spots and sweat stains on her shirt. He let his eyes quickly move, and he took in Marianne, who was not nearly as disheveled, but who was clearly unkempt by her standards, and Sam, who, much like her youngest daughter, looked like she had been through the wringer. He looked quickly back at Elinor, who was fresh as a daisy but wearing a headscarf, something he had only seen her do one other time when she was cleaning the archives at the library. He absorbed what it all meant and smiled. He did all of this in much less time than it took to read that passage, and thus, none of the Dashwoods noticed him process this, and they assumed that the smile had something to do with the answer he was about to give. "It's a gravy boat."

"Really?" Maggie pushed.

"I'm afraid so. Some people collect paintings. Others collect tea sets. Mum collects antique gravy boats. None of us really know why, but it's a thing we have long accepted. Our mother is the crazy gravy boat lady. She has a whole room dedicated to them. It's quite the conversation killer."

Elinor laughed at that, giving the rest of them permission to do so. None of them wanted to laugh at Edward. He was nothing but lovely to all of them, and clearly, there was some kind of relationship happening with promises

and the like between them. While we don't know what was promised, we do know promises were most assuredly made. Still, Elinor hadn't expected Edward to fulfill one of his promises so quickly, but here he was, visiting her as soon as he possibly could.

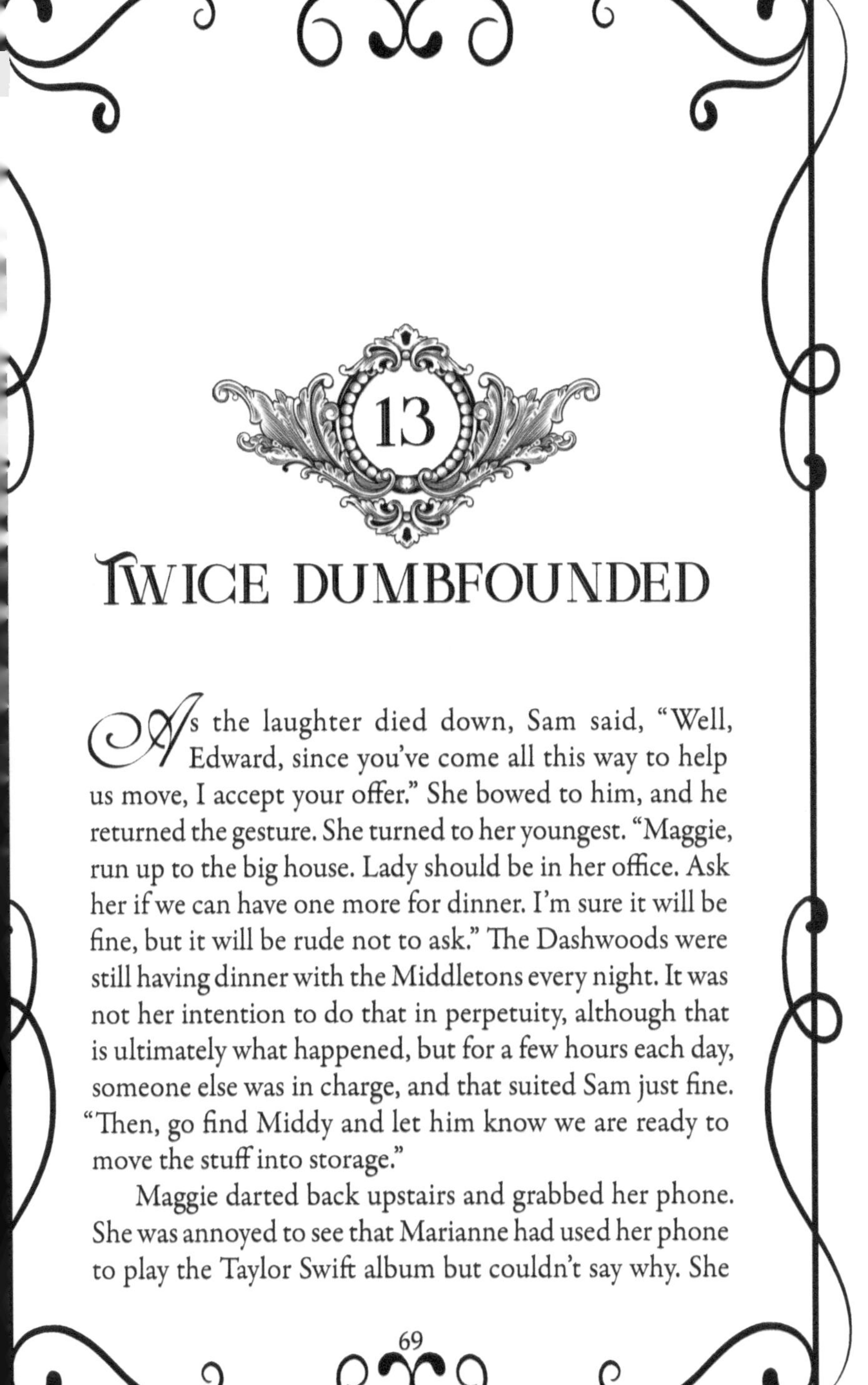

13

TWICE DUMBFOUNDED

As the laughter died down, Sam said, "Well, Edward, since you've come all this way to help us move, I accept your offer." She bowed to him, and he returned the gesture. She turned to her youngest. "Maggie, run up to the big house. Lady should be in her office. Ask her if we can have one more for dinner. I'm sure it will be fine, but it will be rude not to ask." The Dashwoods were still having dinner with the Middletons every night. It was not her intention to do that in perpetuity, although that is ultimately what happened, but for a few hours each day, someone else was in charge, and that suited Sam just fine. "Then, go find Middy and let him know we are ready to move the stuff into storage."

Maggie darted back upstairs and grabbed her phone. She was annoyed to see that Marianne had used her phone to play the Taylor Swift album but couldn't say why. She pulled up her Sara Bareilles mix and pushed her earbuds into her ears. She slipped past Edward and Elinor on the stairs as they were heading up, and she was heading down at a brisk pace. They had to step aside so that she didn't knock them down. "Thanks, Edward!" she shouted as she hit play and heard the opening notes of "Love Song" pound out on Sara's piano.

She bounded out the propped open door, narrowly missing Marianne, who was carrying a box of Elinor's shoes. The lyrics kicked in, so Maggie didn't hear the curses hurled after her. She ran right up the path, trying to land on every other paver, but her legs, which were longer than she knew, were not quite long enough, and she couldn't manage it. She tripped occasionally, but she never did fall.

She arrived at the big house slightly winded but exhilarated. She hadn't realized how much she had enjoyed being outside at Barton Park until she had to spend a few hours, against her will, inside The Cottage. While she was busy not thinking about anything in particular at that moment, it was the first time that she came to understand that choosing to do something and being told to do the exact same thing came with very different feelings.

She arrived at the side door, which once upon a time was called the "servant's entrance." While it was true that the Middletons did still employ people to clean the big house, they had four children and ran a business, time was valuable to them, and cleaning the house was not something either of them enjoyed. However, their employees were certainly not servants. They were a small family-owned cleaning service. When they arrived on Wednesdays, they came in the front door using a key that Lady had given them.

That door was little used by anyone who wasn't heading to or coming from The Cottage, as The Cottage used to be the servant's quarters in a bygone era. Maggie wasn't thinking about any of that as she was still working out the choice/happiness graph in her head when she knocked twice and pushed the door open as Middy had instructed them all to do.

She was looking down, banging her feet against the threshold just to be sure she wasn't tracking more dirt than necessary into the house. She was humming along to the music and stomping her feet to the beat. When she finally looked up, she saw that Gran was standing there, a genuine smile plastered on her face.

"Ahh," she shouted, and she pulled her earbuds out with her left hand while she clutched her heart with her right. "Gran. Hi. I didn't..."

"Yes, dear, I know. I didn't mean to frighten you. I called your name when I saw you open the door, but you were, well... you know what you were doing."

They both laughed. "Yeah, well," Maggie let go of her heart and shoved her earbuds into her back pocket with her phone, "I'm just coming to see Lady."

"Well, I was just coming down to see you girls to see how you were getting on, but since you're here, I'll just walk you to Lady's office, and you can fill me in on all the juicy gossip."

Maggie snorted a laugh. "I don't think anyone would ever say anything we did *was* juicy or gossipy." She held out her elbow, and Gran slipped her arm through it even though she didn't need to as she wasn't remotely unsteady on her feet, but 60-year-old women might as well be ten thousand in the eyes of young people, and they started walking down the hallway. She took a deep breath and said in one long, run-on sentence, "Mum got into a shouting match with the delivery guys today, and she said some stuff about being a woman that I never really thought too much about before, but I can't stop thinking about it now, and then we moved and moved and moved and moved furniture for ages, and Edward Ferrars, this boy that Elinor likes who also sort of is our brother-in-law, so I'm a bit confused on the logistics of that, is here, so I'm up here asking Lady if he can come to dinner, which I guess means he is going to stay the night. Would Mum let him sleep *with* Elinor? And then I'm supposed to get Middy to help us move the stuff we've dumped in the yard."

"Well, dear, that all sounds particularly juicy and gossipy. I am sure Lady will *not* care one iota if Edward joins us for dinner, but it is nice that you will go ask. I can promise that he will *not* be sleeping in the same bed as your sister. There are plenty of couches in The Cottage, are there not?"

"Yeah, like four. We could all take naps at the same time if we wanted."

"Well, there you go. He'll be sleeping on a couch, maybe with a bell around his neck just to make sure." They both laughed at that. "Now, what's this about him being your brother-in-law?"

"Right, well, my dad had an older son called John, and he has a wife called Sissy; she's really the worst person ever, and she has these two brothers, Edward and Robbie. So, since she's my sister-in-law, doesn't that make him my brother-in-law too? If so, is that legal? Can they like each other? I mean, they wouldn't really know each other if not for Sissy and John being married. If we did family holidays, they could all be there, right?"

"It is totally legal. Yes, he could be at a family holiday party, but that doesn't mean much. Even if he were your brother-in-law, which he isn't, by the way, it would still be legal. In-laws are not blood relatives. It might be a bit sticky if one couple splits up and the other doesn't, but what family doesn't have a bit of drama? Yours could just have its own reality show."

"You watch reality shows?" Maggie stopped and looked down at her.

"I am aware of them. I've had to watch a few. I'm an art critic, and so..."

"What!?" Maggie made an explosion sound and mimicked her mind being blown out of the left side of her head.

"Yes, dear. I studied art at Loughborough but got pregnant with Lady shortly after I graduated. I needed something that paid well enough, so I went back to night school and retrained as a journalist. I did lots of freelance work. I covered art shows. I interviewed writers and actors. I got free tickets to lots of shows. I even had a music beat for a while, but that was difficult. My husband, Jamie, worked regular days driving a lorry, so he could be home with the girls when I had to go to events in the evening, but an art opening that ends at 22:00 is much different from a show where the band doesn't start until 22:30. I'm not much of a night owl. Once Charlie, Lady's little sister, was in school, I went and got my graduate degree in film studies. I've written a few books. I'm working on a Princess Grace retrospective right now, in fact."

Maggie hung her head in shame. "I'm embarrassed to say I didn't think about you having a job at all. We've talked and talked about everyone else in the house, and

I just didn't realize that you didn't tell anything about yourself."

"You haven't said much about yourself either. I wasn't worried. I knew we'd get there. I could tell you were curious about everyone and everything. I wanted to help you feel at ease. Besides, that's how it works."

"How what works?"

"Friendships. You start by talking about what you think you have in common, and you eventually learn that you have way more in common than you thought."

"Like art."

"Yes. I'd be remiss if I didn't mention that I've seen you running around the farm with your sketch pad. I hoped to talk about it whenever you were ready to tell me."

"I'd like that, but I've got to do this stuff for Mum and find Middy and..."

"Yes, you do that. This stuff will keep, and the conversation doesn't have to be all in one day. I've years of stories to tell you. I know it doesn't seem like it, and I know you are grieving, but life is long, and I'm not going anywhere, and neither are you."

"Yeah?"

Gran nodded. "Yes."

Maggie extended her elbow again. Gran slipped her hand back through. "Okay. So, reality TV. I had to write a review for..."

They chatted all about it as they walked to Lady's office; Maggie didn't know reality TV was all fake. Gran compared them to the American soaps she watched as a kid and the Australian soap operas her girls watched that she wasn't remotely embarrassed to admit she quite enjoyed as well. She quit watching when they did, but there were some fine actors, and the plots were outrageous, mindless fun, although she preferred films to TV in general. Maggie made a mental note to look up everything Gran said, but she only remembered Princess Grace. They arrived at Lady's office, which was really a converted bedroom suite from the old days. One of the rooms was the boy's playroom. They were constantly making a racket that Lady was somehow able to ignore and do her work. Gran told her that she hadn't missed the comment about what the movers said. She promised that they would talk about that over dinner.

As everyone knew she would, Lady was more than happy to have one more for dinner. She always made a bit more than was needed as there was always someone in the kitchen at all hours of the day and night picking at leftovers. She asked if they needed to put Edward up in the big house. Maggie admitted to having no clue. Lady pulled out her phone and sent a text to Sam, thus relieving Maggie of that duty. She told her that Middy was planning on using the tractors and trailers to pick up the furniture from The Cottage and bring it back up to storage.

"Ever ridden on a tractor?" Lady asked.

"Never ever."

"Want to?" she asked while bouncing her eyebrows.

"Sure!"

Lady texted Middy to tell him that Maggie would meet him in the tractor barn. "Do you want Nicky to show you, or do you know how to get there? Need a map?"

Upon hearing his name, the 10-year-old Middleton boy poked his head out of the door of the game room. Maggie turned and saw him there, smiling a toothless grin while trying to make puppy dog eyes at her.

"How can I say no to that face?"

"Yes!" he shouted. "Wanna race?"

"Well, since I don't quite know where I'm going..."

"Threetwoonego!" he said and took off running.

Maggie waved at Lady and took off running after Nicky, who was very, very fast.

While Maggie did find the run exhilarating and fun, she wasn't really able to pay attention. She had gotten better at understanding where she was on the grounds in the few days they had been there, but she still struggled with directions around the big house and from the big house to anywhere in Barton Park.

When Nicky came skidding to a halt, seemingly not out of breath at all, he shouted, "I won!" He looked up at the metal barn, which seemed out of place as the rest of the buildings were either wooden or made of stone, and said, "This is it."

Maggie, who was not a sore loser, nor was she one to burst the bubble of a 10-year-old who thought he won a clean race, said, "I'll get you next time." She held out her fist, and he bumped it. He had excellent sportsmanship, and competing with Maggie would become a long-standing, fun tradition, as we will soon see.

"DAAAAAAADDDDDDD!!!!!" he shouted at nothing and everything. "MAGGIE'S HERE!"

The sliding door at the front of the pole barn rumbled open on an automatic switch to reveal Middy standing with his arms at his hips, elbows out, waiting for the big reveal. He tied a towel around his neck to serve as a cape. Maggie would remember this moment when she later understood that boys can grow into men, even men as large as Middy, but there is usually a boy still trapped inside. When the door finally opened, he said, "Tractor Man, ready for duty."

Nicky whooped and ran full speed ahead at his father. When he was about four feet away, he launched himself at Middy, just expecting to be caught, and, of course, he was. Maggie assumed that if Nicky had done that to her, she would be flat on her back, and he would be on his face with a bloody nose, although she would have tried to catch him. Middy didn't even take a step back; he just caught his son in his arms and hugged him tight as though he weighed no more than a pillow. "Tractor Boy ready, Commander," Nicky said once Middy set him down. He offered a salute which Middy returned.

Maggie approached the barn at regular walking speed and offered her own salute. "Civilian asks for permission to come aboard."

"That's for boats, silly," Tractor Boy said. "Come on in."

Maggie walked in and accepted a bone-crushing hug from Middy. He was a hugger. He meant well. She learned to accept it. Once she got her wind back, she walked into the barn and let her eyes adjust from the bright outside light. There sat a red tractor straight from a children's novel. It had one seat that looked incredibly uncomfortable. There were metal running boards on each side of the seat with stirrup loops below them. Attached to the tractor was a large, flatbed trailer.

"The sides aren't on. Can I help?" Tractor Boy asked.

"Yes, of course." He patted his son on the head. "Let's go." They walked over to a stack of what looked like prefabricated fence pieces that were leaning against one wall. Middy grabbed the top rail and, with his oldest son's "help," who grunted and pulled on the bottom rail, moved it over to the side of the trailer and slid the panel in place. He did this three more times, and the flatbed had sides and was suddenly ready to be piled high with furniture.

He slammed his hands together and rubbed them. "Are we ready to do some moving?"

"YES!" Tractor Boy shouted.

"Sure," Maggie chimed in with much less verve.

Middy's belly laugh was interrupted by his ringing phone. He looked at the face, saw it was important, and shook himself to get into business mode. He held a sausage-like finger in front of his mouth to make sure they knew to be quiet. "Jack Middleton speaking." He paused and waited. "Mmm." He waited. "Are you sure? Now?" He turned his wrist to look at his watch. "Okay. Sure, sure." Pause. "No problem. Really. I'll meet you in 10 minutes." Pause. "Okay. Great. Thanks for calling. Bye now." He pushed the screen and looked up at Maggie.

"Looks like Tractor Man is needed elsewhere?"

"I'm afraid so. I have an unexpected feed delivery." He pulled his beard and scrunched up his mouth in what Maggie would come to call his thinky face. "You wouldn't happen to know how to drive a tractor, would you?"

"No. My sisters don't even know how to drive a car. Teaching me tractor skills hasn't been a top priority."

"Yes, well, we'll remedy all of that in short order." He looked down at his phone and tapped out a message. "For now, I'm going to get someone over here who can drive the tractor. I'm afraid I won't be able to help with the move."

"It's all good. Edward is here and..."

"Edward?"

"My brother's brother-in-law. He's mad for Elinor."

"Well, showing up to help people move is a good sign of admiration and affection. If she isn't already, she will be mad for him in due course."

"Yeah, I suspect she is already. She got all girled up when she saw him. We'd been moving all day and…"

"Moving all day?"

Maggie offered a quick summary of the day's events knowing Middy had to get moving.

"Yes, well, this is why I love your mother like a sister. I would have been there to help if she had just asked, but she will not ask."

Maggie shrugged and nodded, not sure what to make of any of that and not sure she was the right person with whom he should be conversing about his thoughts on why her mum was doing what she was doing. She added more mental notes to her ever-growing list of things to discuss with Gran.

Middy understood that she felt uncomfortable with the subject. "Yes, well, I'll take Tractor Boy with me, and you wait for Juliet. You'll know it's her because she's the only one coming to drive the tractor." He laughed at his own joke. "Come on, boy. We've got to go do the unfun part of the job." Maggie found it hard to believe that there was any part of his job that he didn't love. "After we're done with the feed, we'll walk down to The Cottage and lend a hand, and we'll drive the tractor back."

"Yeah?" His eyes brightened up. "What if they're done?"

"We'll just take the tractor for a spin to check on the sheep."

"Yes!" He pumped his fist. "Let's go then." He grabbed his father's hand and started pulling him toward the door. "Bye, Mags!"

"Bye, Tractor Boy!" It was the first time anyone had called her Mags. She rolled it around in her head as she waved goodbye. Her parents just always called her Maggie, and it never occurred to her that she could do anything else with it. She didn't mind the name Margaret, but no one called her that. She hadn't really thought about the fact that her name was Margaret until she went to school, as is often the case with children who are called something other than their given name.

She was sitting on the running board of the tractor, thinking about all of this, when she heard the back door open again. She jumped up, not wanting to seem like she was loafing, although there was nothing for her to do, and this Juliet person wasn't going to care one way or the other; she was just doing whatever her boss told her to do. The sun was positioned so that Juliet was backlit when she walked in. Maggie couldn't see her but wanted to seem friendly, so she smiled and waved at the approaching figure. "Hi, I'm," she thought about trying out Mags here but thought it might be weird when she got to The Cottage and some stranger was calling her Mags, so after a short pause, she just said, "Maggie. Maggie Dashwood."

Juliet approached and came into sharper focus as she got farther from the door and closer to Maggie. She wore cargo shorts and had on a long-sleeved Barton Park work shirt with the sleeves rolled up. The rolls fit snugly over her toned arms. Her hair was shaved down to just stubble. Her right ear had earrings from the top of the cartilage all the way down to the lobe. Some were studs; some were hoops. The light behind her made her glow. As she came even closer, Maggie could see that she wore no makeup, and her eyes were so green that they seemed to sparkle. "You sure?" Juliet laughed.

Maggie opened her mouth to reply, but her tongue had turned to sandpaper. She licked her lips and tried again. "Yeah, sorry. I'm sure." She reached out to shake her hand and tried to step forward, but her legs suddenly felt like they couldn't hold her weight. She dared not risk falling down, so she stood and smiled and left her hand out for Juliet to walk to and shake, which she did. It was then that Maggie realized how wet her palms were. She could feel it slide around on Juliet's rough, workworn palm.

Juliet either didn't notice or was too good of a person, so she didn't wipe her hands on her trousers. "Juliet Carpenter." She smiled down at Maggie, who for the second time in a day, stood dumbfounded in front of someone. "I hear you're in need of a tractor driver."

Maggie nodded and tried to make her mouth say words. She eventually sputtered, "Yes, please." She closed her eyes and let her eyes roll to the back of her head. Of all the things she could have said to this person, "Yes, please" was the one that made her sound like a baby. She wasn't sure why she didn't want to sound like a baby in front of this woman, who was at least the same age as Elinor, if not older, who obviously saw a child standing in front of her. She tried to pull it out of the ditch and came up with, "Yes, a driver is just what I need." It came out almost as a whisper. She heard it. Knew it sounded ridiculous and decided then and there that she would never ever speak again. No one needed to hear anything that she ever had to say, especially not Juliet. She would just be mute until they got to The Cottage, and then she would go inside and never come out. Better yet, she thought, she would walk to The Cottage and not ride, and she would get lost in the woods and die alone there without ever having to speak words again.

Once again, Juliet chose not to comment on Maggie's behavior because, of course, this being her first meeting with the youngest Dashwood, she had no point of reference. "Well, I'm here to be your knight in shining armor, then." She started unbuttoning the front of her Barton Park shirt, and Maggie felt her trainers fill with concrete. She tried to look away, but she couldn't. Her brain could not understand what was happening or what she wanted to happen. Her lips were stuck together as every ounce of fluid drained from her face. She tried to swallow. Tried to smile. Tried not to stare. Tried to push her tongue through her lips.

By the time Juliet got to the third button, Maggie realized she had a shirt on underneath, and she felt both relieved and disappointed. She was confused and embarrassed. Her cheeks were burning, but her sweat felt cold. All of this took mere seconds to Juliet and the world at large, but eons passed for Maggie. Once Juliet had unbuttoned it all the way, she rolled down the sleeves, pulled the shirt off, and tied it around her waist. She wore a shirt that read "The Kinks" spelled out in a swoopy font. The bottom of each letter was a shoe.

Maggie knew who The Kinks were. Her mum liked all kinds of music, so she'd heard a few songs here and there, but one of her favorite singers wrote a song that was sort of about them, and so she tried to know more. However, when she saw how many albums they had, and just how prolific they were for so long, she felt overwhelmed, as often happens to people when they are offered too many choices. Thus, she listened to their greatest hits, which she liked very much, but felt that she had enough music in her head as it was.

The shirt though, seen in this light, on this person, made her start to scold herself for not doing the work. Not knowing more than the greatest hits. If she had done the work, she told herself, she could talk about some track that was a hidden gem that had a deeper meaning. Instead, she felt like a stupid fangirl who showed up to the concert, waited for the band to sing one song, the hit song, the one everyone's Grampa knew, and then left before the encore. She'd seen that exact shirt before in a music video of that song that one of her favorite singers made. She liked the video very much, and it made her like the song even more, but still, she didn't learn more about The Kinks. Her heart started slamming against her chest as she heard the chorus of that song play on full blast in her head. "It's the way she walks, the way she talks, can't stop thinking about the girl in the Kinks shirt," Matt Nathanson sang.

"Ready?" Juliet said, silencing the symphony.

Opting to keep her vow of silence, Maggie just nodded.

Juliet put one foot in the stirrup, grabbed the wheel, pulled herself up on the uncomfortable-looking seat, and fired up the tractor. The noise was deafening. Juliet pointed to the running board and then pointed at Maggie. Maggie nodded and put one foot in the stirrup. Juliet reached out her hand to help pull Maggie up. She made the decision that she would rather slime her with her wet, disgusting hand than try to climb up on her own and fall over backward. Juliet was as strong as she looked. Without much effort, Maggie was up on the running board, standing inches from Juliet, who was smiling. "Here we go!" she shouted. "Hang on tight." She pointed at the back of her seat. She put the tractor in gear and jerked it out into a world that looked to Maggie totally different than it had just 30 minutes prior.

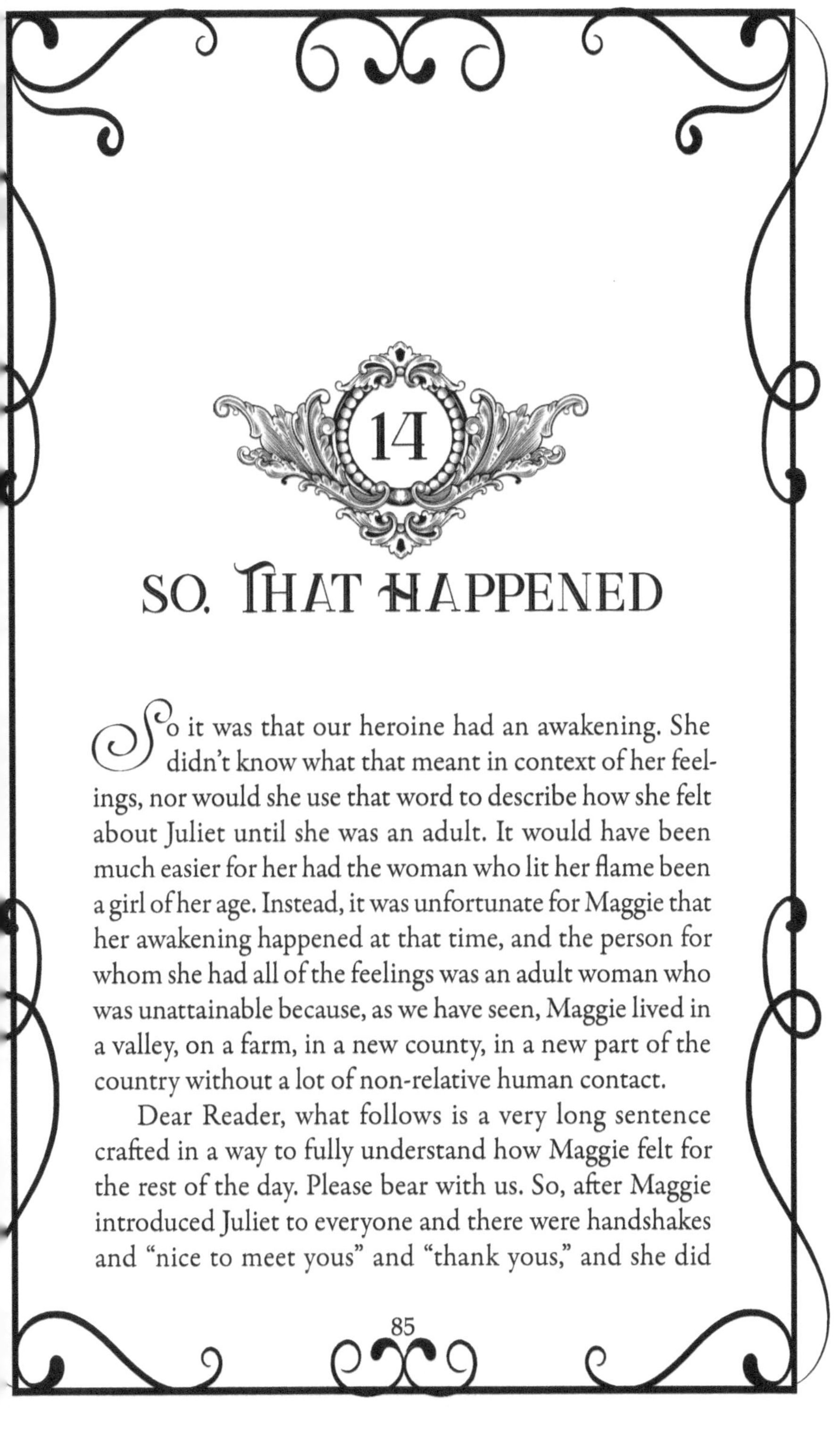

14

SO, THAT HAPPENED

So it was that our heroine had an awakening. She didn't know what that meant in context of her feelings, nor would she use that word to describe how she felt about Juliet until she was an adult. It would have been much easier for her had the woman who lit her flame been a girl of her age. Instead, it was unfortunate for Maggie that her awakening happened at that time, and the person for whom she had all of the feelings was an adult woman who was unattainable because, as we have seen, Maggie lived in a valley, on a farm, in a new county, in a new part of the country without a lot of non-relative human contact.

Dear Reader, what follows is a very long sentence crafted in a way to fully understand how Maggie felt for the rest of the day. Please bear with us. So, after Maggie introduced Juliet to everyone and there were handshakes and "nice to meet yous" and "thank yous," and she did her best not to seem as awkward as she felt, but she kept looking at Juliet while she thought she wasn't looking and imagining what she might look like dressed differently or with hair, or when she was younger, so she knew she was totally awkward and she knew that everyone knew it, and after the trailer was loaded at The Cottage and unloaded into the storage room at the big house, and after Juliet brought everyone back down to The Cottage and had tea and cakes, and after Tractor Man and Tractor Boy showed up, and after Sam and Middy had a not-so-private chat about her not needing to worry about asking too much of him and her explaining that she did worry because she was told she'd be "cared for" the rest of her life once before and she wasn't keen on having the rug pulled out from under her again, and after they hugged and cried a little, and after Middy hugged everyone while his eldest son ate all the "extra cakes" that Elinor assured him would go to waste if he didn't have them, and after Tractor Man and Tractor Boy took the tractor for a trip around the Park, Juliet asked Maggie if she would walk her back to her car.

Having no reason to say no other than all the reasons she couldn't say aloud, Maggie acquiesced, and they walked up the path toward the big house. "So, that happened today," Juliet started without any preamble.

Cold buckets of panic poured down Maggie's back. She ducked her head down and mumbled, "What's that?"

"Oh, kiddo. If I read the situation wrong, then you have an unregulated gland problem, and we should have a talk about that instead. Either way, we should talk."

"..." Nothing came out of Maggie's mouth except for incoherent sounds that shouldn't be recreated here.

They approached the big house, and instead of going in the side door, they walked around the back of the house where there was another worn walking path that Maggie knew led to the sheep barn. "Okay, I'll start. I'll just ask you some questions, and you can just nod or grunt or whatever works for you. Is that okay?"

Maggie nodded. She thought of saying thanks, but she couldn't get her lips to part. She looked up at Juliet's face and tried to convey her thanks, but she was once again struck by her ... everything that she couldn't look for too long.

"Sweet. So, was today the first time you realized you liked girls?"

Nod.

"Ever liked any boys?"

Shake. Shrug. "Maybe? I mean, my sisters talk about boys. Boys are cute. I mean, they even say some girls are cute too, you know? So, I just thought everyone was cute or not cute, but nothing like this." She waved her hands around. "Nothing like you. I..." Her voice died in her throat. She coughed. She waved, indicating she was done.

"Well, I have to say I'm flattered that it was me. I can't say that me in my work cargos and shirt makes me feel particularly fetching. I wouldn't be into me. I mean, for me, the gal was a lady. Skirts and socks and long hair and all. My teacher, actually. That's still my type. My partner, Meg, is the skirtiest and socksiest woman I know. She's even a teacher, so take that for what it is."

"Really?"

"Yeah. It was bad. The first object of my affection was my fifth-year teacher Ms. Hathaway. I would stare at Ms. Hathaway while she was talking so intently that

she assumed I was engaged with the lesson. I mean, I was staring at her all the time, but she only saw me when she was looking back, you know, so she didn't know that I wasn't doing any work. I was just staring. On more than one occasion, she called on me only to have me reply with a 'huh?' It got so bad that she eventually recommended that my parents have my hearing checked. I knew it wasn't the problem, and I wasn't surprised to earn a clean bill of auditory health, but I did have a lot of explaining to do."

"Yeah? Explaining?" Maggie couldn't imagine explaining anything to anyone at any time in the future. "Like, your folks?"

"Sure, them, but mostly to myself. I wasn't really mature enough. I was what, nine? I mean, you're older than nine, right? You must be. You're bigger than the boys."

"Thirteen."

"Right, thirteen with all that stuff in your head and some sense of the world, and you're all confused and stuff. I was nine. My mum was all, 'Oh, don't worry baby. I already knew,' and Da was all, 'You'll grow out of it,' and I was all, 'Not bloody likely.'"

"So?"

"Right." Juliet snapped out of the memory. "Well, the point is, it wasn't for a few more years until I was in secondary when I finally met some older girls who were queer and who..."

"Queer? I'm queer? Do I have to say that? Marianne'll be relentless."

"She the pretty one?"

"Yeah."

"Vain?"

"She thinks all the songs are about her."

"Ha! Deep cut. Nice." She held up a hand. Maggie slapped it.

"Thanks. Owe it to my mum. Music fiend."

"Sure. Sure. Anyway, the queer thing is just a word. It's a word I like. Lotsa folks like it. You don't have to. You can be whatever. At thirteen, even though I knew I was totally into girls, I snogged a few lads just to be sure."

"Snogged a few at thirteen? Ugh." Maggie dropped her head and stopped walking. She put her hands against her temples. "That wasn't even on my mind until just now. I mean, today, I mean... I know I'm not kissing you. You're like an adult, and I'm a kid, and I'm just... Ahhh!"

"Girl, listen, it's your journey. Kiss all the girls or boys, or don't kiss any. That's all I'm sayin'. My journey was different. You're going through some stuff now, and this feels like a rotten cherry on what I'm sure feels like a turd sundae, but it isn't. This could be your way to a new chapter. That's why I wanted to talk. I just wanted to say that I'm here. You don't have to do it all alone, you know."

"Yeah?" Maggie looked up at her with raised eyebrows.

"Just as long as you don't undress me with your eyes again like you did when I was taking off my work shirt." Juliet laughed.

Maggie groaned and dropped her head into her hands again.

"Yeah, yeah. Right. Too soon." Juliet patted her on the back. "Come on. Let's walk again. I do need to get back and head home." Maggie stood up straight, and they continued walking. "Seriously though, you don't need to tell anyone anything, or you can get a pride flag and fly it. This is a pretty great place to be. Lady and Middy are the best. You have allies there. From what I know about Gran, she seems pretty great too. Just don't freak. You're not a freak. You're just a person who now knows that you find other people attractive. It happens. Something about human nature, I suspect."

"Yeah?"

"Yeah. And when you have questions, if you don't want to talk to your sisters or mum about it, I'm here. I work here. Like I was saying, I was a mess until I met some queer older girls in secondary. They really helped me out. I just want to pay it forward. Any questions, you come to me, and I'll be your Queer Yoda."

Maggie laughed really hard at that, and while she was already feeling better, that made her feel good. Once she calmed down, they were at Juliet's car parked behind the sheep barn. "Thank you for being so cool about all of this. I don't think I really knew what it was. I don't think I know really at all; it's just like I was hot and cold and dry and wet all at the same time. Like I just ran a race that I somehow lost and won at the same time."

"That checks out. You started your period already?"

Maggie felt her cheeks heat up again. "Yeah. I started my period last year; Mum was out, and Elinor was home. It was like a very clinical lecture, but I know all about that. Mum had 'The Talk' with me shortly after. It was less clinical but really kind of pointless. I wasn't really feeling all the 'tingles' as she said I would, and I wasn't super close to anyone. We live in the country, well, lived, I guess we do again, and I didn't have a lot of friends at school, weird artist kid, pushed into school early cause of my summer birthday, rich dad, came across as standoffish and unapproachable just because I'm a Dashwood and Marianne's my sister, and all. My brother owns a bunch of media stuff, and so people told all their kids to stay away. They didn't want to end up in one of his gossip rags, as though anyone from Leeds was that interesting."

"Okay, wow." She looked at her watch. "So much to unpack there. I do really have to go, but can we pin that? Your brother is John Dashwood? That means your sister-in-law is Sissy Dashwood? Oh, man." She looked down at her watch again and sighed. "That guy back there was her brother?"

"Umm, yeah? Don't hold that against him. He's sweet and sweet on Elinor. He's nothing like her. I mean, there is hardly anyone in the world like her. Why? Do you know who they are?"

Juliet sighed. "Pin in it. I promise. Just say, I totally get why those parents were the way they were. I mean, screw them for withholding friendship from a kid, but anyone with even so much as an anklebone in the closet could be the target. Her gossip magazines are brutal. I mean, she's the worst, but…"

"Wow. It's like you and Mum share a brain. She says almost the same stuff about Sissy."

"I get that." Juliet's phone pinged with a text. She pulled it out of her cargo pocket. Read it, smiled, and fired off a text. "Well, that's the little Ms. She and I have dinner plans with her sister, and I smell like sheep and moving sweat, as you know, so I promise we'll talk more. Give me your phone." Maggie handed it over. "It's unlocked?"

"Sure. What secrets do I have?"

"Hmmm. Well." She typed a few things. Her own phone pinged again. She handed it back. "There. I'm in your contacts, and I have your stuff." She reached out and ruffled Maggie's hair. "It was good to meet you, and I am glad to know you. Text me when you need to, and I am pretty sure you'll need to. See you around, kiddo."

She climbed inside her car, started it up, honked the horn, and drove off. Maggie looked down at her phone to see that the contact card read "Yoda." She smiled at that. She watched Juliet's car drive away, feeling both exhilarated and exhausted. She checked the time to see she had 45 minutes until dinner. She sniffed her right armpit and grimaced. She would need to get back to The Cottage before dinner and shower. While Gran hardly ate, Maggie didn't want to turn her stomach while she picked at her dinner and peppered her with questions. She pulled out her phone and brought up her music streaming service. She typed in "The Kinks."

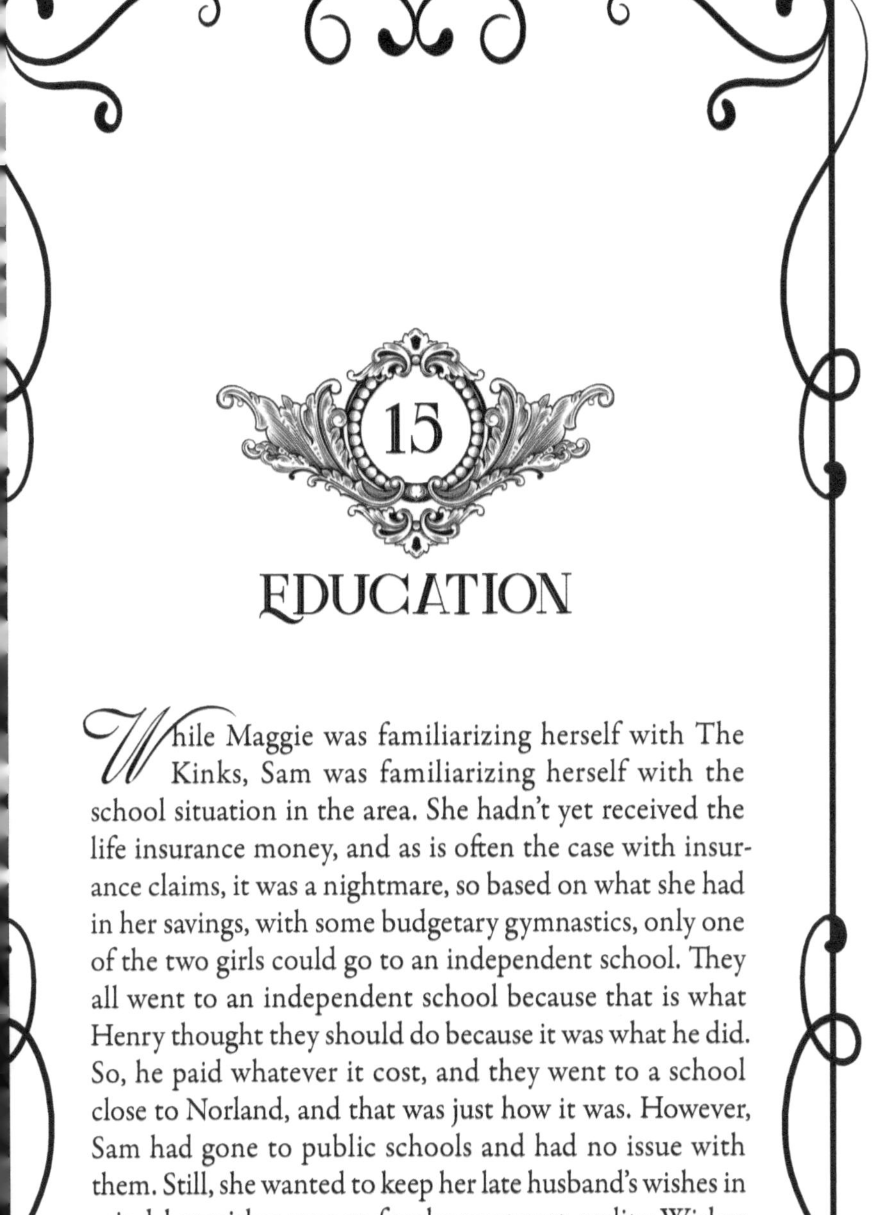

15

EDUCATION

While Maggie was familiarizing herself with The Kinks, Sam was familiarizing herself with the school situation in the area. She hadn't yet received the life insurance money, and as is often the case with insurance claims, it was a nightmare, so based on what she had in her savings, with some budgetary gymnastics, only one of the two girls could go to an independent school. They all went to an independent school because that is what Henry thought they should do because it was what he did. So, he paid whatever it cost, and they went to a school close to Norland, and that was just how it was. However, Sam had gone to public schools and had no issue with them. Still, she wanted to keep her late husband's wishes in mind, but wishes are not, for the most part, reality. Wishes can't pay tuition. Ultimately, she decided that it would be Marianne as she would throw the biggest fit and be the most miserable should she not be allowed to "study drama with the greatest dramatic minds the country has to offer." Obviously, she didn't need to work on her acting skills.

Before they even moved, against Sam's wishes, Elinor withdrew from Aberystwyth. She applied and was accepted to The University of Exeter, where she would study the Liberal Arts with a mixture of on-campus and online courses. She argued, rightly so, that she could still move on and get her graduate degree in library science later. She could live at The Cottage, which would save a lot of money on room and board. She could apply for one of the many student worker jobs that were available in the university's library. The only hiccup in the plan was that they had just one car, and she couldn't drive it. She would need to learn to drive so she could get herself to university and Marianne to college on the days when they both needed to be in town. Middy happily volunteered his time and some work vehicles to instruct them both, and so the Barton Park Driving School began in earnest.

Once all of that was decided and the deposits were made and the paperwork was filed, Sam finally started on Maggie's application for school. The process for going to a public school was quite a bit different. With an independent school, there was a phone call and a meeting, and an exchange of money with paperwork. Not so with a public school. Since Sam only went to a public school but had never sent a child to one, she had no idea what the process would be. Barton Park was technically located in a small village that had a local school system. It was the only option, and so one would think the process would be simple. There was a child of school age who needed to attend the secondary school in the town where she moved.

The internet exists. One should be able to forward records with explanations about Maggie's age and the year she was in and why and how she did at primary school with letters from her teachers, who all liked her very much, and move things around expeditiously, but that was not the case. Sam had to apply to the village council in person and then go through a variety of hoops in person that ended with many a glass of wine drunk. Eventually, Maggie was enrolled in the local secondary school which she would attend in person as well, so it was good that her mum knew her way around the halls so intimately. They qualified for free transportation as they lived far enough away from the school, but that process involved a lot more paperwork for which she didn't have the energy. Lady offered up her services as she had to take two of the four boys to the primary school, which was just down the road from the secondary school, as everything in the village was just down the road from everything else. "Just down the road" could have been the name of the village.

Lady always waited until the last possible moment to buy school clothes for the boys as they were in a perpetual state of growth. The village school opted to have a dress code as opposed to official uniforms as most of the folks in and around the village used charity shops or had hand-me-downs that were clean and presentable but could not afford new required uniforms each year as the children grew. Maggie was in the midst of a mental and physical growth spurt herself, so she was relieved when Sam agreed to follow Lady's lead. She didn't want to be the new girl with clothes that didn't fit, nor did she feel ready to lock in what she was wearing. Elinor wore skirts and socks because that is what proper British girls did. Marianne wore skirts and socks because she thought that is what pretty girls did. Maggie wore cast-off skirts and socks from her elder sisters, but those were the tartan of the old independent school that did require specific uniforms so she had to actually get something new.

She couldn't help but think about what Juliet said about skirts and socks. Did she like girls in skirts and socks? She didn't really know. She tried to think of some of the girls she knew from school up north, and there was nothing. She thought about some of Elinor and Marianne's friends, but she drew a blank there. Just a bunch of same-looking girls who did the same things her sisters did. Elinor hung with self-serious bookish types. While Maggie thought smart was attractive, none of them stood out. Marianne hung out with a bunch of girls who spent small fortunes on cosmetics. She didn't like that at all. Could it be that she didn't like them because she didn't really like her sister, or could it be that she didn't like what her sister represented? She wasn't sure about much. She knew that she liked Juliet, and while she came to grips with the fact that she was born ten years too late for that ship to ever sail, she couldn't help but think about her all the time.

She tied her hair up in a scarf to see what she would look like with no hair. She drew some self-portraits with different hairstyles to get a sense of what she thought she wanted to look like. She liked some, hated some, and felt agnostic about others but made no concrete decisions. She tried on all of her clothes in different combinations. Trousers with button-down shirts. Sweaters and skirts. Sweaters and trousers, and on and on. She couldn't land on anything that made her feel as good as she thought Juliet looked in her rolled-up shirt and shorts. Of course, she tried that look too, but it turns out that toned arms and muscular legs are required to pull that particular look off, and Maggie had neither of those, not yet anyway. She felt that nothing was going to come together for her and that she was just going to end up as a skirts and socks girl so that she didn't have to try anymore. At thirteen, everything seemed so final, and Maggie felt pushed into a corner. She was not in any such corner, but she just didn't know it yet.

Everything changed one day in early August when Sam announced that after breakfast, they needed to join her in the parlor as they had some work to do that must be done together. They had been settled into The Cottage for a full month. The driving lessons were going smashingly for one of the Dashwood sisters and quite poorly for the other. They decided, to preserve their sanity, that Marianne would "take a break" from her lessons and try again next year. It wasn't as important as she hadn't even gotten her provisional. The important thing was getting Elinor ready. She already had her provisional license. She and her father hoped to get in enough practice for her to pass the final driving test before she went off to university. It was something she wanted to do "for him" even though, had she never learned to drive, he wouldn't have cared one way or the other. He wasn't that kind of father, but after one passes on, those who are left behind get to write the narrative regardless of how true or false it is.

After the food was eaten and the dishes were cleared by Marianne, washed by Elinor, dried by Maggie, and returned to their shelves by Sam, the Dashwood girls followed their mother in descending age order, as they often did, into the front parlor. There they found several unopened boxes. They were all confused as they thought they had already unpacked everything, but of course, we know from before that these are Henry's things that Sam boxed up early on.

"Sit." She pointed at the couch, and they marched over and sat. "Girls, these are your dad's things. I honestly don't remember what is in here. Everything from his office. I know that for sure."

"Except for the furniture," Maggie chimed in.

"Yes, save for that."

Marianne said some words about what she hoped her sister-in-law would do with the furniture they were forced to leave behind. While the rest of the family agreed about all of it, we don't need to linger on that too long here. This isn't that kind of book.

"I've been debating what to do with this stuff. Part of me wanted to just store it forever. Part of me wanted to open one box a year on his birthday. Part of me wanted to throw it all away. Ultimately, I realized this isn't just up to me. He was your dad. This is what you have left of him, and I want you to have what you want to have."

Maggie looked at Marianne, expecting her to be the one to make the decision, but she looked to Elinor. There is a saying about a broken clock being right twice a day. This is one of those times. It was Elinor who should lead them. Elinor looked back at her sisters, who were waiting for her to decide. She touched her heart and nodded. She looked at their mother. "Right. We'll do it. One box at a time, one thing at a time. We'll make piles. If there is something more than one person wants, it stays in the box to be decided at another time. Yes?"

"That is just the right thing," Sam said. The other girls nodded. "Okay." She rubbed her hands together. "Let's start," she closed her eyes and pointed her finger around wildly until she stopped and opened her eyes, "here."

We don't need to spend all the time with them as they opened the boxes, but just know that it took all day. Literally the rest of the day and into the wee hours of the next. They didn't end until well after midnight. Fear not; they stopped to eat, drink, and use the facilities. There were fewer fights than one might have expected. We shan't go into a full inventory here, but below are the highlights.

Elinor took his books. He wasn't a huge reader, but he loved what he loved. His favorite writer was Agatha Christie, which may seem like a cop-out to say one's favorite writer is also one of the best-known and best-selling writers in English history, but popular doesn't mean bad. Elinor had only read a handful of Dame Christie's massive library. Her father had the whole collection. By the time Elinor graduated from university, she would also tell anyone who asked that Agatha Christie was her favorite writer as well. There were some other bits and bobs in there, which found their way to Elinor's overstuffed bookshelf. Middy would later bring her two more down from storage that she would fill as well.

Marianne took all the little collectibles he kept on his desk. He had cheap, little figurines and snow globes with which he liked to fidget. He would pick them up whenever he went somewhere new. That is not to say that he picked them up when he went to a new country, which he certainly did, but if he was anywhere that had a gift shop, he would buy something. It wasn't a habit that Sissy thought becoming of a man of his stature, and so when she saw the full box of what she called "roadside trash," she put up no objection. Marianne placed all of them, which numbered in the hundreds, around her room. She asked Middy if she could put up shelves that ran around the full length of her room, just near the top of the wall. Being a man who loved to be amenable, he happily sent Juliet down to install them. It will surprise no one that Maggie was more than happy to help with the installation.

If one would be surprised to learn that Henry Dashwood collected roadside trash, one would be utterly shocked to learn that he had a strange affinity for trashy action films. There was something about the mindless nature of the films, along with, for the most part, a predictable ending that appealed to him. It wasn't quality he sought; it was comfort. He was not discerning. *Die Hard*, a movie that almost everyone feels is the greatest action film of all time, was in his collection, as was every single terrible knockoff *Die Hard* on a ... boat, bus, bicycle built for two, and on and on film. If there was a ninja or a rogue assassin or, better yet, both, odds are he owned a copy. The holy trinity of 80s action, Stallone, Schwarzenegger, and Norris, took up space in his collection. While many of these films were on DVD, for which he had a small, 7-inch, portable DVD player, most of them were digitized and on portable hard drives. He had hundreds of gigabytes of mindless punching and shooting. When they made this discovery, although it wasn't a secret to Sam, there was a bit of awkward silence followed by lots of talking at once.

It was a good time for a snack break. Sam did her best to explain it, but they were all still confused. Elinor thought action movies were misogynistic. Marianne thought they were just sweaty and stupid, although she would eventually change her mind much, much later in life as we shall see near the end of our tale. Thus, it was, with the choice of donating them to a charity shop or keeping them, Maggie said she would take them up to her room and decide what to keep and what to pitch. Nary one movie was donated, and to this day, Maggie Dashwood owns this collection, and it has grown over the years.

When they arrived at his box of clothes, it was decided that it would be best to donate that as there wasn't a lot of practical use. He was taller than all of them, and even if Maggie grew at an exponential rate, she would never get as tall as he was. Still, they went through it all, article by article. Elinor kept what he liked to call his "jaunty hat." Marianne kept his black suit jacket that she thought would look cute with one of her outfits if she rolled up the sleeves and put a belt around it. She was right. Sam had already kept his wristwatch and cufflinks, which she would occasionally wear when she missed him terribly.

Nothing really struck Maggie's fancy until they got to the bottom of the final box, which meant it was the first thing packed when Sam started packing up the room. They found a hanging zipper bag of neckties. Sam almost didn't bother to open up the bag. It was late. They were tired. She didn't think anyone would want the ties, but Marianne insisted, "You said everything." Once she saw them, she lost all interest. Elinor yawned and kissed her mum on the cheek and went off to bed. Marianne followed her out of the room sans kiss. Maggie stood still, feeling not remotely tired but energized. Bowties, skinny ties, and fat ties in all colors of the rainbow. She pulled one out and felt the silk slide through her fingers. She touched them all. They were not all silk, but she needed to know.

"Okay," Sam said, not realizing what was happening. It was late. She, too, was exhausted. "Toss those in the donate bag on your way up. You need help with the movies?" Maggie just shook her head. Sam, of course, thought she meant she didn't help with the movies, which she didn't, but all Maggie heard was the part about tossing the ties. That was the moment it was decided that when she went to school, some days she would wear a skirt and other days she would wear trousers, but every day, without fail, she would wear a shirt and tie, and she did.

16

MOVIES AND SCHOOL: A MONTAGE

So it was, Dear Reader, that the sun was about to set on the first of five summers that we will spend with Maggie Dashwood at Barton Park. While there is plenty that happened to her and her sisters while they were at school, it is the summers of childhood when the real stuff happens. Sure, the UK system only allows for 6 weeks or so for summer holiday, but summer is summer, regardless. The unstructured days followed by first jobs followed by late nights are things of memory. That isn't to say that school doesn't have anything to offer. For some people, time in school was the greatest. Others think fondly of that one particular lecture or that time they scored the winning goal or won the race or did something equally excellent. Those things are of great value, of course, and we would never wish to disparage those moments for anyone. It's just we have only so many pages that we can spend on our heroine's early days, and so we move forward in time, montage style. Music shall be provided shortly.

We shall begin in real-time and speed up and jump time and blur the background characters as needed, as is the way of the montage. Maggie discovered that she, like her father, loved stupid action movies. The first night after the great unboxing, as Marianne had taken to calling it, and as is the way with Marianne, the things she said became part of the permanent record; long after everyone had fallen asleep, Maggie figured out how to work the portable DVD player and played a movie called *American Ninja*. She chose it based on the cover. There stood a white, blonde man, not in a ninja outfit, holding a sword, standing in front of an American flag in the middle of what was clearly a choreo-graphed fight with a person in a ninja costume. It looked like the most ridiculous thing she'd ever seen. She assumed she would watch for ten minutes, get a good laugh, and box up the rest of the movies unwatched. Instead, she found herself strangely mesmerized. It just started. No preamble. The main character didn't talk for ages, and when he did, it wasn't great as the acting was subpar.

There was a kidnapping, a fight between Americans and some local hooligans, and then ninjas showed up in the first ten minutes, and the lead guy still hadn't spoken. The plot was absurd. Yet, there was something compelling in the way the movie carried itself. It was as though it said, "Yeah, I know what I am. Deal with it." Maggie, who didn't know who she was nor was she sure when or if she ever fig-ured out if she would be comfortable saying it with such a boldfaced swagger, felt that she could live vicariously through this movie. She fell asleep finally, halfway through *American Ninja 2: The Confrontation*. She never really found out what "The Confrontation" was, even upon multiple rewatches.

While it would take her years to finally watch all the movies in that box, she eventually did. Many of those movies will come up in conversation in future pages. There will be a lot of ongoing conversations between Maggie and Gran about the difference between movies and films. For now, just imagine Maggie alone in her room, watching movies with sketches of herself in various action movie poses scattered all around the room. Cut those images with some action movie music playing, maybe even Survivor's "Eye of the Tiger" from *Rocky III* while we see Gran and Maggie in deep conversation, cut to them sitting on couches at The Cottage or in the big house with one, or both of them laughing, crying, and making annoyed and/ or incredulous faces.

Elinor discovered that she loved studying the Liberal Arts. She was a diligent note-taker during her lectures, and she was an active reader; although she would never write in a book, she wrote while reading her texts. She filled notebook after notebook with information that she hoped would one day become knowledge that she could use to help future patrons. She realized by the end of her first year at university that she wanted to be an academic librarian. It was a path she would not have followed had she gone to Wales. She would have most assuredly gone on to work in a public library, and she would have, in that split universe, been quite happy, we can imagine, as the library was the place where Elinor Dashwood felt the best. Still, there was something about the quest for knowledge for the sake of knowledge as opposed to information for the sake of information that appealed to her.

As far as her relationship with Edward went, they decided that while technology allowed them to communicate as often as they wished, and they could see each other's faces every day, they wouldn't put that much pressure on themselves. They were five hours apart. They were busy. He was beginning his final year at university, and she was starting her first. They must have said the word "busy" ten thousand times as they justified their choices to each other and themselves. During the year though, neither of them so much as had an impure thought about anyone other than the other. He visited often. What they did in private is between them. However, as we will eventually discover, when some guests arrive from America, there are some minor complications. Nothing can be perfect.

Marianne went off to her independent college where she studied drama and performing arts as planned. She made friends quickly, was elevated to queen bee status, and soon all but forgot about that boy from the beginning of the summer, just as we have. What was he about anyway? Didn't he go to jail? Good riddance, we say. She did have a myriad of crushes. She kissed all the boys who wished to be kissed. Nothing was worth discussing at great length. It will come as a shock to no one that straight teenage boys want to kiss the pretty, new queen bee.

The Dashwoods, Middletons, and Gran attended several performances where Marianne wasn't the lead but where she stole the show. These performances almost always ended with another performance by Marianne in the Barton Park van as she explained why she was so much better than the leads and what she would have done differently and how the director, whose name was Ms. Marks but whom Marianne called by her first name, Christine, told her in confidence that next year, she would be the lead. "The theatre is really quite political," she would say each and every time.

Sam Dashwood eventually got her husband's life insurance payout. She was home alone on the sunny but cold November morning. The notification arrived in her email that the deposit had been made into her account. She felt relieved that she and the girls would be secure for several more years. She could buy Elinor her own car so that she could actually take part in the dropping off and picking up of the kids from school in the village. She could even, if Maggie wished it, get her into an independent school. Then, she immediately felt sick to her stomach about feeling relieved.

She drank several fingers of whisky alone in the parlor and cried herself to sleep in a shirt that was held together with all of Henry's cufflinks while clutching his watch to her chest. She woke up just after noon with her tongue stuck to the roof of her mouth. She drank a lot of water, had some food, showered, shaved, and walked up to the big house to finally have the conversation with Lady about gainful employment. She pitched her some ideas about marketing. She wanted to create a podcast and live stream. Most of the ideas were not fully baked, but by the time they had finished talking, Sam was the new director of communications for Barton Park. She insisted that her wages reflect her housing as income. There was haggling and, ultimately, a handshake, hug, and later at dinner, when the position was announced, a toast.

Maggie arrived on day one of her new secondary school dressed in a skirt with a white shirt, a black tie done in a loose double Windsor knot as Middy taught her, and a black blazer. She didn't feel as cool as she looked, even though even Marianne commented that she looked "pretty cool," which, coming from Marianne, was huge. She did her best to fit in, but the new girl in the tie stood out. While no one ever said it to her, many of the students were intrigued. One girl even called it a "boss move." In fact, several of the girls came back from winter holiday in January with some ties of their own that they got as holiday gifts.

She was friendly enough with some kids in her year that by October she could eat lunch with them but not friendly enough that they invited her to any parties they had. By January, after it was clear that the tie thing was, in fact, a boss move, some kids invited her to parties or back to theirs for tea. She took almost everyone up on these offers. There was always an enjoyable time, but there wasn't one person who, when she returned home to visit after her first term at university, felt the urge to go into the village to see. She didn't collect friends until much later in life, and even then, she only managed to make a few. She never reciprocated offers to go back to hers as she always felt bad about asking someone to drive all the way out to Barton Park or, worse, to have one of her family members drive someone home. However, they were all aware that she lived on the grounds of Barton Park, and so, during summers, they would try to seek her out if they happened to be out that way. This never happened as is often the case that people who live near the tourist attraction rarely go to the tourist attraction. They are, in fact, not tourists.

Maggie Dashwood was, in case we've been remiss and not mentioned it before, very, very bright. School was not particularly hard for her. She wasn't one of those unicorns who could easily write a five-page essay, work out some chemistry equations, and then compose an opera on the same day, but she was a hard-working, diligent student. She took schooling seriously but not so much for the time she spent at school. Save for art class, she felt agnostic about it. It was something one should do and do well, but not something one should feel any pain or pleasure in. Good marks meant very little to her. She never earned any bad marks, so there is no way to know how that might have affected her. School was a means to an end, and as we shall see in the final pages of this tale, and those who already met an older version of Maggie in another book know, it does get her where she wishes to go. The ends did, in fact, justify the means for one Ms. Margaret Dashwood.

However, before we get there, or return there, depending on the order in which we first meet the youngest Ms. Dashwood, it is time to move through the rest of this montage. Let's envision a time-lapsed video with, say, a song by The Kinks playing over the top of it. Possibly "All Day and All of the Night," where we see Maggie in different outfits, trousers, skirts, hats, no hats, red tie, blue tie, tartan tie, and bow tie; her hair changes, but she looks like she is sitting in the same desk. People behind her change, and the teachers in front of her change. The camera pans around her as the music plays. At the guitar solo, we see her in those same outfits, at lunch, on the school grounds, taking self-defense classes that Sam insisted on her taking if she was going to be walking back and forth from school and all around the village, and walking down the hallway.

Again, Maggie moves in real-time while everything around her changes. When the final drum crash happens, we've reached the end of the school year, which also means that it is almost Maggie's fourteen birthday as well. Let's get there, shall we?

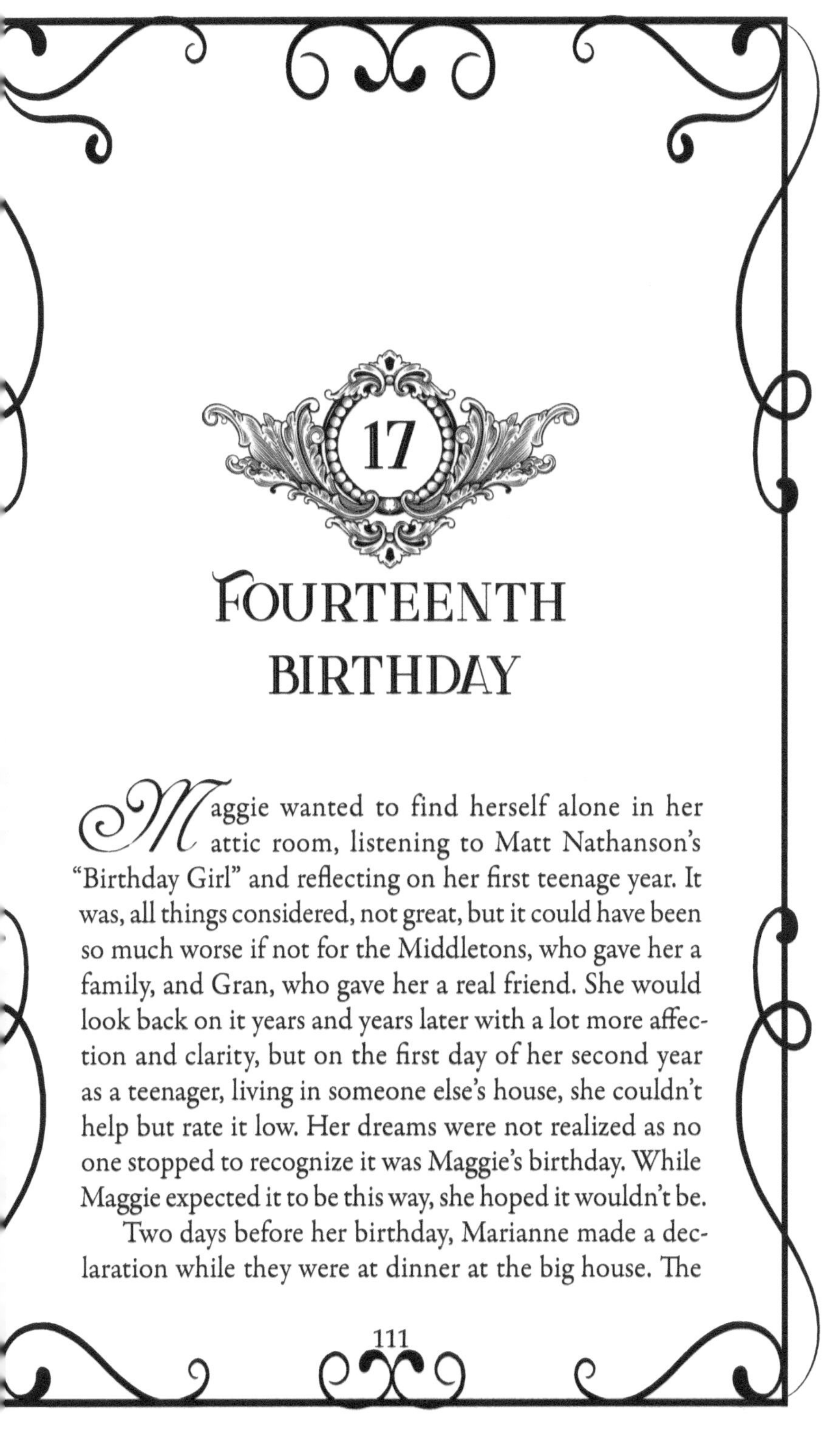

17

Fourteenth Birthday

Maggie wanted to find herself alone in her attic room, listening to Matt Nathanson's "Birthday Girl" and reflecting on her first teenage year. It was, all things considered, not great, but it could have been so much worse if not for the Middletons, who gave her a family, and Gran, who gave her a real friend. She would look back on it years and years later with a lot more affection and clarity, but on the first day of her second year as a teenager, living in someone else's house, she couldn't help but rate it low. Her dreams were not realized as no one stopped to recognize it was Maggie's birthday. While Maggie expected it to be this way, she hoped it wouldn't be.

Two days before her birthday, Marianne made a declaration while they were at dinner at the big house. The declaration was not necessary as they ate at the big house most days anyway. Maggie would occasionally go up and help Lady and Gran in the kitchen. More Gran time was always a joy. When one is about to turn fourteen, one may not be thrilled to admit that one's best friend is a 61-year-old, but it is a fact that people tend to ignore children, specifically slightly introverted, artsy types who are the youngest of three girls. The same can be said for people who are called Gran. Young and old manage to see each other quite clearly while everyone else is busy making other plans.

They were at dinner, sitting around the different tables in the informal dining room as they normally did. Edward was visiting as he normally did during his holiday. Marianne, being overly dramatic, as she normally was, stood up from her seat and banged the side of her glass with her knife. Even the littlest of the Middletons quieted down as though there was some universal understanding that clanging a glass meant a speech was coming.

She took a deep breath, bowed her head, and closed her eyes. She stood there silently for a full ten seconds, which, after one's attention is given after a clanging of a glass, can feel like an eternity. Try it tonight at dinner and see what happens. These people, her old and new family, knew well enough to wait her out. Finally, she raised her head, as if coming from some meditative state where she was communing with the spirits, and said, "Family," and she paused to look around the room at them all, "Friends," another pause with another look around the room, "Loved ones," even she knew this was overkill, but she couldn't help herself, "as you may know, we are two days away from the anniversary of a day that has lived in infamy."

Yes, cringy for sure Dear Reader, we know but Marianne didn't. "While the events of that day have brought us here, to a place where we feel welcome and cared for, we, the Dashwood women, would give it all up in a second to be back home at our beloved Norland with our father," she looked at only Elinor, "her husband," she looked at her mother, "by our side. And so, I would like to propose that, just at the moment I came across his fallen form, we hold a candlelight vigil at The Cottage where we will say a few words in honor of the man and toast him, as we did on the day we spread his ashes, with his favorite whiskey. Will you all join me... us?" She closed her eyes, dropped her head again, and waited in silence for a response.

Lady, who was unsure if she had been insulted or thanked, looked to Sam, who was unsure if her daughter had just insulted or thanked her cousins, who had been nothing but wonderful. Sam mouthed, "I'm sorry," while nodding her head at Lady.

Lady mouthed, "It's okay, love," back to Sam, as they had grown to be quite close during their time in the office, and Lady had taken to calling her "love" in a big sisterly way. Aloud she said, "Of course, dear. That would be lovely."

With that, almost everyone started talking at once, making plans, and doing logistics. Gran couldn't help but notice that Maggie remained silent. Her hands were resting on the table, and she was staring seemingly at her sister, but really, she was looking through her, past her into infinity. Gran wasn't sure if she should make a joke about Scarlett O'Hara, as they had recently watched *Gone with the Wind*, or if she should say something like, "Are you okay, dear?" but then, her brain kicked in, and she realized what day that actually was. So, she did the only thing that anyone could do at a time like that; she put her hand on top of Maggie's hand and squeezed it. With that, a few tears slipped out of Maggie's eyes. She used her free hand to wipe her face and flipped her other hand over, palm up, so she could squeeze back.

The candlelight vigil was as much of a success as something like that could be. "Lovely" was the word that was bandied about the most and, to be fair to our heroine, as this vigil took place, it rolled past midnight and her fourteenth birthday, it was pretty lovely. At the insistence of Elinor, Marianne stood down and let Sam be in charge. All four of the Dashwoods took turns saying a few words about Henry. They told a story about their favorite moment with him while Edward, Gran, Lady, and Middy stood solemnly and listened.

The boys slept soundly in their beds at the big house. They asked Juliet to come over and stay in the big house for the night. As the handyperson of Barton Park, she was the one they trusted the most. She loved the boys, and they loved her. She'd stayed over before on the nights when the Middletons had tickets to a show and when Gran was away on assignment, or when she just wanted to be back in her own house in Exeter. There are, as you may remember, a lot of rooms in the big house. The Yellow Room was designated as Juliet's room. It was so called because it was painted yellow. Much to the relief of the ghost of Charlotte Perkins Gilman, Juliet was not suffering postpartum depression, nor was she married to a know-it-all doctor who was a raving misogynist and obviously having an affair with the nanny.

By the time the vigil was over, there was nary a dry eye. Middy, who only knew Henry tangentially, was openly weeping. He was, and still is, a sympathetic crier. Sam brought out the whiskey and lowball glasses and poured everyone two fingers. "To Henry," she said as she extended her glass. "To Henry!" they all repeated, and they all pounded their drinks. Some coughed, some eyes watered, some felt the warming sensation of the whiskey go down their insides that seemed to loosen their outsides, and tension they didn't know they were carrying left their shoulders. Everyone, save Maggie, was offered a refill. Sam was not against giving her teenagers whiskey and wine, but moderation was still on the menu. Maggie knew she wouldn't be offered a refill, and so, as everyone moved into the parlor, she thanked them all, gave out hugs and kisses on the cheeks, filled her water bottle with cold water from the fridge, and went to her room.

She found a wrapped package on her bed with a card on top. She looked around the room as though she thought someone might jump out at her, but thankfully, the room was empty. She took the card out of the envelope. On the cover, there was a unicorn jumping over a rainbow. It was a card for a child turning four. There was a huge, sparkly number 4 on the cover. The giver had drawn a giant 1 in front of it. Maggie couldn't help but laugh.

She opened the card. On the right-hand side, it read, in the printing from the card company, "Have a magical fourth birthday!" The fourth had been crossed through, and the fourteenth was written over the top. Below the printing was a drawing of a heart and the following words, "Happy Birthday, Dear! Love, Gran."

She assumed she was cried out during the vigil, but as we've learned, the Dashwoods are capable of crying great lakes of tears. She held the card to her chest with her right hand. She put her left hand over her mouth, and she ugly cried until her knees buckled. She flopped onto her bed and pulled her pillow to her face. She cried and screamed into her pillow until she couldn't stand it and was dried out. Sadness and joy sit right next to each other in our hearts, and they both love to show themselves with tears. Feelings are powerful masters.

After a long drink to replenish all the lost fluids, she finally opened the gift. The paper, she noticed, also had unicorns and rainbows. They must have come as a set. Maggie found the whole thing adorable. She wanted to make a collage for Gran as a thank you, even though she knew that thank you gifts for birthday gifts were not necessary; the thank you wasn't for the gift but for the meaning behind the gift. So, she slid her finger under the tape, and eventually, she had the box unwrapped with 95 percent of the paper intact. She pulled the lid off the box, which first housed reams and reams of printer paper. She knew this was not a partially filled box of paper, as it was not remotely heavy enough, and Gran wasn't a psychopath who gave a fourteen-year-old without a printer some printer paper.

She pulled the lid off and found balled-up tissue paper of every color of the rainbow. When Gran wanted to go for a theme, boy did she ever go for it. Most fourteen-year-olds would think this was corny, but Maggie Dashwood would never be listed in the "most" category. She smoothed out each piece of tissue paper, thinking of how she could include it in the thank you collage. When she pulled away the final balled-up piece of tissue, she found several more boxes of various sizes and shapes. They were each wrapped in the same unicorn rainbow paper.

Maggie grabbed the biggest one and tore it open. She was done being careful, and she wanted to have a bit of destructive fun. She discovered it was a boxed set of Frank Capra movies. She flipped the box over in her hands to see what movies were in the set to see a note taped to the back that read, "These are films, not movies." She stood corrected. The rest of the box was filled with similar collections. There was a Buster Keaton collection, a Bergman collection, and The Criterion Collection of *The Before Trilogy* with a note that read, "People today still make films." The final box, which Gran deliberately put at the bottom, was a collection of Kurosawa samurai films. The note read, "Here's where we meet in the middle."

While she wanted to wait to watch them with Gran, she knew that Gran, most likely, already had copies of all of these films herself. She tore the cellophane off the Buster Keaton set, put *The General* into her portable player, set the player on the edge of her bed, flopped onto her stomach, and hit play. She knew who he was as Gran had introduced her to his work with *Sherlock Jr.* during one of their filmstravaganza/movie-palooza sleepovers during winter holiday. She admitted that she loved it, though she found the silent film jarring at first, but she forgot all about it by the end and promised to try more of his work. She hadn't kept that promise, but she was young, and promises don't need to be fulfilled immediately. She fell asleep with a smile on her face.

She woke at the crack of noon, dry-mouthed, sweaty, and sore. She slept in the clothes she'd worn out for the vigil. Her room, the hottest and coldest room in The Cottage, depending on the time of year, was, she joked later in life, like growing up with malaria. As summer was in full swing, the temperature rose quickly, and since she'd slept well past sun-up, she failed to turn on her fan the previous evening, and so she was melting on the inside.

She stumbled down to the bathroom and into the shower. She decided after a quick smell test that the rumbling in her stomach could wait as no one would be able to eat near her in her current state. She tried to drink a little of the water as it came out of the shower head. It was a mistake. She coughed and hacked.

Elinor heard her as she was walking by. She knocked on the door and walked in without waiting for an answer in the way that older sisters, even well-meaning older sisters like Elinor, often did. She shouted, "It's me!"

At the same time, Maggie was shouting, "Get out!"

"Oh, don't be that way. I changed your diaper."

"Did you?" Maggie asked, frozen with her hands in her hair, lathering the shampoo.

"I mean, I'm sure I did. I was a very useful child. Mum treated me more like a sister than a daughter. It's like I was born 19." She sat down on the toilet.

"Well, I don't need you to change my diaper now, thanks."

"Fine, next time I barge in, I'll say, 'I taught you to use a tampon.' Will that be better?"

"Not really."

"Well." Elinor crossed her legs at the knee. "Regardless, I'm your sister and all, and I'm not being lecherous."

"Whatever." Maggie spun backward against the water and dipped her head back to rinse. "So, to what do I owe this great honor? I mean, I'm not moving in here. I will be down shortly to eat lunch. There is another loo." She shut off the water and reached her hand out from behind the curtain. "Towel."

Elinor got Maggie's towel off the back of the door and put it in her hand. "What was your plan to get that if I wasn't in here?"

"I'd just drip and risk a slip and fall."

"Well, I'd have to bust in here anyway and pick you up wet and naked then."

"I guess the fates aligned that we would be in the bathroom together no matter what." Maggie pulled the curtain back. She had the towel wrapped tight around her. "So?"

"Right. Yes. Well. I just wanted to say that I'm sorry."

"Yeah?" Maggie hoped it would be for the right reason.

Elinor nodded. She opened her mouth to speak but couldn't. She cleared her throat. "Well, you know why. It's um... your birthday and we..."

Overcome by the apology that she never expected, Maggie stepped out of the tub and pulled Elinor into a bone-crushing hug. "Thank you." They rocked back and forth. Maggie's wet hair slapped against Elinor's cheek.

"Your hair is wet and gross."

Maggie laughed and let her sister go. "That's what you get."

"Yes, it is just what I deserve. Maybe next time you can do it to Mum or Marianne."

"I don't see them in here apologizing."

"Well, I suspect that will come in due course."

"We'll see," Maggie said, unconvinced.

"That's fair. I make no promises."

"No. You shouldn't."

Not sure how to get out of that hole, Elinor sidestepped it. "Right. Well. Okay. I'll go make you a birthday lunch. What do you want?"

"Big breakfast."

"Done." She smiled at her littlest sister. She turned and headed downstairs to make the biggest breakfast for lunch in the history of all breakfasts for lunch.

We'd like to say that this will be the last time anyone forgets our heroine's birthday, but we can't. We are sorry, but the facts are the facts. We have at least a year before it could happen again, so there's that.

18

BRANDON

It was good that Elinor didn't make any promises because while Sam did apologize profusely and made promises that she would later not keep, Marianne never acknowledged anything. Admitting she was wrong was not a strong suit for her. Still, Marianne wasn't a monster. She didn't hate Maggie, and she did feel bad about missing her birthday for two consecutive years even though she would never, ever say so aloud.

So it was that the day after Maggie's birthday, Marianne arrived at the breakfast table wearing her blue Barton Park shirt. It was the first time she put it on her body. She made toast and sat down across from Maggie, who was finishing her toast and jam, wearing one of the new shirts Middy gave her after she outgrew her last few. In fact, that was the day she planned on asking him if she could actually earn her blue shirt by joining the crew. She wanted a job and the toned arms and legs that could make the cargos and rolled-up shirts look good. She wasn't vain, but she was human. She felt comfortable asking for the job as she was able to be in the same room with Juliet without totally falling apart, but there was never a time in Maggie's life when the sight of Juliet didn't also come with minor palpitations.

Still, Juliet could, as far as everyone could tell, do everything. Maggie, while she missed her dad every single day, understood long before he was tragically taken from them that no one would ever confuse him for being handy, and so she would eventually need to learn to do things from someone else. Finding herself on a working farm with the handiest of handy people meant that she could learn things. Useful things. Things that would allow her to be useful because she, like her mother, didn't like to free-load. While she was still a child and almost all children are technically freeloaders, living in The Cottage just seemed different than living in Norland. Middy was family, and The Cottage did sit empty for 10 out of 12 months a year before they moved in, but there was just something about earning her own money and contributing to the family business that she found appealing.

Of course, when Marianne had plans of her own, the plans of others were always put on hold, and so, when she sat down at the table in her blue shirt, Maggie knew that something strange was indeed afoot at Barton Park. She choked down her coffee and asked, "Am I having a stroke?"

Marianne huffed in a way that isn't unique to Marianne Dashwood but is unique to people *like* Marianne Dashwood. We've all heard it and didn't care for it. She followed up her huff with a petulant, "Don't be that way."

"What way is that?"

"Rude and hurtful."

Maggie managed not to say all the things that she thought of saying about it being the day after her birthday and the other things that couldn't be uttered on broadcast TV. Instead, she said, "Right. Well, did you lose a bet then?"

"No," Marianne said with just enough sincerity that it was believable. "I wanted to spend the day with you out on the farm. We're clearly going to live here *forever,*" she said it like a curse, "so I suppose it's time that I learned a thing or two about this place that is our *home.* Since you've clearly acclimated so well, I thought it would be good for you to act as my guide."

"Really?"

"Really." She went on, "Really, really."

Maggie, who would accept a double really from almost everyone else without question, extended her pinkie for the swear. Even Marianne wouldn't possibly break a pinkie swear. There are lines that one simply doesn't cross, and even Marianne knew that was one of them. Marianne looked her little sister square in her eyes and hooked pinkies. It was seemingly good enough for Maggie, who felt her heart fill with what some might call hope. It would be years before Maggie realized that this was what an apology from Marianne looked like. There are just some people who can't say the words. We've established Marianne is one of those people.

Since Maggie was done with her food and Marianne was just starting her toast, she cleaned up and set about packing them lunch. She ran upstairs and dumped out the messenger bag she used for her excursions alone around the property. Pencils, sharpeners, Xacto knives, charcoal, and notepads went flying everywhere. Normally, she wouldn't be so careless with her tools, but the hope in her heart was making her careless. Hope can do that.

By the time she came down, Marianne was done eating. She even helped Maggie pack all of the lunch items into her bag. "I'll get a sheet so we can have a picnic." She didn't wait for the answer, turning to head upstairs to get it. Maggie extended the strap on her bag so that it would accommodate the sheet on top of the back, which was packed pretty full as it was.

Once they were packed up, with empty bladders and clean teeth, they went out onto the grounds of Barton Park for a big day of exploring. Maggie wished she had more time to plan. She wanted to make it the most special day the two of them ever had, and she worried that doing the wrong thing at the wrong time would crash the day into a metaphorical tree. If she had really thought about it, she should have known that there could never really be a day with Marianne that didn't have some drama. To be fair, not all drama was Marianne's fault; sometimes it just found her. If that is the case in this situation, we shall leave it up to you to decide.

They began the day at the sheep barn. It was Maggie's favorite place. There was ample fencing upon which she could sit and draw. She found that the sheep comforted her. They were nothing flashy, but they were loyal to a fault. They seemed to have anxiety about being alone. They had messy hair that needed a lot of work to maintain. Humidity was not their friend. She could relate.

Marianne had never felt messy or alone. Her confidence was so strong that should scientists be able to harness it, she could power the whole of England through every winter. Still, she thought they were cute enough and enjoyed petting them. She didn't expect that at all. What she liked the most, to the shock of both of the younger Dashwoods, was bottle-feeding a lamb. There were occasionally times when the mother didn't make it, and so the staff had to feed the babies. It was equal parts sad, as there was an orphaned lamb, and adorable, as there is objectively nothing cuter on a farm than a lamb drinking from a bottle. Facts are facts. Look it up.

Maggie assumed that holding a bleating, excreting, sometimes foaming-at-the-mouth animal that couldn't swallow all the milk it was trying to drink wouldn't be appealing to her sister, who seemingly never bleated, excreted, foamed, or spilled anything ever. Yet, there it was. Marianne was overjoyed. She smiled and cooed and baby talked to the lamb. Maggie wouldn't admit it at the time, but she was slightly jealous at the way her sister, who'd never cooed and rarely smiled in her direction, took to this critter that she'd seen for the first time. Still, Maggie's heart was not made of stone, and seeing her sister happy filled her with happiness.

Maggie wished she had brought her sketch pad to capture the moment. Instead, she relied on what most teenagers rely; she pulled out her phone and snapped a few candid photos. She wanted to get them in before Marianne caught her and demanded that the photos be deleted and wouldn't be satisfied until she had the phone in her hands and could check the cloud too. Maggie stood with her back to the barn, trying to get a good shot of her sister in three-quarter profile. It was her favorite angle to draw, and if she could get a few good reference shots, she could really do something special.

A young man's voice cut through the coos and bleats. "She's a natural." It came from behind them. They both turned to see the owner of the voice. There stood a person who was clearly a teenage boy trying out the body of a man. He was trying to grow a beard, but it was patchy and uneven where it had grown in. His Barton Park shirt could barely contain him. Maggie thought of the word "smedium." It was a term she picked up from Gran when they were watching one of the many action movies with Carl Weathers during Maggie's choice night. He was most famous for playing Apollo Creed in the *Rocky* movies, but according to Gran, he was the first person she noticed who always wore a smedium. They were shirts that were always two sizes too small, designed to make sure everyone knew he could lift all the weights and took all his vitamins. If this person grew up to play Carl Weathers in the Carl Weathers story one day, Maggie would not have been surprised. Just to quell curiosity, he did not. It's a shame, really, but he goes on to do good things.

Seeing the blue shirt immediately put Maggie at ease. The blue shirt meant that there was a new person on staff that Middy and Lady hired. They had a perfect track record of hiring people with whom Maggie got along with just fine. While she wasn't a person who collected friends, she wasn't against having allies and being friendly, especially to the Barton Park staff, whose ranks she wished to join.

The blue shirt set Marianne on edge. Even though she liked the way it fit him as he was clearly strong and ruggedly handsome, the patchy beard was not a hindrance to Marianne. He was someone whom she didn't know whose first impression of her was seeing her covered in lamb fluid. She didn't want anyone to think this was who she was. She was a thespian, not a farmhand. Of course, this young man was clearly a farmhand and that didn't mean Marianne was interested in this young, handsome person, but she wasn't not interested either. Farmhand or not, he was male and seemingly near her age and would be around for months or possibly years to come. We apologize for that minor grammatical indiscretion, Dear Reader, but to be fair, Marianne thought in double negatives all the time, and we aim to be as accurate as possible.

Since we are already there, we can tell you that there were plenty of other contradictory thoughts running through the middle Dashwood's mind. Here they are in order. If she stood up, she would be covered in all the lamb filth. Gross. But he knew she was holding the lamb, so he would understand that the fluids and hairs were not hers. She wasn't an oozing, hairy mess. Whew. He said she looked like a natural. Did that mean he saw her as a mother? Gross. How dare he. Maybe he thought it meant she looked caring and nice. Caring and nice was good. And on, and on it went for what felt like eons but was only seconds.

"I'm Brandon. Brandon Christopher. You're the famous Dashwoods."

"Are we famous?" Marianne asked, not realizing that he didn't mean famous in the way she thought he meant it. She turned to face him, which upset the lamb, who threw itself down on the ground and scampered away. She stood up and smoothed out her clothes. She looked him right in the eye and smiled in a way that could have been inviting or a threat.

"Well..." He started to explain, but Maggie saved them both.

"I'm sure Middy and Lady have told you we might be around."

"Exactly," he said to Maggie, but he couldn't take his eyes off Marianne.

"That's Marianne. I'm Maggie. Elinor isn't around much, but you may run into her. Looks like she loves books more than people."

"Does she?" He managed to pull his focus away from Marianne for just a second. He looked right at Maggie for the first time.

Marianne noticed and did not like that one bit, thank you very much. "I think it depends on the book and the person," she said as she walked toward them. She stood next to Maggie, forcing him to look back at her. He obliged. She noticed.

"Yeah? How about you? Do you prefer books or people?" he replied in a tone that made it very clear he forgot that there was a 14-year-old present.

"Oh, I'm into people." Marianne, too, failed to realize her little sister was standing there.

Maggie, who didn't forget she was standing there, decided to intervene before things got out of hand. "So, Brandon, are you here just for the summer, or are you joining the Park full-time?"

The talk of work threw a bucket of cold water on the situation and brought them back from the edge of whatever steamy teen drama was about to unfold. Maggie breathed a sigh of relief as she was worried it would be one of those movies where the cast is played by 30-year-olds instead of real teenagers, so it could be more "edgy." That was fine on her computer screen, but she didn't want to be a walk-on in that picture, especially when her sister was the lead.

"I'm just here for the summer. I'm studying general science at college, and I wanted to see what I thought about becoming a veterinarian. I know working here isn't the same as working in a clinic, but unsurprisingly, most clinics don't hire teenagers to do much. Middy was willing to let me work with his vets here while also letting me learn about animal husbandry."

What did Marianne think when she heard Brandon say the word "husbandry?" That is up to each person to decide. What she said was, "Wow, so you're really smart?"

"Well..." He paused for a moment, trying to figure out the best way to answer this. He was, in fact, very smart. He knew it, but he knew that he worked very hard to be so. He studied and paid attention. He asked questions. Would Marianne be impressed by this or turned off by this? She did, after all, ask the question instead of making a statement. Unsure, he opted for the thing he felt most comfortable saying, which was the truth, which was all the things mentioned in this paragraph, so we don't need to repeat them.

Maggie, who had a good feeling about Brandon, didn't want her sister to get in her own way, so she jumped in. "That sounds pretty smart to us, doesn't it, Marianne?"

"Yes. Yes, of course. Brilliant."

"Well, Brandon, it was a pleasure meeting you. We've got a big day planned, so we're gonna get going. We'll see you around then?"

"I sure hope so," he said to them both while again only looking at Marianne.

Marianne held out her hand to his, and he held it in a way that, if this story was set in a different time, it would have ended with his lips on the back of her hand. However, they were both covered in lamb hair and fluids of all kinds. So, she rested her hand on his hand and looked up at his big, brown eyes, and they both imagined what would come next.

Eventually, they let go, and Brandon went on with his day, smitten, but not totally distracted. He had husbandry on which to focus. Marianne was not smitten but totally distracted. Marianne and Maggie went about their day seeing the rest of Barton Park, the pigs, the cows, ponies, fowls of many shapes and sizes, alpacas, the apple orchard, the hay baling barn, and the tractor barn, complete with a surprise appearance from Tractor Boy.

So it was that for several weeks, Marianne was keen on spending time wandering around Barton Park. Marianne was relieved when Lady decided that Maggie could have a job so she didn't have to wander around the park with her little sister in tow. Also, it allowed her the inside scoop as to where Brandon would be stationed each day since there was an employee logistics center in the office at the big house and another one in the tractor barn. It is true that Marianne could have just visited her mother there at any time, but as was always the case with Marianne Dashwood, the straightest path was not the one she liked to follow; the more twists and turns, the better for her.

She spent so much time with Brandon that, at the insistence of Sam, he was invited to The Cottage one day for lunch. Generally, Sam liked to walk back down to eat there because she discovered early on that the young Middleton boys had grown accustomed to touching their mother's food as she sat and ate at her desk. So, they assumed that all food eaten at a desk in the office adjacent to their playroom was there for their grazing pleasure. While it could be said that Sam loved those boys, she didn't love their dirty, snotty fingers in her lunch.

Marianne tried to negotiate the attendance at the lunch. She wished for it to be herself, her mother, and Brandon, but Sam wouldn't have that. She made sure he got the "Full Dashwood." She personally extended the invitation to Brandon on a day that she knew Elinor would be home. She turned down Lady's offer to help her pre-make lunch the night before in the big house so that it could be a quick and easy affair. She wanted to have him there while they prepared the lunch. They were going to make cheese toasties and tomato soup. It wasn't super labor intensive, but it could be messy. She knew it was a test, and she knew it was silly, but she didn't care. She saw how good of a person Edward was, and the standards had been set very high.

Thus, the "Full Dashwood" lunch day arrived, and not only did Brandon roll up his sleeves and help cook, but he also added an extra flourish to the process by showing them how they could pour some shredded cheese of a different flavor than the cheese that was inside the toastie into the pan after the sandwich was "done" and dropping one side into hot cheese in the hot pan. The result was a crunchy layer of cheese on top of the toastie, making it delicious and extra resilient to soup dunking. Elinor and Sam were impressed but thought it might have been a bit too much cheese. Maggie outwardly called him a magician and would never make a toastie again without giving it the "Brandon treatment."

The meal consisted of the Dashwood women getting all the information they could from Brandon. His mother was a pilot in the Royal Air Force. His father was a non-flying mechanic in the Royal Canadian Air Force. They met during a joint mission in Afghanistan, and sparks and propellors flew. As soon as their tours were over, his father, whose term was up, left the service, moved to the UK, and got a job for British Airways. They were, as Brandon put it, "disgustingly in love."

His older brother was a bit of a rake, and he didn't really like to talk much of him if they didn't mind terribly, and of course, they did not mind. His parents had taken in a girl from his year in secondary school who had found herself in "quite an unfortunate situation," and so he had a "twin sister" called Ellie, of whom he was very fond. He showed them a picture of them together. She was a ginger waif. They laughed at the twin moniker.

Her "unfortunate situation" was now three and called Liza. He showed them a picture of her. They cooed and awed. Sam even made a joke that he best not bring her around as she would fit right into the Middleton Clan, and Lady was desperate to have a girl. Because he was used to people thinking things, he acknowledged that the reason the child looked so much like him was that he was her biological uncle as well as her spiritual uncle, and he would again, not like to speak of it further if that was okay. It was most certainly fine with them. They didn't live in a glass house, but they were never going to throw stones.

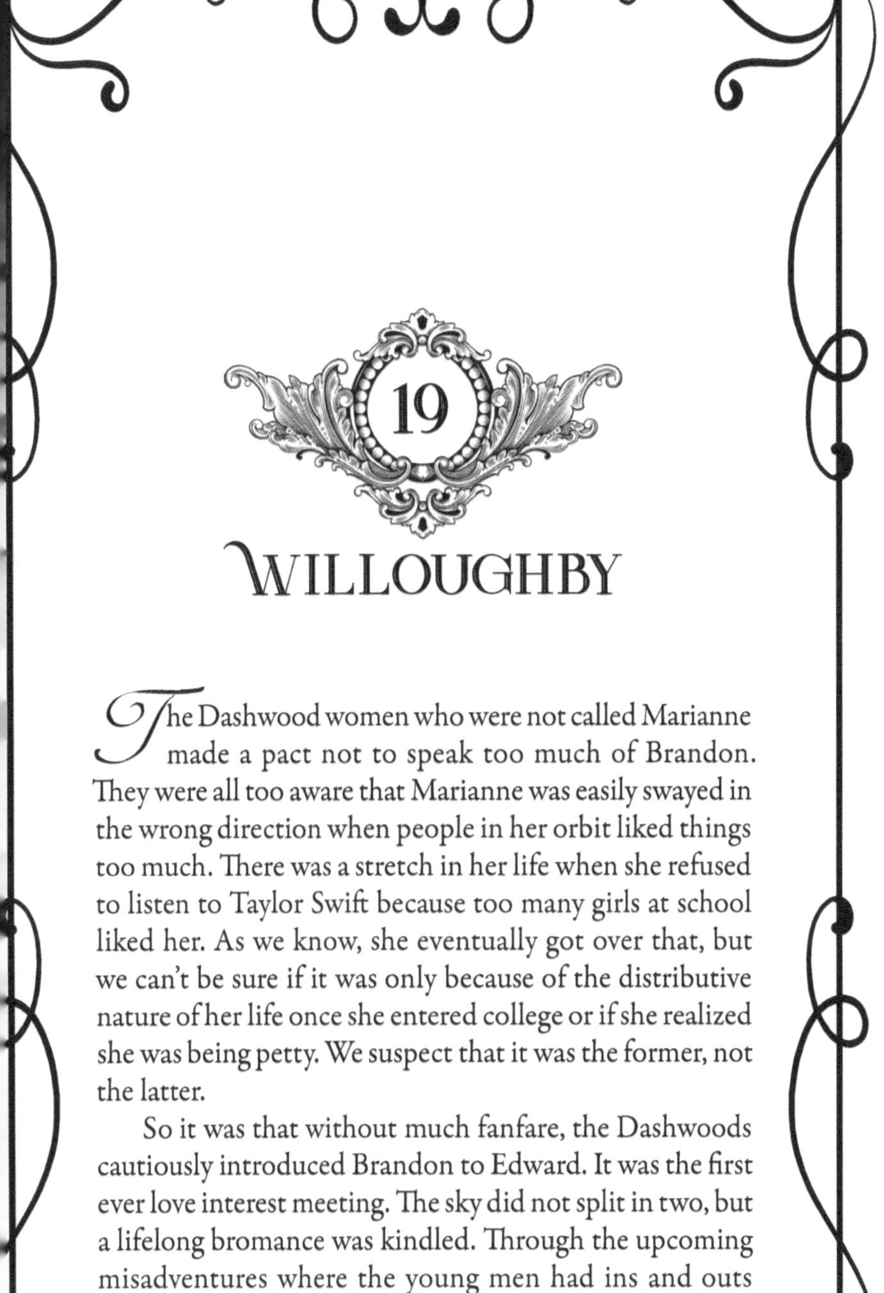

19

WILLOUGHBY

The Dashwood women who were not called Marianne made a pact not to speak too much of Brandon. They were all too aware that Marianne was easily swayed in the wrong direction when people in her orbit liked things too much. There was a stretch in her life when she refused to listen to Taylor Swift because too many girls at school liked her. As we know, she eventually got over that, but we can't be sure if it was only because of the distributive nature of her life once she entered college or if she realized she was being petty. We suspect that it was the former, not the latter.

So it was that without much fanfare, the Dashwoods cautiously introduced Brandon to Edward. It was the first ever love interest meeting. The sky did not split in two, but a lifelong bromance was kindled. Through the upcoming misadventures where the young men had ins and outs with the Dashwood family, they stayed true to each other. Those events, for the most part, happen off the page as it is Maggie's story after all, regardless of what Marianne says. Although, this chapter is still mostly about Marianne. It was roughly halfway through summer holiday and as Maggie was a teenager and time moves differently for them, it seemed to be simultaneously flying by and crawling.

Maggie discovered that the new owner of the property adjoining Barton Park was in town. She heard rumblings from Lady that he and his friends were rapscallions and layabouts who had some offroad motorcycles that made quite a racket. Maggie was baffled as to how one could lay about and do mischief, so she volunteered to investigate. She set off just after noon as she assumed, rightly so, that no rapscallion worth his weight in gold doubloons would make merry before noon. On that particular day, Sam and Elinor woke up early and planned on doing something that was equal parts sweaty, sticky, and boring to Sam's bedroom, involving wallpaper and border. Brandon was off and had other family obligations involving his niece, who did seem to grow more adorable with each new picture he shared with them. If he said he was spending time with Liza, even Marianne had a hard time finding the right to quibble.

So it was that Marianne followed her baby sister into the woods to spy on the neighbors. She freely admitted it was a childish endeavor. She even commented on it on no fewer than three occasions before she finally donned her blue shirt and garden trousers. Most teenagers on the cusp of adulthood would not admit that they actually enjoy throwing off the yokes of impending adult servitude and traipsing about Van Trapp-like, but the fact remains that yokes are cumbersome, and the fear of Lyme Disease does not weigh heavy on the minds of young people although they are those who are most likely to find themselves at risk.

As they headed toward the easternmost property line, the farthest part of Barton Park away from the working tourist attractions, the conversation consisted of Marianne complaining about the heat and what it would do to her hair. Maggie varied her responses, but they mostly consisted of her telling her sister she was free to go home and be alone. Both Elinor and Maggie were often comfortable being alone, but Marianne, who was the one who could most likely benefit from some alone time, rarely took any.

Maggie had gone essentially native in her 18 months on the property, and she could negotiate the woods, the footpaths, both paved and unpaved, the gravel drive, and the grassy parking area without even looking down. While she didn't look as good in her shorts and rolled-up sleeves as Juliet, she was on her way. Marianne could find her way to the big house and to the sheep barn where Brandon was most likely to be found. She would often ask questions regarding what it was that her mother and Maggie did all day while at work, as she often forgot that Barton Park, unlike Norland, was a functional farm and amusement park. Whether she actually forgot or was being passive-aggressive, we shall leave it up to each person to decide.

Due to this navigational discrepancy, the walk to the property line was taking much longer than Maggie would have liked. Marianne, who always chose footwear based on form and never on function, was wearing open-toed sandals as she didn't think boots and shorts created an outfit that was "an appropriate look to meet new people." Of course, every single person who worked at Barton, including Brandon, wore shorts and boots. To that end, she was careful with each step she took. She didn't want to turn an ankle, touch something slimy, or worse, mess up the work she had done on her toenails the night before.

"Just follow my lead," Maggie grumped. "I mean, literally. Just follow in my footsteps. If you see where my foot goes, put your foot there. We should have been there, met the neighbors, had tea with them, and met their mums by now. I can hear the motorcycle buzzing from here. They must be close enough."

"I don't want to be all pit sweaty when I get there," Marianne said with a head nod at Maggie, who was, in fact, quite pit sweaty.

"It's hot. People sweat. Isn't it odd that you don't? I mean, do you want the neighbors, who we're not even sure we'll be meeting, to think that you are an android?"

Marianne's foul-mouthed retort was drowned out by the sound of a motorcycle's engine. It may seem that there is no motorcycle engine that can be so loud that it could mask the sound of one person's voice to another who is only a few feet or meters away, but there are some so loud that the people on the bike can't hear anything. Why are machines made like this? Like the pyramids, it remains a great mystery.

In fact, motorcycle engines, when unregulated, can cause hearing loss after less than an hour. Off-road motorcycles are rarely regulated, and thus, the noise is quite literally deafening. While it is not deafening to a neighbor who hears the constant whirring of the engines from a distance, it can be a constant source of irritation. Many an evening, when Lady and Middy curled up on the sofa to catch up on the day or read or watch the telly, the buzzing of the engines made them both 20 percent more irksome than they normally would be. While neither of them would have been described as a person full of irk, the fact that it registered at all was like a 7 on the irksome Richter scale.

The sound came first, followed closely by the appearance of said motorcycle. The rider had clearly built up quite a run as he came over the rise with such speed that he was airborne. Maggie, whose back was to the rise, turned, sure-footed in her boots, and watched the underside of the bike launch into the sky. She pictured the motorcycle jumps from many an action movie. It was here that she finally admitted to herself that while this was supposedly a fact-finding mission for Lady, it was her hope that she would see this very thing. It was better than she could have ever imagined. She could not wait to tell Gran, who scoffed repeatedly at the bad physics of action movies.

Marianne, who was facing the ridge was not sure-footed in her open-toed sandals, instinctively stepped back as she looked up at the underside of the motorcycle. The tires looked like buzzsaws. If she wore pearls, she would have clutched them. So it was, with her hands in fists over her chest, her center of gravity shifted as she shuffled backward, and the small hole that she carefully avoided just moments before claimed her left foot. The rest of her body tried to do what bodies do and right itself. She turned to the left, which lodged her foot under an exposed root. She went down in a heap.

By the time the motorcycle landed and skidded to a stop exactly the way Maggie hoped it would, the rider, realizing he was no longer alone, cut the engine. The sound was replaced by the sound of Marianne's swearing and wailing. She vacillated between agony and anger. Maggie was to her in a few steps, perfect action movie entrance forgotten. She slid on her knees across the ground and started asking all the questions she thought that Sam would have asked. Can you feel it? Can you move it? Is it broken? She reached into the hole to extricate her sister's foot. She looked down and saw the offending root.

"I can lift the root, or I can pull your foot. Which one?"

Marianne moved her leg and winced at the pain shooting from the base of it. "Root."

Maggie got on her feet and into a deep squat. She reached her hands into the hole and slipped her fingers under the root, which of course, nudged her sister's foot. Marianne inhaled, made fists, and nodded. Maggie used her considerable leg strength to lift the root. Marianne tried to pull her leg back, but tree roots are much stronger than they look, and unbeknownst to them, Marianne's foot and ankle had already started to swell. It didn't budge.

An American voice came from behind Maggie. "Can I help?"

Maggie spun around, having forgotten all about the mystery rider. There stood a young man with long blonde hair hanging over the left side of his face. He held his helmet in his right hand. He wore blue jeans and black leather boots to match his black leather jacket. Maggie had a whole series of biting responses about having done enough, this isn't even your property, and on and on. Before she could say anything, she heard her sister's voice come from behind her.

Before we hear what Marianne had to say, we must spin the perspective as well. From her angle, lying on the ground, supported by her elbows, looking up at him, he glowed. The sun framed him, making his blonde hair seem like a halo. He looked taller than he actually was, and the leather jacket made him look much bigger than he actually was. Maggie could see all of this from her 14-year-old eyes, but from her 17-year-old damsel in distress position, Marianne saw an angel sent straight from heaven to extricate her from her predicament, forgetting the fact that it was his careless driving on property that was not technically his that caused the mess in the first place. So, when she finally spoke, she said, "Why, yes, please" in a baby doll voice.

Taking that invitation, he set his helmet down on the ground and approached. He squatted down in a way that Maggie thought was totally unnecessary. Had either of them looked at her, they would have seen her eyes roll. Having just been squatting down in that exact place, she somehow managed to do it without spreading her knees that far apart in the direction of her sister's face.

"May I?" he asked, pointing down at her foot in the hole.

"Yes" came the baby voice again. "Just be gentle."

"I always am." He reached his hands into the hole, but he looked right at her face.

Maggie groaned in disgust. They either didn't hear or didn't care.

"Does this hurt?"

"Yes, very much."

Maggie had, in the course of her 14 years, heard her sister in pain. She had just heard her in pain, and yet, neither the tone nor the tenor of her voice reflected that sound.

"It looks pretty swollen too. I was hoping I could lift the root out, but my hands are just too big to fit under the root without hurting you." He held his right hand up.

It looked like a normal-sized hand to Maggie, and she was about to say just that when Marianne made an "ooh" sound that seemed to support his large hand claim.

"Maybe I could get behind you and pull, and your friend here can lift the root."

"She's my sister."

"Yes, I suppose she is." He stood towering over her with his seemingly normal hand out. "Let's get you sitting up as best as we can, so I can lift you out while your sister pulls up on the root."

Marianne extended her left hand first, leaving herself propped up on her right elbow. Once he had her hand in his, they paused and looked at each other for way too long for Maggie's liking. He reached for her other hand and pulled her up to a sitting position as though her stomach muscles were made of wet pasta and useless. Again, the long pause.

"Let's get on with it before she loses her foot, shall we?" Maggie interjected, trying to break the spell.

"I won't let that happen," the mystery rider said much too closely to Marianne's face. "Can I slip behind you?" Marianne licked her lips and just nodded. Maggie shook her head. He walked behind Marianne's now seated form and slipped his hands under her arms and around her waist. "Hi," he said in a low, breathy voice in her ear, "I'm Willoughby. Terrible name, I know. It was my mother's maiden name. I was the only Willoughby in school, though."

"Marianne," she whispered back. "I think it's a perfectly lovely name."

"It is so good to meet you," he said as he clasped his hands together around her ribs.

"Wouldn't it make more sense to lift from the pits?" Maggie asked. That finally broke the spell.

"I'm sure he knows what he's doing."

Maggie took a deep breath. She played out all the scenarios in her mind of how that conversation could continue, and they ended with her sister being willingly fondled by a stranger while she pulled up on a root, so she just said, "Fine." She looked at him. "One, two, three, pull or one, two, THREEE?"

"One, two, three, pull."

Maggie squatted back down, managing to keep just enough space between her knees for her arms to fit, and slid her fingers back under the root. She could feel the difference in the texture of her sister's foot. Marianne didn't move at all when she touched it, making her think that she was losing feeling in her foot and that the whole not feeling any pain was real. She didn't like it more than she didn't like Willoughby. She wrapped her hands fully around the root, and Marianne didn't flinch. She fought the urge to turn and throw up.

"Ready?" Maggie looked right at him.

His hands, which had been roaming about her sister's stomach, locked themselves back together. "Ready."

"One," she said.

"Two," he replied.

"Three," they said in unison.

"Pull!" Marianne joined in.

Maggie looked down at her hands and put all her leg and arm muscles into the pull. She felt the root give just enough that she saw her sister's foot come loose and disappear from the hole. She let the root go and stood up. She saw Marianne and Willoughby breathlessly tangled up on the forest floor. "Can you feel anything?"

Marianne tore her eyes away from Willoughby to shoot daggers at Maggie, but upon seeing the look of genuine concern on her face combined with the fact that no, she could not actually feel anything past her knee, her face morphed to confusion and then panic. She had, just moments before, winced in pain and felt the pins and needles of agony. She just shook her head, afraid to say anything.

"Right." Maggie took a breath and channeled her inner Elinor. "You," she looked at Willoughby, "can you ride that thing with someone on the back?"

"I can."

"Have you?"

"Yes."

"Do you know where the nearest A&E is?"

"I don't know what that is."

Maggie searched her mental files for what they called it in America. It clicked. Action movies for the win. "Emergency room. She needs to get to hospital. Like, now. You have to take her. There are a few in Exeter. Find one." She looked down at Maggie. "You call me and tell me which one. I should be back to The Cottage by then, but I need to find Mum too. Call me, not her, just in case." Marianne nodded. She looked back to Willoughby. "Make sure you pick an NHS hospital, not a swanky private one. In this country, swank equals jank. She needs to be well cared for."

"How will I know?"

"I can tell you. I've hurt my foot, not my brain." She glared at Maggie; the moment of tenderness forgotten.

"Whatever." Maggie waved the dirty look away. She was used to what she called Resting Marianne Face. "You, give me your phone. I'll put my number in it just in case they need to put her under or if she needs an x-ray and she doesn't have her phone with her, then help her up." She had her hand extended for the phone.

He looked up at her in stunned silence. He was not used to being directed by anyone, let alone a 14-year-old English girl. He looked at her extended hand, and it clicked what she was doing. He nodded and pulled the phone out of his pocket.

Maggie swiped it with a bit more force than was required. "Get up! Get her on the bike, and she wears the helmet." She looked down, assuming he would follow her orders. She found his contacts and started putting in her information.

He moved up from sitting to squatting next to Marianne. "Wrap your arm around my neck."

"Anytime," she purred.

Maggie reminded herself that Marianne just couldn't help herself. She finished entering her information. She listed her name as "Just Marianne's Sister." She called herself from his phone and followed them over to the motorcycle.

He set Marianne on it side-saddle and then guided her good foot around. He gently put her bad foot on the foot peg. "If you can't feel your foot, it may slip off the peg, so make sure you hold on tight."

"Like my life depends on it."

"It is an honor to have your life in my hands."

Maggie shook her head. She resisted the urge to make a comment about knickers being kept on during the trip.

She handed him back his phone, which he stuck in his jacket pocket. "Be alive when I get there, okay?" She reached out her hand.

Marianne's vacillating emotions swung back. She actually wiped a tear off of her face with her left hand and squeezed her sister's hand with her right. "I will be."

Maggie nodded and squeezed back. She looked at Willoughby, who was climbing on the motorcycle. She let go of her sister's hand and pointed her finger in his face. "If she is more damaged by the time I get there, I will kill you and take your land. Do you understand?"

"She'll be fine. I promise. I got her." He looked her directly in the eyes.

His eyes were deep blue, and she realized why the Ken doll looked the way it did. For just a moment, Maggie forgot herself. She felt a rush of heat come up from deep inside her. She fought the urge to lick her lips. All her internal voices started screaming at her, and she did not lick her lips or step closer to him. She dug her nails into her hands and took a big step back. She just nodded, not trusting herself to say anything.

Willoughby started the bike. He shouted, "Hang on tight" over the deafening roar. Marianne wrapped her arms around his midsection and locked her fingers together in the front. Maggie watched them drive gingerly back over the hill where, just moments before, she saw him soar. She turned on her heel and took off in a full sprint for The Cottage, trying to outrun all the conflicting feelings.

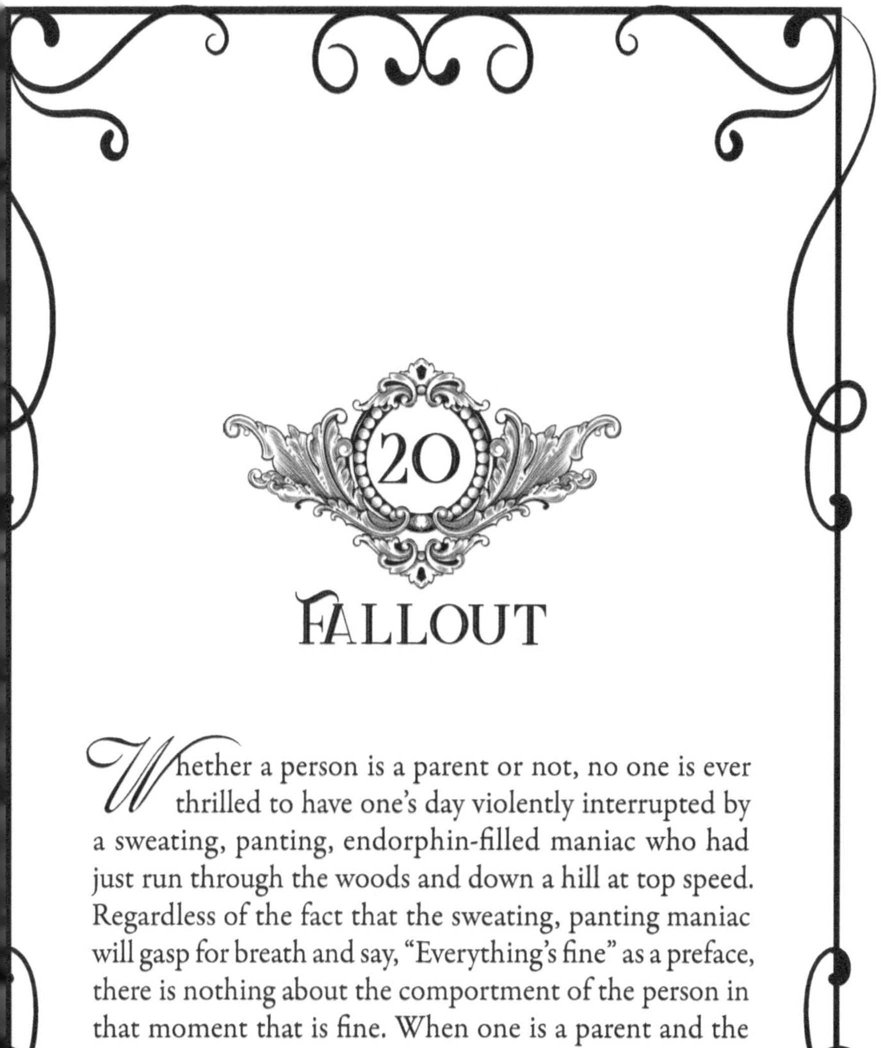

20

FALLOUT

Whether a person is a parent or not, no one is ever thrilled to have one's day violently interrupted by a sweating, panting, endorphin-filled maniac who had just run through the woods and down a hill at top speed. Regardless of the fact that the sweating, panting maniac will gasp for breath and say, "Everything's fine" as a preface, there is nothing about the comportment of the person in that moment that is fine. When one is a parent and the bursting maniac is one's own child, and it is obvious that the news is about one of the parent's other children, "not thrilled" doesn't quite do the feeling justice.

Still, Sam Dashwood, who had, as we've already seen, been through her share of family tragedies, upon seeing the state of her youngest child, managed to remain calm enough to get the information, usher them both into the Range Rover and in the direction of Exeter without shedding a tear or swearing once. She made Maggie bring water and talked in a soothing voice that children every-where know as "teacher voice." By the time Marianne called with the name of the hospital, Maggie had, in complete sentences, explained everything, save for the strange heat feelings she had when she looked Willoughby in the eyes. She would save that one for Juliet or Gran, or maybe she would bury it deep inside. She had not, at that moment, decided. We shall see shortly that she opted for door number one.

It turned out that the ankle wasn't broken, which was good, but the tendon in her leg snapped, which was bad. She would be bedridden for some time. There would be physical therapy followed by time on crutches and possibly a cane which Marianne decided right then and there was not a possibility. She would not use a cane. She reasoned that crutches were for the injured, but canes were for the infirm. She would be back to college by the time the tran-sition to the cane would be on the calendar, and that was not going to happen. The logic was bad and flawed, but it was pure Marianne Dashwood.

The rest of Marianne's summer would be filled with being home and being pampered. All things considered, it wasn't something Marianne was opposed to. Sure, having poor balance for the rest of her life was a real possibility if she didn't keep up with all the exercises she would be required to do, but let's face it; no one believed for a second that Marianne would follow through with those, and we will see, much later in the tale, the ramifications of that choice.

Marianne had what Maggie and Gran called a *Speed* crush. At the end of *Speed,* an American action film that

Gran didn't totally hate but that Maggie adored, the two leads acknowledge that relationships that are bonded in trauma don't last. This is exactly what happens, and only the female lead made it through to the second movie, which was, Maggie admitted, pretty bad even though she watched it three extra times just to "be sure" it was as bad as she thought it was. She could not promise Gran that she would never watch it again because, she reasoned, age can change perception, to which Gran argued that garbage isn't scotch.

Marianne was still in the first movie, and thus, she threw herself at Willoughby with all her heart and soul. Brandon, who was the family choice, was crushed, but because he was a good person, he said he respected Marianne's choices, and he wished her well. He and Edward remained friends and could be found gallivanting around the countryside. However, out of loyalty to Marianne and her capricious whims, the Dashwoods kept their relationship with Brandon totally professional. Secretly, they all hoped Marianne would come to her senses and dump the vapid American for the nice Brit. However, they were a family who respected the choices the others made and so they were nice to Willoughby and never once said, "I miss Brandon."

Sam faked it until she made it and eventually learned to look forward to Willoughby's visits. While she knew he was a trust-fund baby who would likely burn through his family's money rather than grow their wealth, he was fun enough. He made everyone feel at ease around him. True, most of his jokes were made at the expense of others, but the people he made fun of were random Americans that she assumed they would never meet.

He planned on moving to England full-time. He was actually born in the UK, but his family moved to America when he was just a few months old. The land adjacent to Barton Park was his great-aunt's. She left it to him in her will. He came over for the funeral and stayed. He was just the kind of person who thought it was amazing to inherit a large swath of land with a mansion on it but have no idea how to care for it. Lady wished to buy the property for years to build some immersive cabins to create a play-and-stay experience, but the great-aunt had always refused to make the sale as she wanted it to be up to her nephew, who now was smitten with a full-time resident of Barton Park, making it unlikely he would want to sell and move away.

Maggie didn't like him any more than she did upon her first meeting, but she couldn't escape the fact that there was something beautiful about him. It wasn't cute. Cute was cute. Puppies are cute. Some of the sheep were cute. A hat is cute. Shoes are cute. Cute was easy to understand. This was something different. It wasn't quite the same thing as that moment with Juliet, but she couldn't pretend it wasn't not like that either. Thus, to avoid thinking in double-negatives any longer, she wasn't Marianne after all, she made a point to infiltrate Juliet's next overnight babysitting gig.

Maggie walked with her mum up to the big house as Sam, Middy, Lady, and Gran were heading out to London to catch a musical on the West End that came with an overnight stay. She offered her extra set of hands with the boys totally free of charge, using the excuse that she needed to get out of the house as Edward was in town, and she didn't want to be a fifth wheel in their double date/game night. To be fair, she hadn't been invited either and, save for Edward, no one actually noticed she wasn't lurking up in the attic all night.

Juliet, never one to turn down a chance to make all the money for half the work, accepted the help, and the six of them spent several hours playing capture the flag around the big house. The winners and losers were all treated to huge bowls of ice cream, sending them into a sugar high and subsequent crash that forced Juliet and Maggie to have to carry them all to bed. Maggie made a note to talk to Gran about how difficult it was to carry dead weight the next time they watched a movie where the hero ran with an unconscious damsel in distress.

Juliet and Maggie returned to the kitchen, which Juliet called "the scene of the crime," for them to clean up the results of the ice cream extravaganza. "Oof. Feels like maybe some kerosene and a match might be the solution, yeah?" Juliet said.

"I mean, sure, but this is your boss' house, and you love those kids and all."

"Fair point." They both laughed. "So, what do you want? Dishes or sticky surfaces?"

"Dishes. All day dishes," Maggie said.

"Really? No way. I hate dishes. So boring just standing there. Sticking my hands in the hot water with knives and other pokey things. No thanks."

"So, it is both dangerous and boring?"

"Shut it." Juliet laughed again.

Maggie collected all the dishes from the table and stacked them next to the sink. She filled up one side with hot water and squirted in the soap. She turned her back to the sink to look at Juliet, who was wiping everything from the table onto the ground. Maggie cleared her throat. "So..."

Juliet stopped mid-wipe. "Sounds ominous."

Maggie did a fake, all tooth smile. "Yeah, well…" she took a deep breath, turned her back to Juliet, shut off the water, and then exhaled all the words in one long breath, "when Marianne hurt her foot, and I was face to face with that stupid boy she loves now, I sort of wanted to grab him and give him a snog, and I was equal parts repulsed as he is so gross, but burning from the inside out because he is so pretty."

Juliet did a whistle-bomb. She started with a jovial tone, "Well, kiddo…"

"I'm broken?" Maggie interrupted.

Juliet changed her tone to deathly serious. "No. Not broken." She put the towel down, crossed the kitchen, and grabbed Maggie by the shoulders. She looked down into her eyes. "You are not broken. I've told you before, and I tell you again; If you're broken, then I'm broken, and I'm not broken. Never say that. Never think that. Understand?"

Maggie felt some tears leak out. She nodded quickly and looked down. Juliet let her go, and she wiped her face. "Thank you."

"Course." Juliet walked back to the table and attempted to lighten the mood again. "I mean, I haven't actually had the displeasure of meeting that guy, but I've heard that the jury is not out on him. The verdict is in, and he is a tool. However, you are not the only person to comment on how pretty he is."

"Right. It's like looking at the sun for too long. You know it's bad, but you can't stop. I just sort of thought, you know, I liked girls, you know, after…" she let it drift off and pointed to the space between them, "and I'm totally over that. I mean, I'm not, but I know you now, and you're old and..."

"Old!" Juliet laughed and threw the filthy towel at her.

Maggie caught the towel, and the sprinkles that were stuck to the towel kept going, pelting her in the face. Some of them embedded themselves in her hair. She laughed and laughed. Juliet followed suit, and after several minutes of giggling and face washing, they positioned themselves back at their cleaning stations.

Juliet started back up, "So is the issue that you wanted to snog a boy or snog that boy?"

"Can it be both?" Maggie replied without looking at her as she was elbow-deep in hot soapy dishwater.

"Sure. It can be. Going back to what I was saying, it seems as though that particular boy is just snoggable, and there is nothing you can do about it. Some people are just that way. I mean, if I was face-to-face with a young Cary Grant, I think I'd be tempted."

Maggie screwed up her face. She knew who he was. She and Gran had watched *The Philadelphia Story*. They had to stop the movie early on as the opening scene has a part where Grant pushes Katherine Hepburn in the face. Gran said it was of its time and funny. Maggie said it was of its time and sent a message that women should be okay with a little casual violence. Gran pushed back that every single action movie Maggie made her watch was an infomercial for women in peril. After 20 minutes, they finally watched the rest of the film, which, Maggie had to admit, had some of the best dialogue she'd ever heard.

"Okay, that is totally fair. Some people are just classically handsome, and everyone agrees on that. Willoughby is that. He is all of that. Still, this doesn't feel objective.

This feels..." She paused to think of the word. She finished rinsing the last dish and placed it on the rack. She pulled the plug at the bottom of the sink and let the water run out. She turned around to see Juliet, who was finishing up the sweeping-up part and was leaning on the mop handle, waiting for Maggie to keep talking and finish the dishes so she could get to the sink. "I don't know. What's the word?"

"Primal?" Juliet raised an eyebrow.

"Gross." Maggie made a lemon face.

"But accurate?" Juliet posed the question. "Scootch. I need the sink." She waved Maggie away with the business end of the mop and gave Maggie the space to think it over. She filled up the sink again with new hot water.

Maggie dug out a clean towel and went over to make sure the table was totally dry. She thought and wiped the table. She flipped the chairs over and placed them, legs up on the tabletop, then took a deep breath. "I suppose it is. I couldn't control it. I just sort of felt it, and my body couldn't stop it at first."

"Go." Juliet pointed over to the kitchen door with her head. She dropped the mop on the floor and started working backward from the far corner. "Well," she said with her back to Maggie as she worked, "I'd say it means you're most likely Bi. Could be Pan. Won't know until you meet someone who is non-binary, and you get all stomach-turny feelings for them. Right now, it seems you like boys and girls, and that, kiddo, is totally fine and normal."

"Yeah?" Maggie choked out.

Juliet stopped mopping and turned to face her. "Yeah." She broke into a smile and continued, "Some of my best friends are Bi."

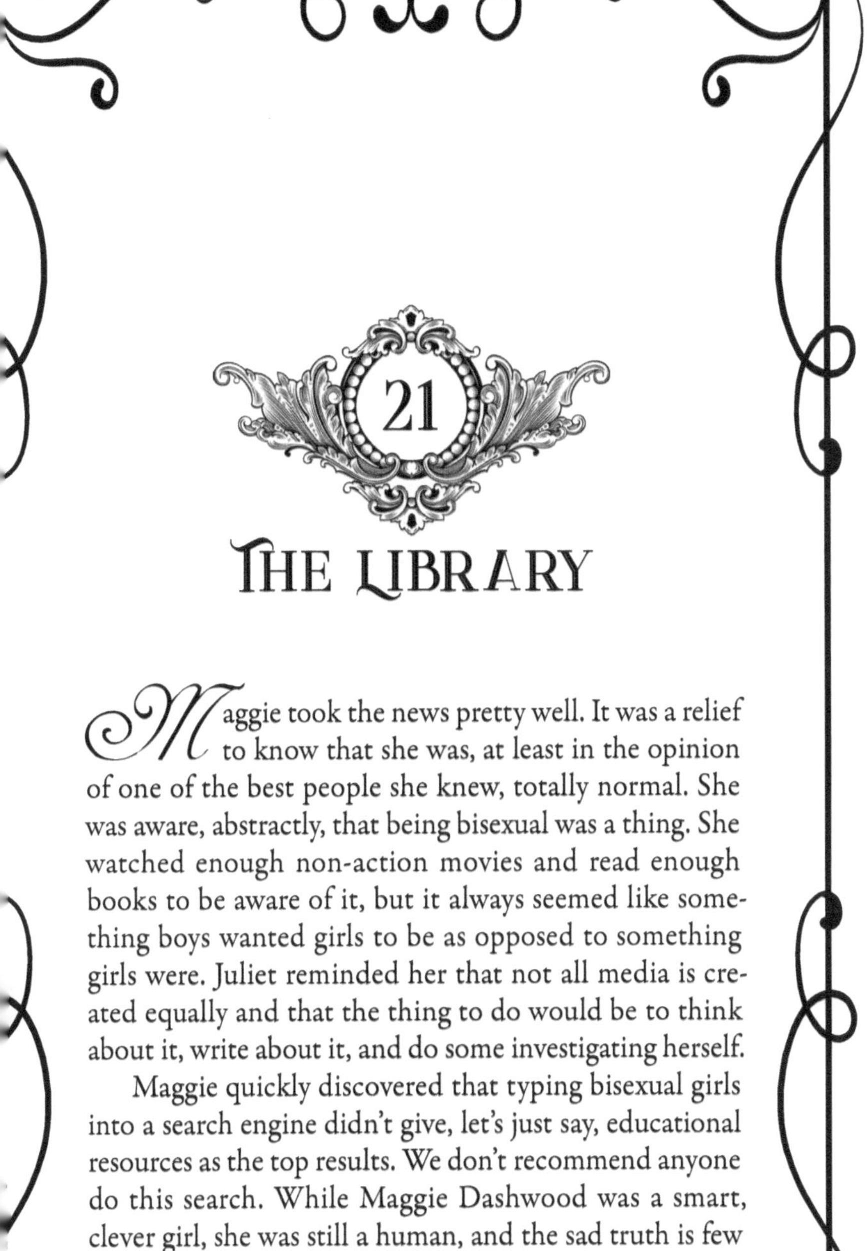

21

THE LIBRARY

Maggie took the news pretty well. It was a relief to know that she was, at least in the opinion of one of the best people she knew, totally normal. She was aware, abstractly, that being bisexual was a thing. She watched enough non-action movies and read enough books to be aware of it, but it always seemed like something boys wanted girls to be as opposed to something girls were. Juliet reminded her that not all media is created equally and that the thing to do would be to think about it, write about it, and do some investigating herself.

Maggie quickly discovered that typing bisexual girls into a search engine didn't give, let's just say, educational resources as the top results. We don't recommend anyone do this search. While Maggie Dashwood was a smart, clever girl, she was still a human, and the sad truth is few people go past the top results when they do an internet search. However, she did push herself through several pages just in case, but she kept finding the same images and videos. She tried different search engines and different search terms, but she was constantly bombarded with the same results. There were some articles about sexuality being a spectrum, but they were often on sites that also had quizzes to find out what Power Ranger one was. Maggie was the White Ranger.

Days of seemingly endless videos only confirmed her feeling that straight men and boys thought bisexuality wasn't a thing a girl was but was a thing a girl said she was to make herself more appealing to boys and men. It was gross. Seriously. Do NOT search for bisexual girls in a search engine. It would take a long time before Maggie actually met an openly bisexual man with whom she could have an honest conversation about the topic. While we will not see that in the pages of this tale, when it does happen, Maggie will cry a little.

With the internet being little help, Maggie once again channeled her inner Elinor and decided to go to the library. Elinor always found answers there. The small village library was, according to Elinor, much more of a library in name only. It was only open three days per week, had a small collection, and didn't subscribe to many online services. It was small enough that it didn't legally need to have an actual degree-holding librarian on staff. They just needed a warm body who was prompt. The woman who ran the village library kept records of every book every person checked out, and she wasn't afraid to talk about one's reading habits in public.

Maggie didn't think that a place like that would have what she needed, and even if it did, she didn't think she wanted that blabbed about. She had only confided in Juliet at that point, and she wasn't sure she wanted this to be the way she came out to her family as well as the employees of Barton Park. She didn't actually think any of them would care very much, but it was still scary and hard, and she didn't want to do it without being prepared. She needed information. She needed support. That meant she needed to gain access to one of the real libraries in Exeter. She knew it would seem more suspicious if she asked anyone other than Elinor to take her, so she cooked up a plan.

First, she needed to make sure she had a day off on a day when Elinor had to work. While she wasn't taking summer courses, the university library was open during the summer, and Elinor picked up as many hours there as she could. It was easy to figure out as Elinor made a family calendar on an erasable whiteboard and hung it in the kitchen. The outline of the calendar was drawn on in permanent marker. Each day then had three lines drawn through it so that there were four rectangles on each day. She allocated the boxes according to age and she assigned each of them a color. Purple for Sam, as it was a sign of royalty, and she was their queen. She gave herself blue, assigned Marianne red, and gave Maggie green.

It had work days, work hours, and visiting hours. The third column down was just filled with red Ws, indicating that Willoughby would be over that day. All day. While Sam did prevent him from staying the night, she was aware that the two of them were home alone most days, and at 17 going on 18, Marianne was old enough to make her own mistakes. She assured her entire family that they had nothing to fear and that Willoughby was nothing but a gentleman. None of them actually cared about how gentlemanly he was, but they nodded and smiled at the announcement anyway.

Sam and Maggie's rows were essentially the same. Work and nothing. They didn't see the point in fighting with Elinor about it. Neither of them imagined having visitors over. When Maggie and Gran did movie nights, they were at the big house, and she was occasionally called on by Lady and Middy to watch the boys when Juliet was unavailable or when it was just for a short time. So, out of respect for the process, Maggie did mark down when she planned on being gone. No one ever inquired about what movies they watched or how it went or what else she and Gran spoke of or how the boys were when she returned. Still, it made her feel part of the family in a small way.

Elinor had to get herself a fine-tipped marker to be able to cram all the information in the space she provided for herself. She lamented not getting a bigger whiteboard so she could include her commute time in more detail. Instead, she had Ls for when she was working so as not to confuse the Ws on Marianne's line. No one ever would, but Elinor just needed to be sure. She used Cs for class, Ts for when she was traveling, and Es for when Edward was going to be around. No one asked for that level of detail, and Marianne most certainly made snide comments about it on multiple occasions, but if every Dashwood folded when confronted with criticism from Marianne, they would never have gotten anything done.

After finding that the following day would fit her needs, she made sure to have her lunch break in the office in the big house to pitch Sam on the idea. She wasn't really worried that Sam would say no. Maggie always told everyone where she was going or asked permission, and she had rarely been told no. She was sure if she said, "Mum, I want to go into Exeter with Elinor tomorrow to learn to fight with swords; after all, I am the White Ranger," she would have been met with a "Fine" or a "Sure, but don't annoy her." The last bit was always added because it was something parents were supposed to say, but both Sam and Maggie knew it was almost impossible for Maggie to be an annoyance. The quiet girl with a sketchbook has rarely been, in the history of the world, an annoyance to anyone. Of course, her aloofness would occasionally unintentionally annoy people who were jealous of her or who were romantically interested in her. She could not be blamed and her mother, had she been there to see those moments, and if she had been paying attention, would have most certainly not said her daughter was remotely being annoying.

Maggie had grown accustomed to these kinds of responses in her short life. When they lived in Norland, and Marianne was going through what could only be called a rage-filled puberty, Maggie essentially moved out to the treehouse and stayed out of trouble. She would say, "Going out to the treehouse, Mum" and Sam would say, "Fine, dear" because it was always fine. Maggie was always fine.

It wasn't that Sam didn't love her youngest daughter. She absolutely did. She loved her with all her heart. Loving someone and giving the person what they need does not always coincide. In fact, sometimes, loving someone can allow one to let the love cloud one's vision. Sam Dashwood's love cloud was more of a fog and thus obtrusive. Maggie was so self-sufficient and capable of doing almost anything; she had gotten a job at 14, and she was never in trouble at school, and her friends were either older than her by quite a lot, or children and she was, in fact, always fine. Sam simply forgot that she needed a mother. Being fine is fine for an adult, but children should never be just fine.

Maggie spent her morning lost in work. She and Brandon spent the morning with the sheep. He fed them. She donned a full jumpsuit, complete with booties, and cleaned up after them. There were jokes made about just throwing the food in the trash to save themselves time. The jokes escalated quickly. Jokes about excrement can be, under the right circumstances, quite funny. She dropped her jumpsuit in the laundry bin in the barn, washed up, and bid him goodbye with a final feces nickname that he shot back at her. She really wished Marianne had better judgment. Later in life, she would joke that "I wish Marianne had better judgment" could have been the Dashwood family motto.

She arrived at the big house. Before she could reach Sam, she lost a quick wrestling match to Tractor Boy and his three sidekicks, Tractor Boy Jr., Tractor Lad, and Tractor Baby; as each of the four boys attacked an appendage, the pin was fast and efficient. Somehow Tractor Boy was both the team leader and the referee as he counted the pin by shouting, "ONE TWO THREE!" Middy had introduced the boys to professional wrestling, and it infected the big house like a sweaty virus.

As she suspected, Maggie gained easy permission from Sam, who in fact, did say, "That's fine dear, as long as Elinor doesn't mind, and you don't annoy her. She is at work." Sam didn't ask why she wanted to go to the library. We can't know for sure if Sam ever wondered why Maggie did anything. It is possible that the love fog just made it impossible for Sam to see Maggie as her own person and not just a lovely child who offered no resistance and caused no problems, thus she wasn't needy, or it could be that she simply had no interest. We suspect, Dear Reader, that it is the former, not the latter, but Maggie couldn't know that. In her mind, every silence felt like an attack, even when it wasn't. Sometimes, ignorance isn't willful.

It was true that most days, all these feelings bubbled under the surface, but because Maggie was feeling particularly confused and vulnerable, she was sure that if anyone had asked her a simple one-word question, she would have told that person everything. She swung by Gran's room, as she knew that she would certainly ask. Much to Maggie's dismay and relief, Gran was out. Her dismay urged her to send a quick text to see if she was around.

Gran's reply was swift. She was at her house in Exeter collecting her mail and taking a break from the wrestling. While Gran was, as we learned, not frail in any way, she was not interested in, nor did she have the energy for, being pummeled by her grandchildren for hours at a time. She said she would come back for dinner as wrestling was prohibited during meal times. They agreed to meet at their usual table. Maggie sighed with relief, knowing that there was no way they would have *that* conversation during family dinner, even when Gran asked her why she was going into town. Her dismay kicked her relief in the shin.

Other than a lot of trash talk from the Tractor Quartet that was shut down with a look from Lady, dinner was uneventful. Gran asked Maggie if she would ever like to come to the house with her in Exeter to help her with a few things. Maggie Dashwood would jump through fire for Gran Jennings, so she said yes without asking what she needed. They made plans for a future day off after she told Gran that she wanted to go explore the university library the next day. Because she phrased it that way, "explore the library," Gran didn't ask the magic question. Exploration needs no future explanation. Exploring is an activity that needs no reason. She knew that Maggie had the map of Barton Park all over her body. It ran through her veins and was printed on her feet. Gran was pleased that Maggie was expanding her horizons. It was why she invited her to the house. She realized, when Maggie texted her earlier that day, that other than her time in the village at school and the trip to A&E for Marianne, Maggie hadn't left Barton Park since they arrived.

On the walk back from dinner, Maggie, who recognized the power of the word "explore," used it again on her eldest sister. Elinor was, as almost all current or future librarians are, on the side of exploration of a library. Many librarians will judge a town, college, or university entirely on the state of the library, both the building and the collection. If a town or village doesn't have a library, even a small, gossip-filled one, that is not a place to live. If a college or university has allowed the library to fall into disrepair, if it is understaffed, or if the collection is missing some essentials, the librarian will, rightfully so, judge the institution harshly. If there is no respect for the institution's repository of all knowledge, why would anyone expect the students there to learn all the things they can learn?

Elinor was, as we expected she would be, thrilled that her little sister "finally" wanted to come to the library. She said it in a way that could have been taken as judgy but was, as Maggie knew, just the way Elinor was. She wouldn't ever tell anyone what to do, which was part of the Marianne issue. No one ever told her what to do, and she assumed the world was hung just for her.

Elinor explained that there was a huge film museum as part of the library system on campus as well as several different libraries. Elinor suspected that once Maggie got there, she wouldn't ever want to leave. Maggie, not wanting to look a gift horse in the mouth and all of that, nor fully understanding the phrase or why anyone was looking horses in the mouth instead of the eyes, thanked her effusively and promised not to be a nuisance. Elinor never once thought of Maggie as a nuisance. She sometimes forgot that she was even in the house as she was up in the attic, out of sight out, of mind, and all of that.

Maggie hardly slept, thinking about all the answers she would discover, and so she was sitting at the table on her third cup of coffee without any food before Elinor came downstairs. She was dressed in what she thought would be "university-appropriate" clothes. She donned a plaid skirt with a white button-down collared shirt tucked in with a matching plaid tie. She burned off some energy in the wee hours polishing a pair of black, calf-high boots. She put her hair back in a high ponytail and had her backpack packed with a sketchbook, an almost blank journal for note taking, pens and pencils for both drawing and writing, as well as several snacks.

Upon hearing Elinor's footfalls on the stairs, Maggie bounced up and started making her toast and poured her a cup of coffee. She was setting it down at Elinor's place at the table when she entered the kitchen. The cup shook a little in her hand, and she splashed just a bit on the table. "Good morning! Sorry. I'll clean that right up," Maggie shouted at an unacceptable morning volume.

"Good morning. No problem. Thank you?"

Hearing the question in her sister's voice, she answered while pulling the toast out from the toaster and slathering on butter. "I'm just very excited. I hadn't realized until this morning that I've not gone anywhere in a long time, and I just..." she waved the knife above her head, "really want to see it. I can't stop thinking about the film museum." She set the knife down on the counter, got the jam out of the refrigerator, and brought the plate of toast and the jam over to the table to see Elinor staring at her with wide eyes. "Yeah, I know, I'm all wound up, but after you told me about it all, I couldn't stop thinking. I looked it up last night, and it looks amazing... and there are so many floors and a lift! A lift in a library! I had no idea that was an option. I mean, that means levels of stuff. Free stuff! How do you stand it?" She plopped down in her chair, realized the knife was on the counter, jumped back up, grabbed it, brought it back over, and set it down on the table.

"Well," Elinor spread some jam on her toast and thought of where to start, "I stand it because I know I am there to work, but I would be remiss to say that there are not days where I go in early or stay late to be a patron, which is what we call people who come into the library, and just marvel at it." She took a bite and did some thinking. Maggie, knowing the look of Elinor's thinking face, waited. "Think of your work here. You love those sheep, and the boys, and spending time with Middy and Brandon and, um..."

"Juliet," Maggie offered and immediately regretted it, thinking that she had essentially shouted, "I'm queer!"

Elinor only heard a name and not an admission, so she pressed on. "Right. Juliet. She's great. You like her, but when you're working, she's your boss, not your friend. It's like that. I just know that when I'm working, I'm there to help the students and public patrons get what they need. Librarians and library staff members do not actually get paid to sit and read. We don't just say shush, and we don't all wear cat's-eye glasses."

"Right, but..." Maggie started.

"Right, if I needed glasses, I would get cat's eye glasses because stereotypes exist for a reason, and I do like saying shush, but college libraries are noisy in general except for the top floors, and everyone knows."

"And you'd be fetching in those glasses should the need arise."

"I would be, indeed."

"Yes, because sexy librarians are a stereotype that is worth emulating as well."

Elinor waved that off. She, too, knew who her sister was. "Let's stop at fetching."

They laughed and ate, and the food calmed Maggie down. They cleaned up the kitchen, used the loo, and headed out to the university a bit earlier than Elinor would normally leave. She wanted to get Maggie situated once they arrived and, what comes as no surprise to anyone, Elinor was an "if I'm not ten minutes early, I'm five minutes late" kind of person.

On the way, Maggie peppered her with questions regarding the maps she saw online, the film museum, how to find books about all kinds of topics, and if there were actual card catalogs or if it was all online and, and, and. It was, to Elinor's estimation, the quickest and most pleasant drive to work she'd had up to that point. People love talking about the things they love to someone who genuinely wants to know. Happiness can be that simple.

They parked on the far side of Streatham Campus so Elinor could walk Maggie across campus and explain things as best as she could. She tried to remember what it was like for her the first time she arrived, just a few days before her first class. It seemed overwhelming. It was beautiful, of that there was little doubt, but for the uninitiated, and for a person who spent almost all of her life on a farm, a university campus can feel like a whole different planet.

Maggie, who had every intention of studying the map last night, was so thoroughly distracted by the library web pages that she never did. She tried to apply her excellent internal compass to the campus. She kept looking behind her to orient herself to where the car was parked. She gave buildings names based on their looks and noticed trees that could be markers. She felt comfortable that she could navigate her way all around campus. Ultimately, all the mental notes were for naught because other than lunch with Elinor at a campus eatery, she only went outside to go between the Old and Forum Libraries. Over the course of the next few years, after that first visit, it would have been possible that if there was not already paving there, Maggie would have worn a path between them.

Elinor set Maggie up with a guest pass so she could access the library databases and use anything she wished. She told her that if there were any physical items she found of interest during the day, she should keep them, and Elinor would check them out on her account; if there was any electronic material that she couldn't get to with her guest pass, she would get those for her as well and download them to her tablet so Maggie could read them at home.

Maggie considered coming out to Elinor by having her check out a bunch of queer articles, books, and movies but ultimately decided that she needed to try it out on Gran before she said boo to her sisters or mum. At that point though, she was more than comfortable having one confidante whom she knew wouldn't judge her for anything. It was a trait she carried with her throughout her life. She would always be incredibly loyal to her closest friends, and she would never need more than three at any given time. Of course, we know that there are some people for whom one person is enough, and we know that for others, there are never enough people paying attention to them. We see that within the same family both kinds of people can exist and thrive.

Maggie felt sure she could bring Gran into her circle of confidence, but she wasn't ready just then. She didn't know much about herself yet, and unlike Juliet, who didn't ask too many questions, Gran asked all the questions. They were not accusatory; she was just interested, and she cared. Maggie needed to know more, and so she began her journey of self-discovery with one step. Well, first, she needed to wander through the film museum for a few hours, and then, definitely after lunch, she would totally take the first step, which, after a lunch where Maggie talked at her sister for 45 minutes about the stuff in the film museum, that Elinor already knew about, Maggie took her first step. It was one small step for girl-kind, but one huge leap for Margaret Dashwood.

She found hundreds of articles. She read through a few of them. There was an option for PDF delivery, but she wasn't comfortable entering her email. She didn't want the record even though she was assured there wasn't one. She watched too many bad movies where someone left a record on a computer somewhere, and someone with glasses came in and banged nonsense on the keyboard and magically found a clue to that person's guilt. On the drive in, she asked so many questions that the questions about tracking search queries and what each person looked at didn't seem out of place. Elinor explained that searches were not saved. Once she had her own library card and account, she could favorite things, or email them to herself, but as a guest, she was a ghost.

What made her day was the print books. There were 12 books total in the system that could be found in The Forum Library that specifically dealt with bisexuality. She took them out one at a time and made sure she put them back on the shelf when she was done. She knew that reshelving was a no-no, but she didn't want one of Elinor's co-workers to find a pile of queer books in the area where her little sister spent the day. She reshelved them anyway and asked the library gods for forgiveness.

A handful of the books took a scientific and socio-logical look at bisexuality. She found them fascinating and read several passages over and over and took copious notes. She really just gave herself more questions to ask, but she felt that she was finally asking the right ques-tions. However, there was one book that felt like it was written just for her, as though someone knew she would be coming into that library on that day, and they dropped it into the collection. She spent a full hour trying to absorb Juno Dawson's *This Book is Gay*. When her alarm on her phone went off, reminding her to get to the ref-erence desk where Elinor was, she wrote down the page number, slipped it back on the shelf, smoothed her skirt, straightened her tie, and went to find her sister feeling lighter than she had in a long time. She felt so good, in fact, that her feelings were not totally destroyed when no one except for Gran asked her how her day at the library went.

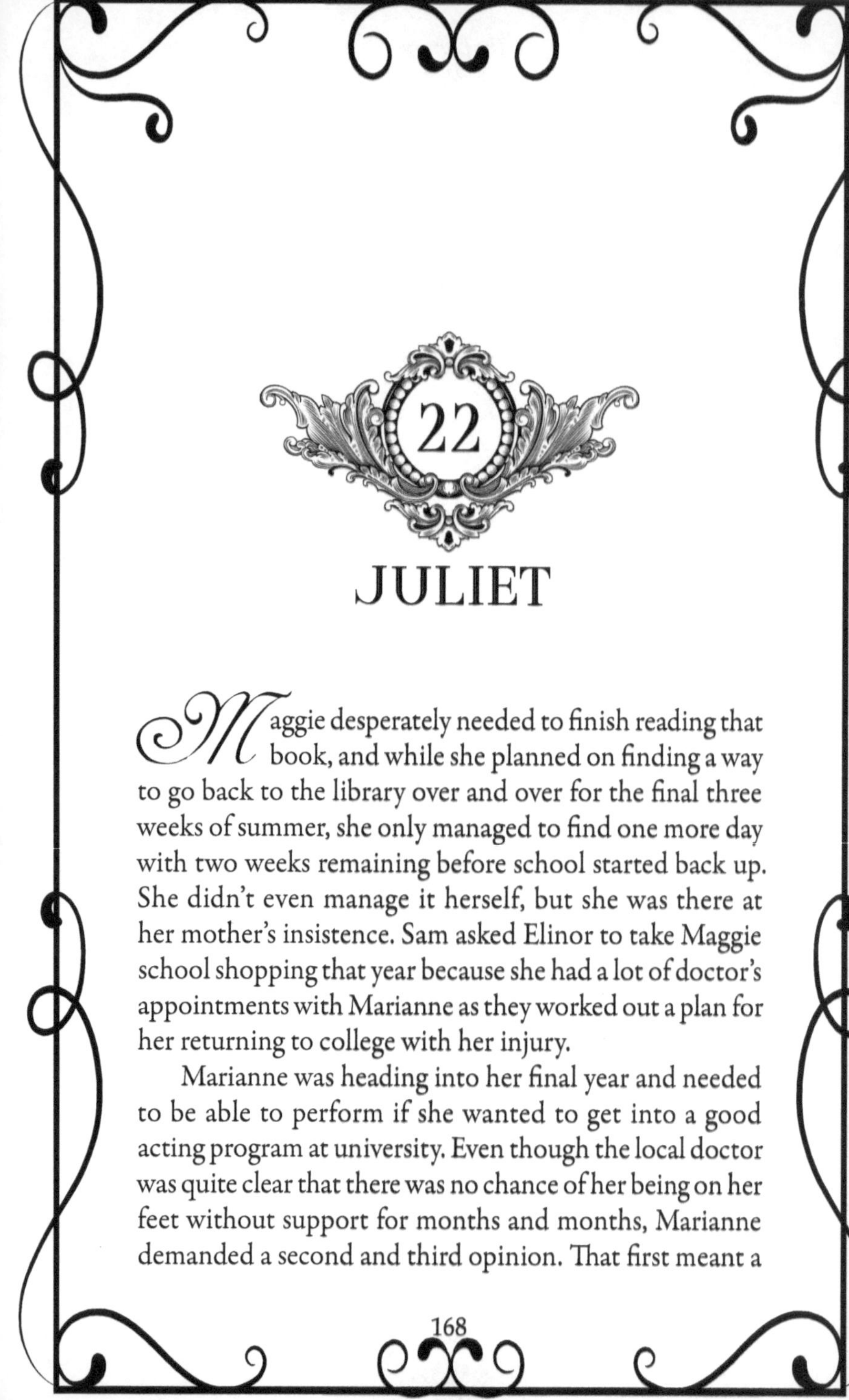

22

JULIET

Maggie desperately needed to finish reading that book, and while she planned on finding a way to go back to the library over and over for the final three weeks of summer, she only managed to find one more day with two weeks remaining before school started back up. She didn't even manage it herself, but she was there at her mother's insistence. Sam asked Elinor to take Maggie school shopping that year because she had a lot of doctor's appointments with Marianne as they worked out a plan for her returning to college with her injury.

Marianne was heading into her final year and needed to be able to perform if she wanted to get into a good acting program at university. Even though the local doctor was quite clear that there was no chance of her being on her feet without support for months and months, Marianne demanded a second and third opinion. That first meant a trip to Exeter, then London. The medical opinions were all the same because they were not opinions. Facts are just facts. Marianne was going to need support standing for some time, and rushing back would only cause irreparable damage. Since Marianne refused surgery, as she didn't want a scar down the side of her leg that would, in almost all performances, be covered by leggings or socks, the slow-heal process was the only option. The tendon wouldn't be replaced, and the body would adjust, but there would always be a weakness, and reinjury would always be a possibility.

Normally, Maggie would think dark thoughts about Marianne's drama queen tendencies. However, she applauded them when she was dumped on Elinor's lap. Elinor obtained a card in Maggie's own name, thus giving her access to the virtual materials, which did include a lot of excellent information, and so without outing herself, she couldn't explain why she needed to get back to the library. Dawson's book told her she was okay, that she was normal. Sure, Juliet said it, but we all need reinforcement. Dawson answered all the questions Maggie didn't even know she had that she needed. Not wanted but needed.

The local village library didn't have subscriptions to the digital services where she could get the e-book or audiobook, and she didn't want to order it via interlibrary loan due to the gossip. She did find a website that had a digital copy of the book online for free, but she couldn't bring herself to read it. Maggie wasn't a Gen Z kid who disliked electronic media. She was fine with it. It was what she knew. She did enjoy the heft of a book and the sound of a DVD whirring in the player, but she was fine with streaming and downloading. While she was a farm kid and would find herself most comfortable being away from big cities for the rest of her life, she wasn't a technophobe.

The issue was that the digital book had the author's birth name before she transitioned. Maggie felt disloyal to read it with the wrong name on each page, even though the book is written from the perspective of James. Maggie assumed Juno wouldn't mind, or at least she didn't think she would mind, as she knew who she was and published the book anyway. Still, she just wanted to see Juno's name on every page. Maggie had been cyberstalking her and read as much about her as she could. She found an old *Guardian* article when the book first came out where Juno was still using her birth name, so Maggie felt sure, in some fictional future where they met and became friends, Juno wouldn't shame Maggie for getting the book in any format, if it was what she needed. Still, Maggie wanted that book. The one that she touched first and that changed her life, as that particular physical copy had magical powers. Some books just do things to us.

Maggie brought the same journal she brought the first time that she titled, *This Journal is Queer,* in honor of Juno. Granted, she only wrote it on the inside page but still. She had taken so many notes before, and she had used her library card to read and read as many journal articles as she could. She made note of another book the library had called *Homoplot*. It seemed that very few libraries had it. She couldn't find a digital copy anywhere, and so she knew that eventually, she would have to go back to the library to get her hands on it. She had made notes of when special events were happening at the film museum so she could use that as her reason for needing to hitch a ride with Elinor, and while she would, of course, actually check those things out, she would hide in a nook and read and make notes.

She finished the book in that second sitting, and buoyed by the knowledge, she enjoyed her shopping excursion with Elinor, who liked shopping only slightly more than Maggie, which is to say 20 times less than Marianne. They made quick work of it. Maggie got some white shirts that fit her better. She was growing, and she struggled to keep the shirts tucked in. She was not, at that time, a person comfortable being in public with a bare tummy. She would eventually learn to, while not enjoy it, but not hate it under the right circumstances, like, for example, a Halloween showing of *The Rocky Horror Picture Show*. So, after two trousers, two skirts, five shirts, and three new ties, which she didn't actually need, there was enough money left in Sam's budget that they were able to pay for dinner before heading back to The Cottage.

The next day, before work, mentally loaded up with so much information that she was sure Juliet already knew, she set out to find her to tell her all about it anyway. She went up to the big house for breakfast to check the big board, and if she wasn't scheduled to work with Juliet, she wanted to request a swap. She was attacked on her way into the kitchen, as wrestling had officially been banned from all places where food was served. She got in a few good blows against the Tractor Quartet and even managed to tickle Tractor Lad into submission, which scared off Tractor Boy and Tractor Boy Jr. into the kitchen and brought Tractor Baby running over for his turn. Ultimately, Middy called the match a draw, making Maggie's solo record against them 0-14-1, although she and Juliet did manage to take them down one time as a tag team.

Lady smiled at her when she entered the kitchen. She was standing at the counter buttering toast while waiting for the next batch to pop. They went through at least one loaf of bread every single day. "You spoil them."

"They are easy to spoil. Wrestling matches are free."

"Well, I appreciate it because Tractor Mum has gone into full retirement after I got a knee to the nose last week. I have meetings with some investors next week, and I don't want anyone to think that anything untoward is going on here. Toast and coffee?" She seamlessly changed subjects in the way that mums do.

"Please." Lady handed her the plate she had in her hand. "Sure? Isn't this claimed by someone? I can do it. I'm the interloper."

"They'll be fine." They turned to look at the four boys at the table. Each of them had something in his mouth. Three of them were chewing with their mouths open. "Nice use of the word interloper, by the way."

"Thanks, it's a good one. I'm fond of 'heretofore' as well. I don't really have a lot of uses for it, but I like it. I'll definitely use it in an essay this year, although I suspect Mr. Turdmonkey will say I've copied it."

"Turdmonkey?" Lady raised one eyebrow in a way that made Maggie jealous. She had spent hours in front of mirrors trying to replicate it, only to eventually relent.

"I suspect that isn't his real name either. Must be witness protection or something. He's, well, the worst writing teacher ever. I am sure he has a mug or a jumper that says that. No one ever does anything right, but he gives no feedback except to claim that we must have copied it from somewhere else. So, it's like, we have to write poorly so he can give us bad marks with no feedback, or we write well so he can accuse us of cheating. Good times."

"Sorry to hear that. It's only one more year with him, yeah?" She continued to butter toast and load the toaster during the entire conversation, and it seemed that she was finally done and ready to sit. "Grab us coffee?" she asked.

She took Maggie's plate back from her and moved over to the non-tractor end of the kitchen table where Middy was sitting drinking coffee and reading the morning newspaper, seemingly oblivious to the goings on of the Quartet. However, he would occasionally say one of their names in a way that meant whatever he was doing was something that needed to stop immediately. He did it without ever looking up from his reading in the way that parents do.

Maggie set the two mismatched mugs down on the table and sat down in front of the place Lady set her plate. She slid Lady's cup over to her, and they both quietly added jam to their toast. After Maggie sipped her coffee and swallowed her first bite of toast, she asked, "So, I'm wondering if you happen to know off the top of your head where I'm scheduled today?"

Middy shook his head even though he knew the question wasn't actually directed at him. He may be out in the field, but even he had to check the big board to figure out where he needed to be each day. Lady patted him on the arm, which didn't somehow come across as patronizing. He knew it and smiled.

"You're in the tractor barn. Juliet is doing tune-ups on the tractors and she, needed your," Lady made air quote fingers, "'tiny baby hands.'"

"Yeah?" Maggie could barely contain her excitement. "Awesome. I was going to ask if I wasn't with her if I could swap. I had a few things I wanted to ask her."

"TRACTORS!" Tractor Boy Jr. shouted, apropos of nothing, which was followed by a loud chorus of the "TRACTORS" battle cry as they all ran out of the kitchen.

Maggie laughed and watched them go out. She said, "I hope nobody pukes."

"Me neither," Lady replied.

Maggie didn't realize that neither of the Middleton parents scolded them for the sudden outburst, and with her head turned, she didn't see the look that passed between Lady and Middy, nor did she see the hand squeeze that accompanied it.

So it was that Maggie's cousins, who treated her like a niece and loved her like a daughter, rejected her offer to help clean the kitchen and sent her off to the tractor barn. The hundreds of things she wanted to share with Juliet were practically bursting out of her. After finishing Dawson's book, she had a sense that she might be ready to come out to her family and the world. She wanted to run it past her Queer Yoda first.

When she arrived, Juliet was already there, and The Doors were blaring from her portable speaker. The hood on one tractor was up, engine parts strew about on a tarp used for that very purpose. When Juliet did anything, she did it all the way. She was not going to just replace the spark plugs and call it a tune-up. She took apart anything she could, cleaned it, replaced every belt, whether it needed it or not, and put everything back together. Most business owners would feel this practice was wasteful, but since they hired Juliet, they had zero tractors break down in action. When part of the business required pulling customers around on a hay ride, a broken-down tractor followed by subsequent refunds and free day passes for a future visit cost thousands of pounds more than replacing a few belts and bearings a month early.

"Oi," Maggie shouted over the music. "Tiny Baby Hands, reporting for duty."

Juliet poked her head up and smiled. "'Bout time."

"I start at 9. It's like 8:45, and I'll have you know that I even battled the Quartet to a draw this morning. So, it's not as though I've been messing about."

"Yeah? A draw? Said who?" Juliet stood up and wiped her hands on her shirt. If there was a new streak of grease there, it would have been impossible to tell.

"Middy."

"Wow, except for that time we tagged 'em, I'm Oh fer. The big one is getting a bit too big."

"The struggle is real."

Juliet laughed. "Speaking of struggle, you're going to do this." She pointed at the pile of parts. "And I'm going to watch."

"Huh? I thought you needed my baby hands."

"Yeah, I need your baby hands to finish this tune-up and then do that one." She pointed with her head at the other tractor. "Then tomorrow, you'll do the other two. You can do so much more than just moving dung around and cutting grass."

"Yeah?" Maggie looked at the pile of parts. The inner confidence she felt about the book and her coming out plan and her entire personhood was fighting to hold up the weight of the image of the tractor breaking down with a load of first years on a field trip.

"I'm not going to let you screw it up," Juliet said.

Maggie looked from the parts back to her. They locked eyes. "Yeah?"

"Yeah." Juliet nodded.

Maggie nodded back. "Right." She took a deep breath and nodded again. "Right."

Juliet clapped her hands together and rubbed them hard. "Right."

For the next three hours, Juliet spent her time telling Maggie what the names of the parts were, what they did, and how they went into the tractor. Maggie repeated everything at least three times aloud and fifty times in her head. In between the lessons, Maggie told Juliet about Dawson's book, which Juliet had not read. She knew who Dawson was because Meg loved YA books and had read some of her novels.

The first tractor started right up, and Maggie and Juliet did a victory dance that, had it been witnessed by anyone, would have looked exactly like a joy-filled victory dance should look. Juliet didn't believe that The Doors were proper victory dance music, so she fired up Prince's "Let's Go Crazy," which is an excellent song for victory dance or any celebration of any kind. Facts, as we keep stating, are facts.

They took lunch after the dance died down. Maggie hadn't brought a lunch, as she normally went back to The Cottage at meal times. Juliet anticipated that and brought an extra sandwich and bag of crisps. It was after they were full and relaxing for 10 minutes that Maggie finally presented her plan.

"So, I was thinking, after reading that book and the articles and talking to you and everything, that maybe

I'm ready to…" In her head, she'd said it a million times. She even imagined telling the story to someone down the line. Her coming-out story was going to be so great, and Marianne wasn't going to make it about her, and that was that. Yet the words died on her tongue. Her throat closed and her eyes watered. She looked to Juliet for help.

Juliet knew exactly what was going on, and she grabbed her hand and squeezed it. "Oh, kiddo."

With that squeeze and with those two words, they both knew that Maggie wasn't ready yet. If she couldn't say it to Juliet, she couldn't say it to her mum, and she definitely couldn't say it to Marianne, who would, without a doubt, make it all about her. No one suspected that Marianne was a closed-minded bigot or that she would have any problem with her sister being bisexual, but regardless of the news, the fact was, Marianne managed to find a way to make it about her. *She* found their father's body. *She* had to go to a new college. *She* was going to have to make new plans.

"Look, kiddo, this is a big deal, and I'm so proud of you for doing the work and thinking it out and coming to me, but this is something you can't rush. I know you said the book says to make plans and do that in a particular way. I'm not going to argue with Juno on that because she really has helped millions of people, but the thing you keep saying, the advice you take from it the most is; it is your story. You are you. There is no right way. There is only your way."

"Yeah?" Maggie wiped tears off her face.

"Yeah. My mum already knew, so it wasn't a thing. She told me. It was so easy. Meg's parents, well, I don't want to tell her story for her, but since she doesn't 'seem' queer, as her da said, it was a bit of a shocker for them."

"What does that mean? Do I seem queer?"

"Hard for me to know because I know you. I think he meant because she is super girly and all. She turns a lot of dude's heads. I think because she's such a looker, her da thought she would have her pick of men. He had a pretty daughter and thought he would have pretty grandkids and all that. You know what it's like being around a pretty."

Maggie nodded and laughed at the term. "Yeah. There are a lot of expectations about her. It's like, she's pretty, so everyone assumes she wants to be super snoggy and all. I mean, in Marianne's case, it's true. She's boy crazy. Like, I can't remember a time when she wasn't talking about some boy."

"I'd say, being boy crazy is stranger than liking boys and girls, or just girls, or just boys. I think most people like to keep their private thoughts private. I love Meg, and I'll tell anyone who asks, but I don't tell everyone my personal stuff. It's our business. I think your sister is, if you will excuse the quick judgment call, a bit of an attention hound."

Maggie laughed and laughed. She told Juliet the term she used, which was much harsher than hound, but started with the same sound. Juliet laughed too and said that was the term she would have used but didn't want to say it. She understood that a person can say whatever they want about their own sibling, but when someone else says the exact same thing, those are fighting words. It makes no sense, but there it is.

With that hard conversation over, they returned to the next tractor. Juliet let Maggie play DJ. Since she was her mother's daughter, the playlist was eclectic. Some of the artists were born in the first half of the last century, and some were born just a few years before Maggie. From singer/songwriters to K-Pop, Maggie could pretty much find something about any song to like. She had favorites, and those appeared a bit more often. They were introspective and subtly sad while presenting happiness. Juliet, who picked up on that trend quite quickly, offered up some suggestions that she could add to her rotation. Maggie had heard "Personal Jesus" before, but she hadn't really stopped to think about what it was saying.

As they worked and talked about music, Juliet admitted that Maggie's obsession with Matt Nathanson, "The American Folk Guy," as she called him, made a lot more sense after she'd heard her favorites on random. Before the last bolt was back in place and the second tractor hummed successfully back to life, The Runaways, The Cure, The Lemonheads, and several other bands that started with "The" ended up on Maggie's playlist.

As they were cleaning up the tarp and wiping down the tools, Juliet said, "Well, listen, Mags..." she opted for Tractor Boy's nickname, which she'd heard him use hundreds of times, instead of "kiddo" which she normally did. The choice was not lost on Maggie, who, having never had the courage to try it out at school as she planned, didn't mind the sound of it coming out of Juliet's mouth. "...Um, look, the reason I wanted you here with me today is that I wanted to show you how to tune up the tractors, and I didn't want to give you that choice, but tomorrow, I need to tune up the other two, and I want you to know that you have a choice about that."

Maggie, who had just finished wiping a wrench clean, turned from the wall where it hung, and looked at Juliet. "Huh?"

"Yeah. Right. Okay. That made no sense." Juliet shook her head. "Put that up, and let's go sit for a second."

Maggie did as instructed and went to sit with Juliet at the edge of one of the trailers where they had lunch. "So, is there some lesson about informed consent you want to teach me that involved tractors?"

Juliet chuckled. "Informed consent. Good lord, I didn't know so many words when I was 14." She took a breath. "No, it isn't that. It's that..." She trailed off and looked away. She wiped her cheek.

"Are you crying?" Maggie exclaimed. She'd cried buckets of tears in front of Juliet, but Juliet had never, even at the end of *The Fault in our Stars,* so much as dropped one tear. "Are you sick? Is Meg sick? Oh, God, Middy? Middy's sick?" Maggie's mind whirled to all of the things that could possibly go wrong, and because the biggest tragedy of her life involved the death of her father, death was always where her mind landed.

"No!" Juliet turned back to her with tears freely flowing. She put her hand on Maggie's cheek, which, had it not already been covered in grease, would have left a grease mark. "Nobody's sick. I'm just..." She wiped her face again. "I'm... Meg... um..." She took a big breath and said in one go. "Meg got into the University of Toronto for a Ph.D. program, and we're moving in a few weeks before the new school year starts. She was wait-listed and just found out. Brandon's da knew a guy who knew a guy who needed a mechanic in Hamilton, which isn't far from there, and Meg's applied for a few teaching positions too and has some interviews lined up, and they are desperate for teachers, some kind of shortage or something, so she feels good that she'll land something and so, I wanted to have this day with you to teach you something new but also give you the choice to spend tomorrow with me too, cause it'll be my last day, but I totally understand if you're mad and don't want to, but I'd like to say that of all the people here, I wanted to spend my final working day with you."

Hearts break in all kinds of ways. Some explode. Little bits of heart residue banging around in one's body, untethered, unable to find its whole. Some shrivel, leaving a space inside one's chest for months or years or ever. Some turn to stone and weigh one down like an anchor being thrown overboard. Maggie, who was thankfully sitting, would have collapsed under the weight as her heart boulder dropped into her stomach. She went cold and broke out into a sweat.

She turned and wretched. We won't linger on that. This isn't that kind of story. Just know, Dear Reader, that it took a while and only after lots of coos and "kiddos," and "it'll be okays" mixed with rubs on the back during the dry heave and wracking sob portion of the aftermath, that eventually Maggie managed to sit up. Juliet handed her some water, which she drank slowly, allowing the water to rehydrate her tongue. She poured some in her hand and splashed it on her face, which felt like it was on fire. It was sticky with dried tears, snot, and some lunch residue. The water felt good, and so she poured the rest of the bottle over her head. The trickles of water ran down her shirt giving her goosebumps that were both unpleasant and life-affirming. Feeling that meant she could feel.

"I'm sorry," Maggie finally said with what she thought was an embarrassed smile.

"You don't have to be sorry." Juliet shook her head. "I suppose I should be flattered. I've never made anyone puke before. Lots of firsts in my life happened with you there."

Maggie dropped her head into her hands. "Too soon. Always too soon." If she could have seen her face, cradled in her hands, she would have discovered that the smile was actually real.

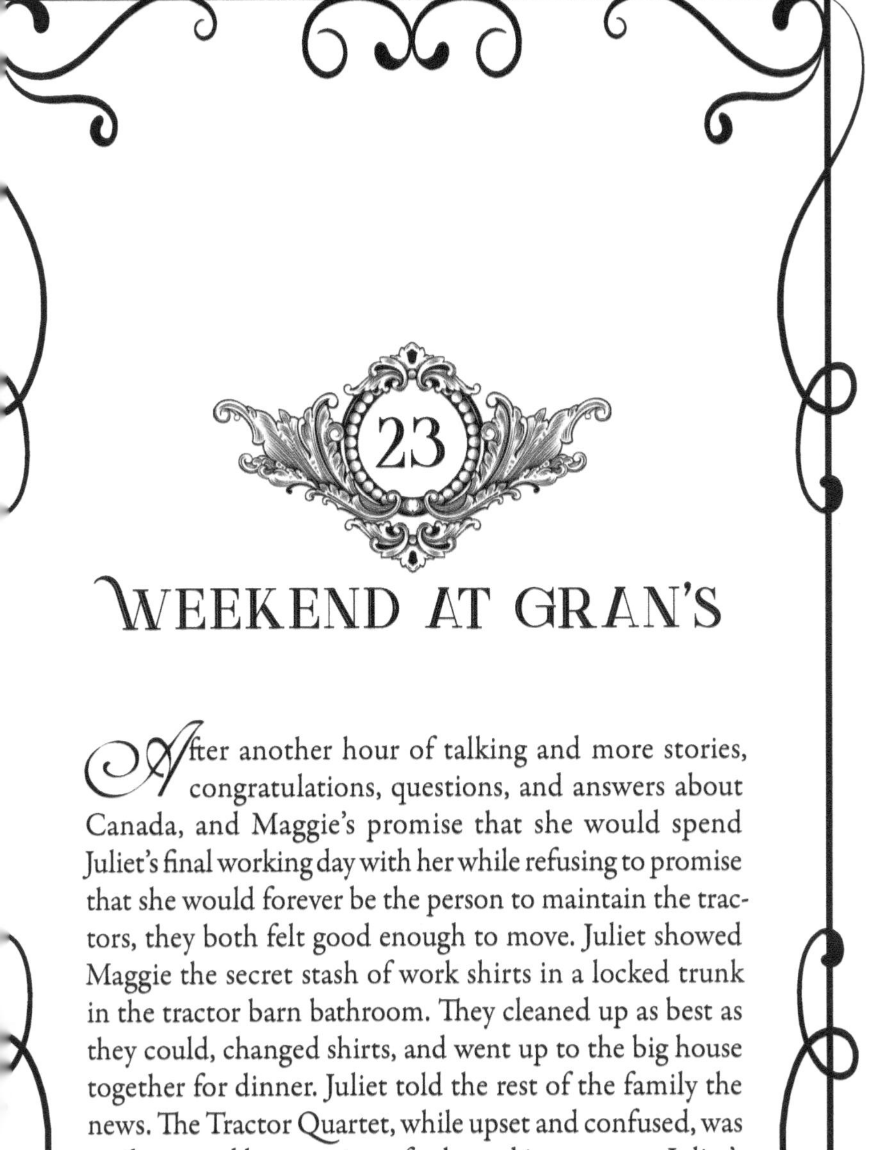

23

WEEKEND AT GRAN'S

After another hour of talking and more stories, congratulations, questions, and answers about Canada, and Maggie's promise that she would spend Juliet's final working day with her while refusing to promise that she would forever be the person to maintain the tractors, they both felt good enough to move. Juliet showed Maggie the secret stash of work shirts in a locked trunk in the tractor barn bathroom. They cleaned up as best as they could, changed shirts, and went up to the big house together for dinner. Juliet told the rest of the family the news. The Tractor Quartet, while upset and confused, was easily swayed by promises of cake and ice cream at Juliet's going away party the next day.

Elinor asked a lot of questions about Meg's chosen field of study, which Juliet could only tangentially answer. She promised to introduce them the next day at the party, and that satisfied Elinor. Sam, who was always happy to see people be happy, was genuinely excited for Juliet. Marianne spent a lot of time talking about how she hated being that cold and how, the doctors said, after her injury, she would likely be more sensitive to the cold in her bad leg. The "doctors" in question were people from the internet, but that didn't stop Marianne from finding a way to make someone else's life-altering decision to move to a new country on short notice about her.

Maggie, who'd had her time with Juliet, sat at her table with Gran during the Q and A section of the meal. Gran, who knew better than anyone how important Juliet was to Maggie, informed her that she'd arranged with Lady for her to have the weekend off so that after Juliet's going away party, she could, if she wished, come to her place for the weekend. Maggie, who, in typical Dashwood fashion, found a few more tears hidden in the recesses of her head, let a few escape.

So it was that after a final day of tractor tune-ups and tears, cake, ice cream, and a special toast with some of the good whiskey, complete with more tears, Gran pulled into her drive at her house in Exeter with an exhausted and sleeping Maggie in the passenger seat.

Gran reached out and rubbed her shoulder. "We're here."

"Merrg."

"English, please." Gran laughed.

Maggie sat up and felt her face. "Oh. I've not had seatbelt face in ages."

"You fell asleep before we were even through the village. I considered driving around for a while longer, but I'm tired too, and while I'm not an old lady, I am no spring chicken. I want to get to bed."

Maggie rubbed her face and cracked her neck as they climbed out of the car. She grabbed her bag out of the back. She said as they were walking up the path to the front door, "Having lived on a working farm for almost two years now, I have to say, I can't see the difference between spring and fall chickens. They look the same and taste the same."

"You're sweet, dear." Gran reached out and touched Maggie's face.

Maggie put her hand over the top of Gran's and held it there against her face. She tried to remember when she'd last been touched just because. The boys were always wrestling her, and Juliet had to comfort her, but she wasn't sure if anyone touched her to just touch her. She found that she liked it more than she thought she would. The saying goes, "We don't know what we have until it is gone," but the inverse is also true. We don't know we are missing something until we have it. In an effort to not cry anymore, Maggie let go and stepped back, but she didn't break eye contact with Gran. She didn't want her to think the wrong thing. Of course, she didn't and wouldn't.

Gran got Maggie set up in what used to be Lady's room but was what she liked to call "the guest room for humans." Charlie's old room had been converted into a "room for future hooligans," complete with two bunk beds and a carpet that was better suited for a soccer pitch. Easy to clean and durable. It had game boards printed on it. Chessboards, Snakes and Ladders, Backgammon, and Life. She had bags of coins kept on a shelf for them to use as game pieces. Gran realized that they were going to lose them or break them, so she showed them how to use different coins for different things, and they had all the fun.

Maggie managed to use the loo and brush her teeth before falling down on top of the bed. She woke, this time with duvet cover face, 10 hours later. She used the loo, showered, and stumbled out into the house to find Gran sipping tea in a highbacked chair reading *Total Film* magazine.

"Good morning, dear." She looked up and smiled. "Sleep well?"

"What day is it?" Maggie joked.

"That well, huh? You'll have to tell Lady that you find her old bed to be more than adequate. She was not fond of it."

"She must hate joy as well as puppies and chocolate too."

Gran laughed in a way that made Maggie feel unadulterated joy. Gran always laughed with her whole body. When something was funny, it was gut-bustingly funny. While the Dashwoods were criers, sometimes solo and sometimes sympathetic, Gran Jennings was a laugher, and it was, like a yawn, contagious.

After the chuckles tired themselves out as they tend to do, Gran asked if Maggie was hungry, which was rhetorical. She asked it on her way to the kitchen. She handed her a basket of strawberries and told her to munch. Maggie asked about the magazine she was reading, and Gran told her about it while she taught Maggie how to make pancakes from scratch. An hour later, with full bellies and a clean kitchen, Maggie and Gran sat in the front room. Gran drinking tea. Maggie drinking coffee, both reading copies of *Total Film*. Since it was new to Maggie, all the issues were new. She riffled through the past editions that Gran had cataloged on a bookshelf.

They broke their silence to discuss different articles they were reading and to ask the other if she wanted a top-off. They stayed that way until it was, in Gran's estimation, time to eat again. Maggie, having no real concept of how much time had passed, seemed surprised to hear this, although the growl in her midsection was not.

They moved back to the kitchen, where they made stir fry. Gran liked to use butter, not soy sauce, to fry the veggies, and since Maggie was not a stir fry aficionado in any way, shape, or form, she offered no argument. The silence in her midsection proved that the butter was, if not a big hit, at least not offensive.

The talk during dinner was about the work Gran needed to be done at the house. She had several closets full of clothes that, at one point in time, belonged to Charlie and Lady. She felt that since Lady was a mother of four and Charlie was living in America, it was past time to bag them up and get them to a charity shop. She thought that Maggie could not only do the heavy lifting, but maybe she would find an item or twenty that struck her fancy.

She also had let her back garden grow wild, and while she didn't spend a lot of time at the house, she didn't want it to look like it had been abandoned. She owned it free and clear and wanted it to remain in good shape so if Charlie ever did come back to England, the house would be there looking like a proper house and not a witch's cabin. She wanted to pull weeds, build some planters, and plant some flowers. She felt that by containing the things planted out there, it would just look more orderly. There were, as there often are for all homeowners, other little things that needed doing. Lights requiring a ladder needed to be replaced. A deep cleaning of all the appliances and carpets was needed. There was work to do for weekends to come once the school year started if Maggie had the desire to help out. Of course, she did, and so they made a plan to do the garden the following day and to go through the clothes that evening.

After the dishes were done and put away, but before the fullness of veggie stir fry wore off, which wouldn't be very long, they moved to the big walk-in closet in Charlie's old room. Gran, who had her whole house set up with wireless speakers, turned on her digital music collection from her tablet. They made three piles. The toss pile was for any bit of clothing that was so tattered that it couldn't be donated. The Maggie pile was for anything she thought she might want to try on. The donate pile was for everything else.

"Charlie had pretty great taste," Maggie said as she eyed the growing pile with her name on it. "What's she like?"

"Oh, she was a handful. Her mouth got away from her brain a lot."

Maggie stopped and looked at her, knowing that she didn't mean it how it sounded.

"I know that was terrible. It's just that, well, I love her so much, but..." Gran waved away her thought mid-stream. "You remember that part of *When Harry Met Sally* when Harry tells Sally she's high maintenance who thinks she's low maintenance?"

"Yeah," Maggie smiled at the memory of having watched it, "you told me I was the exact opposite. I thought I was high maintenance, but I was so low maintenance that sometimes people forgot about me."

"That is still true, dear." They locked eyes and let the moment sit for as long as possible without Maggie bursting into tears. "Well, Charlie is a lot like Sally. She likes things the way she likes them, and she never keeps them to herself. It is a great thing. It really is. I wish more people had that power. I wish you did, dear, but sometimes, in certain situations, the inside thoughts need to stay on the inside."

Maggie dropped two more tops on the donate pile after holding them up in front of herself and looking in the full-length mirror on the closet door. "For example?"

Gran thought about it for a few moments. Maggie didn't push. She just continued to sort while she waited. With her mum, sometimes she would just make a noise or cough to fill the silence just to remind her that she was in the room, or in the car, or at the kitchen table. With Gran, she was never concerned. Gran always knew who was in the room. "Well, sometimes, you know you want to say to your teacher, 'This assignment is bad,' or you want to say whatever you are really thinking to Marianne?"

Maggie snorted at that. "All the time."

"Right, but you don't because you are a person who lives in the world who knows some things are mean, and most of it won't really matter in the long run. The teacher is going to keep doing the same bad lesson. Marianne is going to be Marianne. So, you keep it in."

"Right, I mean, if she was actually putting herself in danger, I would totally say something, but like, her normal state of being her isn't dangerous, just off-putting."

"That's right, dear. That is what most of us do."

"Not Charlie?"

"Not Charlie. I can't tell you how many times I had to meet with the headmaster to discuss her attitude. She left a wake of hurt feelings behind her in every room she entered. It isn't that she means to do it; it's just, she can't help herself. Verbal diarrhea."

"Was Jamie that way?"

"Not at all. If anything, you and he had the same affliction. You wouldn't say cow dung whilst standing in it."

"Well, once you're in it, what good is it to talk about, huh? You can't un-dung the bell."

Gran laughed. "No, I suppose you can't, but it is still okay to say, 'I've stepped in this dung, and I feel a certain way about it.'"

"Is it?" Maggie stopped mid-toss.

Gran nodded. "It really is."

"Yeah, well," she tossed the shirt into the donate pile, "I guess I've saved Mum some time at the headmaster's office then, right?"

"Want to know something?"

"Anything you want to tell me." She held up a pink blazer, looked at her reflection, nodded, and slipped into it. She stood and tried to imagine what it would look like with a shirt and tie. She liked that. She turned and looked over her shoulder at herself from behind. She looked back at Gran and raised her eyebrows.

Gran nodded. "I was never mad about the trip to the headmaster's office."

Maggie took off the pink blazer and tossed it on her pile. "No?" Maggie grabbed the final item in the closet, another blazer, this one navy blue. She didn't bother trying it on. She just dropped it in the Maggie pile.

"No. I wasn't ever mad. I wish she came with a dimmer switch so that she could turn down some of the inside stuff, but I would never want her to turn it off. We worked on her tact. We tried to get her to only offer her opinion when someone asked or to use some softer language, but eventually, we just prepared everyone for her in advance."

"How did that go?"

"She didn't fail out of school. She had some friends. Unfortunately, Tom fell in love with her because she was his manic pixie dream girl. I fear that their marriage can't survive her mouth."

Maggie dropped to her knees and started bagging up the piles so they could be taken to their respective destinations. "How do you feel about that?"

"Oh, that's fine. I don't dislike Tom. I get why he would like her. He is a contracts lawyer. There is nothing manic, nor pixie, nor dreamy about that. She isn't a dream girl, nor a pixie, but she does come across as manic. That can be appealing to someone who doesn't speak his mind. He rarely does, and so I have no real opinion of him one way or the other actually. He's fine. If they have a kid, he'll be a good dad. They live in Cleveland, so I don't love that."

"The Rock and Roll Hall of Fame is there. I'd love to go. Maybe it is something Mum would actually want to do with me. I'm the one who likes music like she does."

"That's true, dear. That would be lovely. I want that for you as well. I'm not saying anything untoward about Cleveland in particular or America in general. It's just, if they have kids, and things end, which I suspect they will, then Charlie is also in Cleveland forever."

"Which isn't here?"

Gran nodded. "Which isn't here. It can be lonely. You know. You just moved a few hours away. It isn't a whole new country. That is just so different. I've been to America. I like it fine. We have some American cousins who are not so far from Cleveland, so Charlie does spend time with them."

Maggie was done bagging and was standing across from Gran at that point. "We do?"

"Well, no, I guess I do. I forget you're related to Middy by blood and not me. I think of you as mine."

She didn't mean to say it in a way that was triggering, but as we've learned, Maggie has a hair trigger. She threw herself at Gran, who, while not expecting a full-body hug, absorbed it without so much as a wobble. Maggie sobbed into her shoulder. She sobbed and sobbed. Gran rubbed her back and didn't say anything. She just let her cry until she felt like she couldn't anymore, and Maggie, who through the silence, heard the echoes of Gran just telling her to say the inside stuff on the outside, whispered, "I'm queer."

Gran said, "I know, dear girl. I know." She stopped rubbing her back and pulled her in as tight as she could just in case Maggie needed to be held up.

Maggie found that second round of tears buried deep inside of herself. It was a part she didn't know existed. She didn't have the spelunking tools to get there nor had she ever had the partner to pull her back up once she got all the way down there. She finally found the part of her where relief lived. She let herself be held as the relief poured out. She was flooded.

Time passed, and Gran eventually got Maggie to the couch and gave her tea. They sat while Maggie caught her breath and wiped her face and sipped her tea. She kept apologizing for crying, and Gran kept shushing her, reminding her she need not apologize for being herself. That led to some more tears and face wiping and tea sipping.

When she thought the time was right, Gran asked, "How are you now?"

"Exhausted?" It came out as a question.

"Yes, I suspect you are. I would be lying if I said I wasn't hoping you'd tell me while you were here, but I wasn't going to push. It isn't about me. I just worried that you'd go into school this year without having told anyone."

"Juliet knows, and so Meg knows too."

"Yes, of course. I meant someone…" She trailed off, not wanting to upset her again.

"It's okay." Maggie surprised herself by not only saying it, but believing it. "She was my gay Yoda, and I thought that without her, I'd be lost, but you know, like, maybe it'll be better for me? I can't believe I'm saying this, but maybe I don't need a gay Yoda. Maybe being queer isn't all I am?" She looked to Gran for support.

"Maybe you just need someone to see all of you. I told you when we first met that I'd be your Gran, and I meant it. I want to be whatever you need me to be. Your Yoda and friend and Gran."

"Yeah…" Maggie's voice caught in her throat, and she felt the tears start to come again. She wiped her face and sipped her tea, not wanting to stop where this was going. She nodded at Gran. "Yeah… Yes. That's just what I need."

This time it was Gran's turn to tear up. Maggie sprang into action and scampered into the kitchen. She made more tea and brought in some biscuits. By the time she returned, Gran had composed herself. They spent the rest of the day and well into the night eating snack foods and talking and talking. Tears were replaced by laughter. Maggie went to sleep feeling lighter than she ever had. Gran went to her bookshelf and pulled out her copy of Whitman's *Song of Myself* that she would slip into Maggie's bag before she returned her to The Cottage.

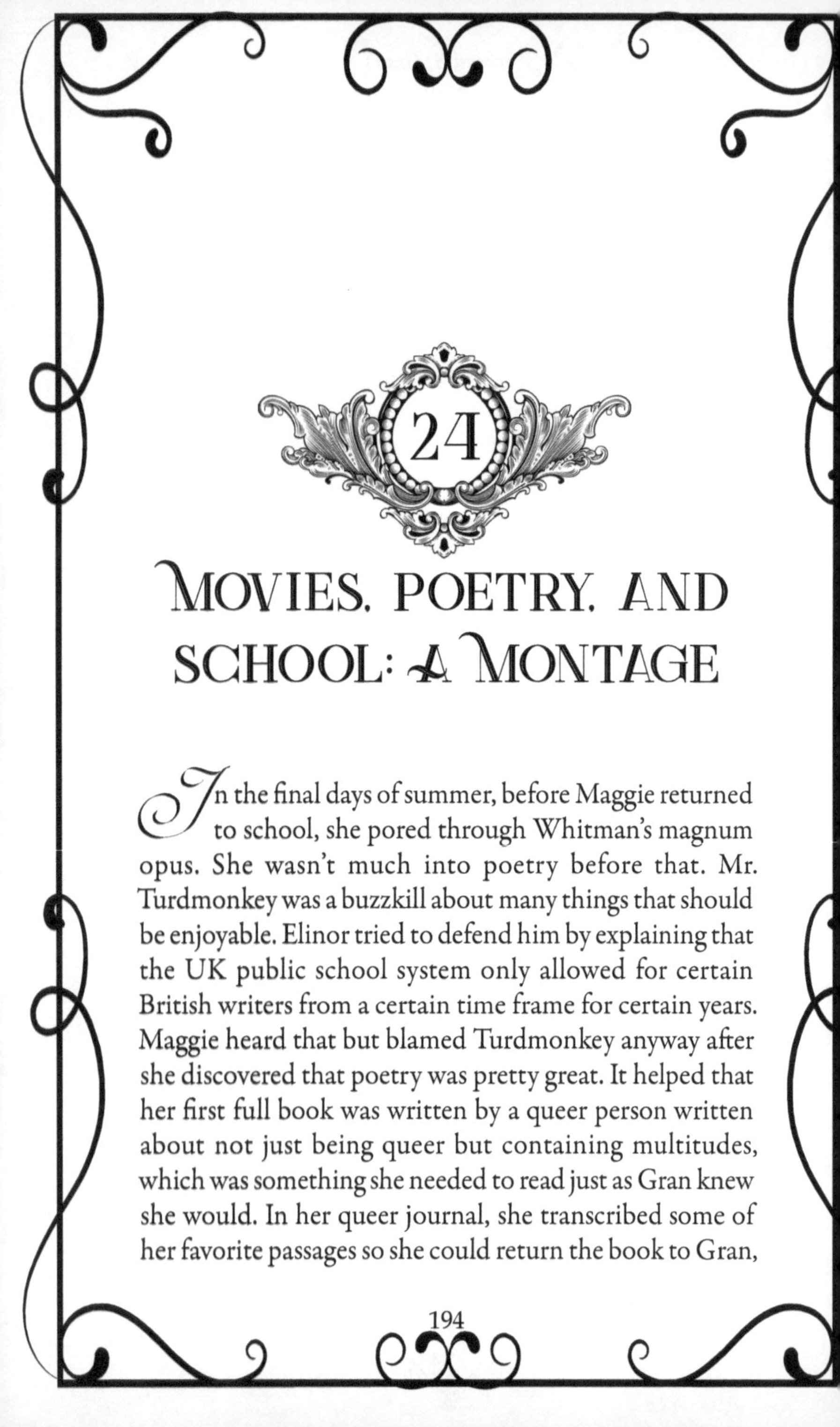

24

MOVIES, POETRY, AND SCHOOL: A MONTAGE

In the final days of summer, before Maggie returned to school, she pored through Whitman's magnum opus. She wasn't much into poetry before that. Mr. Turdmonkey was a buzzkill about many things that should be enjoyable. Elinor tried to defend him by explaining that the UK public school system only allowed for certain British writers from a certain time frame for certain years. Maggie heard that but blamed Turdmonkey anyway after she discovered that poetry was pretty great. It helped that her first full book was written by a queer person written about not just being queer but containing multitudes, which was something she needed to read just as Gran knew she would. In her queer journal, she transcribed some of her favorite passages so she could return the book to Gran, who flatly refused it, and instead, she gave Maggie the collected poems of Audre Lorde.

After Lorde, she introduced her to Dorothy Parker, whom Maggie loved more than she thought possible. Once school began, Maggie was reading poetry almost daily. She found plenty of free poetry websites. Some of them were well-curated poetry by published masters like Hughes, Keats, Shelley, and the Brownings. She rightfully thought Elizabeth Barrett was much better than her husband Robert. Some of the other poetry sites she found allowed people with the inclination to publish raw, not always great, but always honest, poetry. All of this made her less grouchy when Mr. Turdmonkey told them they would be doing a unit on Shakespearean sonnets. We shall not recount all the books of poems that Maggie read for the rest of the tale but know she kept it up. Space is limited, and we are just at that halfway part.

During our second of five summers at Barton Park, we should check in with the rest of the cast as well before we wrap back around to our heroine and catch up on her 15th birthday, which, we all know, will not go smoothly. Imagine something from Bob Dylan playing; reader's choice. He is much more of a poet than a singer anyway.

Edward finished up his time at university and decided that he would like to continue his studies by earning a graduate degree in classics and history at the University of Exeter. Edward loved to learn, and learning about learning was something he found appealing. More appealing was being close to Elinor Dashwood. While Sam was a liberal woman, and she didn't mind Edward coming down to visit whilst staying in Elinor's room, she didn't want him living with them all the time. She didn't want them to get the wrong sense of what it was like to live together as all of their bills were paid, and the chores were divided up among three other people in the house.

Always sensible, Edward agreed. He found himself a two-bedroom flat near campus, and he and Elinor agreed that while she would stay over now and again, she would make sure to *live* at The Cottage. He opened the second bedroom to Brandon, who was starting his first year at university. Elinor, who always liked Brandon, was thrilled to have the chance to see him without having to feel as though she was betraying a beloved sister. The three of them spent many an evening engaged in rigorous talk about big ideas. They were the breed of 20-something academics for whom a two-hour discussion about the way the patriarchy was alive and well in the modern superhero movie was a delightful way to spend an evening after watching said superhero movie.

Elinor went into her second year studying Liberal Arts. She kept working at the library, where she led several book clubs and discussion groups. She used the wide-ranging possibilities of her degree plan to dabble in all kinds of subjects that she would normally skip over. She said it made her feel more well-rounded. She would regale them with all kinds of facts and educational mysteries during dinner. Marianne said it made her seem like more of a know-it-all, which dampened Elinor's spirits to share, although she still did, just with truncated versions of things. Maggie almost asked why it was a bad thing to know things, and since she didn't really know about the salon-level discussions at Edward's flat and since her mother didn't intervene, as she never said a word against Marianne, Maggie swallowed it but made notes to ask Gran.

Marianne, determined to find a way to star in all the productions, without the use of a cane to walk, used her incredible ability to charm anyone she met to convince Christine to choose plays where the female lead either had a disability or sat for most of the performance. They settled on Tennessee Williams' *The Glass Menagerie* and then did a gender-flipped rendition of *Cyrano de Bergerac*, where, instead of a big nose, she was wheelchair-bound. Marianne was magnificent as Laura and as Crystal de Bergerac. The gender-bent play was such a success that the entire troupe was asked to perform it the following summer at The Exeter Festival. More on that later.

Willoughby was, just as Lady suspected, a layabout and a rapscallion. We won't spend too much time on him here as watching him wake up just in time for Marianne to get home from college, stumble down to The Cottage, and whisper sweet nothings into her ear whilst eating all of the Dashwood's food only to head out to who knows where until the break of dawn over and over would get annoying. Well, it appears we've spent just the right amount of time on him, for now. Unfortunately, we are not done with him.

As we rejoin our heroine, we will play in The Kink's "Wonderboy." Imagine the jangly piano playing and the Davies brothers singing the "la las" as we see her arrive at school for the first day of school kitted up in one of her new skirts, a white shirt, and a blue tie while sporting the pink blazer. She chats with some of her school friends, who see the pink blazer and, once again, go into clothing envy, totally unbeknownst to Maggie.

She takes her seat at her desk as Mr. Turdmonkey approaches the front of the room at the 25-second mark, and as Ray sings about days and nights and time, the outfits change, and the teachers change, and Maggie takes notes, sketches, paints, reads from books, looks bored, looks engaged, and eventually gets up and packs her bag as things flash around her. We see the seasons change out a window over her shoulder when the lyrics change to mention the sun.

We cut to a similar montage of lunches, martial arts practices that were the next logical step after self-defense classes, and walks to and from school. The groups of kids change around her as Maggie is, once again, always welcome but never part of any particular group. We see her sitting on the stone wall, legs kicking against it in rhythm with the song, chatting up some boy or girl, killing time, being a teenager, trying to figure herself out. As the song starts to lose the beat and the lyrics bang on about life being lonely, we see a mash-up cut of her in different outfits, walking down the drive to The Cottage until the song ends, and she walks in the front door. It closes behind her as the song ends.

Of course, Maggie and Gran spend another year learning about each other and themselves while watching as many movies as possible. As Maggie's love for action movies has only solidified, she has discovered that a lot of what Gran says about films makes sense, and she finds that she is equally compelled to watch the high art movies when she is alone as her trashy, muscle-bound, shoot-'em-ups.

Gran's book on Princess Grace came out that summer and was well received. She earned back her advance and then some. Not really needing the money, she put it in the bank and wouldn't think much about it for a few years. Maggie read the whole book in one night, and they spent several weeks watching the late, great princess's filmography in order. It isn't as long as it could have been. Maggie loves those movies still.

In honor of the maturing of her tastes, we shall queue up Strauss' "Also Sprach Zarathustra," which plays as the opening theme to *2001: A Space Odyssey*. We can start with an image of a theatre marquee that shows the name of the film playing, and we can imagine watching Gran watch Maggie as she sees that film not just for the first time but for the first time on the big screen. Gran smiles over at Maggie, who cranes her head up, gobsmacked.

We can imagine plenty of other nights of them at cinemas, in the big house in the viewing room, at Gran's house, watching and talking and reaching for the pause button to start a conversation mid-movie. It became a tradition that unless they were in public, they never once made it through an entire movie without having to pause and discuss it. Imagine a lot of wild flying hand gestures and good-natured finger-pointing at the screen and each other as they bicker like sisters who actually like, not just love, one another.

As Strauss' masterpiece comes to a close, we see Maggie asleep with her head on Gran's lap. Gran finishing a movie she's likely seen hundreds of times, scratching Maggie's head and smiling happily. It is time now for us to wake up our heroine as the school year has ended, and she is about to turn fifteen. Taylor Swift wrote a heartbreaker about being fifteen. We will hear that during our next montage. It is the most packed summer holiday for our heroine, and so we will spend the most time there. Grab some tissues.

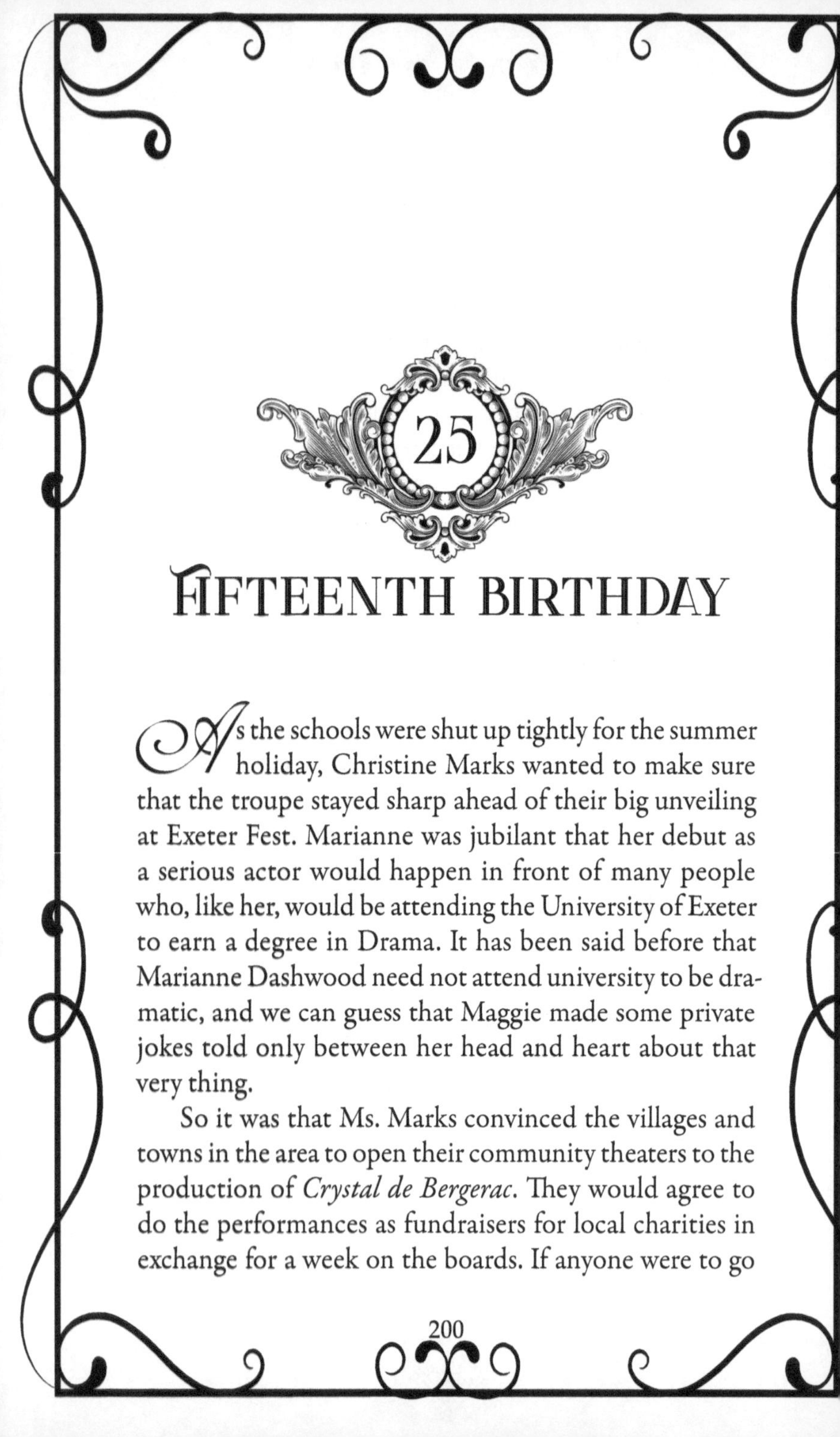

25

FIFTEENTH BIRTHDAY

As the schools were shut up tightly for the summer holiday, Christine Marks wanted to make sure that the troupe stayed sharp ahead of their big unveiling at Exeter Fest. Marianne was jubilant that her debut as a serious actor would happen in front of many people who, like her, would be attending the University of Exeter to earn a degree in Drama. It has been said before that Marianne Dashwood need not attend university to be dramatic, and we can guess that Maggie made some private jokes told only between her head and heart about that very thing.

So it was that Ms. Marks convinced the villages and towns in the area to open their community theaters to the production of *Crystal de Bergerac*. They would agree to do the performances as fundraisers for local charities in exchange for a week on the boards. If anyone were to go to a small town or village and ask to perform something at no cost whilst raising money for the town, they will almost always say yes.

As bad luck would have it, their local village agreed to host the performance on the day before Maggie's birthday. They agreed to include the performance as a huge village-wide celebration with a street fair and carnival that would shut down for the two-hour production, which would begin once the sun set to help the performers get used to using outside lights, as they would during Exeter Fest. After the performance, the rides would start back up, there would be fireworks and merriment, all to support the new annex for the town library. Real librarian or not, it was a good cause.

Maggie had to agree that Marianne's performance was exceptional. She had somehow gotten better with each show. Maggie thought the choice to rename the characters wasn't necessary and leaving them be would have added an extra layer to the gender bending, Roxanne, played by a boy, whom they call a woman, would have a treat, but still, she couldn't fault much about it. Marianne managed to move around in the wheelchair in a spectacular fashion. If one reads the words "wheelchair" and "swordfight," one would assume this is the setup to an insensitive joke, but alas, in the case of Marianne Dashwood as Crystal de Bergerac, there is nothing about which anyone can joke. There is no punchline.

As Crystal died and fell out of her wheelchair, and her unrequited love, Rex, not Roxanne, who had joined a monastery not a convent, held her and professed his love for her, there was not a dry eye in the house. The curtain fell and the crowd rose. They stood and applauded as the curtain rose again and the supporting cast, hands locked, took a bow. Then the actor who played Christine, the Christian role, took her bow and the crowd stayed steady with the clapping. Rex got a few "woos" as he took his bow, but when Marianne came out, walking, slowly, but without a cane, much to the chagrin of the Dashwood contingent in the crowd, the applause became adulation. Flowers were thrown. There were whistles and whoops and feet were stomped.

She wiped away tears and bowed and waved. Her co-stars each came to one side and took her hands. The three of them bowed. The rest of the cast joined hands. They all bowed. They turned to stage right and applauded and waved and pleaded until Christine Marks came out.

A hand mic was found, and Ms. Marks made a speech thanking the residents of the town for such a lovely reception. They were honored to be there and proud to be part of what, she was told, would be the first of an annual "Spring into Summer" festival, held at this time each year where fun would be had, funds would be raised, and the community would come together. She thanked her cast and crew and finally because this is how things go for Marianne Dashwood, she thanked her personally for pushing them to do this play this way. She handed the microphone to Marianne, who seemed to demure, even though Maggie, who knew when her sister was acting and when she was faking, saw that she was doing the latter. After more whooping and stomping, she "reluctantly" took the mic. It will be important to capture her words in detail here.

"Thank you all for this lovely reception. We've felt so welcomed here this week as we've been setting up and rehearsing. As some of you may know, this is my home village, but I only just moved here two years ago, and while tonight has been amazing, it has been a bit bittersweet." She wiped away a real tear from her face. She paused to let the murmur run through the crowd.

Maggie, knowing what was going to happen next, felt her stomach drop to her knees, and she felt the urge to follow it down and sit down. Gran, who also knew what was about to happen, reached out and grabbed her hand. She leaned over and whispered into Maggie's ear, "I'm sorry, but you have to bear it. Stand with me. I've always got you." Maggie intertwined her fingers with Gran's, and she looked at her, jaw set, tears welling, and nodded. She couldn't trust herself to talk. They rested their foreheads together for a moment. When Marianne started talking again, they turned, shoulders back, feet planted on the ground, hands clasped, physically ready for the verbal attack that was sure to come.

"It was two years ago, on this very night, when I came home after a late night out with my dear sister to discover our father..." She let it trail off, and the crowd was silent. She shook her head. "No, I won't go into details, but I will tell you that it was two years ago tonight that I lost my father and dedicate this performance to him." She reached into her pocket and pulled out a flask. She touched it to her heart and lifted her hand to the sky. "I know he is looking down and proud of me." She looked down and wiped her cheeks. The audience held its collective breath. "So, tonight, in honor of Henry Dashwood, I want us to celebrate, not be sad. I love you, Dad!" The crowd roared. She drank the whiskey, alone, surrounded by strangers, instead of with her family.

Maggie dug her nails into Gran's hand. Later, she would apologize profusely. At the moment, she didn't know she was doing it. Gran, who was a woman and quite accustomed to bearing the pain of others, bore it without complaint. Later, when Maggie apologized, she waved it off with an "It's nothing, dear."

The cast collapsed on Marianne and hugged her and kissed her cheeks. If it didn't seem inappropriate, Maggie would have thought they would have carried her out on their shoulders singing "She's a Jolly Good Fellow." Instead, they all moved backstage. The Chair of the Village Council came to the stage and directed everyone's attention to the sky for the fireworks display, after which the carnival would remain open all night or until everyone called it a night. The crowd, once again, roared.

As the fireworks began, the family made the move to stage left, where Marianne instructed them to meet up after the performance. Middy and Lady stayed behind with the boys who, while tired and grouchy, were not about to miss out on fireworks after sitting through the play. To be fair, they loved seeing Marianne in it, and they thought the sword fighting was so inspiring that the Tractor Quartet would, for several weeks and months following, leave wrestling behind for epic sword fights with anything they could find handy and ultimately plastic and foam swords. It would only be a trip to A&E for Tractor Lad that required a line of stitches on his back, following an after-hours bout with Tractor Boy Jr. using straightened-out wire hangers, that ultimately led to Tractor Lady's cancellation of swashbuckling.

Sam, Elinor, Edward, Willoughby, Gran, and Maggie stood looking up at the fireworks as they waited for

Marianne, who was, despite the colorful explosions in the sky, being mobbed by villagers. Mobbed and villagers has a bad connotation, but it wasn't that kind of mob. They all wanted to touch her and tell her how amazing she was. Sam, who wanted her off her feet or on her crutches as soon as possible, eventually pulled out the Mum card and told everyone, in the nicest way possible, to sod off.

Marianne, who was a person for whom all press was good press, was equal parts mortified at the way her mother acted and thrilled that she gave the villagers something to talk about. An artist with an overbearing mother wasn't a terrible image to have. So, Marianne threw herself down into the wheelchair and slumped over to one side, mocking her mother as though she were unable to move. Maggie thought it an ableist move, but something about Marianne's form reminded her of Andrew Wyeth's *Christina's World*. She made a mental note to do something with it later.

They all took their turns coming up to her, now sitting in her wheelchair, hugging her and telling her how great she was even though they easily could have done it once they all got back home. Maggie, who wanted to watch the fireworks instead of telling her sister how awesome she was and how terrible it was that she did the whiskey toast without them, lingered at the edge of the group, and looked up. Gran nudged her when it was time to back up a step to get closer to her royal sister on her wheeled throne.

She couldn't really enjoy the show as she could feel the eyes on their little group as they were now the family of a village celebrity who would star in a production in front of thousands and who would, they had no doubt, go on to be the most famous British actress of her generation. It didn't matter that she'd only stepped foot in the village when she had no other choice, she claimed to be theirs publicly, and as is the case with those who wish to be famous adjacent if they can't be famous, the villagers were happy to have her.

The grand finale was just coming to a close when Maggie finally had her chance to talk to Marianne, who looked up at her baby sister with a smirk, enjoying the attention as much as she possibly could, but even more since she was about to be told, publicly, by the only member in the family who didn't think she was perfect, that she was in fact, just that.

As anyone who has experienced it knows, when the grand finale ends, the voices of the people who were talking during the show all burst forth into the sudden silence like a verbal avalanche. So it was, just as Maggie was squatting down to talk to Marianne and tell her, that yes, she was a good actor and yes, Maggie thought her death scene was better this time than it was last time, but no, she didn't think Willoughby was jealous about the "crackling electricity" that she and the boy who played Rex seemed to have, and yes, she was sure he knew it was just acting, that a small band of villagers, who were, instead of watching the finale, watching the youngest two Dashwoods talk, were speaking loudly to each other. They wondered who it was who could be so privileged to have alone time with Marianne Dashwood of Barton Park as she was soon to be known. Not one villager ever said, "That must be Tractor Lad of Barton Park," even though he would eventually be one of the two who took over running the park, and it was his progeny who kept the farm running for years to come. When the final crash of the final rocket faded out, Maggie heard, so clearly as though the person was speaking from inside her brain, "Oh, that must be *that other Dashwood girl*. I heard there were three, but Marianne only mentioned the one sister."

There is no official record of what Marianne's face looked like upon hearing the comment as 99 percent of the audience was still looking sky-high, and Maggie turned to shoot daggers at the woman who said it. We would like to say that it was uttered by a young person, someone who could maybe be forgiven for saying such a terrible thing about another girl, but alas, Dear Reader, it was an adult woman speaking to an even older woman. We can report, as there were plenty of witnesses that Gran also heard the remark, and she found her body moving, leaning forward, toward the woman at a pace that would be called brisk. Because it is not that kind of book, we will not repeat here what she said. As the clock struck midnight, that string of profanity was to this very day, the best present Maggie Dashwood would ever receive on any birthday. It even topped what Gran did for her the next year. We shall see, that is a doozy.

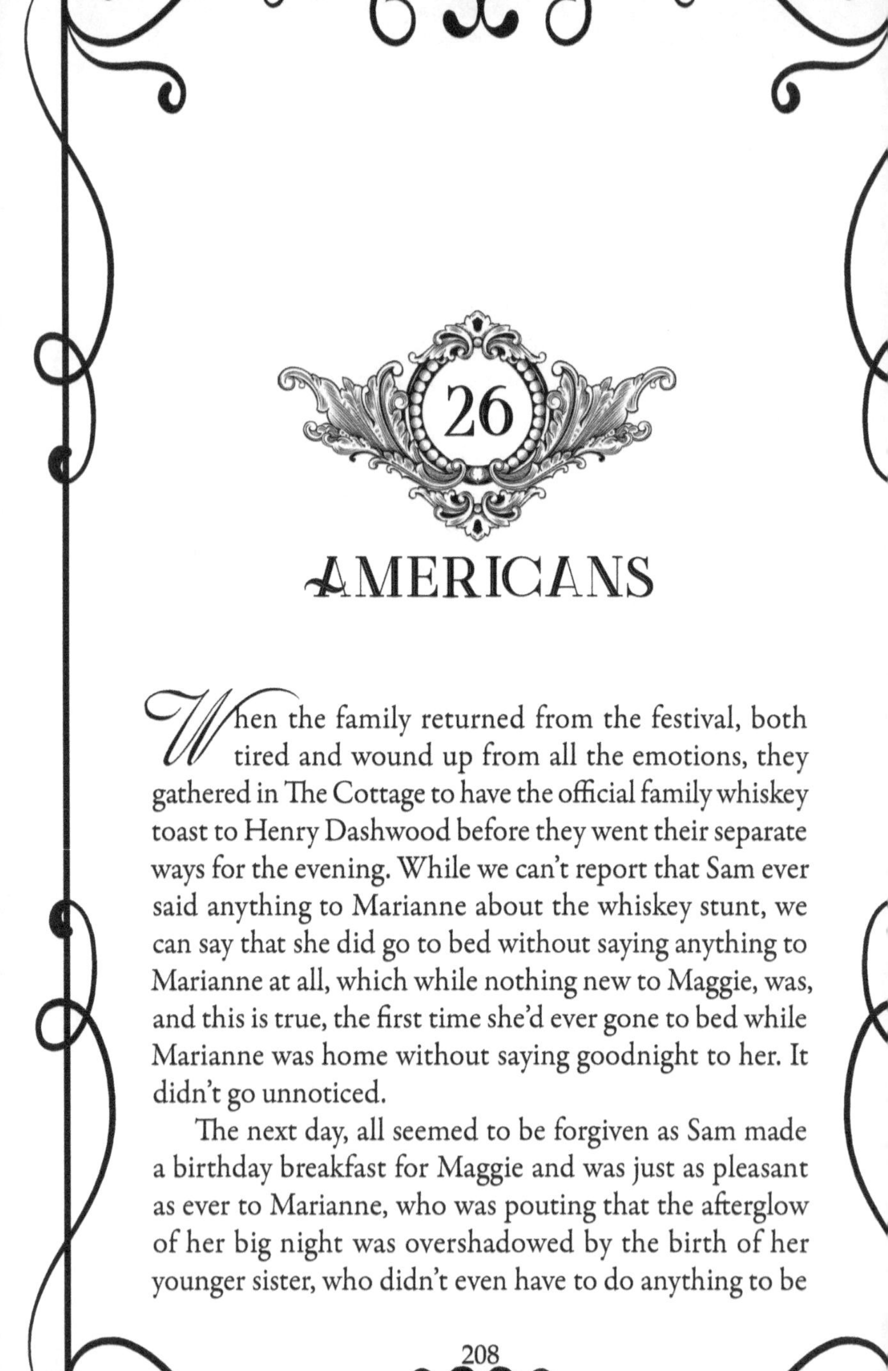

26

AMERICANS

When the family returned from the festival, both tired and wound up from all the emotions, they gathered in The Cottage to have the official family whiskey toast to Henry Dashwood before they went their separate ways for the evening. While we can't report that Sam ever said anything to Marianne about the whiskey stunt, we can say that she did go to bed without saying anything to Marianne at all, which while nothing new to Maggie, was, and this is true, the first time she'd ever gone to bed while Marianne was home without saying goodnight to her. It didn't go unnoticed.

The next day, all seemed to be forgiven as Sam made a birthday breakfast for Maggie and was just as pleasant as ever to Marianne, who was pouting that the afterglow of her big night was overshadowed by the birth of her younger sister, who didn't even have to do anything to be born while she was a master thespian. Sam patted her on the shoulder and said, "She doesn't ask for much. We can give her a nice breakfast," and with that, the scales were balanced, and the clouds moved on, and all the other trite phrases that remind us that all is well. Marianne enjoyed not only the birthday pancakes, but the actual birthday cake Lady made that they had after lunch in the big house. She even sang aloud during the birthday song.

After the cake was eaten and the ice cream was consumed, Maggie was doing battle with the Tractor Quartet at wooden spoon fencing. She was doing quite well as longer arms win the day with shorter weapons. The reverie was interrupted by a sound seldom heard echoing through the big house; the doorbell rang. For a family that was used to friends and staff just walking in at all hours of the night, the doorbell was a shocking sound. They all froze as though they thought one of them installed an alarm system behind everyone's backs. Tractor Baby, who was the first one out of the fencing match, who had curled up on Gran's lap to watch the rest of the battle take place, was so surprised by the sound of the doorbell, which was in fact an actual bell installed centuries before when the house was built, that he covered his ears in surprise.

When the bell rang again, they all sprang into action as they simultaneously realized what was happening. While the house was big and the doors were large, there was no reason for the whole troupe to open the door. Still, the shock of it saw all the Middletons, Gran, Maggie, and Sam head through the warrenous hallways to the seldom-used front entrance. Marianne and Willoughby used that as their way to escape the festivities and head back to The

Cottage while Edward and Elinor stayed behind to clean up. Alone time is different for different couples.

The bell rang again as the group made their way to the door, and by the time they arrived, someone on the other side was pounding and shouting Lady's name through the door. It was long and drawn out. "LAAAAADDDDDYYYY!" Lady and Gran knew who it was, and they sped ahead of the group, each wearing huge grins. While some families disliked pop-ins, the Middleton/Jennings family adored them, especially when the person popping in was on an unannounced trans-Atlantic visit.

Lady pulled the door open to reveal her sister, Charlie Palmer, fully and unexpectedly pregnant, with her arm back ready to pound on the door again. Behind her stood her husband, Tom, and two young women, who could have been dead ringers for each other save for one had raven hair and one had orange. They were tall, pale, seemingly pore-less, and angular. They had pointy ears that shot straight up from their heads, and they both had their straight hair pulled back into matching high ponytails. Their noses were triangles jutting out from their faces. Their shoulders poked out and pointed down to their tiny waists. Maggie's first thought was, "Charlie knows elves?"

"Lady!" Charlie shouted and threw herself at her sister. "Mum!" she shouted over her sister's head. She let herself be hugged around her considerable belly and opened her arms to pull Gran in to make a Lady sandwich. They all hopped in a circle and laughed and cried and talked at the same time.

"Good to see you, Tom," Middy boomed over the noise. He reached out a hand and Tom's disappeared into it.

"You too, Middy." He smiled at Middy. Everyone smiled at Middy. He was the gentlest of giants and made everyone feel at ease. After he was done shaking hands, he looked at Sam, Maggie, and the boys. "I'm Tom and this is Anne and Lucy Steele."

"Ahh yes!" Middy opened his arms to them. "The American cousins. Welcome to Barton Park, ladies!"

The orange-haired elf sister stepped forward and extended her hand, not sure about being wrapped in a Middy hug, which was, as she suspected, hardy. "Thank you. Anne."

Middy took her hand and gave her a hearty shake. "Hello, Lucy," he said to the black-haired elf.

She didn't step forward for a handshake, but she bowed and whisper-shouted, "Hello. Yes. Lucy." She smiled and nodded and bowed at the rest of them while her sister and Tom shook hands and said hello.

Middy wanted to get everyone inside, so he did what all people do to lure people places; he offered them sweets. "Well, you've come on a perfect day. It is young Maggie's 15th birthday today, and we just so happen to have plenty of leftover cake and ice cream in the kitchen. Who wants some?"

They all agreed they would love to have some cake and ice cream. The Jennings sisters each slipped an arm through one of their mother's arms, and they walked toward the kitchen like a human chain followed by the Tractor Quartet to find out why Charlie was in England and why she kept her pregnancy a secret and all the other things loved ones ask when they catch up after a long time apart.

We can quickly jump in here to explain why Charlie decided to show up, very pregnant in the middle of the day on Maggie's birthday. She didn't know it was Maggie's birthday, so she wasn't grandstanding. She wasn't that kind of sister. She kept it a secret because it turns out that she had been pregnant several times in the past few years, and she miscarried each time. She and Tom bore it alone, and it made them closer in some ways and more distant in others. Still, they realized they wanted a child, but they were not going to keep trying to climb up a slippery tree, so this was the last attempt. If she made it past seven months, which is where she was when she arrived at her sister's house, they would pack up, with the doctor's blessing, and get to England so the child could be born with dual citizenship. Plus, she only really trusted the NHS to deliver her child.

One might be concerned that Maggie would feel a pang of jealousy that her best friend was going to have someone else to occupy her attention, but fear not. Maggie isn't Marianne. She was happy that Gran would get to spend time with Charlie. She liked being useful, so grabbed a few bags and helped Tom, Sam, the Steele sisters, and Middy bring them in.

Once the pile had moved from just outside the door to just inside the door, Maggie asked, "Who's going where?"

Middy scratched his beard. "Well, I think we should keep Charlie near her sister and mum, but she should have her own bathroom considering her, uhh, condition."

Tom nodded. "Thank you, yes. That would be ideal."

"Ladies, do you want to share, or would you like your own rooms?" He turned to the Steele sisters.

They looked at each other and had a silent conversation the way some sisters do. "Share," they said at the same time. Maggie felt that pang of jealousy of the way some sisters are and some sisters are not.

"Okay then. Sam, can you take Tom to the Blue Room?"

"Of course." Sam picked up some of the bags and Tom followed suit. "Follow me." They had a perfectly fine adult conversation about the weather and the traveling and airports and taxis. There is no reason to get into it here. Everyone has had that conversation a million times, and it is forgettable.

Middy and Maggie looked at each other and, showing off their own cousin telepathy, said, "Green Room." They laughed. It was the room she crashed in whenever she stayed over.

Middy explained, "It is on the top floor, so there are several flights of stairs, but there is a private bathroom, two beds, a couch, and..."

"It is far enough away from the boys that you won't hear them first thing in the morning," Maggie finished.

"Oh, we don't mind," Anne said. "We like children." She looked to Lucy who was nodding and smiling.

"Yeah, well," Maggie said, "the boys are great. I love them all so much, but they are..." She looked to Middy, not wanting to insult his children.

"A lot. They are a lot, especially in the morning."

"And in the afternoon," Maggie added.

"And at night." Middy laughed. "So, the top floor is best."

"I stay up there sometimes, and not only do you not hear them, but they don't like to climb up there. They think it is haunted, so they won't surprise tackle you or rope you into a spontaneous wrestling match." Maggie smiled fondly as she thought of all the times they tackled her as she turned a corner. She looked at the Steeles who were not smiling fondly. One might actually call the look gripped with fear.

"Don't worry, ladies. It took at least a few months before they started beating up on young Maggie here, so you should be fine," Middy boomed.

"Yeah, besides, I let them do it. If you don't engage, they will be little angels."

With those calming words, the quartet climbed the three flights of stairs. Middy narrated the climb by pointing out all the things that were on each floor of the big house. Middy, being Middy, didn't ask why it was that they were in his house or for how long they were staying. Maggie certainly wondered, but she followed his lead and decided that all would be revealed when they all arrived back in the kitchen.

However, she couldn't be totally silent. Once they got in the room and while Middy rummaged in the storage closet for towels and toiletries, Maggie asked, "First time to the UK?"

Lucy looked from Maggie to Anne. While they looked like twins, it was obvious to a younger sister that Lucy was a younger sister. Anne made a face that older sisters make and looked back at Lucy and nudged her to go ahead. "Yeah. We've been out of the US before but never to the UK. Our dad is a math professor, and he has summers off, so we travel a lot. Our mom is out of the picture, so it's just us and he likes to, 'keep us cultured.'" She dropped her voice and tucked in her chin as she mimicked her father's voice.

"We say maths here." Realizing she was being rude, Maggie quickly followed up with a question. "Is he here? Where does he profess?"

"Do you? Why?" asked Lucy.

"Well, you know, it's mathematics and so that 's' is there on the end… maths."

"Hmm," Lucy said in a tone that made it seem as though she didn't believe it. Anne remained silent, looking down at the ground seemingly trying to dissolve through the floor. The awkwardness hung in the air.

Maggie plowed on, "But you know, we say 'sport' not 'sports' so, words are weird. Anyway, your dad?" she asked again, hoping it would break the tension.

Feeling unsure of anything at that point, Lucy clamped her lips shut and so Anne looked up and replied, "He isn't here. There are some summer programs this year he wanted to do at Mansfield, that's the college where he works, and so, when the chance to travel here for a few weeks was offered up, Dad said we could come. He and Charlie are cousins somewhere, so whatever that makes us."

"That is pretty great that he let you come over. I'd love to travel. I've never left England, not even to go to Scotland, and my brother has a house there." Maggie laughed, thinking they would laugh too because they didn't know John or Sissy and wouldn't know that they were nothing to laugh about. She was desperate.

Instead, Lucy said, "Oh, we've been there. Lovely country. We spent a whole summer there five years ago when I was in 8th grade. The most magical summer of my life. Did you know that there are unicorns in Scotland? It's their national animal, so that is something. I didn't see one, but I looked very hard." She smiled brightly, happy to be part of the conversation again.

Maggie, not sure how to unpack all that information, looked to Anne who was once again very interested in a spot on the floor between her feet. Maggie opened her mouth. Closed it. Opened it again. Heard the snarky words form in her head about their dad being a maths teacher and not a geography teacher. She wasn't even sure how to comment about the unicorns. It was, and is, true that the official animal of Scotland is the unicorn, but she didn't know how to explain to a person who didn't know that Scotland was in the UK. Maybe she was joking? It was impossible to be sure. She closed her mouth. Opened it, realized she looked like a fish gasping for water, closed it again, and was saved by Middy who returned with the towels.

"Here you are, ladies." He held the towels aloft like a trophy. "Let me show you the tricks of the room." After ten minutes in the Green Room where Middy showed them around the room and where they could store their clothes, and after he explained the proper setting of the shower handle to ensure optimal pressure and heat, the four of them walked down the back stairs which would lead them directly to the kitchen. Middy talked more about the history of the big house and explained that the top floor was once servant's quarters, hence the direct passage to the kitchen.

When they neared the bottom of the stairs, they heard the sound of knives scraping against plates and spoons on bowls as well as jovial conversation that comes from the happiest of family gatherings, be they planned or spontaneous.

Middy led them through the door followed by Anne and Lucy with Maggie bringing up the rear. Even though they were not talking when they entered the room, anytime Middy entered a room, everyone looked up. His hulking size always shifted the air and light in a way that forced everyone to look his way. So it was that the entire group was watching when they filed in.

Maggie, expecting to follow Lucy in, ended up smacking right into her back. If she could have seen Lucy's front, it would have somehow gone paler. She stood, feet rooted to the floor, utterly gobsmacked. Across the kitchen, also paler than normal stood Edward Ferrars, equally shocked.

"Edward!" Lucy exclaimed.

"Lucy!?" Edward interrobanged.

Because it isn't that kind of book, we will leave off what Elinor exclaimed just as Maggie was rubbing her nose.

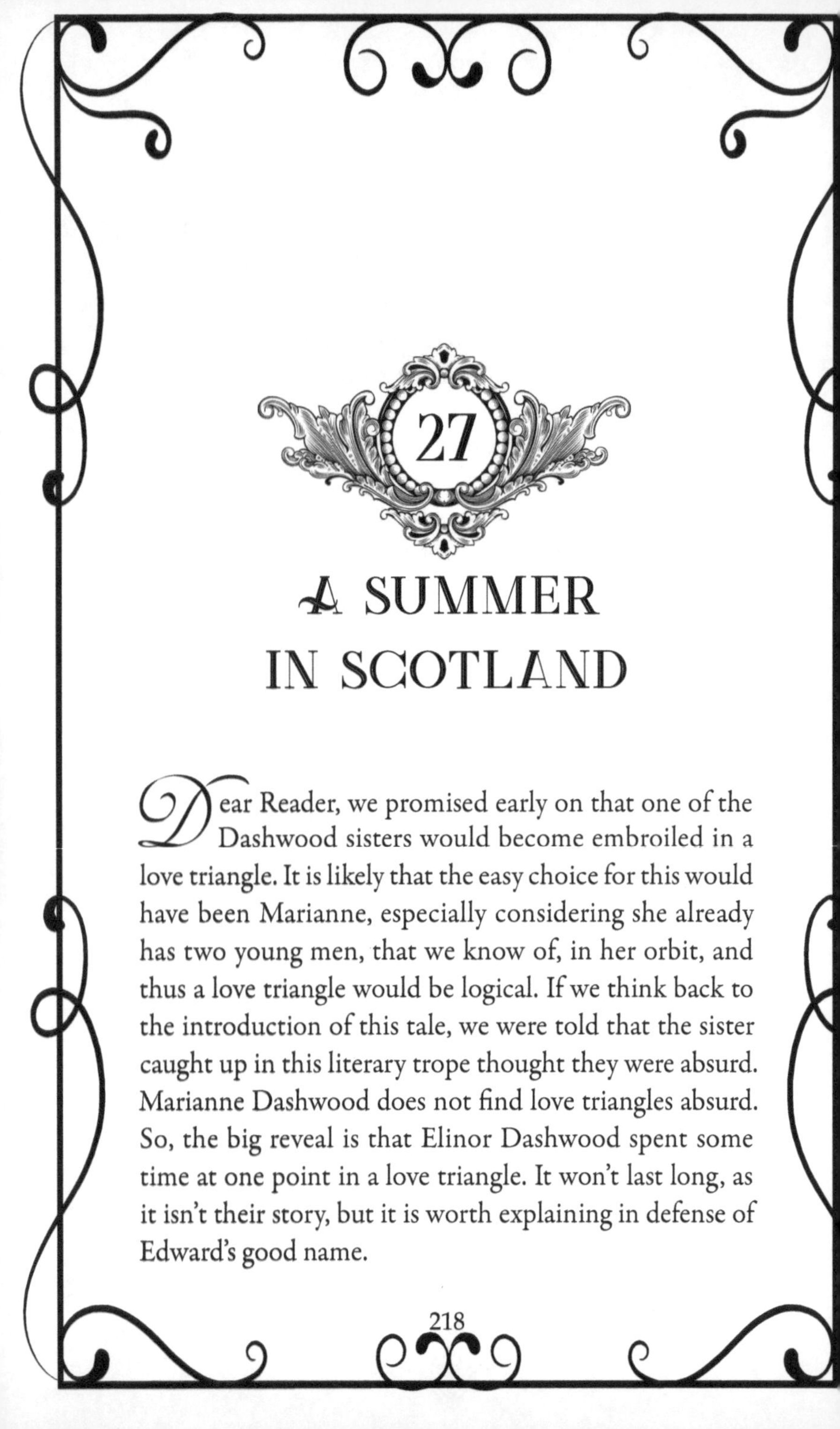

27

A SUMMER IN SCOTLAND

Dear Reader, we promised early on that one of the Dashwood sisters would become embroiled in a love triangle. It is likely that the easy choice for this would have been Marianne, especially considering she already has two young men, that we know of, in her orbit, and thus a love triangle would be logical. If we think back to the introduction of this tale, we were told that the sister caught up in this literary trope thought they were absurd. Marianne Dashwood does not find love triangles absurd. So, the big reveal is that Elinor Dashwood spent some time at one point in a love triangle. It won't last long, as it isn't their story, but it is worth explaining in defense of Edward's good name.

As the geographically challenged Steele sister mentioned, five years prior, when she was the tender age of 14, she, Anne, who was 16 at the time and, their father, Dr. Steele, went to Scotland for the summer. Dr. Steele did the best he could as a single father raising his children in a small Midwestern college town in the United States. While the educational and cultural opportunities on the college campus were vast, they were not all appropriate for young girls in content or in educational level.

The Steeles attended the annual Shakespeare performance as Dr. Steele had no inclinations against his children, regardless of age, being exposed to the Bard. However, the student art show and film festival were often off limits as there was often part of the anatomy exposed that he wasn't comfortable seeing and language used he wasn't comfortable hearing from his own students, and thus, he wouldn't take his children. While the local private school, The Rushworth Academy, offered a rigorous education and had a robust extracurricular slate of offerings, Dr. Steele felt that his girls should see the world and get out of their own bubbles.

In fact, much to the chagrin of his campus president, Dr. Mary Bennet, he discouraged his girls from attending Mansfield College. He wanted them to be their own people and not Dr. Steele's daughters. Dr. Bennet, a Mansfield Alumnus, and Dr. Steele spent many an hour in her parlor at the presidential residence, Pemberly, drinking wine and debating this point. In the end, parents have the final say, and ultimately, when the Steele sisters arrived in this story, Anne was attending a small, private, liberal arts college in the American Southwest and Lucy was preparing to spend a year with Tom and Charlie in Cleveland. She did not have many plans for the future and Dr. Steele thought that a new venue would be helpful.

The trip to Scotland was an opportunity for the girls to see if they wished to attend university abroad, which he would have liked for them. He was offered the opportunity to advise and act as a final reader for several graduate students who were finishing up their doctoral theses at the University of St. Andrews. The girls were then enrolled in as many summer educational activities as they could be that were either sponsored by the university or sponsored by local schools and libraries. The family was offered campus housing, which they were used to since living in Mansfield.

It was there that the Ferrars brothers met the Steele sisters. Edward was enrolled in a boarding program at the university where he and a bunch of fellow history buffs of various ages, spent each day digging through the archives at St. Andrews. It is Scotland's oldest university. The archives are, to borrow a term from many a historian, literally epic.

Robbie was rooming with him. He was supposed to be part of the history program as well, but he found libraries and archives to be dull, and so, after checking in and being counted each morning, Robbie would, for the most part, run off and play football with some local kids until lunch, when he would return and eat with Edward and his other "classmates." Edward, who found this to be a huge waste of money, didn't mind too much as he didn't want his enjoyment to be hampered by a bored and annoying younger brother.

Edward first encountered Lucy Steele in the library. She was there because her father told her that the library had all the answers. It is true that it does, they all do in fact, but Lucy wasn't looking for answers one could find in books; she was looking for the romance she found *in* books. She loved love stories. If a movie, song, book, or TV show featured love in any way, she loved it. Big romantic gestures were her favorite thing. She wanted to fall in love in Scotland and be chased to the airport. She longed to be loved, and she felt she had so much love to give. She had no idea how to find love, keep love, or what love meant. Her father, whose heart was broken when his wife left, didn't discuss matters of the heart with his girls. One would think then that Lucy could have turned to her older sister Anne, but because Anne took very much after her father in attitude, but not remotely in looks, and was such a serious student, she never allowed herself much time for romance. Dr. Bennet was her hero, and Dr. Bennet, as we shall discover in another tale, didn't think much about romance. Friendship yes, but not romance. Thus, Lucy was left to her own devices, the internet, and other girls her age. All of those things offered a lot of bad advice.

Lucy's plan that summer was, once she picked the boy she would make fall in love with her, and hopefully if he could drive or at best take a bus or train or something, he could chase her to the airport and beg her not to leave. Her plan was to simply agree with whatever he said. One of her classmates at Rushworth Academy had an older sister who managed to "snag herself a man" by being agreeable. The sister in question said yes to everything her target said, agreed that everything he liked was the best, and whenever asked if she'd read/watched/heard anything, she would simply give a non-committal grunt and ask what he thought of it. To which, he would launch into a diatribe about the thing to which she could reply,

"Exactly" or something equally affirming. This plan was anecdotally foolproof. The woman in question married a rich Mansfield graduate, moved away, and was only seen on holidays driving a luxury SUV and wearing a lot of jewelry that she called bling.

So it was that one day, she set her sights on young Edward as he and his younger brother sat and had lunch on the steps of the library. He was laughing at a story Robbie was sharing. He knocked his head back, and when he brought it forward, he brushed his floppy hair out of his face. For Lucy, the scene played out in slow motion. He was every lead in every movie she'd ever seen. She walked right over to them and stood so the sun shone on her pale face and reflected off her black hair. She looked down, hand extended, and said, "Hi, I'm Lucy."

Edward was a hormonal, inexperienced 15-year-old boy who, like many hormonal, inexperienced 15-year-old boys, had a not-so-secret crush on either Arwen or Galadriel or both. He looked up at the tall, pale, angular, elfish girl and forgot his own name. Thankfully, Robbie knew it, and he, equally smitten, introduced them both. She joined them for lunch and set her plan in motion.

She asked questions, and Edward answered. She said yes or nodded emphatically while never breaking eye contact. She followed Edward around the rest of the day as he dug through the archives, asking him about everything he touched and listening intently while he answered in a long-winded, self-important way that suddenly overconfident boys often do. Thankfully, Edward would learn to grow out of that habit in short order, whereas a multitude of men have not.

Anne felt slight approbation upon first meeting Edward, but that is the way of some big sisters. She ultimately approved of him as she felt "history nerds are harmless." Robbie made almost no mark on her. She was much too old to care about him, and he was much too afraid of her, as he saw a grown woman, not a girl, to say more than "hello" to her. Robbie did remember Lucy quite well though because, although she was quite taken with his brother, he was quite taken with her. He wished to be "yessed" to and looked at the way Lucy looked at his brother. It is fair to say that for the rest of his life, Robbie Ferrars was on the lookout for someone exactly like Lucy Steele.

As the summer went on, Edward and Lucy spent a lot of time together. Edward practiced his professing, Lucy practiced her "yessing," and they practiced their kissing. They kissed a lot in a lot of places. He talked. She listened. They kissed. Sometimes, they never bothered talking at all. On her final night in Scotland, they kissed on the coast of the North Sea, and they made promises to each other. Due to the fact that he had to leave St. Andrews a day before she did, she forgave him for not rushing to the airport to beg her to stay.

Email addresses were exchanged, and an international correspondence began. It became evident in less than two months that when required to say more than "yes" or "that's interesting," Lucy Steele didn't have much to say. This went on for several more months at which time when Edward realized that he was a dumb, hormonal boy who didn't find anything appealing about Lucy Steele save for her appearance and her kissing ability. He wrote a polite, incredibly self-deprecating email explaining that while he would always look back on his time with fondness, due to geography and situation, there was not a future for them, and so, he released her from any promises she made to him.

Lucy, thinking this only made him more appealing, wrote back thanking him for being so big-hearted and wonderful. What Edward failed to do, in his overly polite way, was to ask to be released from the promises he made to Lucy. He assumed, wrongly, that the release of promises was reciprocal. Because Edward was not, and is not monster, he and Lucy eventually became followers of each other on several social media platforms. He even occasionally liked a picture or a post. Because he didn't pay close enough attention to those likes, he didn't realize that she liked almost every single one of his pictures and posts.

So, we may not forgive Edward for being a dumb hormonal teenage boy who wanted to hear his own ideas said back to him. We may not forgive him for not being clearer with his feelings about the young American. We may not forgive him for being virtual friends with Lucy Steele and giving her false hope. However, we can, at least we hope we can, forgive him for not having a clue that according to Lucy Steele, their long-distance love affair had never ended.

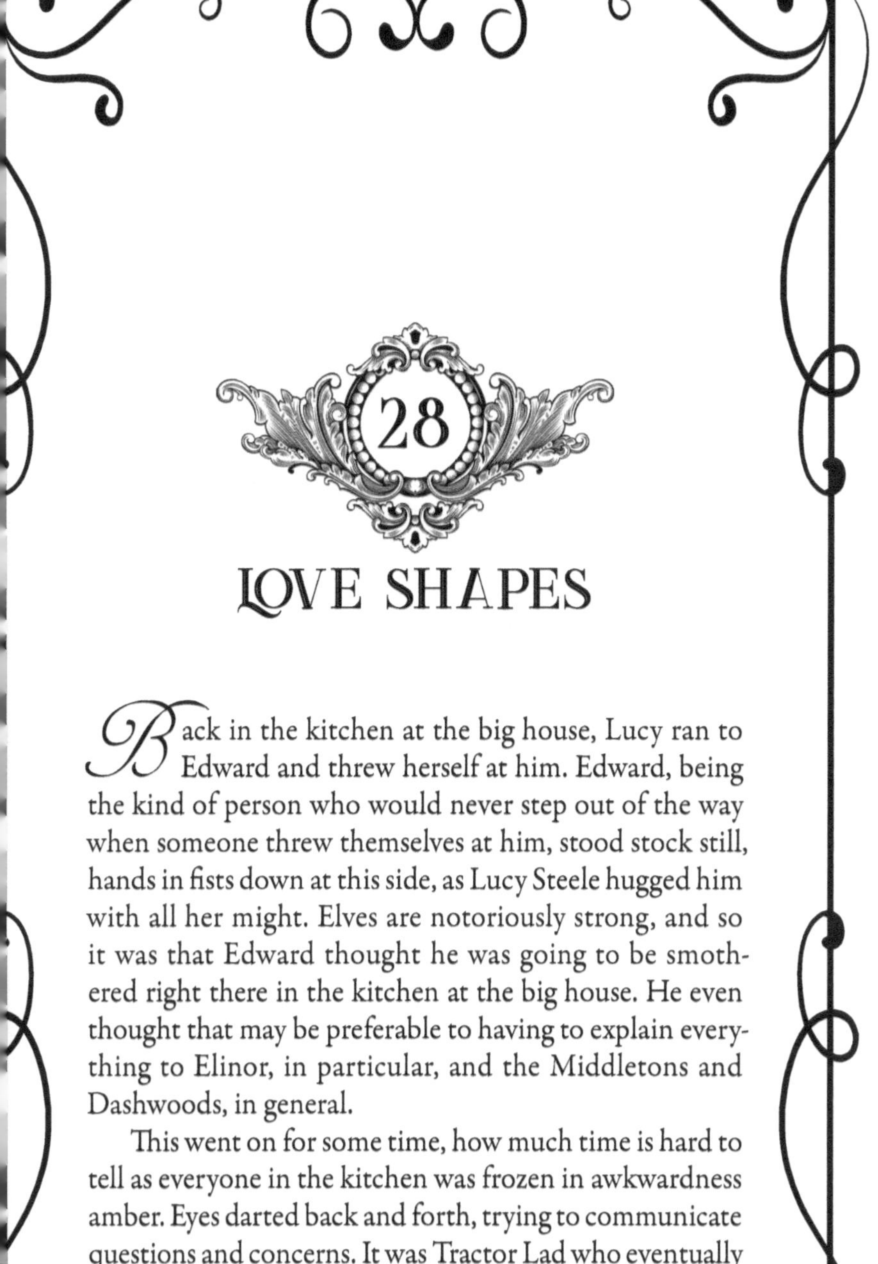

28

LOVE SHAPES

*B*ack in the kitchen at the big house, Lucy ran to Edward and threw herself at him. Edward, being the kind of person who would never step out of the way when someone threw themselves at him, stood stock still, hands in fists down at this side, as Lucy Steele hugged him with all her might. Elves are notoriously strong, and so it was that Edward thought he was going to be smothered right there in the kitchen at the big house. He even thought that may be preferable to having to explain everything to Elinor, in particular, and the Middletons and Dashwoods, in general.

This went on for some time, how much time is hard to tell as everyone in the kitchen was frozen in awkwardness amber. Eyes darted back and forth, trying to communicate questions and concerns. It was Tractor Lad who eventually broke the tension in a way that young children can. He asked, "Why is that tall lady hugging Edward? Can I get a hug too? I like hugs." It is true, he did like hugs, but the tall lady was not interested in hugging him. Still, it did enough to cause everyone to become unstuck in time, and things moved rather quickly from there.

Edward, never one to speak over the top of anyone else, allowed Lucy Steele to tell her version of the story, which was remarkably accurate, and thus we have no reason to repeat it here. However, it was, as we know, when the two young lovers parted that the realities split. Lucy was convinced that Edward had, as she had, been pining away for her and waiting for the day for them to be reunited. While she didn't know that England and Scotland were part of the same country, she did know that they were on the same island, and her reason for gladly accepting Charlie's offer to come to England was that she hoped to find a way to Scotland to be reunited with Edward.

Upon hearing this news, Anne Steele dropped her head and once again tried to bore herself into the floor, making it clear that she was not privy to this information, and had she been, she would have done her best to talk her sister out of coming on the trip. Anne could not count the number of times in her life that she tried to run damage control for her little sister, whom she loved dearly, but whom she didn't fully understand. She didn't want her to embarrass herself, but of course, Lucy Steele was never embarrassed. It never occurred to her to feel that way. Some would consider it a superpower. If that made her a superhero or an anti-hero is up to each reader to decide.

Maggie Dashwood, fully understanding how the actions of sisters often affect one's life even when the sister doesn't consider her siblings, put her hand on Anne's back and gave it a rub. Anne, sensing that the touch was not pity but empathy, locked eyes with Maggie. An understanding passed between them. They both smiled out of the side of their mouths. Maggie's lips smirked up to the left and Anne's did the same up to the right. While the two were separated by many years, that simple touch by Maggie and the shared smirk would change the trajectory of Maggie's life as we shall see in the coming pages. Compassion is free and so the return on investment is infinite.

After Lucy finished speaking, all the eyes in the room turned to Edward for his side of the story. He stood, mouth in a line, grim-faced, lockjawed. Edward didn't contradict Lucy's story. He wasn't interested in making a fool of anyone. He was genuinely shocked to learn that she thought they had been in a relationship for all those years. In his own way, he thought it was kind of sweet that Lucy carried a torch for him all those years. He didn't feel he deserved it, but it was nice nonetheless.

It was lucky that Marianne wasn't present when everything went down in the kitchen as she would have had some hot takes, and her influence over her elder sister and mother was exponential. Had she been there, she would have stood, ruddy-faced, between her elder sister and her suitor and shouted all kinds of words that Edward would have taken to heart, thus running him off for possibly ever. Instead, when he looked at her with his sweet smile and kind eyes, with his hand extended to her while jerking his head at the door, Elinor reached out and took it. They silently left the room while Lucy Steele shouted his name in exasperation and attempted to follow them. Charlie stepped in front of her and wrapped her in a hug that Lucy didn't know she needed until she was in it. She started weeping on Charlie's shoulder. Gran walked over and put her hand on Lucy's back in the same way that Maggie did on Anne's. The two women led her back up the stairs to Green Room, leaving those behind in the kitchen to physically and metaphorically clean up the mess.

It will not surprise readers to learn that Elinor Dashwood took little convincing to the truth of the matter. There was nothing Edward had ever done that would have led anyone who knew him well to think he did anything nefarious. She understood the situation, and she felt empathy toward Lucy. She even apologized for the cursing we adroitly dodged sharing earlier.

Because, by the time the news finally reached Marianne, the issue was resolved, and she immediately started making snarky jokes about Lucy Steele. It didn't matter that only Willoughby laughed at her jokes, no one told her to stop, and so it was that Lucy was the butt of many a joke for quite some time. While Marianne Dashwood may be a bit of a monster, she is not so monstrous to make jokes to Lucy's face. At least, not the jokes that she fully grasped. Anne grasped them just fine, and thus it was her lifelong dislike of Marianne Dashwood that began the summer Maggie turned 15. The Steeles and the Dashwoods would end up staying linked for the rest of their lives after that summer. Anne and Maggie for reasons we shall see soon, and for eagle-eyed readers from a previous tome, already know why, communicated the most. Whenever they spoke or sent messages, Anne pointedly didn't ask about Marianne. Anne Steele could have earned her Ph.D. in passive aggression instead of physics but chose the latter as it is much more useful.

So it was that the love triangle that Elinor Dashwood ended up being trapped in was fictional, but it was still incredibly annoying. Lucy thought there was one, and they didn't want to be rude to Lucy. She was a guest of Lady, whom they all loved and respected, but they didn't want to encourage the behavior either. They still took most dinners at the big house and that made things problematic. She always made sure to sit as close to Edward as possible. It didn't matter that he had pointedly said to Lucy that he only had platonic feelings for her and that any chance of rekindling their brief but "not unpleasant" relationship was not going to happen. He was with Elinor. He loved Elinor. That was that.

We can't know for sure if Lucy knew what platonic meant, but she heard "not unpleasant" and that was all she needed. Lucy pranced about the big house and Barton Park trying to catch Edward's eye whenever he was around. She wore revealing clothes and dropped a lot of things in front of him so she could bend over in such a way that was designed to cause his eyes to linger. She tried to speak longingly of the kisses she and Edward shared many moons ago, but they came out as far too graphic descriptions of make-out sessions. While the families liked to loiter and have coffee and watch the Tractor Quartet do something dangerous after dinner, Lucy's antics often brought abrupt endings to many of the evening festivities.

Even Maggie, who was desperate for a snog, as she was sure she was the last kid in her school to kiss anyone in any romantic fashion, found the descriptions revolting. Lucy was beautiful, but Maggie thought of Edward as a brother and she didn't have a thing for elves, so there was nothing particularly appealing about either of them, but she didn't want the whole idea of kissing to be a turn-off. She eventually pleaded with Gran to do something. She rarely asked for favors, and Gran knew that if she was asking, it was serious. Still, as much as Gran hated to disappoint the girl she treated like a granddaughter, she wasn't going to get involved. The Steeles were not her guests. Maggie knew she was right, and so she and Gran promised that they could spend at least one night per week when Maggie didn't have to work the next morning at the house in Exeter away from the drama. We shall soon see that that wouldn't be necessary, as Lucy would be otherwise occupied. Still, they had fun together, so they still spent one night each week away just because.

Fortunately, the news of Lucy Steele's sudden reappearance reached Robbie Ferrars who, as we learned, had been searching for a woman who was exactly like Lucy and couldn't resist the urge to try his hand at wooing Ms. Steele himself. He was unemployed and undecided about any direction in his life, so he headed due south and arrived at Edward's flat quite unannounced one day, and he installed himself in the lives of our cast for a time.

He was determined to "win Lucy" from his brother. He made the mistake of saying this in front of Elinor, who happened to be at the flat when he arrived. While she clearly had no love lost for Lucy Steele, the idea that a woman was a prize to be won rubbed her the wrong way, and she gave him quite a lecture about women's bodies and souls. Both Edward and Brandon chimed in, and by the time the lambasting was over, the lecture made no difference to him. Robbie was determined to "steal" Ms. Steele, and that was that.

So it was that at the next dinner, just one week after Maggie's birthday, and one day after Gran and Maggie had spent the night at the house in Exeter, that Robbie showed up at the big house with his brother and Elinor and began his attempt to win over Ms. Lucy Steele. What happened next is exactly what everyone assumes would happen.

Robbie first played it coy and slowly wormed his way into Lucy's confidence. He charmed her. He said she was stunning and statuesque. He made jokes about first Elinor and later Edward. When she laughed at those jokes, he knew he'd done it. The two of them sent furtive glances at each other across tables and texts across the stratosphere. They bumped feet all while Lucy outwardly pined for Edward. She didn't want to seem like she was "that kind of girl" even though she and Robbie met in the dark of closets around the big house, fumbled in the dark, and spoke in whispers.

Eventually, after what to them felt like an eternity but was really only a week of clandestine meetups and stolen kisses, they announced quite publicly at dinner that they couldn't keep the secret any longer. Lucy even said, "It's tearing us apart" while flinging her head back and pounding her chest. They announced that they were in love, that they never meant to hurt Edward, but they simply couldn't help it. They were destined for one another.

Robbie said to Edward, "No hard feelings, brother."

Lucy said to Elinor, "You can have him."

Maggie stifled a laugh into Gran's shoulder. Gran, as a theater critic, had seen her fair share of melodrama and saw this whole thing coming from miles away and was relieved to finally have it over. She patted Maggie's head while she smiled the way she hoped she was supposed to.

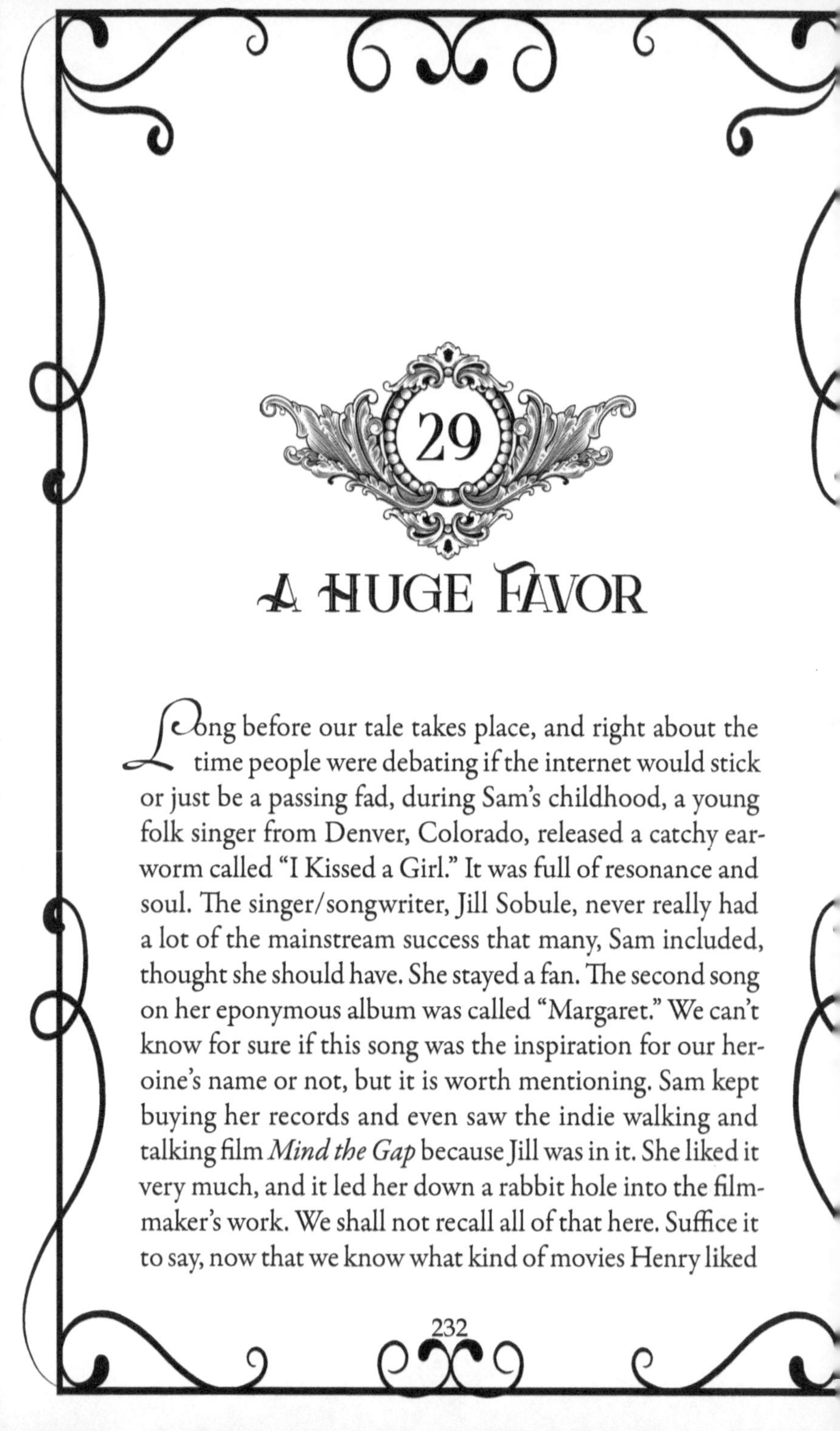

29

A Huge Favor

Long before our tale takes place, and right about the time people were debating if the internet would stick or just be a passing fad, during Sam's childhood, a young folk singer from Denver, Colorado, released a catchy earworm called "I Kissed a Girl." It was full of resonance and soul. The singer/songwriter, Jill Sobule, never really had a lot of the mainstream success that many, Sam included, thought she should have. She stayed a fan. The second song on her eponymous album was called "Margaret." We can't know for sure if this song was the inspiration for our heroine's name or not, but it is worth mentioning. Sam kept buying her records and even saw the indie walking and talking film *Mind the Gap* because Jill was in it. She liked it very much, and it led her down a rabbit hole into the filmmaker's work. We shall not recall all of that here. Suffice it to say, now that we know what kind of movies Henry liked and the films that Gran liked, we are pleased to report Sam eventually found someone to chat with about those films.

Many years later, one year after the first iPhone and the same year as the first Android was released, most people still had phones connected to their walls in their homes, and the phones in their pockets flipped or had slide-out keypads, which was not quite a long time before our tale takes place, and thus well into Sam's motherhood, all three of her daughters having been born, a young pop star from Santa Barbara, California, released a song called "I Kissed a Girl." When people of a certain age first saw the song title, they assumed it was a cover song. Sam even said aloud to Henry, "Why remake a perfect song? Who is that tart anyway?" She wasn't proud of herself for calling a stranger a tart. It wasn't a feminist thing to do, but she said it, and she owned it.

When she finally heard the song and discovered it wasn't a cover, she thought it was fine and catchy but always said to no one in particular, how much she liked the Jill Sobule song. While she assumed no one was listening, Maggie heard everything, and she sought both songs out. The only rule on Sam's music collection was to return it when you were done. Maggie always did. At that age, she had no opinion of her own. It was only much later, especially during the summer she turned 15, that she spent a lot of time with these songs that she realized that she agreed with her mother. Maggie felt the Sobule song was sweet and honest whereas the other song felt like a gimmick which, as someone who wanted very much to kiss a girl, felt like an insult.

Slightly before the time our tale began with a birthday and a tragedy, when most people of means had mini-computers in their pockets, and music was discovered on YouTube instead of on the radio or TV, a young country singer from Golden, Texas released a single called "Follow Your Arrow." It was a song that advocated girls should be kissing boys and girls and smoking pot and doing whatever they wished. It was a risky move given country music, known for its conservative fanbase, had several years before kicked three women out of its "club" for daring to have political opinions. Yet the song, co-written and performed by Kacey Musgraves, went on to win all kinds of awards, became a huge crossover anthem, and made people feel seen. Sam Dashwood cried a little when she first heard that song. She had forgotten that her youngest child was in the backseat of the Range Rover. When Maggie asked her mum what was wrong, Sam said, "More people need to be brave and speak up like that girl there." She wished she'd said woman, but she said what she said. Mums of girls often say girls about women.

So it was that Maggie knew that her mum was not going to have a problem with her wanting to kiss boys and girls, and yet she just couldn't bring herself to tell her. She and Gran talked and talked about this when the two of them were alone in Exeter. Sometimes Maggie felt like it was all she spoke about. It wasn't true at all, but she saved it all up for the safety of the sitting room or the garden in the old house that she had slowly thought of as a lovely second home. She even told the story of those three songs and her mum's reactions to them all.

Gran told Maggie the story of the first time she heard that Sobule song. She went on to tell her about the other songs that she thought Maggie should hear. They listened to them and talked and talked. On the way back to

Barton Park, Gran, being supportive and loving, told her that she would do it whenever she felt ready. In the meantime, Maggie should keep talking to her and not worry. Whenever Maggie told Sam, Gran just knew that it was all going to be fine. She always said, "It will be okay, dear. I promise. It will be okay."

Maggie wanted to believe Gran, but she still just couldn't make the decision to share it with the person she felt she should tell. She and Sam were not close like Sam was with Marianne and yet, she felt she should tell her before she told Elinor. It felt good to tell Gran, essential really, and Gran had already known, so it helped with the guilt that Gran knew and her mum didn't. Maggie was only 15 and knew that secrets were not something she would enjoy keeping, but this one, this truth, was just something that she couldn't figure out how to share. She didn't have to tell her mum her eye color, her dominant hand, or her shoe size. Those were just who she was and so was this, and yet, there was something different here. She knew, objectively, if only because of her mum's musical taste, that she wouldn't care, but was not caring the same as accepting? We shall not have a great answer to that question, but it will come up again shortly. Sorry.

Thus, it was with all of this on her mind that one morning Maggie walked into the big house for breakfast, and after a swordfight in which she was roundly defeated because she agreed to fight with her non-dominant hand, Lady asked her for a favor that seemed simple enough. No one could have known what would happen next.

Maggie had, until that day, enjoyed her dirty work at Barton Park. She took the role of future Juliet seriously. She tried to learn how to fix as many things as possible.

She loved feeding the animals, and she didn't even mind cleaning up the pens because while shoveling; she was alone, sometimes listening to music, sometimes alone in silence. She would go home each night exhausted and able to shut off the noises and the stress about coming out and what that would mean for her and her family dynamic. She was able to be outside and observe the world. She tried almost every day to draw something from a memory that she came across while working. It could be a tractor tire or a member of the Quartet. It could be a goat hoof or a hawk feather. She always tried to do it from memory, and she never went back to see if it matched. While other kids of her generation had digital hordes of photos they never looked at once they posted them online, Maggie Dashwood had books and books of sketches that she liked to pore over from time to time to see if she'd gotten any better. She did share some online, but mostly, she liked to touch the drawings and paintings and think about what was hidden just over the horizon.

So, soundly beaten and stabbed quite to death multiple times by the Quartet, she'd walked into the kitchen and saw Lady sitting next to a plate of toast and jam with a cold glass of juice and a steaming cup of coffee next to it. They made eye contact, and Lady patted the empty seat.

Maggie smiled at the woman whom she thought of as her aunt, came over, and plopped down. "Thanks." She took a sip of juice. "They're getting good. I don't know how much longer I can take on all four of them without having two swords." She took a big bite of her toast. Sword fighting was hungry work.

"Noted. I'll make sure to hide an extra in the big vase in the hallway. Girl power and all that." She flashed some

Spice Girlesque hand gestures while singing "Spice up your life."

Maggie laughed and choked on her toast. Lady laughed too and pounded her back. The toast dislodged, but the laughing, coughing sounds continued. This went on for long enough that Middy called timeout on his sword-fight to come in and check on them. They both had their heads on the table snorting and giggling. If asked why they thought it was funny, they would have said different things, but sometimes laughter is just contagious.

When they finally got themselves calmed down and food was being eaten and the Quartet was lying in the hall playing dead with their father lording his foam sword around, lovingly trash-talking his own children, Lady said, "Remember how you feel right now because I need a big favor."

"You need me to watch the boys?"

"No, you'd enjoy that. I wouldn't call that a favor. I'd say, 'I have a job for you.' This is a favor I need you to do for work."

"Well, you're my boss, landlord who charges no rent, food provider, and everything else, so I would submit that you could just say it the same way. You are essentially the feudal lord to my serf."

"Not this." She clenched her teeth together and smiled a full-toothed fake grin at Maggie. "This is the thing that I can't possibly pay you enough to do, so I have to ask it as a favor."

Maggie knocked back the rest of her juice like it was a shot of whiskey and wiped her mouth on the back of her hand. She slammed the cup down, rim first, like

Marion Ravenwood in *Raiders of the Lost Ark,* and she said, "Hit me."

"Jimmy quit."

Maggie dropped her head into her hands and mumbled, "Fine."

Lady rubbed her back. "You're a good, good girl. I tell anyone who listens."

Who was Jimmy and why are we just hearing of him now? He has not been germane to this tale until this point, so he wasn't mentioned. It is possible that Jimmy could have made a brief appearance earlier so that this moment didn't feel like it came out of the blue, but sometimes, just like the sudden appearance of Lucy Steele, the whole backstory doesn't come into focus until it is absolutely necessary. Sure, mentioning Jimmy before would have been reasonable. There were plenty of chances to bring him up, but he wasn't so important that most folks would have remembered him, and then, there would be some explaining to do anyway. This is a pretty full cast, and Jimmy is most important here because he leaves. Don't worry. He is fine. He just fulfilled his lifelong dream of landing a costumed role at the House of Mouse's amusement park in France.

Jimmy was the resident mascot. He spent most of his days rotating duties as most of the front-of-the-house staff did. He sold tickets and trinkets and parked cars. Lady was great about rotating people so they didn't get bored. However, whenever there was the need for a person to wear a costume for a field trip, educational trip, or as it was that day, a birthday party, Jimmy was the man. There was a collection of animal suits that he happily donned. He danced, he juggled, and he took pictures with guests. He did it all in mime because he was quick to remind anyone who asked, "Animals don't talk." Yes, of course, animals don't dance, juggle, or hug guests while posing for pictures. Logic isn't for petting zoos or amusement parks. Still, Jimmy considered himself an artist. He took the job 10 years prior to gain the mascot experience he needed. Middy wrote the letter of recommendation himself which ultimately landed him the job. They were in the process of finding a new permanent mascot or deciding if they wanted to open it up to the staff as part of the rotation.

Not surprisingly, none of the full-time staff were keen on wearing the suits, doing mime work, or getting hugged by strangers and their children while sweating out five liters of water. They never considered that option when they applied for the job. Some of the summer workers toyed with the idea as having fun at a kid's party is often joyous, but they were mostly teenagers who were nervous about being found out and worried about what nicknames they may garner from their time in the suit. For teenagers, being called animal names rarely came with positive connotations.

The Middletons thought they had more time after Jimmy tendered his resignation, but they received a frantic call just that morning from a parent who explained that the venue where he planned on having his son's party had flooded overnight due to a ruptured pipe and so he was willing to pay double if they could pull off a themed birthday party that afternoon for 20 5-year-olds plus five chaperones. Lady said yes, because, if Maggie had said no, she would have climbed into that costume herself. It wasn't that they needed the money, although she did accept the double fee with the intention of giving the overage to Maggie if she said yes. Lady just loved children so much, as evidenced by her having four and opening her home up to the Dashwoods and Steeles so readily. She simply hated the idea of a ruined fifth birthday party even if none of them would really remember it. She would never have said any of this to Maggie, and it was, in fact, a huge favor to ask. Maggie had already heard a lot of nicknames being the girl with ties and blazers, who worked in a zoo, drew pictures, and didn't have friends. Plus, her love for Lady and Middy was so big that it eclipsed any issues she may have regarding hearing more.

Thus, Maggie Dashwood, who was, in fact, a good, good girl found herself dressed as a chicken leading a group of 5-year-olds in the brain-breaking polka known as the "Chicken Dance." It was, like many other songs for children, written in such a way that once one hears it or even thinks about it, as we are all undoubtedly doing right now, it will buzz around in one's brain for at least the rest of the day if not for several days to come until it is finally beaten into submission.

There were other chicken-related duties in between the endless rounds of "Chicken Dance" for her to do that did not involve dancing. Pin the tail feathers on the chicken was a big hit. Maggie put blindfolds on the kids, spun them round and round, and turned them loose as they dizzily tried to stick Velcro tailfeathers onto a plush chicken who was, sadly, tail featherless.

She had the kids play a chicken-based variant of the Duck-Duck-Goose game of Chick-Chick-Rooster, which wasn't an exact 1 for 1 name swap as Geese and Ducks were not the same things and a Goose is female. The game is not called Duck-Duck-Gander, but Maggie was supposed to remain mute while Middy was the MC of the party, and so she reminded herself to ask him later, which, we will pretty quickly see why she did no such thing.

Being inside the chicken suit was hot and challenging. The eye holes were not the actual chicken eyes but were through the grinning teeth of the chicken head. Of course, chickens don't have teeth, but they don't do the chicken dance either, so it was something else for her list of questions and/or grievances for the management of Barton Park over dinner. Her narrow field of vision meant that was constantly afraid of stepping on people on any side of her. She tried to look forward and move forward. Since the suit didn't come with a backup beeper, she didn't want to even try it.

She threaded her arms through big wings and so when her wings were up, the people she was facing could see her hands. She could hold her hands up and do the chicken mouth gestures during the song, but she had to resist the urge to put her hands under her armpits to make wings during the second part of the dance. She just flapped her wings before she wiggled her hips from side to side. Really, doing the chicken dance in a chicken suit was, for all intents and purposes, pointless. The song is about becoming a chicken sans suit. As soon as one dons a chicken suit, any dance, be it polka-based or even the fox trot, is a chicken dance if not *The* "Chicken Dance." Still, Maggie performed the dance to start the show, between each game, and one last time before the presents, cake, and ice cream portion of the day began under the pavilion and not in the hot, hot sun.

During the final, final dance of the day, Maggie gave it her all. She do-si-doed with everyone she could. Little kids, several random adults that she assumed were part of the party as Middy wouldn't have let them get close if they were not, Middy himself, Lady, who had come to witness the "great favor," her mum, Gran, and even a very pregnant Charlie.

When the music stopped and the entertainment part of the party was over, Middy took to the microphone and said, "Thank you all for being here to celebrate Raymond's fifth birthday." There was a round of applause. "I want to take a special moment to thank the co-star to Raymond's special day, Barton Park's very own, Camille the Chicken!"

He pointed at Maggie who found out in that moment that her character had a name and that it was Camille. Afraid of bowing over and having her head fall right off in front of all the kids, she put her wings out wide and dipped into a curtsy. This was followed by another round of raucous applause. She waved her wings and pointed one to Raymond who ran over and gave her a big hug. More applause mixed with plenty of "awws" and pictures.

"It is now time for everyone to move to the pavilion where we will open Raymond's presents and have some cake and ice cream." Middy gestured in the direction of the pavilion and the sound of 40 little feet running filled the air.

Maggie waved and waved until she thought it was safe enough for her to get back to the costume shed and take the costume off. She turned to go but felt a hand at her side and she froze. The hand was firm and was clearly a warning to stop walking. A young, female-sounding voice said, "Careful, Camille." It wasn't accusatory as in "Careful, you fumbling fowl" nor was it angry as in "Careful, you bird brain" but it was a soft, calm warning as in, "Please, proceed with caution, there is someone here."

She put both of her wings sky-high and turned around slowly. In normal circumstances, she would have immediately started apologizing for being in the way as Maggie always felt in the way even when she wasn't. However, because she didn't want to break character, she didn't speak and hoped her wings-up gesture would be good enough. Because she was so concerned with making sure the kids had a good time, she hadn't really paid much attention to the chaperones. They were five, grown-up-shaped blobs around the edge of the party, and she had certainly danced with some of them in the area that she would forever call the chicken coop so when she turned and tried to focus on the face of the person whose hand was just touching her back, she expected to find a person of a certain age standing there. She imagined all of the chaperones looked like Gran or her mum. Chaperoning a fifth birthday party was the job of folks at least one generation above the subject of the party and all the invitees. Who else would spend hours at a petting zoo all day listening to the "Chicken Dance" on repeat?

Imagine her surprise when she found instead a golden-skinned teenage girl with long black hair and hazel eyes. She said, "I was trying to stay out of the fray. I didn't mean to startle you." She smiled. Her lips parted, showing off a few crooked teeth that Maggie found inexplicably adorable. She never, until that moment, thought about teeth as attractive or unattractive. They were, until then, only functional. She liked the way that this person's teeth were framed by her plump, shiny lips. Maybe it was the lips and not the teeth? She couldn't think clearly.

Thankfully for Maggie, her face remained hidden inside the chicken head so that this girl couldn't see Maggie stare at her mouth while she licked her own. Maggie didn't even realize that she'd done it. Her heart knew exactly what was going on and so it took control over her body, fending off her brain which was still shouting, "Don't talk! Don't take your mask off! Don't talk! Don't take your mask off! You're supposed to wait until you get to the costume shed!"

Maggie's heart told her brain to take a seat and pipe right down. She placed one wing on each side of her mask and lifted the giant chicken head off of her own head. "Right, sorry. I didn't see you there. This thing needs to come with a backup camera or at least a mirror." She laughed at her own joke and was surprised at her confidence.

The girl's smile somehow got even bigger when she saw who was inside the suit. "Maybe you could invent that and make a mint."

"That would be great. Then my days as professional chicken would be over."

"Well, I for one would be sad to see that happen. You were, and I mean this sincerely, the best professional chicken I've ever seen. It would be a tragedy to professional chickendom everywhere if you hung up your beak."

"Would you believe this is my first day in this suit?"

The girl clutched her imaginary pearls and gasped an exaggerated gasp. "Just imagine how magnificent you will be the next time."

"We've got some other suits too." Maggie gestured with the detached head in her hand to the costume shed at the edge of the party space which is where she was supposed to exit for the party and enter after the party in full costume. "I could just as easily be a sheep or goat next time."

"Well, if past is prelude, then I suspect you'll be amazing." She looked right into Maggie's eyes.

"You think?" Maggie stared back mesmerized.

"I know." The girl smiled that big smile again and Maggie smiled back. "I'm Polly, by the way. Older sister." She jerked her head toward the party but didn't look away from Maggie at all.

"Maggie. Youngest sister."

Polly laughed. It was a sound Maggie liked very much.

30

POLLY

Polly Ansari was born and raised in Exeter. Her mum, whose surname was Campbell, was also born and raised in Exeter much like all the people on her side of the family as far back as Queen Victoria, was a florist who met her dad, sadly enough, at his dad's funeral. Her dad was the first Ansari to be born in Exeter. The previous generations were born in Jaipur, India. His parents both came to the UK for university, fell in love with the country, then each other, and decided to stay.

Meeting one's future spouse at his father's funeral is not ideal, but florists are incredibly empathetic and so this happens more often than one might imagine. Her normal delivery person was out sick, so she took the flowers herself. She entered the funeral home hours before the service was due to start, and she found him sitting on a bench outside of the funeral home, head in hands, weeping. He hadn't seen her. She could have gone right past him, gone around the back where deliveries go, and moved on with her life. Instead, she set the wreath down and sat next to him. She gently placed a hand on his back. He looked up at her, saw her big, compassionate, hazel eyes, and fell in love.

They married within a year and had Polly within a year of that. They always said they were just going to have one child. They were each only children and loved the autonomy it brought them. So, before Polly was even born, her father had a vasectomy. Her mum carried on with her flower shop, and her dad carried on as a pastry chef. Polly was the only girl in her school who knew how to arrange a wreath and decorate a cake. They lived a very happy life and Polly's parents were already planning on what an empty nest would look like while they were still in their 40s. They made big plans and talked about them and that was going to be that. Except, that wasn't that because in some rare cases, vasectomies spontaneously reverse and "surprise" children show up years later. So, when Polly was 11, her little brother Raymond was born. Two years later, she came out to her parents, who were surprised but supportive, and three years later, she ended up at Barton Park smiling at a girl in a chicken suit.

After Maggie changed into her regular clothes, they spent the remainder of Raymond's birthday party innocently knocking knees under the table whilst eating ice cream. They told each other things about each other that new acquaintances with friendship on their minds share. They gave each other furtive glances. They found ways to touch each other in ways that new acquaintances with nothing more than friendship on their minds don't. They could not, during the party surrounded by adults and over-sugared, worn-out five-year-olds, have the "do you like girls because I like girls?" conversation out loud, but they did their best to convey it to each other. At the end of the party, they exchanged numbers, and Maggie went home to The Cottage for a long, cold shower.

They texted little notes to each other that night and, in the way that people of their generation do, sought out and followed each other on social media. Polly had a lot of friends and even more followers. She was active in a lot of extracurriculars. She had two jobs, one for each parent, and she shared a lot of the work she did there. Maggie's page was much sparser, but by the time it occurred to her that this might be a bad look, Polly had already liked five of her drawings and three of her lamb videos.

It is well documented in this tome that Barton Park and the city of Exeter are relatively close. However, without transportation, they might as well be separated by an ocean. Maggie Dashwood, while an expert tractor driver, had not started her driving lessons, nor was she old enough to drive nor wealthy enough to own a car even if she had been old enough. So it was that as Maggie was crafting a long message about coming into town with Elinor to spend some time at the library and film museum and maybe they could meet up there to "hang out," Polly sent a photo of a burnt orange Vespa.

Out of context, Maggie didn't know what it meant, so she deleted her long missive already in progress about the University of Exeter library and responded with a simple question mark. A video call request came in. Maggie accepted.

Polly's face appeared on her phone. "Hi!" She was wearing a headband and a top that slipped off her left shoulder.

"Hi," Maggie replied. She absolutely noticed the exposed skin and thinking about what that meant did her best to stare directly at Polly's face on her screen instead of at the curve of her neck. She kept looking down at her own image to make sure she wasn't looking and then she caught herself doing that, assumed she looked like a crazy person, and opted to stare directly at her camera. "So... Vespas?"

"I like them a lot, you know?"

"I didn't know, nor do I know enough about them to form an opinion, but I am Vespa curious."

Polly laughed. Maggie liked it. She wondered if there would be a time that she would not like her laugh. Time is infinite when one is fifteen.

"Well," Polly continued, "I hope you like that one in particular as it is mine."

"Yeah? Cool."

"My parents wanted me to get it because I work for both of them, and their shops are not super close. One of them normally has Raymond after school, and so I usually go to the place where he is to be the extra set of hands running the shop while they look after him. They prefer to do the parenting while I do the laboring. I don't mind because they pay me and gave me the Vespa. They can just send me a text after school and tell me which place needs me the most, and I can zoom on over there. You know?"

"Is it fun to drive?"

"She is."

"She?"

"Yeah, I named her Tori."

"Like for Tori Amos? Because of the orange hair?"

Polly's face almost broke open she smiled so big. "Ding Ding Ding. You got it in one. No one gets it."

"Mum's a bit of a music buff."

"Yeah. Mine too."

"Ladies of a certain age I suppose."

"And their daughters obviously, you know." They stared at each other and smiled. Polly continued, "I love to ride her around when the weather is fine. It feels amazing to buzz around and feel the breeze. During the winter, it is really cold, but I bundle up. It doesn't snow much down here, you know, but I've even taken her out in a flurry. That was a mistake." She closed her eyes as she described these temperature swings as though she was reliving the events.

Maggie smiled at the way she seemed to be lost in her own story. "Sounds amazing."

Polly popped her eyes back open. "It really is. So..."

"So?"

"I was wondering if maybe you wouldn't mind if I brought Tori over sometime this week. You could meet her, and we could take her for a ride in the country, and maybe you could show me around Barton Park. I'd love to see some of those critters you've drawn in person, you know."

"Yes! Yeah! Yes, please, I'd like that so much."

"What about tomorrow?"

"It so happens that after my turn as Camille, I have the day off for good behavior, so my day is wide open."

"I have to work in the bakery in the morning, but I could easily be there by lunch?"

"Lunch. Yes. Great. I'll make us lunch."

"You cook?" Polly seemed genuinely impressed.

"I mean, I don't burn food, and I make a mean cheese toastie."

"Excellent! I love those. It's a date."

Maggie's tongue turned to dust in her mouth. She choked out, "Is it?"

"Do you want it to be?"

Maggie nodded emphatically. "I really do. It's just that my family doesn't…"

"Me too." Polly kissed the air in front of her.

Maggie's brain short-circuited. She wasn't sure what she was saying. She didn't realize that she hadn't finished that sentence. Her heart was racing.

"See you tomorrow!" Polly hung up.

Maggie stared at the blank phone screen with her hand on her heart, trying to keep it from pounding out of her body. She checked the clock. It was far too late to call Gran, although we all know that it is never really too late to call Gran in case of an emergency. Maggie wasn't sure if this qualified. It felt like one, but was it? She decided to ride it out and find out the next day.

31

DATE

*M*aggie stumbled downstairs at the literal break of dawn having no idea if she managed to sleep at all. She woke up at least four times just before her dream self kissed dream Polly. There wasn't any need to do a deep dive into Jungian theories about what her dreams meant. She made coffee and nervously picked at her toast while sketching Polly from images she found online and listening to The Kinks' song "Polly" on repeat. She got good enough at her face that she was eventually able to draw a picture of her driving Tori, leaning forward into the wind. Polly's eyes squinted against the wind. Her mouth, a closed-lipped smirk. Maggie drew herself on the back of the seat, arms around Polly's mid-section, her head on Polly's back. Her forehead was just below the nape of Polly's neck. Of course, she knew, that in real life, she would totally wear a helmet, but in the drawing, their hair, tangled together, was blowing wild in the fictional wind.

Sam wandered in, pulling out her sleeping earplugs that had become a necessity since moving into The Cottage and dropping them in her robe's pocket, while Maggie was finishing her fourth piece of toast and sixth cup of coffee. The second pot of the morning just finished brewing. Maggie was not one to leave just the dregs of a pot for anyone, unlike other members of her household whose name rhymed with Ferry Fan. Sam looked at her youngest daughter, on her day off, having clearly been up for a while based on the state of the kitchen, hunched over her sketch pad, earbuds in, totally oblivious to the world. "Oi! You okay?"

"Fine!" Maggie shouted as she sat bolt upright, slammed her sketchpad closed, and yanked out her earbuds by pulling the cord where the split hung in front of her chest. The left bud landed dangerously close to her coffee mug. The right one landed in a blob of jam. She swore under her breath, a skill she learned from Marianne, and wiped it on her napkin.

Sam stopped and looked over at her through squinted eyes. "You sure?"

Maggie nodded. "Yeah, um... Yeah." She smiled a big toothy grin.

Sam filled her coffee mug and opened the fridge to get out the eggs. She set the eggs on the counter and pulled a pan down from the rack that hung above the stove. "Sounds convincing. The second 'Yeah' sealed it," she said with her back to Maggie. She clicked on the gas, opened the butter dish, and cut a dab of butter off the stick they left next to the stove for this very purpose. While she let the butter melt, she turned to Maggie and said, "Wanna try again?"

Maggie inhaled a big breath and launched into an epic run-on sentence. Even in a story full of run-on sentences like this one, it is worth noting that this one was intentional. "Well, I am fine, but it's that yesterday at the party I met this girl called Polly, she's the older sister of the birthday boy, and we started talking, and she asked to come over to hang out, and so I said yes and I invited her over for lunch, I said I'd make toasties, and I thought I would go full Brandon with them, it was late last night and I didn't want to wake you up to ask, I figure you wouldn't mind, but I know I should've asked first so sorry but can she still come, I mean I can stop her, she hasn't even gotten off work yet, but it would be great if you let her come, she has a Vespa called Tori after Tori Amos so she likes good music, and her mum is a florist and her dad is a baker, not serial killer stock by a long shot, plus you know she was here as a chaperone for her brother's birthday party so she isn't a nutjob either, so can she come?"

Sam blinked, trying to process the information stream. She turned her back on her daughter, cracked two eggs into the melted butter, and put the shells back into the container which was the way in The Cottage. All three of Sam's daughters would continue to do this for the rest of their lives much to the consternation of their partners and friends who would much rather see the rubbish, at worst, in with the other rubbish, at best, in the compost bin. She watched the eggs take shape. She dropped some bread in the toaster. "You promise she isn't a serial killer, but what if she's a mass murderer? Edward and Willoughby are likely to be here today, and that would qualify as a mass murder."

Maggie felt the tension go out of her shoulders that she didn't know was there. "I promise to throw myself in the way so that you all have the best chance to get away."

Sam flipped her eggs over when the toast popped. She dropped them on her plate and flipped the eggs back over quickly. She liked her over-easy to be very easy. "Also, you have to make toasties for everyone, not just your new friend Polythene Pam."

"Pretty Polly," Maggie corrected before she could stop herself. She held her breath. Her own words circled around the kitchen, making a declaration she wasn't ready to declare.

"Right, The Kinks, not The Beatles. Either way, if you become the toastie technician, and you don't call the Brandon by name, your alliterative friend is welcome." Sam shut off the gas and put her eggs on her plate next to her toast. She opened the drawer next to the stove and pulled out a fork which she set on her plate as well. She topped off her mug with some hot coffee. She picked up the plate and the mug and turned back to the table.

Maggie exhaled as quietly as she dared. "Thanks, Mum. I'll check with you next time."

Sam sat her plate on the table in front of her chair. "Yeah, yeah, old Mum is furniture until you need something." She sat down and cut into one of her eggs with the side of a fork. The yolk spread all over her plate. She would later soak it up with her unbuttered toast which was her way. "Whatcha sketching?" she asked through a mouthful of runny egg.

"Just now?" she asked, guiltily stalling for time to find a way to answer truthfully without telling the full truth.

Sam took a sip of her coffee and looked quizzically at her youngest daughter. "No, last month at three in the morning. Yes, now. You were hunched over it when I came in. Your hair was on the table and everything, you were so close."

"I was shading. I like to get close when I do the shading. I turn the pencil," she picked it up to show her, "like this so I can go from the side you know. I don't like to shade from the point. It rips the page and can mess up the stuff on the other pages too if it doesn't rip through. It's a mess. I've ruined plenty of good stuff that way."

Sam shoved another forkful of egg in her mouth. She nodded. "Makes sense. Just you know, next time, hair tie. We all have to eat here."

"Right. Sorry. Will do," Maggie said. She didn't say the inside stuff outside about Marianne's bag always being on the table, the bag that she sets on the stage, which must be disgusting, nor did she mention the hundreds of times Willoughby sat with his feet on the table while rocking back in a chair. She dodged the bullet about having to explain what she was actually drawing. "More coffee?" She stood up with her own mug.

Sam looked down into her cup, picked it up, took a big gulp, and handed it to Maggie. "Thanks."

"Sure, no problem." She filled up both mugs and set them both down on the table.

Sam looked up at her and she smiled. "Thanks."

It was a genuine thank you. Maggie felt there was an opening there. She thought that maybe this was the time. Maybe she could tell her that Polly wasn't just going to come over as a friend. She nodded to herself and opened her mouth to speak when the front door, which they rarely locked, burst open, and she clanged her teeth shut in surprise.

"Morning, Dashwoods!" Willoughby's booming voice rang through the house. "I've a big surprise for you all! Wake up! Wake up! We're going to see a show!"

Maggie resisted the urge to make a remark about Willoughby being the show just as she resisted the urge to say most things about him that she thought. The show was a concert in Bournemouth. It might please readers to know that this will be one of the last times we see Willoughby in this tale. The first domino gets knocked down at the concert when Willoughby runs into Sophia Grey, a young woman that he used to know, while in line for the loo. There will be a lot of drama and gaslighting with Marianne at the center of it all. It isn't going to be pleasant, we can put a pin in it for now, but we needed to explain it some-where, so this seemed like the right place. Willoughby's sudden arrival meant that Maggie was going to have The Cottage alone for her first date as there was no chance she was going to cancel even though she would have loved to go to an all-day music festival.

Of course, after the family gathered around the table, Marianne was already in full makeup but still in her pajamas when she was "surprised so early in the morning" with Willoughby's "sudden and generous day out for the family." They offered Maggie's ticket to Lady who was more than happy to spend a day with people who didn't constantly want to stab each other with foam swords.

Bournemouth was several hours away by car, and the event was a music festival where the gates opened at noon and the first show started at one, so everyone was sud-denly very busy. Elinor called Edward. Sam called Lady.

Marianne and Willoughby went into Marianne's room to go through her whole wardrobe and try everything on four times. She was still not at 100 percent on her bad leg and so flats were the only option. Sam shouted through the doors that she should wear boots to which Marianne shouted back something about boots with a few salty adjectives attached. Maggie was left alone in the kitchen to clean up. Normally, being left to pick up after everyone would have made her quite angry, but when she realized that this afforded her a whole morning to prepare and the rest of the day to be alone with Polly, she literally whistled while she worked.

Within an hour, Maggie found herself next to the Range Rover with everyone who was going to go. Lady asked five more times if she was sure she didn't want to go. It was her ticket after all, and after five emphatic refusals, the concert-going party was ready to go. After hugs from Lady, a kiss on the cheek from Sam, a "have fun" from Elinor, a two-fingered salute from Marianne, and nothing from Willoughby, the five of them headed out to pick Edward up on their way to the show. Maggie scampered back into the house and up the stairs to the shower before the taillights were even out of view.

While she had several hours to get ready for Polly's arrival, Maggie was so concerned about the order she wanted to share the sketchpads that she lost track of time, and so she wasn't remotely ready for the knock on her door at a few moments before noon. She was sitting on the floor in the front room with her sketch pads everywhere looking like they had been thrown in the air and landed at random. She gasped, looked at the clock on the wall that confirmed that the only person it could be was there, looked down at the mess, cursed in a way that would have made even Marianne proud, realized she couldn't do anything about it, so she skipped over to the door and pulled it open.

Before Maggie could say anything, Polly was in motion coming straight toward her and before she knew exactly what was happening, she felt Polly's hands on the side of her face, turning her head slightly to the left. Before she could think about how she liked the feeling of her rough, calloused hands on her face, she felt lips on hers. Her eyes were still open. They opened wider, and then closed, and she let Polly lead and figured out what to do. This isn't that kind of book, so we won't linger, but it was not the most chaste first kiss ever, but it was not going to steam up any windows either. It was clearly a kiss between an experienced person and an inexperienced person.

Polly pulled back. Maggie was leaning forward; her hands were on Polly's hips. She didn't remember putting them there. If Polly knew it was Maggie's first kiss, and of course she totally knew, she didn't say anything about it. She was certainly impetuous, but she wasn't rude. "Hi. Thanks so much for having me over. I'm starving, you know. Didn't you promise me toasties? You said this was your cousin's house? Wow. It's lovely. Give me a tour?" She smiled at a bewildered Maggie Dashwood who was staring at her mouth trying to figure out how words could come out of there after what just happened. She walked past her into the house spewing rat-a-tat non-sequiturs that are not all that important and would fill up more pages than necessary to list them all here.

Maggie's face was tingling. She touched her own lips to see if they felt different to the touch as they did on the inside. They remained lips. She nodded at that new information. She closed the open door and turned to find Polly on her way upstairs. She had apparently started the tour on her own. Maggie followed Polly around the house telling her whose was what and where it came from. They shortly found themselves at the top of the stairs in the attic where they lost track of time after they crossed the threshold into Maggie's room. It turned out that Polly wasn't quite as starving as she let on as they managed to spend a good 20 minutes up there.

Eventually, her stomach did protest, and it growled the growl that transcends all other bodily functions, causing them both to laugh and bonk heads while laughing, which made them laugh even more. Maggie left her phone on her desk, not wanting to be remotely distracted for the day, and they found their way down to the kitchen where Maggie made the promised toasties, which were as excellent as advertised. Polly liked to talk and so she did. She talked and talked about flowers, cookies, brothers, other girls she kissed, her Vespa, the music she liked, the books she'd read, the cool spots to hang out in Exeter, the kids at her college, the college itself where she was studying accounting since her parents each had a business, and she thought it would be a good skill to have for when she owned them, making it very clear that she wasn't ever going to leave Exeter or likely go to uni.

Maggie tried to make sense of it all or get words in, but Polly liked to end sentences with a sing-song "you know." Sometimes it was a question; sometimes it was a statement. It was just a verbal tick. People have them. They are not often nefarious, and Polly's was not. However, this one often, but not always, made Maggie instinctively nod, making Polly think she'd agreed. We know this sounds like

Maggie was pulling a "Lucy Steele," but we assure you that was not the case. If and when she could answer, she didn't nod because she contributed to the conversation, but if and when she didn't or couldn't answer, she nodded. Polly saw the nods as confirmation and agreement as one would.

They cleaned the kitchen together and matriculated to the front room where they looked through Maggie's sketchbooks. They sat on the floor, back against the couch, leg to leg, hip to hip, shoulder to shoulder. They extended their legs straight out and piled the sketchbooks on their shared lap. Polly turned her word flood on the images, asking questions. Where did she make this one, how old was she when, where was she when, why did she when, and on and on. Maggie did the best she could to answer them all, but it was a lot for an isolated introvert whose best friend was a woman in her 60s.

Hours sped by. They got snacks as they were hungry like girls who work two jobs while having a five-year-old brother or who dress like chickens and do battle with four boys on a daily basis can be. They moved from the floor to the couch and back again while always making sure they were touching in some way or another. When they got to the last book, Polly saw the sketch of the two of them on Tori, and she finally stopped talking. She touched the drawing of their hair, tangled together, flying wild. She ran her hands over the indentations on the page. She set it on the ground, slid forward, and put her hands on the side of Maggie's head to feel her hair. Maggie did the same. They spent the rest of their time there in the front room not talking at all.

When Polly's alarm went off, reminding her that she needed to be home within the hour, they groaned and booed and made disapproving sounds about time. It was only then that they realized that they hadn't actually left the house or done any of the things they said they would do. Since Polly didn't have a lot of days off and her parents didn't want her on the Vespa on the country roads after dark, they made plans for Maggie to find a way to Exeter which wasn't really all that hard to do. Between Gran and Elinor, she had ways to get to town.

They kissed one last time in the same place they had their first kiss many hours before, and Maggie watched Polly ride off into the gloaming. She knew it was too late to go up to the big house for dinner, so she made herself a small something, cleaned up her sketchbooks, and took them back to her room. She saw a few missed calls from Middy and a text that said, "Nothing important. Wanted to invite you two to dinner. Hope you are having a good day." She texted him back with thank you hands and a smiley face. She got the text from Polly that she'd arrived home, and exhausted and exhilarated, she fell asleep so soundly that she didn't hear a sound when her mum and sisters came into The Cottage, all of them a bit loopy from drink and music, belting out the chorus of Paloma Faith's "Only Love Can Hurt Like This."

It wasn't until morning when Maggie found herself alone again at the table drinking coffee, reflecting on her date, when her head wasn't spinning, when her hands were not sweating, when there was blood in her brain and it was functioning as brains do, she realized that when Polly first arrived the day before, there was no way for Polly to have known that no one was home and that there wouldn't be a line of Dashwoods standing there to greet Maggie's "new friend," but she'd kissed her all the same. She didn't know what it all meant, so she did the only thing that made sense to her; she called Gran. She didn't even look at the clock because it was an emergency.

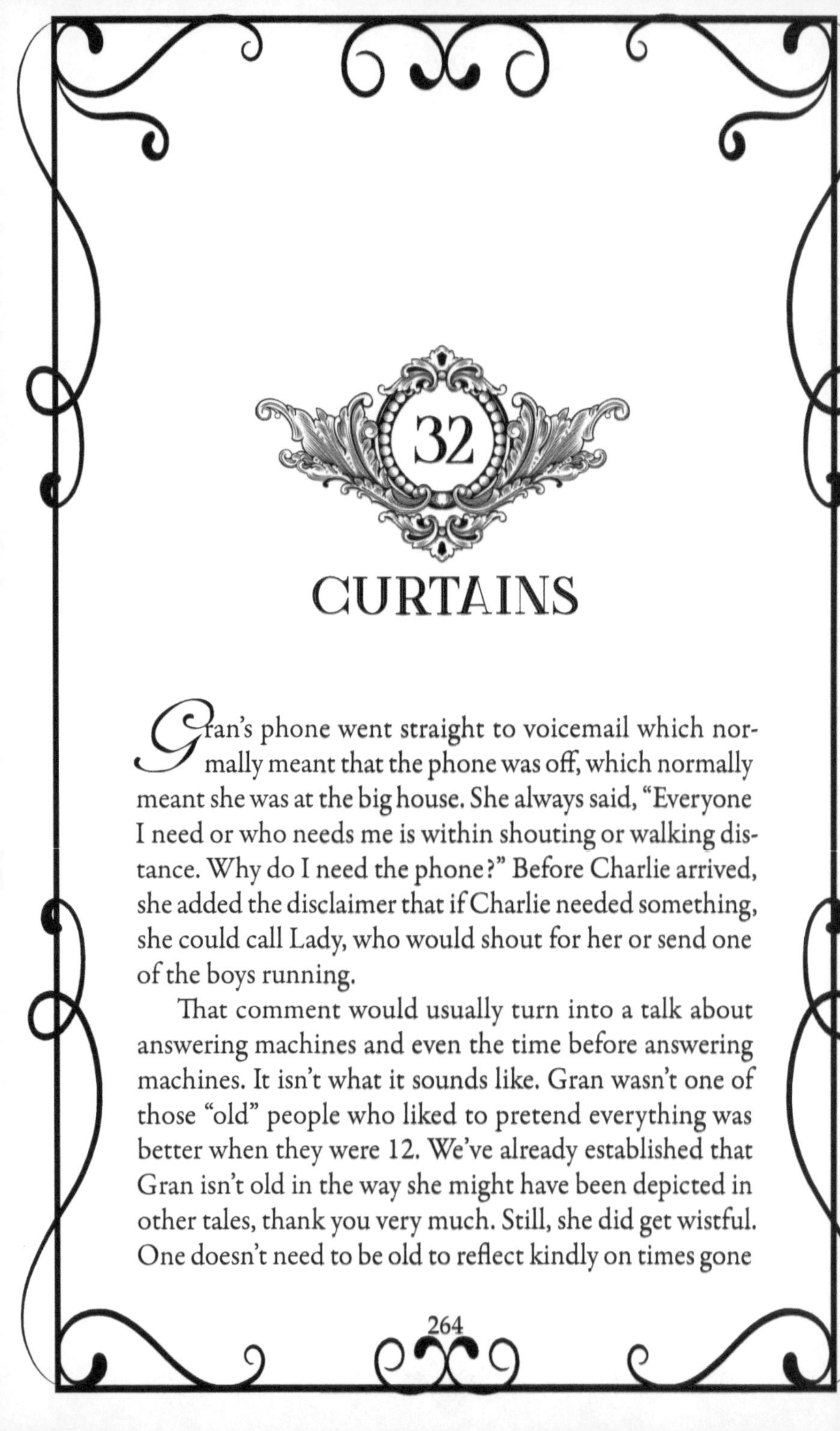

32

CURTAINS

Gran's phone went straight to voicemail which normally meant that the phone was off, which normally meant she was at the big house. She always said, "Everyone I need or who needs me is within shouting or walking distance. Why do I need the phone?" Before Charlie arrived, she added the disclaimer that if Charlie needed something, she could call Lady, who would shout for her or send one of the boys running.

That comment would usually turn into a talk about answering machines and even the time before answering machines. It isn't what it sounds like. Gran wasn't one of those "old" people who liked to pretend everything was better when they were 12. We've already established that Gran isn't old in the way she might have been depicted in other tales, thank you very much. Still, she did get wistful. One doesn't need to be old to reflect kindly on times gone by. Sometimes people long for last week when things were not so complicated. She knew that there was a give and take. She could see her daughter who lived across the ocean on a device that fit in her pocket. Still, she did miss being disconnected from everything and everyone, so she took advantage of it whenever she could.

Maggie wrote "BIG HOUSE" next to her name and schedule for the day on the whiteboard. She even drew a little picture of a big house, which she assumed rightly would go uncommented upon later, but it made her happy to do it and that is why we make art anyway. She slipped into her boots and clomped her way up there, hoping to catch Gran before the Quartet woke up and she had to do battle.

She headed straight for the kitchen, for she knew that if Gran were up, she'd be there having her morning coffee and reading the paper. She and Middy both still preferred to read the paper in its dead tree form and since they could use the paper for all kinds of things around Barton Park, they didn't feel terrible about the dead trees. She tiptoed down the hall just in case there was an ambush waiting, but as it so happened, Tractor Boy had actually slept over at a friend's house, leaving the Tractor Trio to stay up late in the playroom having their own sleepover, which consisted of tent construction and junk food. They were, at that moment, all asleep on the floor curled up around Middy, who had pulled tent duty and ended up joining the fracas.

She pushed the kitchen door open to see Anne Steele sitting at the table with one of Lady's old-timey teapots sitting on the tea mat, steaming and seeping. She was reading something on her tablet. She had her orange hair pulled up into a high ponytail, drawing even more attention to her elf ears. She looked up when she heard the door open. They made eye contact for a second, neither of them sure if it was okay to speak first. Anne's severe expression changed to that of genuine surprise and pleasure to see it was Maggie. She patted the chair next to her.

Maggie nodded and held up one finger. She went over to the counter to start the coffee and to throw some toast in the toaster. She turned, held up the bread, and raised her eyebrows at Anne in the way that people who don't speak sign language make up new signs for things when they are trying to be quiet.

Anne nodded and mouthed, "Yes, please." The kitchen was so far away from any of the living quarters that they could have shouted through megaphones, but they made some silent pact, and they were clearly determined to see it through until they sat together.

Maggie got to making the toast. She got out the butter and a collection of jams and brought them over to the table with two knives. She went back, pulled out the coffee pot with her right hand, and slid her cup under the stream in one practiced movement. It was a trick Middy showed her; she didn't do it perfectly, but the drips were negligible. The toast was ready, and she put it on one plate that she'd stacked up on the other and carried that in one hand and her coffee in the other. Finally situated, with all the things she needed to break her fast and her short vow of silence, Maggie sat down next to Anne and said, "Morning."

Anne poured herself some tea from the pot and lifted it to clink mugs. "A toast over toast."

Maggie clinked. "Cheers." She took a sip. She started to put butter on her toast. "Funny that you're drinking tea, I'm drinking coffee. Who needs stereotypes, right?"

"Who needs them indeed," Anne said with a laugh. "Although, some stereotypes exist for a reason, don't they?"

Maggie had a mouth full of toast, so she made a face that was supposed to infer she wanted Anne to go on with her point.

"Well, I know that I look like an elf, and I am tall and strong and when I tried archery during a summer camp, I was, according to the instructor, a natural. You're a tomboy, who's all rough and tumble with the boys, you get dirty most days at work, and you're gay. Sometimes, you know, things just..."

Maggie's throat closed around the toast that was going down. She pounded on her chest and coughed. Her eyes teared up as they do when one is choking. She took too big of a drink of her hot coffee, as she hadn't bothered to bring over any water or juice. It did the trick to open her throat up and push the food down, but it gave her mouth not quite a scald but a quick burn that made her hang her tongue out to cool it off.

Anne sat, stock still, not sure what to do. She was never good in a crisis. She felt if she just held still and didn't get in the way, the issue would eventually resolve itself or someone would come to the rescue. That is, by the way, terrible advice, but in this case, and quite often in Anne's life, it worked out just fine as most things do come to resolution without much interference from outside help.

Once it was clear that Maggie could breathe and her tongue was back where it belonged and the tears cleared her eyes, she looked at Anne, who at that point still was thinking the toast just went down the wrong pipe as it does sometimes. Maggie couldn't figure out what to ask. A million questions ran through her head and crashed into each other on their way to her mouth. Most of them started with either "why" or "how." Whether it was the power of the alphabet or that "how" is easier to form with a burned mouth, Maggie asked, "How?"

"How...?" Anne asked back, leaving room for a follow-up, but quickly playing back the incident realized that Maggie hadn't just been a poor eater. "Oh, dear." She covered her mouth with her hand. "Oh, Maggie. I'm..." She knew that sorry wasn't the word, but it was the word she had. "I'm sorry. I just thought..."

"You thought what?" Maggie raced through every action she'd ever taken in front of Anne Steele that would have tipped her off. Then she raced through every action she'd taken since that day with Juliet, whom, as is the way with young people who think they found the most important person in their life only to discover much later that the person was just an important person in a roster of important people, she hadn't thought about for months and months.

"Well, I wondered, you know because of the Tomboy stuff, and the action movies, and the martial arts, and the stuff with the boys and the dirt and all, but I know better than to believe in stereotypes, and so I didn't say anything, but yesterday, when I went down to The Cottage to..."

"You went to The Cottage yesterday!?" She leaned forward, her hands in claws on the tabletop.

Anne didn't want to be part of this conversation any longer, but since there was nothing for it, as Maggie was clearly agitated and upset, and there was no one else to diffuse the situation, she lowered her voice to a whisper, thinking that would emulate calmness. "Yes, well, um, Middy called you when you didn't show up for dinner. He knew you'd not gone to the show, and that you had, um," she paused to think of the best word that wouldn't freak Maggie out, "company, and he wanted to make sure you knew it was okay to invite her up for dinner too. When you didn't answer his calls or his texts, he just wanted someone to go check on you. I wanted to get away from Lucy and Robbie, so I volunteered."

Maggie's eyes widened as her brain figured out what time that was and where she was around that time. The tears welled. She dropped her head into her hands. "The curtains," she muttered as she wiped her leaking face.

Anne, remembering the kindness Maggie showed her on the first day they met, reached out and rubbed her back. "Yeah, the curtains were open, and so I walked by and saw you and that girl, um... well, you know. So, I just came back up and told Middy you were 'just fine.' He didn't push for more information, and I didn't give any, but you know, I just figured that the curtains were open and all, who does that out in the open if they don't care if people know, so I figured that everyone must know, so I thought the joke about the stereotypes..."

Maggie sat back up straight. Anne's hand plunked down on top of Maggie's half-eaten toast. Maggie put her hand over the top of hers and squeezed. "You didn't, um... say anything at all? Like to anyone?"

"Well, not to Middy or the boys, or Gran..."

"Gran already knows. Gran knew before I told her."

"Okay, but not them, because you know, I figured they already knew, but..."

"Lucy!" Maggie said her name like it was a curse.

At that moment, the door opened and she walked in as though being summoned. "That's me! I'm Lucy." She spun around like she'd been introduced on a catwalk.

Maggie jumped up from her seat. The tear streaks on her face and puffy eyes made her look slightly unhinged, which, to be fair, she was. "Listen... Lucy..." Robbie followed just a few steps behind her and seeing her twirling around, he grabbed her hand and danced around the kitchen to a song only they could hear. Maggie, eyebrows up, turned at looked at Anne who, understanding completely what the eyebrows were asking, grimaced and nodded. Maggie groaned. She muttered some curses that would make Marianne blush. She tried to get herself under control. She held up both hands, trying to get the two of them to stop dancing. They twirled and whirled right past her stop sign. "OI!" she shouted. "STOP!" She heard the tone of her own voice. She took a breath. "Please. Stop. Just for one second. I really, really need to talk to you."

They stood, frozen, mid-twirl, and looked at her. Neither was mad. Neither of them was really capable of being mad. They were confused for sure. They didn't like shouting and didn't know why this child, out of whom they'd heard a total of 30 words in all the time they'd known her, would be shouting at them.

"I need to say..."

The door burst open again, and Tractor Lad came running in. "BABY!!! Baby!!" He didn't mean that there was something wrong with Tractor Baby, although for one heart-freezing moment, Maggie thought that is what he meant. She had to focus on his face to realize that it was joyous. Charlie was in labor. All of this would have to wait.

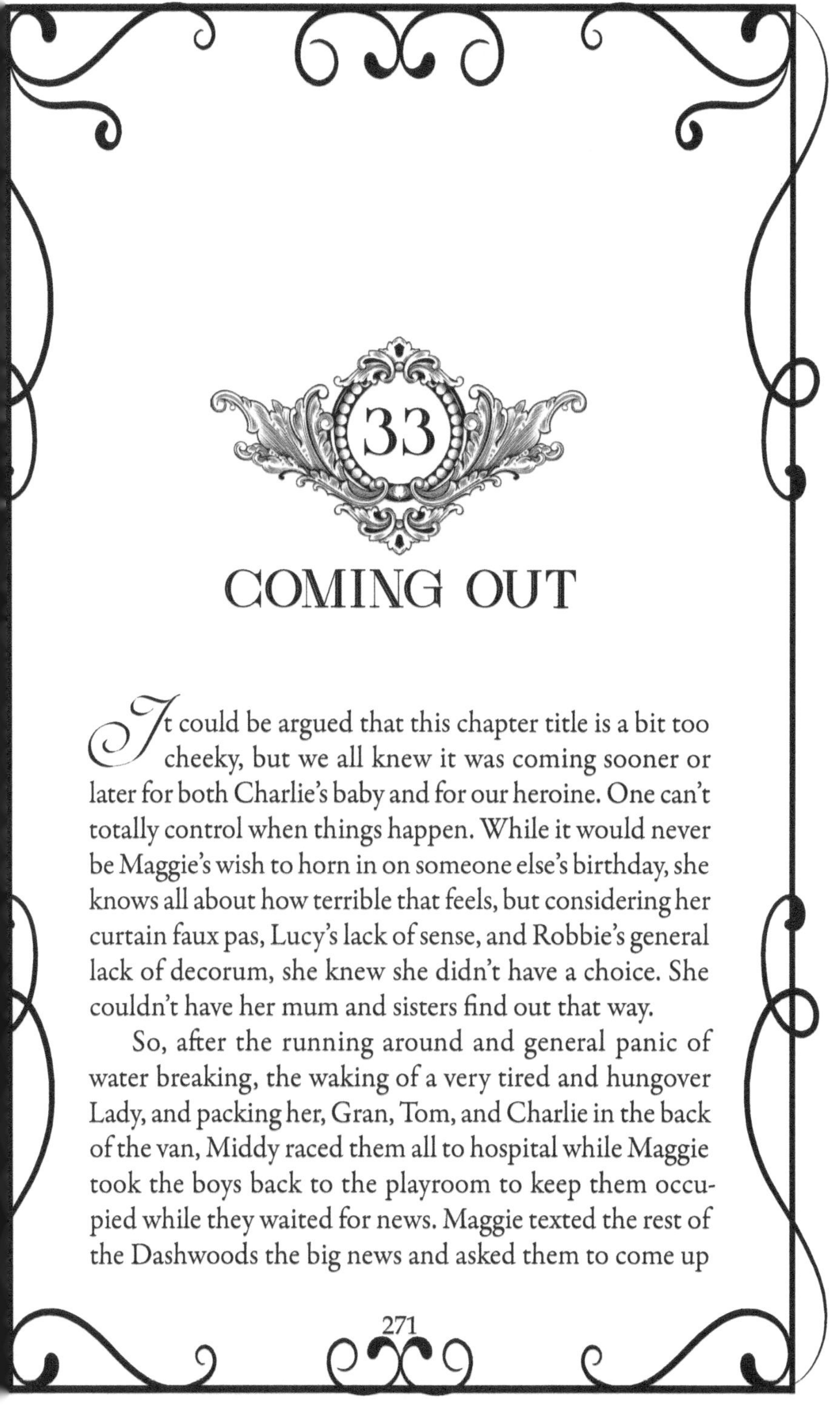

33

COMING OUT

*I*t could be argued that this chapter title is a bit too cheeky, but we all knew it was coming sooner or later for both Charlie's baby and for our heroine. One can't totally control when things happen. While it would never be Maggie's wish to horn in on someone else's birthday, she knows all about how terrible that feels, but considering her curtain faux pas, Lucy's lack of sense, and Robbie's general lack of decorum, she knew she didn't have a choice. She couldn't have her mum and sisters find out that way.

So, after the running around and general panic of water breaking, the waking of a very tired and hungover Lady, and packing her, Gran, Tom, and Charlie in the back of the van, Middy raced them all to hospital while Maggie took the boys back to the playroom to keep them occupied while they waited for news. Maggie texted the rest of the Dashwoods the big news and asked them to come up to the big house so they could all wait together and take turns keeping the boys, who were all pretty excited about a new cousin, occupied. The Quartet wished for a girl. We can all extrapolate the influence of Maggie on that overall decision as much as we'd like. None of them would ever confirm this, and once they found out later that day that it was a boy whose birth name was Jamie after his grandfather, they ignored those previous wishes and christened him Tractor Baby Jr. before he was even home and envisioned all the roughhousing they could imagine, which was quite a bit as we know.

Anne did manage to get Lucy and Robbie out of the picture to give Maggie some time to do what she knew she needed to do. Anne told them that she wanted to have flowers delivered to the hospital, but she was very specific about what she wanted so she only trusted Lucy to follow her directions to the letter and only trusted Robbie to deliver them. That, she hoped, would buy Maggie at least two hours for which Maggie was appreciative.

Maggie had just finished off Tractor Boy Jr. with a nifty spin and thrust that got him right in the heart when Sam walked into the playroom. "You need to let them win sometimes."

"They win all the time, don't cha lads?" Maggie said in her best pirate voice.

There was a lot of talking and whooping and retelling of excellent fighting skills all at once. "So much for dead men telling no tales." Sam laughed as she said it.

"Yeah, these are the chattiest bunch of corpses ever." Maggie patted Tractor Baby on his backside with the flat of her sword. He giggled and wriggled and came over with his arms up indicating he wanted a hug and/or call a truce.

Maggie picked him up and hugged him tight. He wrapped his legs around her back and buried his head in her neck.

Of the four members of the Tractor Quartet, he was the one who didn't have an inkling of life before Maggie. He was toddling around and just out of diapers when she arrived. As adults, the 10-year age gap would disappear, and they would stay very good friends; he always thought of and often spoke about her as his big sister. The first time he says it will actually happen during one of the upcoming school years, so it won't show up, as the montages are just not that detailed, and thus, it might be good to mention it here. She was picking him up from school and she had the van windows down and he was sitting on a wall with some pals waiting for his ride, as kids do, as we've seen Maggie do. She pulled up and shouted "OI" at him. When the pals asked who that was, he said, "Maggie, my big sister." She shed all the tears.

"Right, well boys, can you all head down to the kitchen? Elinor and Marianne have been making waffles. Who wants…"

Tractor Baby let go of Maggie and dropped to his feet like a ninja whose only mission was to get waffles. They were heading for the door, making double the noise that three boys should make. Maggie and Sam turned to watch them go, both smiling and feeling different kinds of love for those boys. They represented different levels of joy for each of them.

Maggie set about picking up the swords and the remnants of the tent that Middy hadn't had time to clean up what with the abrupt exit. "How was the show?" she asked her mum, who joined the clean-up.

"Oh, it was delightful! Lady can really let loose when she isn't in boss mode."

"But she still was *a boss,* right?"

Sam laughed. "100 percent. Edward even danced a little, which was both adorable, terrible, and hilarious."

"They're a perfect fit."

"They really are. I think Elinor and Marianne both found someone who fits them just right."

Luckily, Maggie's face was turned away so Sam couldn't see the face she made at the thought of Willoughby being a perfect fit for anyone but the man in the mirror. "You didn't say what kind of time you had, Mum." Maggie deftly changed the subject.

"I was happy that everyone else was happy. I may have had a few too many overpriced cocktails. Lady had to drive us home. Paloma Faith was divine."

Maggie let the image of Faith wearing a glittery hip-hugging dress fill her up. She could hear her smoky voice growling out the lyrics. "She's something."

"You would've loved it." Sam tossed a pillow on the couch. "Right, so how was your little play date yesterday?" Sam asked in a joking way, thinking she was being funny and clever, which to be fair, would have been pretty funny in different circumstances. Humor is subjective of course.

Maggie, knowing she was on a clock, heard the ticking and tocking in her head and saw the open window her mother had given her, so she jumped out of it. She stepped in front of Sam so she couldn't look away from her. She wanted to see her face. She put her feet flat on the floor and squared her shoulders. "It was a regular date, Mum, and it was exceptional. I'm queer. I like girls. I kissed one yesterday. It was my first kiss. I like boys too, but I've not kissed one. Anne saw us through the window and told Lucy, who told Robbie, so I wanted you to hear it from me, not them." She felt the tears come again. She bit her lip to try to keep the tears at bay, but we know by now that Maggie has little control over that part of her body. Her tears have a mind of their own. She watched her mum's face absorb the information.

Sam's joking brain was still in control, and her mum brain had to elbow its way back into control. She plastered a smile on her face. She knew enough to know that a frown was wrong. She didn't feel like frowning, but she didn't feel like smiling either. She felt like a shocked umm feels when it comes out of one's mouth, so she said, "Umm."

We all know fake smiles when we see them. It is worse when we know the person because we've seen their real smile. We know all the reasons why someone would use a fake smile and rarely, unless playing poker or posing for a school photo, is the fake smile acceptable. When one says the most important thing one will ever say, a frown would be better than a fake smile. At least a frown is real. We don't only frown when sad. We frown when we are confused, or when we think, or when we are told some big thing right after cracking a joke. Frowns can be explained. Fake smiles are harder to reconcile.

Maggie knew her mum's fake smiles well, and she didn't care for them at all. They didn't play poker, and Sam always looked genuinely pleased in her school photos. She fake smiled when speaking to Sissy or about Sissy or anything Sissy or John Dashwood-related when in public. She didn't want to make her mother feel the way that Sissy made her feel, so she needed to address it head-on. She wiped her face with the back of her hand and released her quivering lips from her teeth. She looked down so that maybe it would be better not to see Sam's reaction. "Mum, you're making the 'Sissy face.' Is it that bad? I mean, I know it's not what you want or what anyone wants, but…"

"No!" Sam said loudly. "Oh, Maggie. You are not Sissy. I just… I'm just…" She paused. "Can we sit?" She sat down on the edge of the couch, hoping that it wasn't a command but an invitation.

Maggie sat down next to her and wiped her cheeks again. She looked up at her mum who was now looking down at her fingers that she'd intertwined with each other. She was shaking her head. There was a conversation going on in Sam's head that Maggie would've given all of her chicken suit bonus to hear. She was normally quite good at sitting quietly, but that clock sound was banging away in her head, or it was her heart rattling her brain around inside her skull. Either way, she needed it to be quiet, so she opened her mouth to speak at just the same moment that Sam finally nodded at whatever the voice in her head was saying. Maggie closed her mouth shut with a teeth-rattling clang.

Sam looked up at her youngest daughter and said the three words that she thought were the right words to say in the moment. Parents don't always get it right. There are some pretty terrible parents out there. Some parents just don't have it in them to be parents. The aforementioned Sissy for example. She is just bad.

Other parents are as perfect as whichever TV parents we can conjure up. Remember that one episode where that TV mom said the perfect thing? That was incredible, wasn't it? Wow. We all wish she was our mom.

Parents are people and people have flaws. Sam is one such parent. Is it true that she gave Marianne a pass on things? Yes. Is it true that she treated Elinor like a sister and not a daughter by the time Maggie was born? Yes. Was that good for either of their relationships? Maybe; maybe not. Is it true that she thought the three words Maggie would want to hear upon coming out to her were the best words? Yes. Of course, she thought that. The words were true. They were words that reflected how she felt about it. They were the words that she thought her youngest and most reclusive child would wish to hear.

She said, "I don't care."

Now, Dear Reader, we can read those words, and they can echo around in our heads and we can feel all sorts of ways about Sam Dashwood. We can hear them as "I don't care what you think. None of this queer nonsense in my house." Or we could hear them as "I don't care, but other people will so maybe only kiss boys in public." Or we could hear, "I don't care as long as you are happy. Nothing matters but that. I love you thank you for telling me." Or we could hear "I have no opinion on this in any way shape or form. This is like telling me you also like chocolate or sunshine or joy. This is just a thing that is. I don't care because it isn't important. I don't care because you are you, and that is all that matters to me." It could be that Sam meant any of these, save for the first one. We all know she didn't mean that, and we likely can guess she didn't mean the second one, but supporting Kacey Musgrave's right to kiss boys or girls was different. Kacey wasn't her daughter. It was abstract. That was up to Kacey's mother to decide about how she felt about all of that regarding her daughter.

We don't know for certain which of these things or any number of other versions of these three words she meant.

We do know that Maggie Dashwood heard, "I don't care." Full stop. She felt a cold hand reach into her chest and crush her heart a little, and she realized that she wasn't crying anymore. She heard the next words that Sam said and that made her interpretation of "I don't care" move from wet to dry cement in a second.

Sam asked, "What will we tell your sisters?" She thought she said, "When will we tell your sisters?" but she said "What." Was it a Freudian slip? We don't know. To decide, we will play the rest of the conversation out here as well.

"What?" Maggie asked incredulously for she heard exactly what Sam said.

"When will we tell your sisters?" Sam asked, saying "when" not "what" because it was what she thought she said the first time. She followed up with, "Do you want me to go get them now? Do you want them at the same time? Do you want me here with you?"

Maggie still heard what she heard, which was the thing Sam said the first time. She also heard what she said the second time. "Yes, please. Yes, on all." She nodded, the hand let go, and she expected the tears to come gushing, but they didn't. Something shifted, and it found a way to dry up her tears in a way that no other kind of growing up could.

She and Sam never, ever talked about it. Sam never knew that she said "what" instead of "when." Later that night, when she and Lady talked about it while having bourbon over ice, she thought she did really great job, all things considered. They both agreed it was terrible that

Maggie was pushed out of the closet like that, and they talked about the moments in the past two years when they both suspected she was gay but didn't dwell on it as they didn't care either way. They both spent plenty of time tomboying around as kids. They had to admit they never thought she was bi. Even still, thinking something and knowing something is different. Besides, most people don't think about bisexuality at all until they are faced with it directly. It's the nature of the binary world that was constructed by the patriarchy all those eons ago.

Back in the playroom, Sam reached into her pocket and pulled out her phone. She reached out with her other hand and placed it on Maggie's knee. She squeezed it in a way that was meant to be reassuring. She wasn't sure if the lack of tears meant something or not, so she made another decision not to hug her youngest child, who seemed to be holding it together really well, and she did not want to throw that off by putting too much contact into the mix. She sent out a missive to her elder children, telling them that she needed them in the playroom right away, but they needed to leave the boys downstairs, so if Gran wasn't there, they were to find her first. Sam was an excellent one-hand texter in the way that Gen Xers who learned how to text using alphanumeric buttons on flip phones are.

They sat in uncomfortable silence. Maggie wanted to bounce her leg up and down, but her mum was holding it in place. It felt like a crowded psychologist's waiting room. Everyone there will soon be spilling their guts, but in that moment, they can only breathe shallowly and look down, wondering what the other people are thinking and have to say.

Elinor and Marianne came in sooner than expected. Sam squeezed her knee again.

Elinor said, "Gran was in the kitchen. Is everything okay?"

Marianne said, "What's so important? Make it quick. I'm expecting Willoughby."

"Girls. Your sister has something to tell you," Sam said. There are some children for whom the talking is almost always done on their behalf as though they can't be given the floor without permission first. Maggie was such a child.

Elinor, reading the room, sat down next to Maggie and put her hand on her other knee. Marianne was looking at her phone, scrolling through social media, trying to stalk Willoughby who was not actually on his way over regardless of Marianne's expectations. More on that soon.

Maggie cleared her throat to get Marianne to look up. She didn't. Sam squeezed. Maggie pushed ahead. "Well..." She licked her lips and coughed. She didn't remember swallowing sand, but it seemed to be the case. She didn't have the chance to think about it when she told Sam and she'd spent the past five minutes that felt like 500 eons waiting for her sisters. She almost wished it had been one of them who peeked through the window. She didn't really wish it, mind; she just almost wished it.

Marianne made a huffy sound that Maggie knew meant "hurry up" with two words that constituted seven letters total crammed in between.

"Right," Maggie replied to the unsaid demand. "I'm queer. Like, not odd, but I guess I am that too, but not because of this, but like I'm queer, like bisexual. I like girls and boys and um..."

"How do you know?" Marianne interrupted, making it about her while seemingly making it about Maggie.

"Um?" Maggie asked. She turned her head sideways the way babies and dogs do. "What?" she asked for the second time in ten minutes, even though she heard everything clearly.

"How. Do. You. Know?"

"Know what?" Maggie would have jumped up, but her mother pinned one leg down and her eldest sister held down the other. Stopping a fight was apparently more important than speaking up.

"That you are bi or whatever. I mean, you're just gay, right? I mean, we've all thought it at one time or another. It's not a big deal. I know lots of gay girls and boys. I'm in the *theatre* after all. Queers are everywhere. I'm sure I'll have to kiss a girl for a role at some point. No one cares anymore. No. One. Cares. Can we go now?"

The question was for Sam, but it was Maggie who answered, "No." She wasn't answering the "can we go" question at all, of course. She was responding to the first question. She wanted to explain that no, she wasn't just gay. She knew in the way that she knew she wanted to draw and in the way that Marianne knew she wanted to act and in the way that Elinor wanted to be a librarian. She knew in the way that she loved her mum and the boys and Gran and even her sisters, who didn't always seem to love her back, or at least like her. She knew in the way she knew that she needed air and her heart beat in her chest. Saying she was "just gay" felt like putting shoes on the wrong feet or a jumper on backward. Sure, it did the thing it was "supposed to do," but it wasn't quite right. She wanted to say all of that after she made her declaration of "no."

We know, Dear Reader, what Maggie actually meant. It could be that Sam knew. We can be almost sure that Elinor knew. If Gran had been there, she would have known with certainty, but Marianne didn't. She didn't hear the "no" in the way it was intended. She, of course, heard it as a challenge to her leaving the room. She'd never really been told no by anyone, let alone her kid sister. It will not come as a surprise that she didn't like it one bit. "Whatever," she said to the no that she heard the wrong way, and she turned and walked out, head down, refreshing the page to see if Willoughby magically appeared.

The remaining Dashwoods watched her go. One was shocked into silence, one was not surprised at all but disappointed, and one who shouldn't have been shocked, surprised, or disappointed was somehow all three. We can leave off here. While Elinor had different words to say that were somewhat better, she never contradicted her sister or her mother regarding the three words. Let that simmer on a burner. Be it back or front burner is irrelevant really. Something simmering is still hot and can still boil over if the heat is increased.

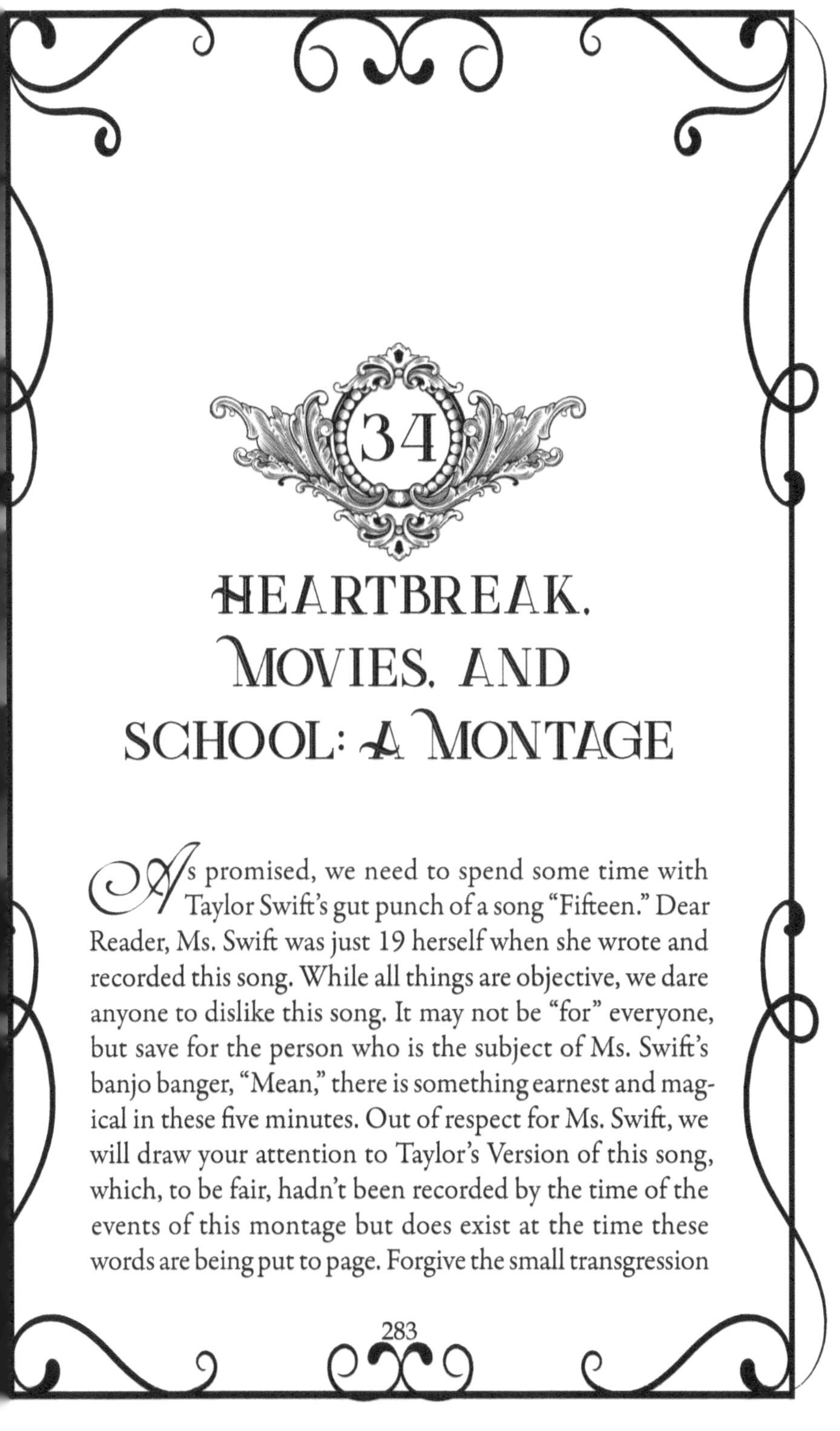

34

HEARTBREAK, MOVIES, AND SCHOOL: A MONTAGE

As promised, we need to spend some time with Taylor Swift's gut punch of a song "Fifteen." Dear Reader, Ms. Swift was just 19 herself when she wrote and recorded this song. While all things are objective, we dare anyone to dislike this song. It may not be "for" everyone, but save for the person who is the subject of Ms. Swift's banjo banger, "Mean," there is something earnest and magical in these five minutes. Out of respect for Ms. Swift, we will draw your attention to Taylor's Version of this song, which, to be fair, hadn't been recorded by the time of the events of this montage but does exist at the time these words are being put to page. Forgive the small transgression in continuity. We felt it best to just acknowledge it here instead of risking you all pulling out your pocket computers and looking up dates. There is just something even more wistful and powerful about the fully formed adult Swift soul coughing, and it fits our scene even better.

Imagine as this song plays, we see Maggie and Polly spending the final week of summer together on the Vespa, in Barton Park, at the museum in Exeter. The song plays over the entire rom-com montage that will melt the coldest of hearts as they look so happy. Young love is hard to hate when it is pure and good.

However, as the song continues and swells, and Swift relives all the pain and angst and admits that she and Abigail both cried in a way that only a woman who'd once been a fifteen-year-old girl can, we see Polly's image on Maggie's phone making hand gestures and doing all the talking. Maggie, tears streaming, silently taking the terrible news, knowing that fighting won't get her anywhere or anything. Polly always had all the power. She always knew what she was doing. It was young, but it obviously wasn't love. The song fades out with the lyrics and advice from Ms. Swift. Maggie, dressed in her uniform, tie, jacket, and black boots, entering not her first as in the song, but her final year of secondary school, takes a deep breath and walks through the doors.

At that moment, a toy piano jangle, this time from our old friends and constant reminder of things lost, The Kinks. "Just Friends" plays as Maggie sits at her art desk drawing as all the faces from previous years approach her and walk away as she keeps her head down. The outfits change, the seasons change, and Maggie stays hunched over her desk, with them but apart from them.

The haunting song continues with the cynical lyrics as we see Maggie at school, at Barton Park, and in the village with a variety of cuts while she leans forward, bent at the waist, hands behind her back, wooden doll style, eyes closed, lips slightly puckered, ready to kiss boys and girls of various sizes and shapes. Each new cut is a new person leaning forward in the same pose as Maggie. They could be stone statues carved from her heart. Their lips, inches apart, never quite reach. We never see any of them actually kiss because it isn't that kind of book, but we are meant to understand that if her mum doesn't care, and her sisters don't care, and Polly doesn't care, then why would Maggie care? When the song comes to its sob-inducing end, we see Maggie, alone at lunch, tie pulled down Sinatra-style, wearing her sadness like a noose.

Maggie's final year at public school in the village was not the best year of her life. Not to dwell on it, but to drive the nail home, fade in on Maggie at her desk again, practicing for and taking her GCSEs while The Police's "So Lonely" bangs over the top. Four minutes and change of reggae, pop, and punk all smashed together in a cry for help that no one hears is the perfect vehicle for this final time we will see Maggie with these people in this location. We watch her inflict more damage than she needed to on her sparring partners in martial arts class. She felt so low, so low, low, low indeed.

Of course, not everything was clouds and frowns; she did still work weekends, she did have holidays, and most importantly, she and Gran spent time together. Even though Charlie and the new baby did decide to stay for a while, they spoke every day. They still shared their own table at dinner, and at least once a month, they went to

Gran's house for movie night. Queue up the new wave kings Duran Duran's "Girls on Film." As Maggie grew into young adulthood, Gran started a project of rewatches. She wanted to see what Maggie noticed the second or third time through a film. Picture them on the couch, at the table, in the chairs, in the garden, in Gran's room in the big house, walking through Barton Park after hours. When you envision them watching, talking, smiling, hands waving in animation never in anger, as each one of them tries to make a point to the other, make sure you see what it really is; love and friendship.

While they did watch a lot of movies, they didn't only watch movies. They did projects like building a crib for Tractor Baby Jr. They went to different school plays, martial arts demonstrations for her and the older two boys started to study at her dojo as well, musical performances, as well as other spectacular things that four school-aged boys do. Gran took Maggie to some art shows she was covering in London. It was Maggie's first time there without her mum and while Gran was both her gran and not her gran, she still felt like being there without Sam was a step into adulthood that she needed.

They talked about more than just movies. Maggie told her everything about the misery at school and the kissing and the emptiness it brought and how she just thought if she just kept kissing frogs, one of them would be royalty of some kind, even if it was just a Baronet. While Gran did her best to convince Maggie that things would be okay eventually, there was nothing for it. Sometimes hormones win out over solid advice and unconditional love. However, when there is unconditional love, hormonal teenage overreactions are easily forgiven and forgotten.

Before we find out what scores Maggie got on her GCSEs and where she decides to go to college, it would be good to check in on everyone else as is the way with a montage and a big cast. Hawai'ian singer/songwriter Jack Johnson's college friend Zach Gill is quite the magnificent musician himself. He came to prominence when he joined Jack's band on the 2005 *In Between Dreams* album. His first full solo album, *Stuff*, featured some excellent tunes. The best one for this current montage is the first track off that album. It is simply titled "Family." It starts with an infectious piano riff that carries the whole song. Johnson himself can be heard singing backup and playing drums on this track. It's a good, good song. Let us let it play while we catch up with everyone.

We already know that Charlie and TBJ stayed behind at Barton Park, but Tom returned to America to get some in-person things worked out. As a contracts lawyer, he could actually be anywhere in the world and do his work with a secured computer, which he didn't bring with him. His employer insisted he pick up the secured computer in person and go through all the rigmarole with the IT woman in person. She didn't insist on it because she was in IT and knew she could ship it to the UK no problem, but their boss was the type of person who thought that the internet was a bunch of invisible tubes in the sky, so Tom headed home for a short period. He comes back into the story, but he might as well be furniture. He really doesn't have much to do regarding Maggie.

Lucy and Robbie will factor in more soon. Suffice it to say, Lucy decided to stay behind too. Since her "job" was to attend to Charlie, she felt it granted her a free pass to stay. Dr. Steele, who would have liked to see his daughter again at some point, had already come to grips with the fact that she was going to go where her heart took her, and he was relieved when he found out that she would be staying with Charlie at Barton Park and not moving in with Robbie in Scotland.

Anne Steele decided to apply for a year abroad. "Decided" is the wrong word here. Her father "strongly suggested" that she "consider it" while Lucy was still here. Yes, he felt fine that she was there "helping" Charlie, but he still wanted there to be some kind of guiding hand on hers. He trusted Anne with the task, and to be fair, she had nothing waiting for her back in the American Southwest and so she agreed she would try. Dr. Steele always wanted this for his children and Anne's small liberal arts college loved it when students did things like this. The marketing team immediately started making new brochures about the Exeter Exchange as they would call it, and so, after a few emails and transatlantic phone calls, she was enrolled in the University of Exeter for a year. While faculty may take the summer off, the staff and administrators do not.

Anne was a bright spot in the school year for Maggie. As seemingly overlooked siblings, they felt a kinship. Anne was very studious and spent a lot of time on campus, but when they were both around after dinner or on the weekends or when Maggie was in the big house watching the boys or up late after a movie night with Gran but unable to sleep, they talked about all things as friends do. It would be during one of these many talks that Anne first told Maggie about their hometown of Mansfield and the small, midwestern college where her dad worked. Much more on that to come.

Edward continued with his graduate degree while Elinor entered her final year at university. They were happier than most people their age. Not everyone finds their soulmates at such a young age. Not everyone even believes in soul mates. Of course, some people do and for those who believe in soul mates, they all agreed that Elinor Dashwood had found hers. Their thing and Robbie and Lucy's thing are linked and it will, unfortunately for the Dashwoods, bring Sissy back into the fold. Batton down the hatches, Dear Reader.

Marianne was, as everyone expected, amazing at the next level. The family was collectively surprised when she decided to go to university instead of jumping at one of the opportunities her success that summer on stage would have afforded her. We could speculate why she made the choices she made, but everyone already knows that her reason was an American with a last name for a first name who had wandering eyes, and Marianne feared that should she be too far away, it would have been more than just his eyes that went wandering.

Sam's marketing genius combined with Maggie's semi-permanent role inside the animal costumes made Barton Park's online and in-person traffic continue to swell. Lady hired more workers. Middy bought another tractor to accommodate the number of trailer rides and school trips. It was, for almost everyone not named Maggie Dashwood of The Cottage on Barton Park, a pretty great year.

For Maggie, the best news came when she found, based on her scores, that she would be able to attend an arts college. The village on the other side of Barton Park, thankfully, had a public college that had an art and design path. While technically there was plenty of money for Maggie to attend an independent college should that be something she wished, it was never discussed. Likely, it was never discussed because, unlike Marianne, she didn't demand anything from anyone. Public college was fine with her if it had the program she wanted and so it was that Maggie Dashwood smiled for the one and only time at school that year on the day she opened the brown envelope that showed her that her dreams were still alive and well. That was a lot of songs, but it was a long montage. We said 15 was a big year. We are well past the point of no return now. Let's finish strong.

35

SIXTEENTH BIRTHDAY

On the day before Maggie's birthday, Sam made the executive decision that the "celebration of life for Henry Dashwood" tradition would continue, but it would not wait until evening. They would do it after dinner in the big house. The whiskey was purchased, the glasses were cleaned, and the new guests were invited. It was set. There was no conversation as to why, but Maggie felt it inside her. Of course, Marianne, oblivious to anything that wasn't called Willoughby or Marianne, complained quite loudly to anyone and everyone.

The decision was made via furtive glances and active eyebrows that Elinor would handle it. The conversation between the eldest Dashwoods shall not be reproduced here, but Marianne was not on her best behavior nor was she even on good behavior during dinner and the toast, but she wasn't outwardly hostile and so it was taken as a win. It didn't help that Willoughby was suddenly busy just moments before dinner was served. Regardless of what any of the family members thought of him, which we know was varied, everyone agreed that having him there meant that Marianne was much more pleasant, and her potty mouth was kept to a whisper, usually in his ear, which caused often uproarious laughter from them both. Also, regardless of what any members of the family thought of him, it was universally agreed upon that he had a good, infectious laugh. Maggie had thoughts about why she only shared with Gran. Something about being an adult who didn't even have the problems of an infant.

The dinner was quite pleasant. Those who knew Henry told stories to those who didn't. Charlie and Anne asked a lot of thoughtful and sensitive questions. Lucy asked several insensitive questions that caused Anne to once again stare at the floor, her default escape mechanism. Sam found ways to talk around Lucy's impertinent questions while protecting her feelings. It was a bit of magic that everyone in the know, that is everyone but Lucy and Robbie and the Tractor Quintet, although, one could argue that Tractor Boy, who was almost a teenager himself, was aware that something was up, silently acknowledged and admired. After dinner, the whiskey was poured for everyone save the original Quartet who had fizzy drink and the toast was made. While 12 was the age for drinking in Sam and Middy's family, Lady had a teenage policy and so that was that for Tractor Boy. He would have to wait. Tears were shed and hugs were doled out freely. Everyone had a second whiskey and moved to one of the many sitting rooms to sip and talk and dry tears. Around 11 that evening, the party broke up with promises to reconvene the next day for a birthday feast with cake and ice cream, and the Dashwoods and Edward, having received a myriad of hugs and back pats and kisses on the cheek, left for The Cottage.

Thus, on the night before Maggie's sixteenth birthday, she was once again alone in her attic room. Matt Nathanson's album, *The Last of the Great Pretenders*, played. She timed the start of the album in just a way that the song she wanted to play would roll around as close to midnight as it could so she didn't feel the need to watch the clock. She lay on her bed, hands on her stomach. She contemplated the past year and cried for the heartbreak and the stupid, empty, emotionless kisses that she'd wasted on so many frogs that she knew, deep down, would never be royalty.

She didn't know that Polly would break her heart. She knew, objectively, that she didn't love Polly, but that she loved what Polly saw when she looked at her. Maggie loved Polly's laugh and being the cause of the laugh. She loved talking until their phones died and holding hands while walking through the museum. She understood right then that it wasn't really the kissing that she loved. That was nice and it was true that some of the frogs were interesting enough that she gave them a second or third go before she gave them the "just friends" speech and moved on to the next one, but what she really loved about Polly and not the frogs was the companionship. For a short time, someone saw her, even if it didn't mean the same thing to Polly that it meant to her, there was no way the laughs were empty, stupid, or emotionless. They were real. The laughs, the smiles, the joy was everything.

It was decided just then, with her eyes closed, that Maggie Dashwood knew what her heart wanted. She would never again waste a kiss on lips that were not attached to a mouth that made her laugh first. While it wasn't a foolproof plan, it was something that served her well for the rest of her life. There were some frogs because we all know that some frogs in real life, unlike horses, can actually change colors. While some of those frogs hurt her feelings and made her cry, she always held fast to the fact that at least for a moment, she laughed and maybe one good laugh was worth a few tears, which, let's face it, she was going to shed anyway. She fell asleep smiling, hands not just on her stomach but wrapped around herself in a hug, and so she missed midnight and hearing "Birthday Girl," but when she woke in the middle of the night, needing to use the loo, she didn't even mind, so maybe we won't be too upset about it either.

When she woke up properly, showered, shaved, and dressed, she came down to the smell of coffee and the sound of spoons clanging against the side of bowls. She expected to see Sam in the kitchen, but instead, she found Edward.

"Ummm," she said before she could help herself. She didn't mean it as an accusation, but of course, the shock couldn't be denied so she just leaned into it. "Hi?"

Edward turned around, not a speck of flour on him even though he didn't have on an apron. "Happy Birthday! I thought I'd make waffles."

"I won't say no to birthday waffles." She smiled at him and wasn't sure what to do next, so she stood rooted in place. They'd always gotten along, but she never really thought that he considered her as her own person. She was just a side effect of his love for Elinor, one that he would willingly put up with, as many people do when they become entangled with someone's family. You can love the person, but you deal with the racist uncle.

"Excellent!" Edward said without seeming to notice the awkwardness that maybe wasn't there at all. "Sit." He pointed at her chair with the spoon he'd been using to mix the batter. "I'll pour you some coffee."

"I could get used to this," she said as she took the steaming cup from him.

"Well, I hope you will. I secretly love birthdays. Sissy has always been, well…" He paused to think about what to say.

Maggie finished, "Sissy."

Edward nodded. "Right. You know."

"Unfortunately."

"Yes, well, she's always been like that and so anything that was remotely celebratory or joyous was not something she supported. She wanted all holidays and birthdays to be done at a tea room or out to a meal at a place with a dress code. Mum was fine with it. Sissy is an alpha, you know. Fun just isn't her thing. You know as well. It's like she's allergic to it or something. Like making a mess or laughing aloud is somehow beneath a family of our station. I'm not sure exactly." He opened the waffle maker and poured the batter in.

"I'd like to point out that you have not made a mess here so, and I don't ever want to defend my sister-in-law, but something worked. When I bake, I look like I've crawled out of the sack of flour. I sneeze it out for weeks. Like, how does it get up there?" She pointed to her nose.

Edward sat in Elinor's chair. He laughed. "That's a good point. I don't like things to be messy. It's why Brandon is such a good roommate. His military mum really trained him to be tidy."

Maggie looked over her shoulder to make sure Marianne wasn't there. She whispered, "How is Brandon? I've missed him. Since I started working at the front of the house instead of the back, I don't see him much."

"He's doing well. Getting ready for his final year at Uni. Thinking big thoughts. Deciding what to do next. I'll tell him you asked after him. He'll like that." He got up and opened the waffle maker and placed it on a cookie sheet and popped it in the oven to stay warm. He poured the next waffle into the maker, closed it, and sat back down. "Maybe next time you come into town with Elinor, you could come over and have dinner with us."

She wanted to say yes emphatically, but she knew Elinor got a pass for spending time with him as he was Edward's roommate. She didn't go out of her way to see him. She thought about what Marianne would say and knew it wouldn't be good. Still, she did want to see him. She hemmed and hawed.

Before she could decide what to say, the answer came in the form of a voice from behind her. "Waffles! Oh Edward, that is so nice. What's the occasion?"

Edward looked up at Marianne genuinely perplexed and unsure how to answer. He opened his mouth, looked to Maggie, who was shaking her head, and back to Marianne, who was pouring herself some coffee.

"I'd love to," Maggie heard herself say.

"Love to what?" Marianne asked.

"Edward asked me to do something with him and Elinor next time I'm in town." It wasn't a total lie, and thus she only felt a small pinch of guilt in her heart.

"Something boring, I'm sure," Marianne said as she headed out of the kitchen with her coffee as though she might be able to catch boringness. "Call me when the waffles are ready." She fished her phone out of the pocket in her sleeping clothes, and she padded out to the parlor.

Edward got up and repeated the waffle routine. Hot one in the oven. Batter in the waffle maker. He clearly wanted to ask Maggie a lot of questions, but he also knew that sound traveled around the ground floor of The Cottage quite easily. He poured Maggie another cup of coffee. They made eye contact. He hoped he conveyed the desire for her to say more. She just shook her head. He nodded.

They chatted about other things like what Maggie hoped to do on her birthday and what she thought of her college and how his grad program was going and things that brothers and sisters discuss, for that was how they felt about each other at that moment, until Sam and Elinor woke up and came into the kitchen. Earplugs can't stop the smell of waffles.

He pulled out one of the folding chairs they kept in the front closet for the rare occasions when there was an extra body at the small table in the kitchen. He poked his head into the parlor and told Marianne that the waffles were done. Edward Ferrars was not a shouter, even when shouting was requested.

Sam insisted on cleaning the kitchen so she sent everyone away with no real lunch plans. Since the big birthday celebration was later that night, the day was sort of a free-for-all. Maggie thanked Edward again. They exchanged their first hug. It wasn't awkward at all. She grabbed a full cup of coffee, a tin of pencils, and a new pad and headed out to the front porch to sit on the porch and see what struck her fancy. She considered heading out into the woods and up a tree, but Marianne had stomped off toward Willoughby's place, and she didn't want to come upon them in the woods.

She decided to draw without any earbuds. She wanted to get a sense of the natural sounds. She wanted to try to incorporate some of that into her work. She'd been reading a lot in preparation for college and the idea of making the whole picture come to life kept coming up. She wanted to notice if the wind was making a sound and find a way to represent that in the sketch by having the trees bend. If there was a bird somewhere or some other critters making noise, she wanted them to be represented with some little nugget, a nest, or a bump in the lawn or smudge in the sky. She was trying to figure out how to share what was hidden with other people who saw her work.

She thought to do a POV image, so she looked straight up the drive and got a sense of what she could see out of her periphery. She started sketching and lost herself in the exercise. She had a good basic sketch and started with the shading. She was hunched over, hair dangling over her pad, which she had to admit was her favorite part; it blocked the light, true, but it gave her a little protective bubble. She was rubbing some of the shading with her fingers when she heard the buzzing sound that she knew all too well.

She looked up and didn't see anything, but the clear sound of a Vespa was echoing around the valley where The Cottage stood. She always heard Tori before she saw her. She knew that Polly knew when her birthday was, but it had been months since they'd even liked an image of each other's on social media. Maggie wondered if she thought that with the summer came the opportunity for another summer fling. She was not interested even if Polly made her laugh. Not with her. Fool her twice and all of that.

She closed her pad and set it on the porch. She didn't think Polly deserved to see her work and ask about it and distract her from her firm resolution of not being a fool. She put her pencils away. The buzzing got closer. The sun glinted off the front windscreen. She argued with herself about standing and crossing her arms or sitting calmly and being aloof. She opted for sitting. She leaned against the stair post and tried her best to look as disinterested in a way that Marianne would.

The Vespa came into focus, and it was not orange but a royal purple. Maggie felt a pang of sadness that something happened to Tori or that Polly had decided to paint her. Regardless of how she felt about Polly, Tori didn't deserve to be harmed in that way. The rider came into focus, and Maggie realized it wasn't Polly at all. She was on her feet and running.

Gran, not wanting to zig when Maggie zagged, stopped the Vespa where it was and cut the engine, letting Maggie come to her. She put down the kickstand. She didn't have time to get the helmet off when Maggie was upon her, wrapping her in a lung-collapsing hug. Gran was not frail in any way, but she wasn't a 16-year-old tree climber with a job on a farm and in martial arts training. Art critics use different muscles to work.

They hugged and rocked back and forth, and Maggie said all kinds of words of thanks in jumbled order that didn't really make any sense. Eventually, Maggie let go, and Gran took off the matching purple helmet. She caught her breath and said, "Happy Birthday, my sweet girl."

"Thankyouthankyouthankyouthankyou!" she shrieked. "GRAN! I can't believe it. I don't even know. Wow. Does Mum know? We should tell her. I need a permit and ohmygosh." Her brain stopped working and words quit coming. She pulled Gran back into another hug that lasted for a while.

Eventually, Sam broke it up. She did know, of course. Gran would never buy someone else's child a gift like this without the approval of her parent. She wasn't a fool. She wanted to be in this child's life for the rest of hers. She had plans for her. Giving gifts that could be considered dangerous was a surefire way to be kicked out of the picture forever. Once Maggie was accepted into the college that was in the opposite direction of the boys' school, Gran hatched this scheme. She bought the Vespa, and Sam would pay for the license, the compulsory basic training course, insurance, and everything that came with it on that side of things for the first year. After that, Maggie would take over those payments herself.

Of course, they both knew that Maggie already had driven Polly's Vespa and so, they let her drive it around Barton Park until she completed all the CBT requirements. They'd already booked into training in Exeter and set up a schedule with Lady to accommodate it. She would stay with Gran for two days in town. They signed her up for the one-day training. It was a long day, so they still wanted her to have a day off on each side of it. The idea was, once she passed, she could drive the Vespa home herself.

Gran spent the day at The Cottage while Maggie drove in circles all around the property. She went up to the big house and gave each of the Quartet a ride. They wore the helmet and she promised to go as slow as a walk. While

Vespas have excellent petrol economy, they do not have infinite tanks, and so, Maggie had to push her birthday present back to The Cottage once she hit empty. She was hot, sweaty, and happy when she finally reached the top of the hill by the back of the big house. She put it in neutral and rolled down the hill going faster than she actually had all day.

She ended up skipping lunch due to her two-wheeled excursions around Barton Park so, after the second shower of the day, she shoved a few granola bars in her mouth as she looked at her closet. She decided to dress up to celebrate her big day. She put on a crisp white shirt and a purple tartan skirt with a matching purple tie, slipped into a black blazer, and headed to the big house.

The dinner was delightful, and the cake was perfect. It turned out everyone was in on the present. Lady and Middy bought her a purple leather jacket. The boys gave her purple driving gloves. Elinor and Edward gave her a purple storage case/mini-trunk for the back. Charlie, Lucy, Anne, and Robbie have her purple sunglasses, hair ties, and other accoutrements that would be helpful while riding a moped. Maggie cried and cried tears of joy even though Marianne only gave her a purple key chain. It has been years since she cried because she was happy, and she had to admit she liked it very much.

After the three youngest boys were tucked in bed, the family moved to the viewing room where Maggie requested that they watch a movie to celebrate her Vespa. She'd thought of the name as soon as she realized that it was Gran and that it was a gift for her. All the gifts only certified that she named it correctly. They popped corn and settled in. Maggie hit play. The Warner Brothers logo appeared. The ambient noise of the crowd cheering played over the top of it. The announcer's voice said, "Ladies and Gentlemen; The Revolution." The keyboards played, and Prince's silhouette appeared on the screen. "Dearly beloved..." he said, and the movie began in earnest. Even Marianne had a good time, though she would never admit it.

36

BIG ANNOUNCEMENTS

The first week after her birthday was incredibly blissful. For a whole week, she felt seen by everyone in her family. Even she and Marianne had no beef. They didn't hug or hold hands or skip through a glade or roll down a hill while giggling, but for seven consecutive days, Marianne threw nary a barb. Maggie finished her CBT training. She passed her written tests, and she drove Prince home on her own. There is little that can compare to the freedom and joy one feels when one takes one's first solo trip. It was just a ride home from Gran's place. She did it countless times as a passenger, but that day, for that short time, she could go anywhere and do anything. In fact, she drove right by Barton Park and took the country road into the next village to scope out her new college. It was a waste of petrol, but what teenager with wheels and spending money hasn't wasted petrol? She felt one with her pocket of the universe, and she was incredibly grateful.

One week after her birthday, she came down with a sketchpad and tin of pencils with plans for coffee and shading to once again find Edward in the kitchen making breakfast. The coffee was brewed, and instead of a spoon, she could hear a whisk banging against the side of a bowl. "Umm. Hi?" She really needed to work on her game when it came to surprise entrances. Granted, "Umm. Hi?" was the right thing to say. Most people who find their sister's partner cooking breakfast in the family kitchen would say the exact same thing.

"Morning, Maggie!" he said without turning to face her. "Coffee's done."

She set her pad and pencils on the table, poured herself a cup, and tried to peek over his shoulder to see what he was making, but he was taller. He threw his elbows out wide to block her view. She set her cup down at her seat and went to the front closet to get a folding chair to give him, and whatever he was doing, some privacy. She came back in, and he was closing up the oven, smiling a big, cheesy, cat-like but genuine smile at her.

"Curiouser and Curiouser," she said through a smirk and a raised eyebrow.

He laughed. "Yes, we're all mad here." He took the chair from her, unfolded it, and moved Elinor's chair to the side to get his where he normally put it.

"Maybe we just need to get you your own chair? I guess that would mean we'd need one for Willoughby too, though." She shook her head at that. "Still, it'd be worth it for you to have your own place here. I mean, breakfast two weeks in a row is pretty huge. I know you have more than a drawer in Elinor's room; you have a few hangers in the closet as well. It seems like a no-brainer."

Edward smiled at that. "Wow, and that was before you even tasted my quiche."

"Quiche, huh?" She made a face that was supposed to convey surprise and approval, but it was just a small frown and a head nod.

Thus, Edward asked confusedly, "You don't like quiche?"

"I'm all about that quiche, bout that quiche, no frittata," she sang and laughed at herself. "Well, that's a lie. I would totally crush a frittata too."

He was relieved. "I don't have the frittata skills yet. There is a balancing act. Stove to oven, and if you don't time it right, it is burnt or raw. There is a lot of watching and worrying, and after an hour, it could be a huge bust, and everyone is eating bran flakes. Quiche is much easier. Bake and sit and drink coffee."

"I would rather eat a raw frittata than bran flakes." She made a face he could easily understand. "Do we have bran flakes? Is that even a thing? Did you sneak in bran flakes?"

Edward held up both hands. "No, I swear. I didn't sneak them in."

Maggie pointed two fingers at her eyes and back at him. They both laughed and fell into an easy conversation. Elinor and Sam, lured from slumber by the smell of goodness, came in and joined the pre-breakfast chat. The conversation ranged from Prince, the Vespa and, by extension the artist, his final thesis for his master's degree, if he was going to go forward for his doctorate, where they thought Elinor would go to graduate school, what they thought of the last show Marianne did, what Maggie was working on at the moment, which of the costumes she preferred to wear when performing for the kids, what new marketing material Sam was going to make based on said performances and on and on.

When the second pot of coffee had finished brewing and the quiche was out and settling, Sam went to get Marianne. Waking her was always an adventure, and it often went better when she was roused by her loving mother than one of her sisters who were much less gentle and said exponentially fewer kind words depending on which sister it was and how their interactions with her had gone the day before.

By the time Sam and Marianne came into the kitchen, Edward had cut one of the quiches and had them on plates on the table. He knew Maggie wasn't joking about the destruction of a frittata. He'd seen the Dashwoods eat. He knew that one wasn't going to do the trick. He also poured them each a mimosa. None of the elder Dashwoods were unfamiliar with day drinking, but it was new for Maggie. She had to perform later that day in the pig suit, which was her least favorite. It had a big pig belly that was hard to control, and often times she felt the head and the body were going in opposite directions. She decided, regardless of how good her champagne and orange juice tasted, she was only going to have one, two tops.

Once all Dashwoods were seated, Edward stood back up with his glass in hand. He looked down at Elinor, who smiled and nodded at him. He held out his other hand, and she took it. He cleared his throat. "Sam, Marianne, Maggie." He looked at each of them as he said their names. "I want you to know that it has been the greatest honor of my life to get to know you over these years. I've always appreciated that you didn't hold Sissy against me."

"Or Robbie," Marianne chimed in in a tone which, through their Marianne to English translators, they understood to be a joke.

Edward laughed politely. "Yes, or Robbie." He cleared his throat again. "Anyway, I hope you all know I love Elinor so very much and that I consider you all my family."

Sam gasped when she realized what was happening. She put her hand to her mouth. "Sorry." She nodded at him as the tears started to flow. "Go on, but hurry." She wiped her face.

Edward nodded. "Right. Yes. Well. Elinor has done me the honor of accepting my marriage proposal! We wanted you all to be the first to know. She graciously agreed to let me do it this way." He squeezed her hand and gestured to the breakfast with his drink hand. "So, if you please, raise your glasses and celebrate with us."

Maggie, overcome with joy, joined her mum with tears of joy, the second time in a week she'd experienced those, whooped, and raised her glass. She couldn't think of a better couple in the history of the world.

"Huzzah!" Marianne joined in. She did think they were both boring and would go on to live boring lives and have boring children but also knew that there were hardly any perfectly paired people in the world and that Elinor and Edward would never become a divorce statistic. She'd never heard them fight. Their disagreements were always about plot points in books or over hidden meanings in movies, and thus, they were not even disagreements but reasonable, and, yes, often boring to the outsider, debates.

Sam was crying freely. "To Elinor and Edward," she said through the sniffles. "Welcome to the family, officially, but you've been a member for quite a while now. I hope you know that."

They clinked glasses and drank. Elinor set her glass down and stood up to get hugs from her mother and sisters who found something upon which they could finally agree. With cheeks wiped and racing hearts calmed, they sat back down to enjoy their magnificent breakfast and discuss wedding plans. They'd like to do it by the end of the summer at Barton Park if possible, maids of honor outfits for the two sisters who would be sharing the duties, Maggie could wear a tie if she wished, an admission that Brandon would serve as best man followed by a nod from Marianne who could read the room well enough to keep her thoughts to herself just then. Maggie definitely had a second mimosa. She reminded herself to hydrate later. No one wants to see a pig pass out during a children's birthday party.

After the successful party and after Maggie took a long, cold shower, and after she drank more water and ate a late lunch, she headed up to the big house to do battle before dinner. She and Lady agreed that on days she had to wear the costume, whenever the event was over, that was the end of her day, but she was paid for the full day. Due to Sam's ability to use the magic of the internet with SEO keywords and all the other stuff that no one understood, Maggie's parties were a big deal. People booked early and paid more. No one was losing any money by paying Maggie for a few extra hours of work she didn't do. There wasn't anyone clamoring to climb inside the costumes. On days she didn't wear the costume, she worked a full shift.

Because Tractor Boy and Tractor Boy Jr. started martial arts training, and because Maggie was not quite a black belt but was very good, the Quartet often wanted to do some Kung-Fu fighting, which was nothing like what they studied at all, and their sensei would be annoyed to find out that they called it that when they were not in the dojo, but Maggie was their primary babysitter, and she had introduced them to action movies full of terrible dialogue, baddies with paper-thin motivation, and lots and lots of Kung-Fu. Tractor Baby Jr., who was quickly approaching one and would be heading back to America at the end of the summer with his parents and Anne Steele, sat on the floor and made squawking noises.

Lady made some ground rules regarding Kung-Fu fights. No contact above the shoulders or between the waist and knees. No blows to the head had always been a loose rule for wrestling and during the summer of sword fighting, but for Kung-Fu, Lady was adamant. Three direct hits equaled a kill. Blocks on arms didn't count as hits. Everything needed to be done in slow motion at best and half-motion at worst. When fighting Maggie, it needed to be one at a time, which they were fine with as that is generally how it happened in the bad action movies. One hero took on one baddie, while 3-10 stood around them in a circle or at the end of the hall, or at the back of the airplane, or train car, or cargo truck until the hero soundly beat the one baddie and then another one came forward to get creamed. If Maggie did the special handshake with one of them, that member of the Quartet was her partner for that particular battle, and they could go back-to-back and take on all three of the rest at the same time.

She tried not to play favorites on that, but when she and Tractor Boy teamed up, the fight was over quickly. One adult-sized girl and one three-quarter-sized man were no match for three boys. When she was in a hurry, she gave the handshake. When she had nothing to do, she took them all on one at a time or she did the handshake with Tractor Baby, who was much more of a lover than a fighter, but he loved to be Maggie's partner so much that he gave it his all each time, even though they always lost.

They had three hours before dinner so when Maggie snuck into the playroom, ninja style, gave Tractor Boy Jr. the secret handshake she promised them that after the battle ended, she would take them all on rides on Prince. The terms were agreed upon and the battle commenced. Maggie and Tractor Boy Jr. took out Tractor Lad pretty quickly, but Tractor Baby fought dirty and went for the belly tickle. Maggie was down for the count, leaving the two who actually took classes to spar. The rules went out the window, and it was a pretty good match with the older boy winning, but only because they both ended up being forced to do battle while standing on one leg, *Karate Kid* style, due to some last-minute rule changes by Maggie.

When dinner came around, all of them were starving, happy, and tired. Maggie wanted to get them worn out so that after Elinor shared her big news that night, the adults and Maggie could have some celebration time without worrying about the boys being occupied. Exercise and fresh air are nature's sleeping pills.

It was good that she did it, although the evening didn't really go how any of them planned. Before dinner, Elinor got everyone's attention and asked them all to retire to one of the sitting rooms before they dispersed for the evening as she had a big announcement. They were all on summer time and so, save for Marianne, who was anxiously hoping to have a meet-up with Willoughby who had been "unexpectedly called away on family matters" for several weeks, none of them had a lot planned. Lucy and Robbie were not there for dinner but had sent a message saying they were on their way back and would most assuredly be there in time for the big announcement.

After dinner was done and the dishes were cleaned, folks milled about in the sitting room making small talk, killing time, and trying not to clock watch as they waited for Lucy and Robbie. They enjoyed each other's company and were happy to spend time together, but ultimately, waiting around for "something" to happen often made people fidgety. People can't be in a heightened state of awareness for too long.

Just as Edward pulled out his phone to call Robbie and find out where he was, they heard laughter and running footsteps coming down the hall. Lucy and Robbie appeared, she in a white dress, he in a suit. "We just got married!" she shouted as she launched her bouquet into the air. As luck, or irony, or whatever would have it, Elinor reached up and caught the flowers.

The doors were already open, so there was no door bursting, but years later, when Elinor told the story, she said, "Lucy burst through the door and stole my thunder." She tried not to be bitter, but for a planner like Elinor Dashwood, ruining her plans was the equivalent of throwing wine on a rare book. Well, she would be much more upset about the book thing. Still, she was pretty annoyed.

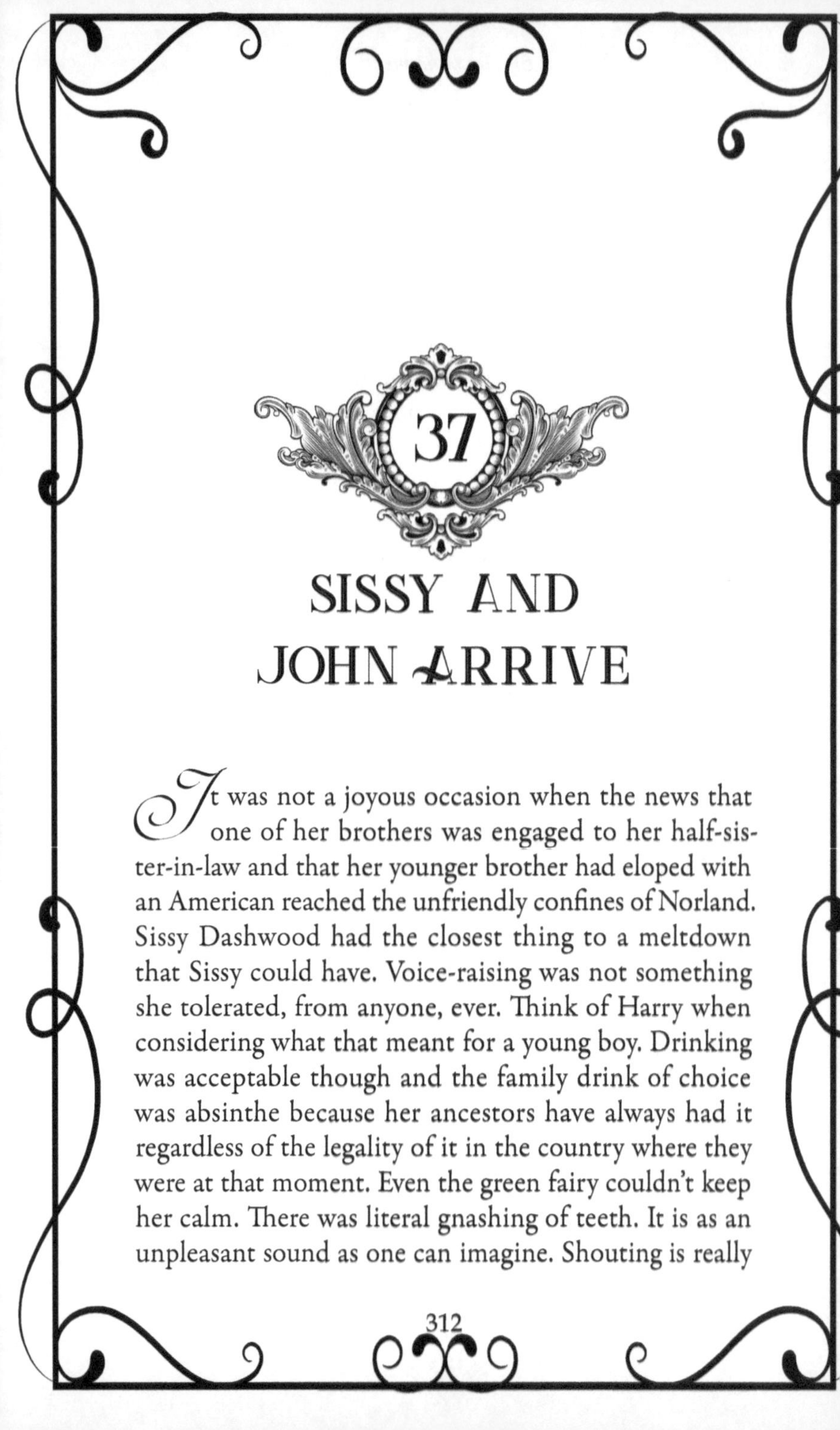

37

SISSY AND JOHN ARRIVE

It was not a joyous occasion when the news that one of her brothers was engaged to her half-sister-in-law and that her younger brother had eloped with an American reached the unfriendly confines of Norland. Sissy Dashwood had the closest thing to a meltdown that Sissy could have. Voice-raising was not something she tolerated, from anyone, ever. Think of Harry when considering what that meant for a young boy. Drinking was acceptable though and the family drink of choice was absinthe because her ancestors have always had it regardless of the legality of it in the country where they were at that moment. Even the green fairy couldn't keep her calm. There was literal gnashing of teeth. It is as an unpleasant sound as one can imagine. Shouting is really more dignified regardless of ancestry. People don't need to spend thousands of pounds on dental work to deal with shouting, do they?

Sissy unleashed the full power of her media empire, pretending that it was John's at all except in name is beneath us all, on Lucy Ferrars née Steele. She needed to find, if not a full skeleton, at least a buried femur. Unsurprisingly, a relatively silly person who was born in a small American Midwestern town and raised by a single professor has little to hide. The most embarrassing thing Sissy's minions could find on her were some ill-advised online makeup tutorials she made when she was just into makeup at age twelve. The rest of her social media platform consisted of liking makeup tutorials and sending on memes that the famous people she followed made or liked themselves.

Sissy did find it disconcerting that the majority of the cultural icons that Lucy followed were reality stars, influencers, and fabricated famous people. While it was uncultured and absurd to Sissy, there were literally billions of people who felt exactly the same way Lucy did. More people knew who the fifth most famous member of some show about angry rich people in Miami than knew who the afternoon anchor was for Sissy's TV network or who covered 10 Downing Street for any of her news outlets. Maybe those people knew something about getting attention in a way that Sissy never could.

Similarly, Anne Steele and Dr. Steele were boring nobodies. Anne was studying physics and comported herself well during her year in Exeter. She'd even been published as co-author of a paper. It was, apparently, quite an honor for a foreigner. The team included the paper in the dossier. Sissy found it unintelligible. She woke several people to have them explain it to her. The reasoning was sound, and one of the scientists said he wished he could have written that clearly at her age.

Dr. Steele seemed to only have an online presence in academic journals, on his college's website, and on a few professor-rating websites. He was a hard but fair grader who had bad fashion sense but seemed to genuinely care. The overwhelming majority of students at Mansfield College would either take him again or recommend him to a classmate. Sissy could respect that. Dedication was admirable even if it was teaching polynomials to undergrads in that godforsaken part of flyover country in the States. She did discover that he used to teach at an Ivy League school, and he purposefully moved his two daughters to Mansfield. While her team did a full inspection on the mother, they said there was nothing there, and optically, it wouldn't be worth it. None of them had the courage to say this directly to her face, but an anonymous sticky note on the front of the folder made it clear enough. Further investigating taught her that Mansfield College was considered elite by "People in the Know," which Sissy understood meant her wealthy and powerful consumers and investors. She could work with that.

By the time John woke up, Sissy had already run a story on the early morning radio show and a first-page story in section three running in the morning edition about her brother being married to the daughter of a professor of some renown who had managed to raise two daughters on his own while having taught at least one astronaut how to do maths. Regardless of what one thinks about space travel in general or if it is a good use of funds, be they private or public, almost everyone is in awe of people who strap themselves into metal tubes and rocket out of the atmosphere. While Dr. Steele wasn't an astronaut, he was responsible for one. It would've been better if he had raised one. Anne certainly had the potential.

By the time John woke Harry and had him fed, Sissy confirmed the family's reservation of a neighboring property to Barton Park. The young American who owned it was only too happy to extricate himself for the summer so that the Dashwoods could be there to supervise the upcoming wedding and continue to do damage control on the one that already transpired. What was it with all these Americans. Were they being invaded?

By the time Harry was cleaned and dressed, the belongings Sissy saw fit to take with them were packed and loaded into their SUV for a summer in the south. She had told which staff members needed to meet them at the rental address by that evening and which staff members needed to come stay at Norland and which staff needed to go close up the house in Scotland. So, without so much as a conversation, Harry Dashwood was on his way to get to know his aunties.

The courteous and decent thing to do when going to visit people is to call ahead and let them know you are coming. It is really just good manners. Sure, Maggie arrives at the big house without calling first, but it is sort of a standing invitation. They don't consider her to be a guest, and while she knows on a guttural level that the big house isn't her house, she still to this day calls it the big house and thinks of The Cottage in particular and Barton Park in general, not Norland, as home even though she was born in one and spent only a few years at the other, the big house feels like it is hers. She only ever knocked the one time.

She knows where all the secret hiding places are. She slept on several of the beds and most, if not all, the couches. Popping in up there isn't really popping in at all when one is considered family, and those who are considered family don't pop in or visit. They come over. They hang out. They are expected for dinner. They have their favorite mug, and they have food in the pantry that is just for them.

Blood and marriage can make families, it is true, but they don't always mean family. So it was that when Sissy showed up at the front door of The Cottage the next morning, the Dashwood ladies considered it an unwelcome pop-in. It is worth spending a bit of time on this moment even though we are long on story and short on space, but it was something that stuck with Maggie for the rest of her life. It went thusly.

Maggie was drinking coffee and having toast and jam, which was her jam and a joke she liked to say to only herself and Gran when she heard a rattling at the front door. It surely sounded like someone was trying to walk in. She looked at the clock. 7 on a Saturday morning in the summer. No one who would walk into The Cottage as if they lived there would be up at that hour. She knew everyone who lived there was sound asleep and would remain that way for some time. Willoughby had been missing in action lately, and he did walk in like he owned the place, which is why the door was locked. Marianne was mad at him, not mad enough to say anything, but mad enough to passive-aggressively lock the door that they never locked. So, while Maggie hoped he would try to walk in and smack his dumb, beautiful face against the door, she knew he wouldn't show up at this hour. Three or four in the morning was much more likely than seven in the morning.

Maggie was almost always up at this hour; she wasn't one of those teenagers who liked to sleep in. The light was good in the morning for shading at the kitchen table. She had a job that she took seriously regardless of what her costume proclaimed. She was at that time and would remain a morning person. It would end several relationships. One young man was suspicious of everything and thought she was up early to rifle through his things, as if she would. How dare he. One woman, much too old for her behavior, liked to stay out very late drinking and dancing. Not that Maggie minded such things; she just didn't want to do it every night. She found a place where the light was just right for shading at the kitchen table, and she had a job at an animation studio that she took very seriously even though she spent most of her days drawing talking ducks with the express purpose of making children laugh. To be fair, at one point both of them made Maggie laugh, so they were worthy. Some frogs are funny, but they are still frogs. Facts.

The rattling of the door knob happened one more time before the pounding started. If one shows up unannounced at someone else's home, there are two ways to announce one's arrival. One is to ring the bell and the other is to knock politely. Three or four knocks, raps really, with the front of one's knuckles or even a door knocker if one is hanging there, asking to be used, followed by an adequate waiting period of at least 20-30 seconds before knocking again. Trying to walk in as though one owns the place followed by a second attempt at illegal entry followed by a full side-of-the-fist pounding as though the dinosaurs have escaped the park is not an acceptable third way. Yet, that is just what happened.

Maggie, not wanting the noise to wake the rest of The Cottage, although there was little chance that even Sam's earplugs did the trick for this racket, pulled the door open to see who it could possibly be. She had just about convinced herself it could have been Lucy. She was strong enough to rattle the house with her fists and was silly enough to think that walking in unannounced would be socially acceptable. She turned the deadbolt and unlatched the chain, not taking chances that Willoughby had finagled himself a key, and pulled the door open only to be struck by the side of the angry fist of her half-sister-in-law, right in her third eye, as the Yogis might say.

Getting a fist in the forehead would have sent Sam tumbling, would have dropped Elinor where she stood, and would have most assuredly resulted in years of post-incident commentary if it happened to Marianne. For Maggie, who was a 16-year-old who climbed trees, jumped over fences, took martial arts, rode a Vespa when she needed to go far, which is the most core-centric mode of mechanical transportation, dressed in animal costumes and danced for hours, worked on tractors, fed animals, shoveled their excrement, moved bails of wire, straw, hay, or anything asked of her, lived on the top floor of her house which required more stairs in a day than most people walked in a week, watched more action movies that involved hand-to-hand combat than anyone she had ever known, and who had engaged in some sort of combat with four, hungry, growing wild boys almost every day for several years, a fist in the face from an angry TV executive and propagandist was merely a shock.

Her muscle memory took over. She absorbed the blow by lowering her center of gravity. She bent her knees and crouched down. She brought her right hand to her right shoulder. Her left was up by her left temple.

Sissy Dashwood was trying to regain her balance as the momentum of missing the door and connecting with Maggie left her wobbly. Her knees were locked, and her arms were swinging like someone who got off the merry-go-round after being on there for too long. She was looking down, trying to will her feet to find steady ground. Her focus was not on her half-sister-in-law as it should have been.

Maggie was coming forward, silently like the ninja she knew she was, core engaged, momentum going forward, with the full weight of her body into the punch. Most people want to punch in the face. When people watch a lot of action movies, they romanticize a punch in the face. They love the idea of leaving a black eye on the villain. They can imagine some blood trickling out of the side of someone's mouth with some teeth splayed out on the ground around the fallen body. Maggie, having followed the no-hitting-the-face rule for years, regardless of the fact that the Quartet didn't always follow it themselves, and who had all kinds of professional training, knew better. Face punching can often lead to broken hands. So, she focused on the center of mass in front of her. Her right fist connected squarely into Sissy's solar plexus, and within half a second, her left fist hit Sissy on the side of the ribs.

There was never a day in her life that Sissy could have withstood that 1-2 punch. If she had stood still, with padding on, feet firmly on the ground, legs bent, core engaged, she would have been sore for a few days. However, being off balance and moving forward into the blows meant that she would indeed be sore for weeks not just because the first punch knocked the wind out of her or that the follow-up bruised a rib, but because she collapsed onto her left side, moving with the momentum of the second punch and banged her face hard against the uncarpeted floor in the entryway of The Cottage. She still ended up with a bruised face and loose tooth without Maggie having to break her hand.

By the time Maggie's brain caught up with her body, she was stopping herself from dropping into a straddle over her fallen foe and pummeling her. John, who stood motionless on the porch watching the whole thing, also was catching up to the reality of what happened. He shrieked "Sissy!" as he dropped to his knees to check on his fallen spouse. Harry Dashwood, the person for whom Maggie had to leave her ancestral home, stood, mouth open, eyes wide in shock.

Maggie looked down at Sissy who was gasping for air so hard she was unable to wail. She gingerly touched her head where Sissy's fist struck her just moments before. It was tender and would swell if she didn't get some ice on it. She looked at her nephew who didn't appear to have relieved himself in his trousers, thankfully, "Heya, Harry. I'm your Auntie Maggie."

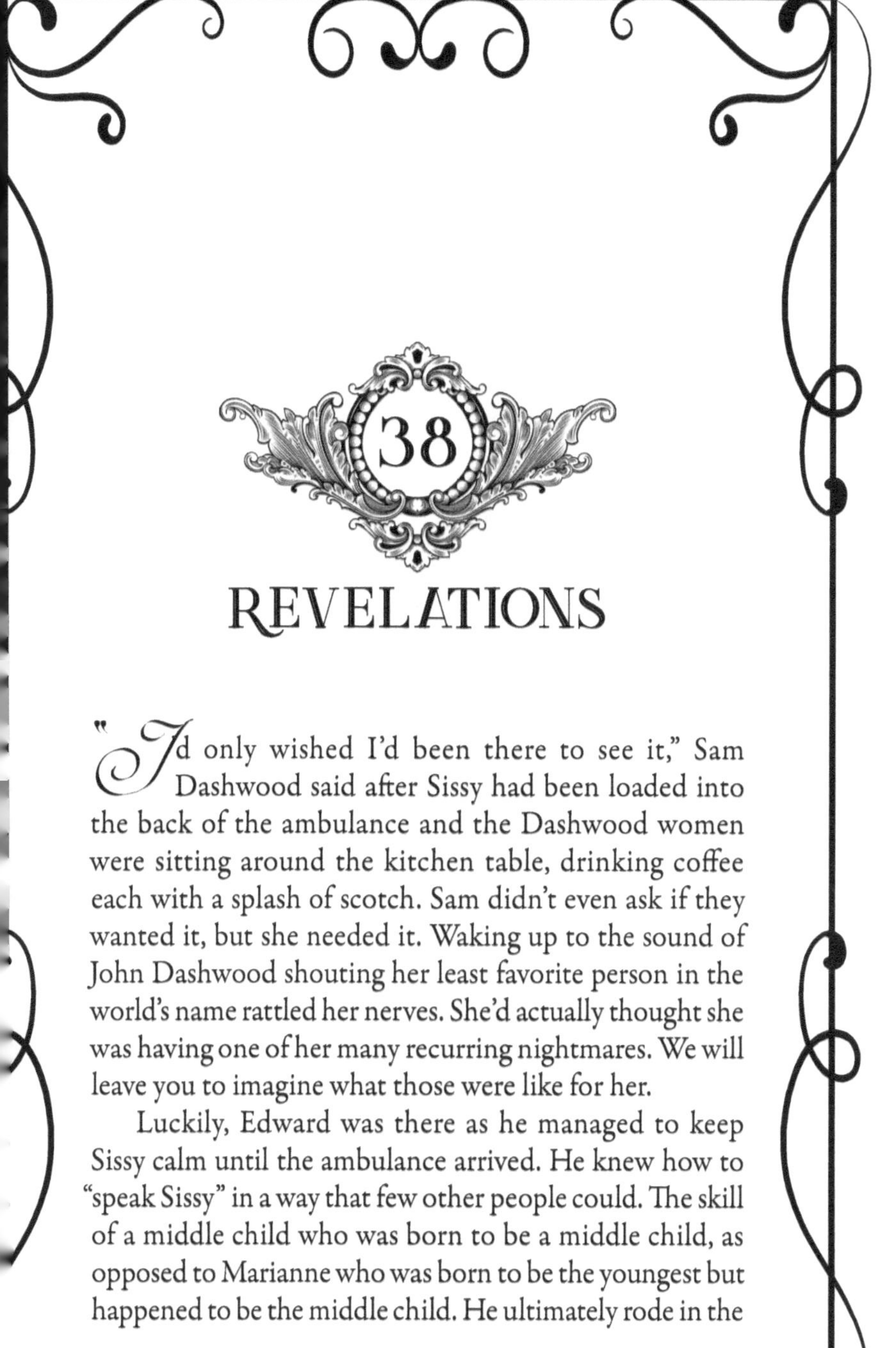

38

REVELATIONS

"I'd only wished I'd been there to see it," Sam Dashwood said after Sissy had been loaded into the back of the ambulance and the Dashwood women were sitting around the kitchen table, drinking coffee each with a splash of scotch. Sam didn't even ask if they wanted it, but she needed it. Waking up to the sound of John Dashwood shouting her least favorite person in the world's name rattled her nerves. She'd actually thought she was having one of her many recurring nightmares. We will leave you to imagine what those were like for her.

Luckily, Edward was there as he managed to keep Sissy calm until the ambulance arrived. He knew how to "speak Sissy" in a way that few other people could. The skill of a middle child who was born to be a middle child, as opposed to Marianne who was born to be the youngest but happened to be the middle child. He ultimately rode in the ambulance with her while John drove behind with Harry. While they all may have thought a trip to A&E wasn't necessary, except for having Harry, Sissy hadn't really experienced physical pain in her life before, and even then, she took all the drugs. For some children of Sissy's generation, a punch in the ribs and a face plant was just a Saturday. Sissy was not like anyone else.

"No, Mum, you wished it had been you to do it," Elinor said.

"Hmmm. Yeah. That's it," Sam said. "Still, not being able to do it, seeing Maggie do it would've been second best." She lifted her glass and toasted her youngest for the third time since she'd poured the scotch into the mugs.

Maggie clinked her mug with her mum's. "Salud." She still held the icepack on her head at Marianne's insistence. It wasn't that she cared so much about how Maggie was feeling, but she didn't want there to be any bruising or swelling in the wedding photos. The wedding was still weeks away, and the bruise would be on her head, Maggie reminded Marianne, who made pishing sounds that were supposed to explain everything.

Sam snorted. "To your health, baby girl. How's the noggin?"

"I've been hit harder by a sprinkling rain."

"Well, just the same, have Georgia check you out later."

Maggie nodded. Georgia was the Barton Park nurse. Lady knew it seemed like an extravagance to pay a person to sit in a medical tent all day, but Barton Park had never received a negative review online about someone being hurt and left to bleed out on the ground. Of course, no one had ever been hurt that extremely. Mostly Georgia gave out headache medicine or feminine hygiene products.

She covered up minor scrapes and removed enough splinters to build a new barn. There was a lot of getting out of the sun in the summer months and reminders to hydrate.

The conversation turned to why Sissy and John were even there in the first place and what that meant for the weeks leading up to the wedding. They all had their own theories about an 11th-hour legal injunction or a dramatic objection during the ceremony. Marianne, who really was an amazing actor and brilliant mimic, slipped into Sissy's muted Scottish accent, the one that she worked on to acknowledge she was Scottish but told people that she wasn't *that* Scottish. Marianne was working out a Shakespearean-level soliloquy about why she absolutely objected to the marriage. She even rolled out an imaginary scroll. It was epic, and they all laughed and laughed while secretly, or not so secretly, worried that the nail was being struck directly on the head.

Watching her sister take center stage, where she belonged, made Maggie sit with the fact that Sam had been quite attentive and even called her "baby girl" which was not something she'd heard very often. She watched her mum watch Marianne, and she saw the joy she felt watching her be amazing. She looked at Elinor, who was much more resistant to Marianne's charms, but she wasn't immune. No one could be totally immune; even Maggie admitted that Marianne could charm a rampaging bull and turn it into Ferdinand with ease. Still, she saw it for what it was just then, having accidentally taken some of the glow away from her for a few minutes. It wasn't just that Marianne sucked all the air out of every room she was in, she did and always would; it was that her innate desire to be the center of attention at all times was the perfect emotional storm for the ship of Sam.

Sam lived vicariously through those she loved. While it was true that she passed on her love of music to Maggie, she never said, "Listen to this." She didn't, as far as Maggie knew, have a favorite band or album or song. She surely loved *Rumours* best as did most fans of the Buckingham/Nicks Fleetwood Mac era, but she never declared it. It was possible that she thought *Tusk* was a masterpiece, and there is an argument one can make for that case. It was possible that she thought the Peter Green years were somehow superior. It was not possible though that she felt that the 1995 *Time* record made without either Buckingham or Nicks was very good. There is not having an agenda, and there is reality. Let's be real.

She wasn't a parent who forced her kids to like anything she liked. Her husband had a secret stash of bad action films that she most assuredly watched with him, and yet, until that box of magic was opened, the girls didn't know. As was the case for the majority of Dashwood men, they let their wives, for as of this writing they all married women, lead them. They were happily led. They were malleable, and they wanted their person to set the agenda. The men were generational Betas. Sam didn't push her agenda; therefore, Henry didn't push his. The one thing he ever asked any of his children to do ended up with us at this stage of this story. A Beta asking a Beta to do something ends up with a family living on a farm in the south of England. Not always, of course, but in this particular instance, that is what happened. Different Betas asked other Betas favors all throughout history, and it can be reported here that less than five percent of those favors came to fruition exactly as they were posed.

If asked what their mum's favorite anything was, the only thing the kids could agree on would be that Marianne was her favorite. Anyone who knew Sam would have answered that exact thing, save Gran who knew everything all the time. Maggie was sure when she shared her big revelation with Gran later, she would say, "I know, dear." They all thought it because that is what Marianne wanted everyone to think and so everyone thought it. She got all the attention because she demanded it, and she had two sisters who asked for very little. Trite phrases are what they are, lazy, overused, and perhaps meaningless, but the reality is that the squeaky wheel does get the grease just like the noisy door hinge gets the WD-40. Lubricants abound on squeaky things because they are squeaking and loud and obnoxious and possibly broken. Attention is demanded and it is given. It doesn't mean the person likes that thing best. That person just does what needs to be done for that thing at that moment.

Maggie realized that morning over coffee with scotch and a bruised forehead and sudden violence that Marianne wasn't Sam's favorite. She didn't have a favorite kid. She liked them all. She didn't have a favorite song. She liked them all. She wanted everyone to be happy, and she wanted to give everyone what they needed to *be* happy. We are sure there are lots of theories as to why Sam is this way, and we can neither confirm nor deny any of them.

Maggie always knew her mother was human; she was never a kid who believed her mum could stop bullets or lift cars, but she didn't know, until right then, watching her mum watch her sister make fun of her arch nemesis, that she knew she was a person. Personhood and humanity are often used as stand-ins for each other, but they are not remotely the same thing, and they shouldn't be. From that day forward, Maggie Dashwood was extremely aware of the difference between the two and never again used the words interchangeably.

Not all revelations are flashes of aha moments that change one's life. For our heroine, that day at breakfast was the first in many revelatory steps about her mother. It wouldn't be until she was much, much older that she finally understood what it was that Sam meant when she said, "I don't care." Upon first reading those three words, some among us might have understood it immediately. We do have the privilege of objectivity from our great heights, and while we love our heroine and we understand her, we are not her. Some things just must be learned when the time is the time. That doesn't mean it is when the time is right; it is just the time. Maggie's time for that will be later. We won't see it happen in these pages, but we wanted to share that it absolutely shall happen. Unsurprisingly, Maggie will cry and cry. She won't be alone, so fear not; someone's arms will be there to hug her and let her cry. It won't be Gran. Sorry. She will call her shortly afterward though, and Gran will say, "I know, dear." Maggie will cry again while laughing. Later, she will call Sam. They will talk and talk. It will be lovely.

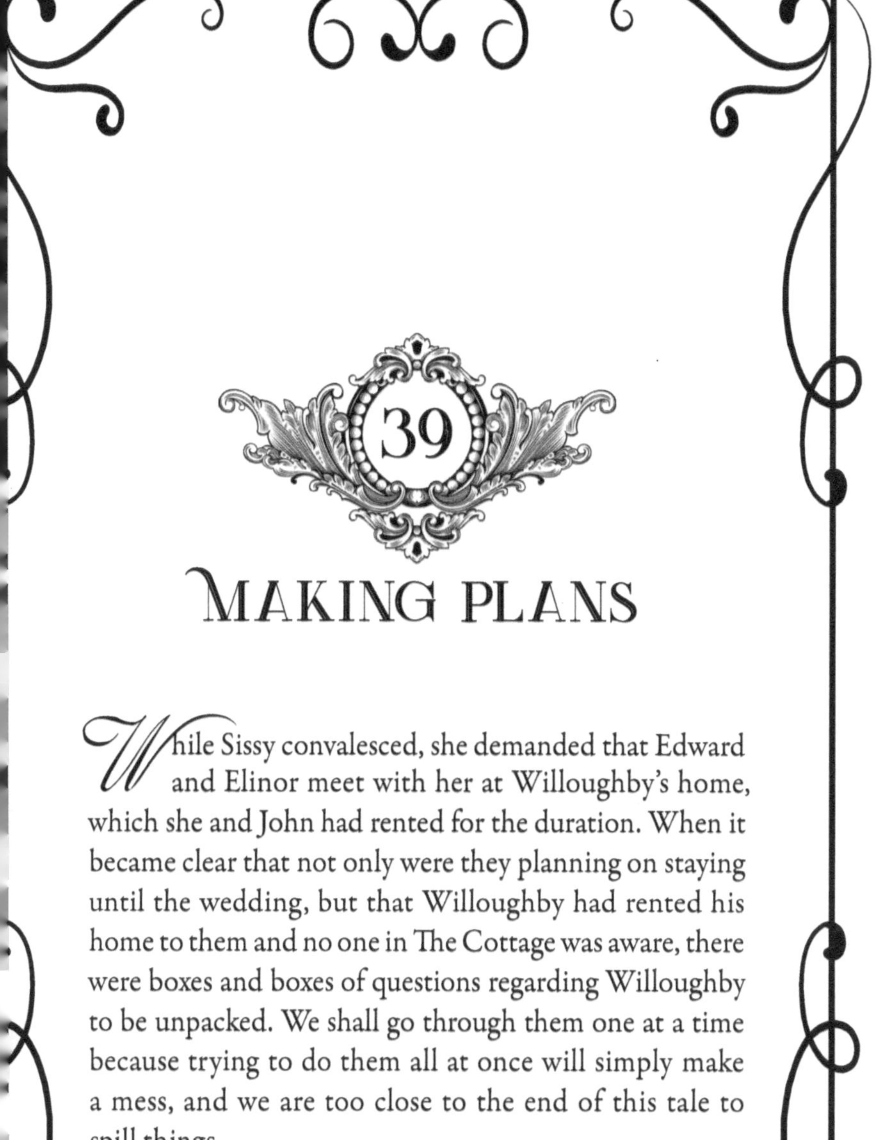

39

MAKING PLANS

While Sissy convalesced, she demanded that Edward and Elinor meet with her at Willoughby's home, which she and John had rented for the duration. When it became clear that not only were they planning on staying until the wedding, but that Willoughby had rented his home to them and no one in The Cottage was aware, there were boxes and boxes of questions regarding Willoughby to be unpacked. We shall go through them one at a time because trying to do them all at once will simply make a mess, and we are too close to the end of this tale to spill things.

We know everyone has burning questions, and some of them may be far too detailed for a story like this, so we shall address the following essential questions and leave the rest for speculation. Where has he been? What has he been telling Marianne? Why would she lock the door if she was expecting him? Did he already know John and Sissy?

Obviously, Willoughby was stepping out on Marianne. She knew he had that in him and gave up her chance to start her film career as a young ingenue to attend university near him. We might see that as a declaration of love and devotion, or we might see it as a sad and pathetic grasp to hold onto a person who isn't worth it. Both could be right. Willoughby himself saw it as an attempt by Marianne to put a leash on him while holding a pillow over his face as he slept. He still mixes his metaphors.

Instead of simply saying this to Marianne, he took up with several women, including the person he ran into at the music festival, Sophia Grey. She found herself in the family way, and so she and Willoughby were off to Europe to figure out what to do. Of course, Marianne didn't know that. He told her he was away on "business" and would be back "soon." She told him to come over whenever he arrived, but in her dramatic, passive-aggressive way, she wanted to punish him by making him knock or at least text from outside her window and have to ask to be let in.

He did not already know John and Sissy, but of course, Sissy knew everything about him as was her way to keep tabs on everything all of them were doing. She didn't want the Dashwood name to be blemished by a bad match. She didn't so much care about Marianne as she did about her last name and so, through her various "contacts" around the south of England, she was aware of Willoughby's escapades and Sophia's condition. Sissy had never met a scruple she couldn't stare down or a law she couldn't bend to her will. It is a travesty that medical professionals are not paid well enough that they could resist the bribe offered by one of Sissy's associates. It was with the money paid by John and Sissy that Sophia and Willoughby could afford their trip to the continent. He had, unsurprisingly, burned through most of his inheritance by gambling and living lavishly. The only thing of value he still owned outright was the property that he rented all too happily to the elder Dashwoods. We wish we could say he won't be back, but he will. It will be just one more time, near our finale.

We know already that Sissy felt the need to "supervise" the wedding. She called it supervising; Elinor called it meddling. Her injuries at least kept her off the property so Lady and Sam could do the actual planning. That part of the story is unnecessary to follow. Lady ran a successful business for years; she planned events every single day, and Sam was a communications expert. They were fine. We'll catch back up to them at the wedding. It is going to be a great day regardless of Sissy's presence. Sure, both Sam and Lady spent the whole day slightly drunk, but everything worked out fine. You'll see.

While those plans were being made, our heroine, fresh off her revelation that her mum actually liked her, which is no small thing for her, did her best to stay out of the wedding plans. She knew what she was wearing. She knew her role. She would show up when told to show up and have her hair and makeup done however Elinor, not Marianne, wished. That was a point of contention that ended when Sam asked Marianne not to be… let's say… difficult. She said it in a way not fitting for this book but in a way fitting for Marianne. Considering that Sam had never, ever said that word to any of her children, it landed with authority and finality. Sam had been saving it for the right occasion.

When she told Lady about it later, they laughed and laughed about the first time their mothers said it to them.

So it was that Maggie found herself alone with Anne Steele who had very little to do as well. They had become quite friendly over the past year. Anne felt terrible about outing Maggie, who could only blame herself really. Curtains close for a reason. She wondered aloud if maybe she'd left them open on purpose. Maybe she'd wanted to be "caught." Anne thought it was possible, but still, she felt bad, so she always put the blame back on herself. It was a whole thing.

They generally talked about pop culture and kept things light and friendly. Anne had even spent some time with Gran and Maggie during movie night at the big house. Gran and Maggie were not in an exclusive movie club. Occasionally one of the boys wandered in and, depending on whose choice it was, stayed or left. Anne was open to new experiences and so she watched steroid-filled rage monsters shooting faceless baddies and German experimental films.

We don't need to spend a lot of time with all of their conversations. They are, like most of our conversations in a day, banal to the outside listener. No one really cares except for those in the conversation. However, there was one in particular that is important enough that we should zoom in and spend time with them. It happened two weeks after what Sam was calling "The Great Beat Down" and one week before the wedding.

There was a lot of commotion at The Cottage that morning as Marianne was not being difficult but was having an issue with her dress. There was a refitting, and she was being dramatic. In the time since Willoughby's disappearance, Marianne hadn't been taking the best care of herself. While he was on the continent, he had gone completely dark, without so much as a false promise. His social media accounts were active, but he only liked memes. He posted nothing original. It was enough for her to know he was alive but not enough to know where he was. She wasn't eating well, she was drinking a bit too much, and she had lost some weight. Her dress no longer fit the way it should, and there was a concern for her health and well-being but also that people would show up for a wedding and end up at a burlesque show. Yes, of course, Sissy knew exactly where he was, but she didn't share that with anyone because, she is, well, difficult.

Thus, Maggie walked up to the big house for breakfast. She arrived before the boys were up and about, so she entered the kitchen without having to do battle and found Anne Steele there, reading on her tablet in much the same way she was on the day of the coming out. Just like that day, and quite a few days in between, Maggie made toast and coffee and joined Anne at the table for breakfast.

"How are things down at The Cottage?" Anne asked.

"Mad," Maggie said through a mouthful of toast. Friends don't have the same manners as they do with strangers.

"Mad angry or mad crazy?"

"Can it be both?"

"Sure."

"Both. Marianne is having a dress catastrophe, and she is trying to be on her best behavior, but the closer we get to the big day, the harder and harder it is for her to not make it about her."

"I totally get it."

"I know." Maggie lifted her mug and Anne clinked her tea cup to it.

They ate and sat and were amiable. "So, totally random question," Anne started.

"Shoot." We've already established that Anne and Maggie would remain friends forever, so it could be that this was the moment that began in earnest.

"College. You're like 16 but going to college. In the States, my dad works for a college, you know, but here, you call that university. My credits here at Exeter will transfer back to my college out west because university, college, is sort of the same thing, for me."

Maggie chewed and listened and nodded. She took a sip of coffee and waited a beat. "Yeah. Is there a question in there?"

"Oh, right, sorry, well, could you go to an American college after you finish up at college, or like wouldn't that work? Like, we go to high school, and some kids dual enroll taking classes at two-year colleges at the same time so they go into college with some credit. Would it be like that for you or would you have to like, take all four years?"

"I've no idea. Uni is generally three years, so I suppose that I could do it in three. I really have no clue. I could have to start over at nursery as well. I'm sure Professor Internet could tell us though. Why do you ask?"

Anne was about to say something that often leads to people taking things the wrong way. However, because Maggie trusted Anne enough to chew like a cow in front of her, she won't take it the wrong way. It will be fine. Better than fine actually. It will be great. Anne began, "Well, and don't take this the wrong way, but, um, you and your family sort of live here for free, right? Like, you don't pay rent, and you don't, um, have, a lot of, money?" She ended it with a question mark, and all those commas are intentional. She was nervous about the wrong way thing even though she told Maggie not to take it that way. If only she'd paid attention to the subtle cues as we did. Still, Anne can be forgiven. Asking about money isn't done in polite society. Impolite society is lousy with people asking about how much people make and how much they paid for a car and what their house payment is. To prove the point, Willoughby asked how much the Range Rover was worth while Edward didn't ask or even think about it.

Maggie didn't take the question the wrong way at all. She wasn't remotely embarrassed about her situation. She knew that everything she had in her life was possible out of the charity of the Middleton family and that if Sissy were not such a villainous monster, she would be living at Norland and going to an independent college next year with no friends in front of whom she felt comfortable enough to eat and talk to at the same time. She wouldn't have Gran, or the boys, or have been destroyed by Polly, or kissed anyone, or wore ties, or dressed like farm animals, or had a Vespa, or been thankful for all of it. All of that was there, racing through her head as she thought of a witty response, but she ended up just saying, "That's the long and short of it." It wasn't a saying most girls her age would utter, but she picked up on a lot of Gran's idioms as people do when they are around others a lot.

Anne nodded, knowing that she already knew the answer, but she wanted to find a way to actually share the next bit of information with some context. She didn't want to just blurt it out without preamble or explanation. "Well, okay, at my dad's college, I mean, not his college, he doesn't own it, but you know, where he works, there is this thing that they do for smart kids who are not well off. It's called the Mansfield Gift. Every year, five people from the pool of applicants from all around the world win The Gift, and they are given a full tuition scholarship. They have to pay room and board, which isn't cheap, but you know in America, room and board is pretty much the same every-where. If your school is a public university with low tuition or if you are a private school where a kidney transplant is cheaper than tuition, room and board is roughly the same."

"So, it's like Wonka but for Uni?"

Anne snorted. "Sort of. There is a lot more to it. You can't just find one and Veruca and Mike would never be in the running. I mean, those kids totally go to Mansfield. If you don't have a record and your parents can afford the tuition, you can go. It is easy to get in but hard to finish. Mike would find a way to pass, but Veruca would be out on her ear in a year."

"Daddy couldn't do her work for her?"

"Exactly. It is tough but prestigious. A degree from there opens doors, and Gift winners in particular are big deals, and most of them are super successful. Not like world-famous, although some of them are, it's just, they work so hard and the teachers are the best of the best, and the classes are small, so they get all this expert instruction. Like, the school where I go uses a book my dad wrote. My dad doesn't use a book in his courses because, you know, he's there."

"Why didn't you go there again?"

"Dad didn't want us to. He wanted us to go our own way and I get it. I mean, plus, I know all those teachers, so I can call them and get help. Lucy and I were like unofficial mascots. Dad was unique. Single dad with two daughters doing it on his own. The community is pretty tight. People stepped up. Dr. Bennet in particular. She's the president. She's like my spirit animal, but Dad and I agreed I would try something else, you know?"

Maggie nodded. "I'm the girl who wears ties."

"Right." Anne nodded. "Anyway, so with that in mind, that doing something different is good and going your own way is best, I thought, maybe, you could, you know, apply for The Gift whenever the time is right. Whatever Professor Internet or Edward or Gran, whoever knows that stuff says. I just think, well," she paused and considered the exact right words, nodding when they came to her, "you are not the person you could totally be, and I worry that, if you stay here, even with Gran, who so loves you, and the boys, who worship you, and Lady and Middy, who would give you the keys to the kingdom if you only asked, that maybe you'll never have the chance to find out who Margaret Dashwood could be. Like, Maggie is awesome, but maybe, Margaret is in there, or Mags or maybe even Peggy is trying to get out, and the only way she can get out is if you, um, leave?"

You will not be surprised to discover that Maggie, who would never, ever, ever, never in a billion years go by Peggy, regardless of the lovely sentiment, thank you very much, had, after that heartfelt speech, tears streaking down her face. She was nodding without even knowing she was doing it and licking her top lip and sniffing.

Anne smiled. Maggie smiled. They both said, "Okay" at the same time and got down to the business of making plans.

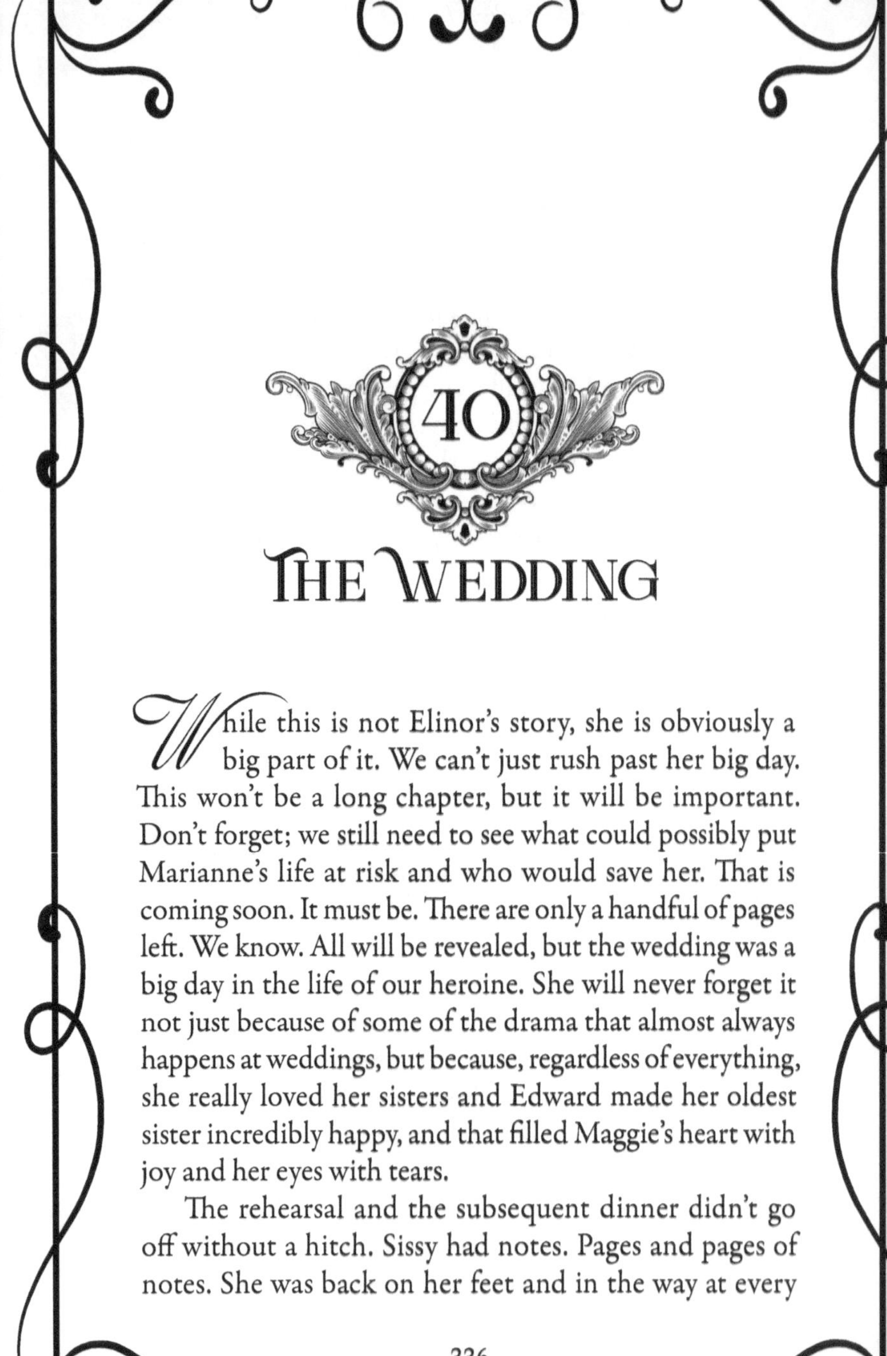

40

THE WEDDING

While this is not Elinor's story, she is obviously a big part of it. We can't just rush past her big day. This won't be a long chapter, but it will be important. Don't forget; we still need to see what could possibly put Marianne's life at risk and who would save her. That is coming soon. It must be. There are only a handful of pages left. We know. All will be revealed, but the wedding was a big day in the life of our heroine. She will never forget it not just because of some of the drama that almost always happens at weddings, but because, regardless of everything, she really loved her sisters and Edward made her oldest sister incredibly happy, and that filled Maggie's heart with joy and her eyes with tears.

The rehearsal and the subsequent dinner didn't go off without a hitch. Sissy had notes. Pages and pages of notes. She was back on her feet and in the way at every turn. Edward, while not proud of himself, as he was and is a feminist, knew that his sister thought that word was dirty, leaned into her bizarre take on gender roles, and claimed that there was nothing he could do. Weddings are, historically, all about the bride. He was only required to show up and say, "I will or I do," depending on whatever the officiant told him to say.

Sissy thought back to her own wedding day and the fact that, besides making promises to his father that he didn't keep, John did that very thing. He stood, smiled, said "I do," and gave her a chaste kiss. As much as she wanted to argue, she privately swore, vented, and vowed revenge while publicly she complained loudly and essentially heckled the entire run-through in a loud, fake stage whisper.

During the dinner, she discovered that her pain medication and copious amounts of wine didn't mix. If someone from her own tabloid had been present, she would have been front page news and a meme within minutes. Of course, there was a very strict policy against covering the Dashwoods in any way that was remotely unflattering, and thus, it went unreported until now. It was only because of Edward that Sam didn't ask Maggie to give her another kicking. Her being a minor and all would have kept her from being prosecuted. Maggie would have happily obliged, but again, Sissy Dashwood was a permanent fixture in their lives no matter what. There was no reason to make her a bigger enemy than she already was. Plus, they loved Edward and didn't want to make his life harder.

Eventually, even Robbie thought his big sister had had enough so he and Lucy lured her back to Willoughby's by offering to stay there with her and listen to her complain all night long. Once she was gone, the party relaxed. Elinor and Edward gave out their gifts to the bridal party. Maggie's gift was a tie with the Dashwood crest on it. She loved it so much that she wore it the next day, which, is what they hoped she would do when they picked it out for her.

Willoughby, who was still Marianne's plus one, surprised no one by not showing up. The ratio of disappointment for Marianne and relief for everyone else was equal. It wasn't her weekend and his absence did nothing to dissuade her from that. Of course, it did not help matters either, but his vacant seat sat silently, and Marianne couldn't question it.

While Elinor held no antiquated beliefs about seeing the bride before the wedding, she and Edward leaned into the tradition to keep Sissy at bay, so they had no choice but to sleep their final night as an unmarried couple in separate beds. He retired to Willoughby's and Elinor sat up with her sisters, trying to have one final day of her childhood, even though most would argue that Elinor Dashwood was never a child; she'd been born and turned 30 the next day.

They opted to have the wedding early in the day so that the reception could take place during lunch. There were five young children there and keeping them fed and well-regulated was, while not top of mind, part of the conversation when Lady and Sam did the planning. Elinor and Edward had no objections to saying "I do" at 11 in the morning as opposed to 2 in the afternoon. They would've eloped if they thought Sissy wouldn't have found a way to have it annulled.

The wedding itself was brief and beautiful. There was a bit of last-minute drama when Marianne insisted that she walk down the aisle with Brandon instead of Robbie. She and he had, out of respect for the happy couple, been cordial and distant. Well, he had been distant and cordial. She spent a lot of time staring at him while sulking and looking away quickly when he turned his head her way. No one could blame her. He looked good on a normal day, but he was one of those men for whom a suit changes the way he sees himself, and he projected that into the room. He stood taller and more confidently in a suit. If a stranger walked into a room and Brandon was in a suit, that person would walk up to him to ask directions because he just seemed to be in control of everything. He learned from watching his mum. She stood much differently in her dress uniform than she did in her flight gear.

It was hard enough for Marianne to ignore him when he was wearing a regular suit, but when he walked into the staging area in his tuxedo, he caught everyone's attention. No one is supposed to upstage the bride on her wedding day, and Brandon wouldn't ever consider it, but had a modeling executive been present, he would have been offered a job on the spot. Maggie jokingly wolf-whistled at him, forcing Marianne to look over at the door, and her knees actually buckled, and she plopped onto the nearest chair. Regret can manifest itself in lots of ways. Sometimes it makes our faces flush, or gives us butterflies in the stomach, or makes us physically ill, or in the case of Marianne Dashwood, it made her shaky on her legs like a fawn. Of course, when one has a bum leg anyway, that can be dangerous. She didn't think she could walk behind him and not want to touch him.

"Oi!" She didn't bother to whisper-shout at Maggie.

Maggie who, being used to quickly turning her head when hearing that particular exclamation come from one of the other women in her family, turned to face her sister with an annoyed face, ready to do battle only to see something she'd never seen on Marianne's face before because if you recall, Maggie was upstairs in her attic room when Marianne came in that fateful day that set this tale in motion; terror. Her scowl became concern, and Maggie skittered over to Marianne. "What? Are you feeling faint? I knew you didn't eat enough breakfast." She reached into the inside pocket of her jacket and pulled out a granola bar she was saving to eat herself just before the show got started. She didn't want a growling tummy to disrupt the ceremony. It was at elevenses after all.

Marianne swatted it away, and being so distraught, she didn't even bother to make a crack about bringing snack food to a wedding. "We have to switch."

Maggie couldn't think of anything they could switch, so her brain threw her a lifeline. "I can't fit in that dress."

"No," Marianne hissed. "Not that, you idiot. I can't..." she interrupted herself and looked over at Brandon.

Maggie followed Marianne's eyes. "You can't what?"

"I can't... I made a mistake." She looked directly at her little sister, her eyes wide and tear-filled, and hoped that regardless of what they'd said to each other or done to each other over the years, there would be something there, some kind of bond that coursed through their genetic code that allowed her to convey everything without any more words.

Maggie felt herself nodding before she knew she was doing it. "Yeah. Okay." She resisted the urge to say all the things she wanted to say about the colossal mistake and bad choices she'd made over the past few years. Instead, she wiped her sister's cheek and went to get their mum.

Whispers quickly spread through the staging room as the news spread. While Sam was explaining to Elinor,

Maggie grabbed Brandon by the hand and led him over to Marianne so they could sit and talk in hushed tones. There was no time right then for Marianne and Brandon to have a private moment, which would happen much later that night, and Marianne would explain that it wasn't just how amazing he looked in his tux, but how amazing he'd been the whole week leading up to the event and in the past years and what a good friend he was to Edward and Elinor without making it weird for them, and if there was ever a chance he'd forgive her and give her another chance, she would love that. Brandon, who'd gone on plenty of dates in the years since he and Marianne didn't work out, had never really gotten over her even though their time together was short. Some torches burn bright and strong regardless of reason or bad weather.

The wedding was beautiful. Sissy didn't object when given the chance. The reception in the big house ballroom, because of course it had a ballroom, was big fun. Maggie's speech was funny and lovely. Marianne's was not safe for work, and the boys had to be ushered out for a few minutes before she started. Brandon's was heartfelt, and while it was about the happy couple, whom he considered his closest friends, one could, if one listened closely, hear a promise to Marianne in there too. Robbie, who tried to write a funny, charming, or dirty speech, failed miserably and just stood and raised a glass to his big brother, whom he wished he could be more like. Tears flowed like champagne at a wedding.

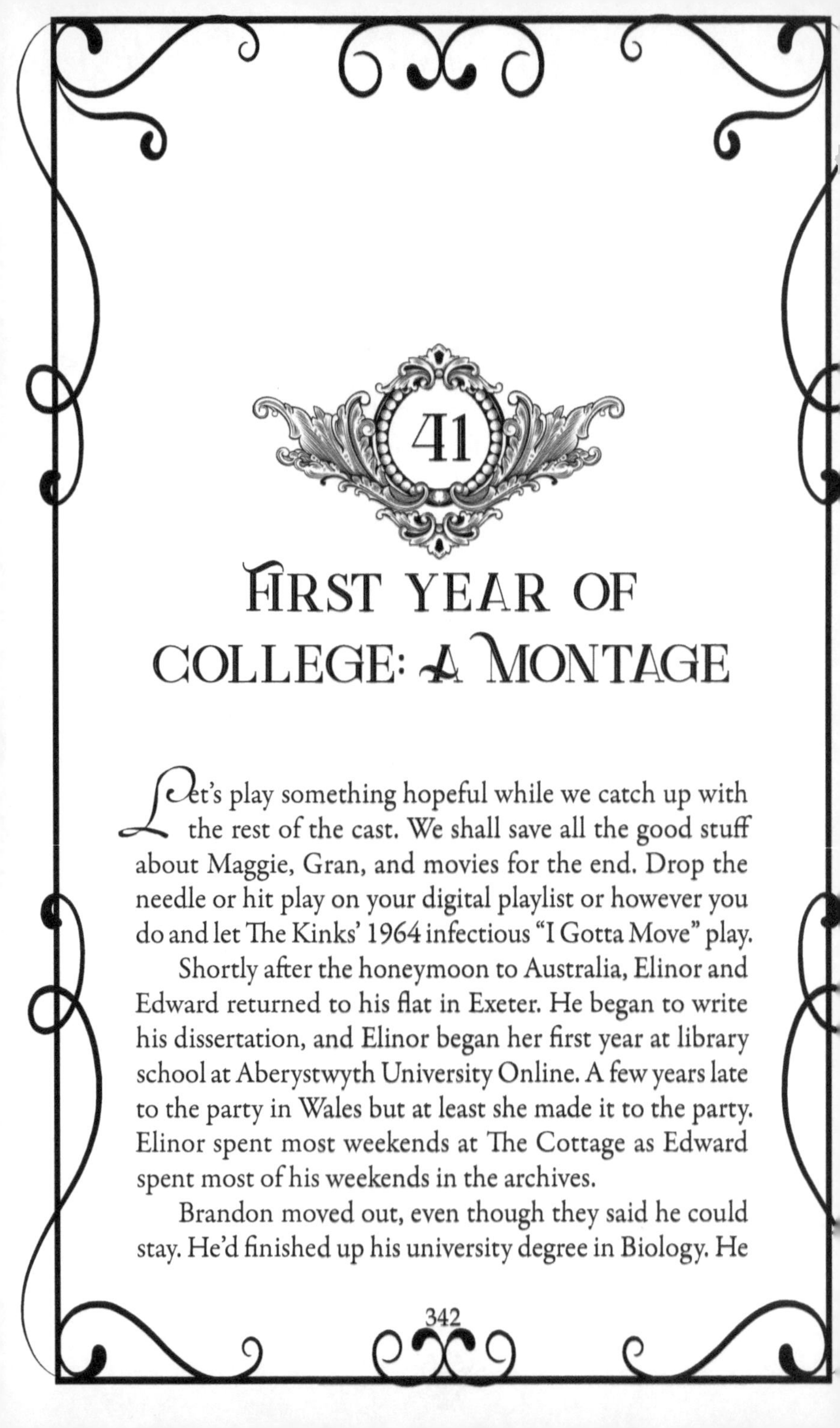

41

FIRST YEAR OF COLLEGE: A MONTAGE

Let's play something hopeful while we catch up with the rest of the cast. We shall save all the good stuff about Maggie, Gran, and movies for the end. Drop the needle or hit play on your digital playlist or however you do and let The Kinks' 1964 infectious "I Gotta Move" play.

Shortly after the honeymoon to Australia, Elinor and Edward returned to his flat in Exeter. He began to write his dissertation, and Elinor began her first year at library school at Aberystwyth University Online. A few years late to the party in Wales but at least she made it to the party. Elinor spent most weekends at The Cottage as Edward spent most of his weekends in the archives.

Brandon moved out, even though they said he could stay. He'd finished up his university degree in Biology. He asked Middy and Lady if he could work full-time at Barton Park while he decided if he wanted to pursue veterinary science or animal behavior. He wanted to take a year off. They were thrilled to have a biologist on staff. He planned to rent a small house of his own in the village, but they put him in the Yellow Room. Like Juliet before him, he didn't go mad.

Anne Steele moved back to America to finish her final year of her undergraduate degree. She and Maggie kept in touch using What's App and other social media. She won't appear physically in this tale again, but just know, her presence isn't gone. Think of her not so much as Maggie's Jiminy Cricket, as that is Gran, but more of her Blue Fairy.

Similarly, Lucy and Robbie exit, stage left if we look at a map of the world with the UK in the center, as they decided to spend a year in America too. They began by visiting Dr. Steele in Mansfield as he had yet to meet his son-in-law in person. They used some of the "traveling money" Sissy gave them, which was the equivalent of a year's salary for many a reader, to see the sights in America, visit Anne out west, and ultimately end in Cleveland, where they stayed. Sissy made him "Senior American Correspondent" and paid him to go to parties where rich and famous people were so he could get all the dirt for one of her American tabloids. The jet-setters had no idea that the call was coming from inside the house because, once in a while, Sissy would scandalize her brother and sister-in-law on the back pages of her publications. Not enough to make any noise but enough to give them plausible deniability. Lucy just liked going to parties. She became a successful social media influencer.

Tom, Charlie, and Jamie, no longer Tractor Baby Jr. because there was no chance Charlie would ever call him that no matter how much she loved her nephews, were back in Cleveland as well. Jamie, a dual citizen just as his mother planned, would eventually make his way back to the UK for some time with Gran because, well, everyone needs time with Gran. Charlie settled into a busy life as a stay-at-home parent who was incredibly involved in little Jamie's life. She would eventually become a pillar in the community, a school board member, and educational reformer. Not every kid learns the same way, and she was determined that they all got a fair shot. Cleveland was rocked.

Sam and Lady kept at their work and were at the point where Barton Park needed to expand, or they were going to have to dial it back. They most assuredly were not going to dial it back. It was abundantly clear by that point that if the right offer were made, Willoughby's place could be procured and not only could they have some new animals, they could, as was Lady's big plan from the beginning when she sent Maggie to spy on him all those years ago, turn Barton Park into a residential park big enough and important enough that Jimmy might want to move back from Paris to don the costumes again. Calls were placed. A lowball offer was made and accepted within hours. Willoughby will make one final appearance when he comes to sign the papers.

Marianne Dashwood couldn't let being at university hold her back from stardom. She did decide to finish up her degree at Exeter, but she managed to land an agent who was booking her in small roles that she could shoot in a day or two. She had several speaking roles on TV shows.

She shined in a period drama where she played the pleasant but clueless visiting cousin from America. Her accent was impeccable. She did a few Danish commercials as her agent didn't want British folks to think of her as "that girl in that commercial." As the Kinks fade out and remind us that the Davies brothers have gotta move, over and over, we do a slow fade on Marianne and Brandon leaning in to kiss. They spent a lot of time together and were, as Gran would say, "an item."

As we fade back in, we can hear the grooves crack and pop as The Jam's 1977 jam, "Art School" fades in. This song is the perfect song for this part of the montage. It is two minutes long and the lyrics really capture exactly what Maggie feels for this first year of college. Go and listen. Go. We'll be here.

Back now? It is so good, isn't it? Let's listen again, shall we? Okay. Hit play and let those four chords reverb out, and we hear the count in followed by that snare drum drop, and we see Maggie parking Prince in the student lot on her first day of college. Under her purple jacket, she has on a black, button-down, untucked shirt, and a purple tie in a double Windsor, fat at the neck, pulled up tight. She has a tie pin in the shape of Prince's symbol when he was The Artist Formerly Known as Prince, when, and this is true, he wasn't allowed to use his real name because his old record company owned it. His name was Prince. That wasn't a nickname.

Maggie walks up to school, helmet under her arm as the background behind her changes with the days and the seasons. We see her pull open the door to school, and we cut to her at her art table, and we spin around her as her outfits change, and the year goes by. Kids come and go, and like before, none of them stick. She doesn't have anything against them, but she doesn't have anything for them either. They are, as we see in the montage, background extras.

Maggie didn't need permission from them to do anything she wanted to do. She did what she thought was right, and she realized that Anne was absolutely right. School could be what she made it. It didn't have to be snogging and drama. It could be, but it could also be her golden ticket to something bigger. Unlike years past, we see her smile the whole time. Learning about art, not just doing art, but learning about it. She loved being in college not because of anyone else but because it mattered to her. Those final drum crashes happen as we see Maggie pack up her portfolio bag and strap it to her back. We fade out as The Jam wails on the whammy bar, and we see Maggie drive Prince away from school toward home.

It is time once again to join Maggie and Gran watching movies. For reasons about to be apparent, it is appropriate to let everyone's favorite jam band, Phish, accompany this with the manic and frenzied "Dinner and a Movie." Of course, Maggie and Gran still spent plenty of time at the big house in various rooms watching movies together with the Tractor Quartet and even occasionally with Sam, Middy, Lady, or all three. They decided, because Maggie had her own transportation and could get herself to and from after work and after school, that they would meet up once a week to see a movie in the theater, which was something they always loved but could do with more frequency. One week Gran would pick. The next week Maggie would pick. Afterward, they would go out to eat, almost always Gran's treat although sometimes Maggie could get the bill while Gran was in the loo, and they would talk about the film in depth. The dinners and talks were almost always longer than the films they saw. As Phish rattles to an end, in what may be one of their shortest songs, we see Maggie and Gran hug hard and kiss each other on the cheek before Maggie climbed aboard Prince and drove directly into her 17th birthday.

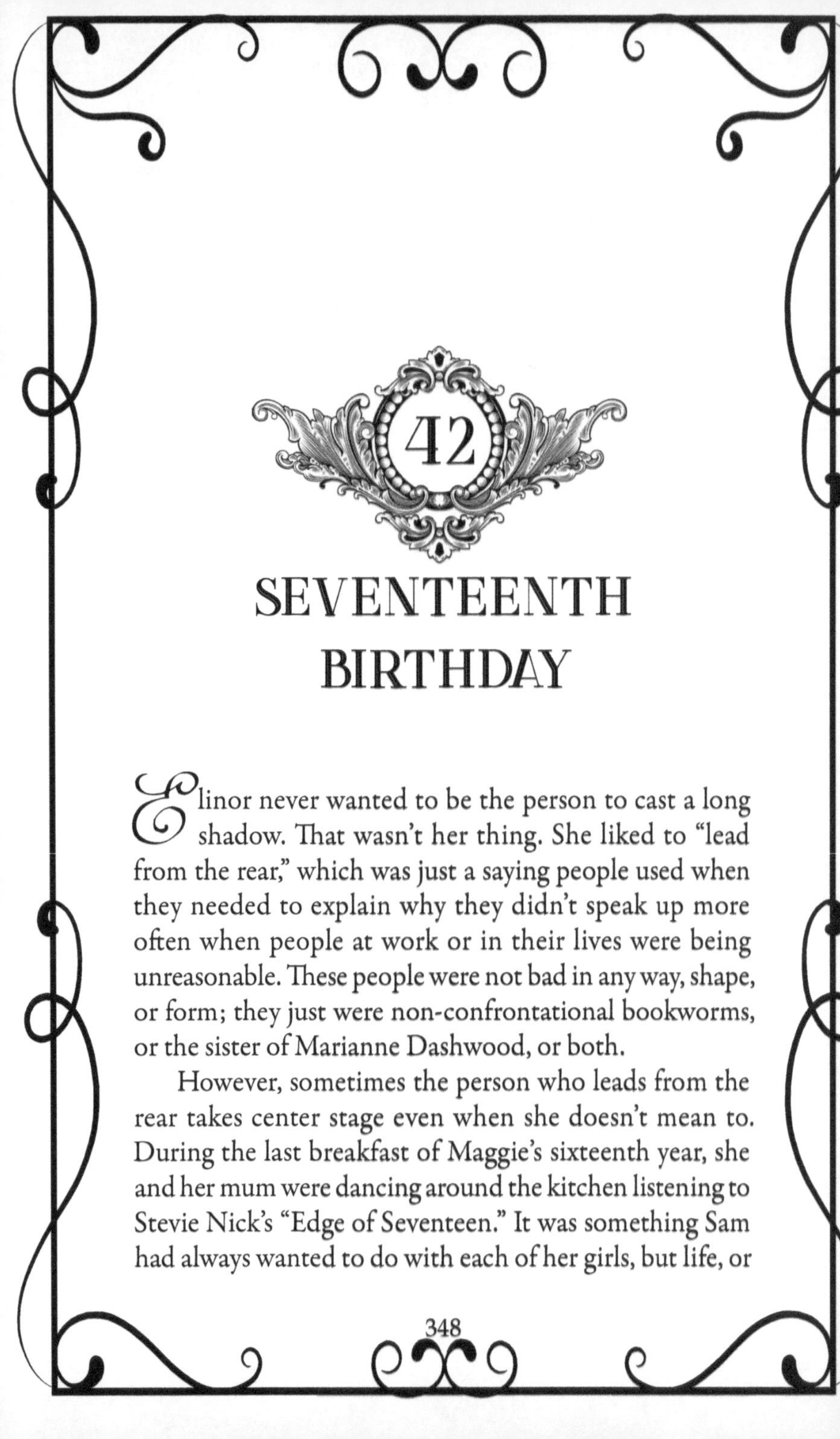

42

SEVENTEENTH
BIRTHDAY

*E*linor never wanted to be the person to cast a long shadow. That wasn't her thing. She liked to "lead from the rear," which was just a saying people used when they needed to explain why they didn't speak up more often when people at work or in their lives were being unreasonable. These people were not bad in any way, shape, or form; they just were non-confrontational bookworms, or the sister of Marianne Dashwood, or both.

However, sometimes the person who leads from the rear takes center stage even when she doesn't mean to. During the last breakfast of Maggie's sixteenth year, she and her mum were dancing around the kitchen listening to Stevie Nick's "Edge of Seventeen." It was something Sam had always wanted to do with each of her girls, but life, or bad attitudes, or both got in the way, and so it was, her last chance to do it fell to Maggie, who was happy to have a memory that was just for her and her mum.

Of course, we all know that the day before Maggie's birthday was a different, sadder anniversary. They knew that they would toast the whiskey and say nice things about Henry later in the day, but they planned to spend five minutes and change, singing into spoons and dancing like banshees. Unfortunately, Elinor, who had stayed the previous evening as she hadn't ever spent that day away from her mum and sisters, was upstairs getting sick in the bathroom and Marianne, who was never confused with someone who was a caretaker, scuttled her way downstairs to get Sam who was ooh, ooh, ooing like the white winged dove.

Marianne shouted from the top of the stairs but was drowned out by the wailing and shrieking coming from the kitchen. She pounded down the stairs, stepped wrong on her bad leg as she hit the final step, twisted her ankle, tweaked her knee, and crashed on the floor with a flood of curses that would have made the filthiest of stand-up comics blush.

Before the final refrain could pour from the speakers, Sam was on her knees in front of Marianne who had forgotten that her older sister was on her knees upstairs resting her sweaty head on the cold toilet seat. By the time it was determined that Marianne could not stand on her own, she remembered and Maggie was dispatched to find out how bad it was.

It was not so epic that a Greek would write a poem about how sick she was, but it is possible that a drug-addled person might write an incoherent poem about it.

Thus, breakfastless and hangry, Maggie found herself holding Elinor's hair as she bent forward over a pail in the back seat of Sam's Range Rover on the way to the A&E. It was, she thought, not a fitting end to her personal calendar year. She had other plans, but little sisters, even when they tower over their big sisters and who could easily pass as a full-grown woman, don't make the plans; they follow the whims of their older siblings for seemingly ever.

Eagle-eyed readers who are good at deduction or are just great guessers will know that this was the day that Elinor Dashwood, for she kept her last name, thank you very much, and the conversation she had with Sissy about it was not something we could reproduce here, discovered that she and her most beloved husband, Edward Ferrars, were going to be parents. She wasn't sick at all. Well, she felt ill, and she had not one but two little parasites inside her, making her feel like garbage with no concern about their future mother at all.

Maggie was tasked to call him but not to spill the tea. For the second time in our tale, Maggie started a conversation with "Everything's fine, but..." Thankfully, they were in Exeter, so he wasn't too far away, and he need not drive like a manic to reach the hospital to finally be told the joyous news. When he heard the news, he cried and hugged Maggie as hard as he possibly could, as he was afraid to hug his wife at all out of fear of harming one or both of his impending children. Maggie, who was, as we've discussed, incredibly sturdy, withstood the hug and gave back better than she received. If he were not sobbing so loudly, everyone could have heard the sounds of his back popping in his sister-in-law's hug. Maggie felt the pops and was convinced at that moment to never, ever become a chiropractor.

Meanwhile, Marianne had not done worse damage to her leg, but unsurprisingly, she never really let it heal properly. The damage was permanent, and while, for the most part, she would be fine and it certainly wouldn't hamper her career, she would have occasional setbacks and that was the first of many. There would be some swelling, and she was released with an explicit promise to either use her chair at home or at least crutches. If there was ever a person who was the human embodiment of crossed fingers behind one's back when one makes a promise, it was Marianne Dashwood. She even crossed her legs when making the promise just out of habit. Even after all her success in the wheelchair and even after becoming quite an expert on the crutches, she still hated them and was determined her hubris could trump medical advice every day. Ask Ahab about hubris and a bum leg.

So it was that when they returned to The Cottage for the celebration of Henry Dashwood, Elinor toasted with cider and Marianne had her shot and a few more. The day turned to night and the celebration continued regarding the soon-to-be Dashwood-Ferrars twins. The Middletons and Gran were summoned, and the party raged well into the night. They so rarely had events at The Cottage as the big house was just part of home to them all, but it seemed appropriate, and there was no way Marianne was getting up the hill without her wheelchair that she was refusing to use.

Pizzas were ordered and celebration won the day. Tractor Boy had his first and last shot of whiskey. He didn't care for it at all. Not everyone needs to be taken behind the woodshed and forced to drink a whole bottle of something until they are sick. He felt pretty terrible immediately and went back to the big house early to brush his tongue and gargle. He was destined to be the designated driver for all time, and he was such a good person that he didn't even mind.

Eventually, a very drunk and sloppy Marianne Dashwood, who had done her best to make the night about herself and her reinjured leg, was carried up to bed by her very sturdy younger sister who wanted to drop her unceremoniously on her rear end but opted to be the bigger woman, plopped her on her bed, and left the room without so much as a backward glance.

By the time Maggie brushed her teeth and hair and felt decent enough to climb the stairs to her bedroom, the clock had already struck pumpkin, and she was no longer at the edge of seventeen but fully into seventeen by a few hours. When she saw that her clock read 3:07, she sighed and sang a few lines from "Birthday Girl" as she dropped her clothes on the floor and slipped into a T-shirt and shorts. She turned on the fan that was pointed at her bed and flopped down on top. She starfished as much as her bed would allow and stared at the ceiling. She switched from "Birthday Girl" to "Whiskey Bottle," which is a bit of a waltz, and while waltzes are made for dancing, when slowed down, they are for slowly rocking oneself to sleep. She didn't have to work in the morning, nor did she have any real plans. There would be cake and ice cream at the big house, and they would likely let her pick a movie. She'd already decided she was going to finally introduce the boys to *Commando*. Schwarzenegger's absurd action flick where he chases some baddies who kidnap his daughter was, for her money, which wasn't a lot, but was a phrase everyone used regardless of how much money one has, the best shot-for-shot 80s action movie of all time. Even Gran, whom she'd forced to watch it, admitted it was well cut and was paced almost perfectly even if the villain was dressed as a low-rent Freddie Mercury.

Just before she drifted off, she realized that she didn't even feel annoyed about missing midnight anymore. Being a teenager had been a big adventure, but she discovered something many adults learn later in life that, regardless of how hard one tries to make one's own birthday special, it is just a day to someone else, and there are many more someone elses in the world who just can't help but have things happen to them. Think of how many unexceptional birthdays happen each day. It is someone's birthday right now. Someone is somewhere having the best or worst or most likely just a so-so birthday. They are all days that end in Y of course. We hope that spending time with Maggie brings some joy, but it could also cut too close to the bone. Birthdays are like another B word that often is associated with families; no, not that one. Birthdays have baggage that we all carry around with us forever and ever.

Of course, we are not totally done with birthdays or baggage here. Maggie will have one more birthday, and Marianne has to deal with some baggage before we end our tale. The birthday will be pretty good, maybe not better than her sixteenth but still really good. That and the opening of and repacking of the baggage will bring this part of Maggie's story to a satisfying close. Hang on tight. We will be there soon. Time is flying.

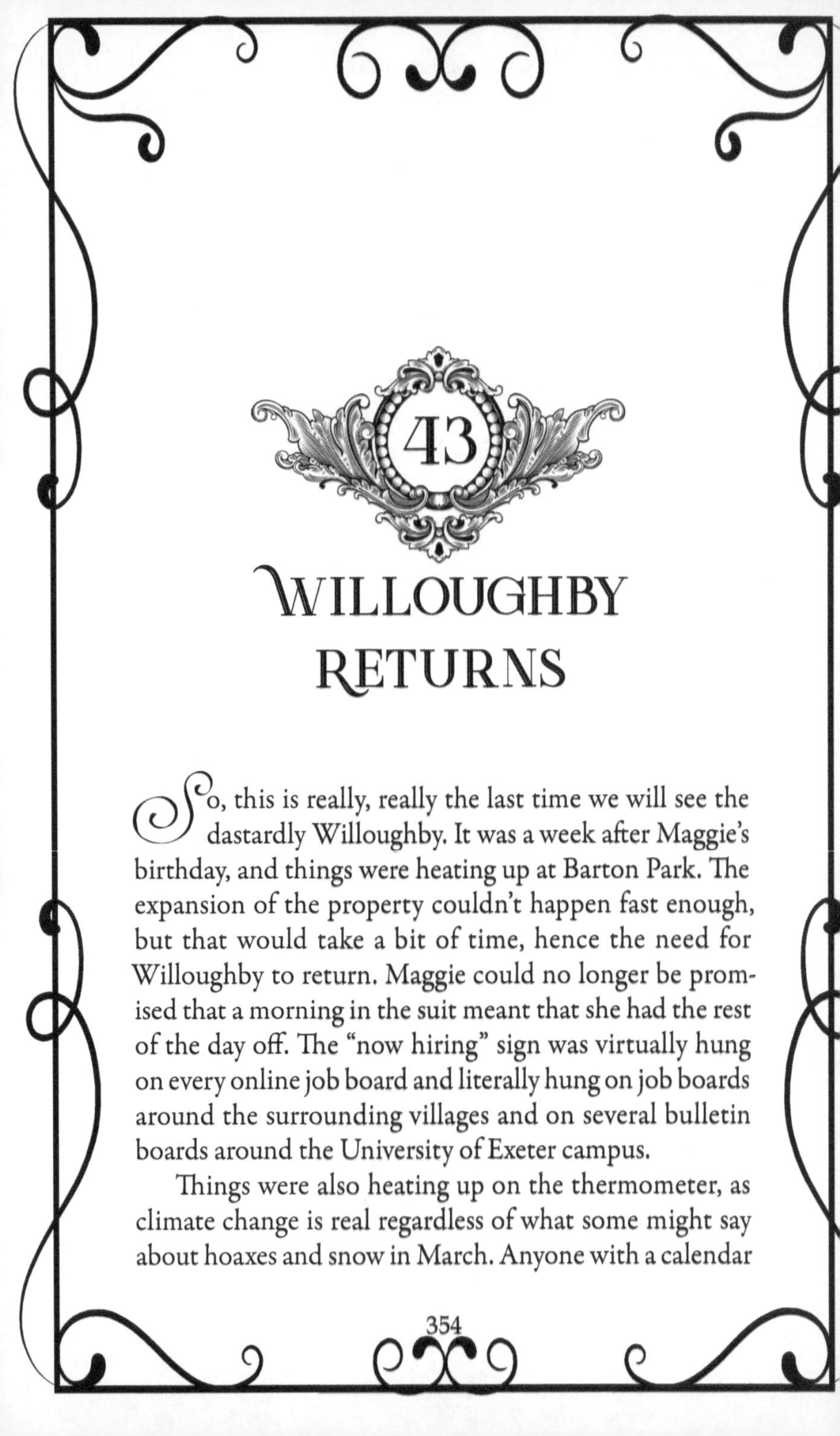

43

WILLOUGHBY RETURNS

So, this is really, really the last time we will see the dastardly Willoughby. It was a week after Maggie's birthday, and things were heating up at Barton Park. The expansion of the property couldn't happen fast enough, but that would take a bit of time, hence the need for Willoughby to return. Maggie could no longer be promised that a morning in the suit meant that she had the rest of the day off. The "now hiring" sign was virtually hung on every online job board and literally hung on job boards around the surrounding villages and on several bulletin boards around the University of Exeter campus.

Things were also heating up on the thermometer, as climate change is real regardless of what some might say about hoaxes and snow in March. Anyone with a calendar knows the vast majority of March is in winter and so snow in March isn't that much of a shock, nor is snow in April or May in some places. When the solstice comes, Mother Nature doesn't notice. Calendars are an arbitrary human invention anyway. Leap year. Really? Still, it is all we have. So, in that particular July in the northern hemisphere in southern England, one week after Maggie's birthday, there was a heat wave that was made worse by a myriad of pop-up storms that didn't cool anything off but did succeed in increasing the humidity by, according to the unofficial barometer of Maggie's hair inside the head of an animal costume, fifty million percent.

So, it was on the day that this chapter title came to fruition, it was hot, wet, and muggy. A trifecta of misery. It will not come as a shock to anyone that Lady made arrangements to meet Willoughby at her solicitor's office and that he failed to show up that morning. He called her solicitor ten minutes after the appointed time to explain that he'd been otherwise detained and that he would be able to come by Barton Park later that evening to sign. Had he simply agreed to E-sign like 99 percent of humans did in situations like this, this entire chapter would be unnecessary, and there would be no drama. We know though that Willoughby is a moth to drama's flame.

The delay wasn't a huge problem other than the waste of time for Lady who dressed in "outside" clothes, as she called anything she wore when she left the property, drove to town, waited around, apologized profusely, collected the documents, and returned to the park without a deed even though there would be no money to change hands that day anyway as everything was being done via wire transfer. Still, the landscape architect was chomping at the bit to get started, and she was waiting in the office annoying Sam when Lady returned empty-handed and grumpy. While Willoughby's property remained empty and the sale was all but completed, she wasn't about to have someone so much as cut the grass without the liability insurance in place. Willoughby could have made a phone call directly to Lady, Sam, or any number of people that morning as he obviously knew long before the 10 minutes after the allotted time that he wasn't going to make it, and yet he made his choice not only to miss the appointment, but to come later in the day so that he had the best chance of seeing, or more likely being seen by, the Dashwoods in general and Marianne in particular.

Sam sent out a message to her daughters through the Dashwood women's group text thread. She told them the situation and asked that they all be together for dinner. Elinor, who had no plans on being at Barton Park that day, called Edward and told him the situation. Marianne was his family too, so he wanted to come as well. They agreed to head over after work for dinner at the big house and a sleepover in The Cottage. Maggie, who didn't see the notice at the time it came through, was dressed like a bunny leading a group of kids around the party area doing the bunny hop. When she was back at The Cottage, freshly cooled down from an icy shower, having been defeated by her hair and stuck it in a hat, even though everyone knows hats retain heat, she saw the message while eating lunch. She was ready to head back to the goat barn which would mean she would need to shower again before dinner. She dropped in some not-so-veiled threats about Willoughby and included some ninja emojis.

Problematically, Marianne didn't respond at all. The read receipt option on some brands of phones is possibly the most passive-aggressive bit of technology in the world. We can assume that it was created so that people knew, on their end, that the message went through. However, most people shut this feature off for privacy and because they don't want the person on the other end to get the wrong idea when they don't, or can't, respond right that second. We are not slaves to our tools regardless of what the tool makers want us to think. There is a small group of people who don't know how to shut this option off. We all know them. We don't worry about it. However, there is a smaller group of people who leave the read receipt on to prove a point. Shocking to no one, Marianne Dashwood was, and still is, a member of that group.

So it was that everyone knew she saw the message and chose not to respond, sending them into panic mode. They all started sending her messages to the group and privately. All of them were read but lacked a response. Sam, being a woman of a certain age, picked up the phone for its intended purpose and called her middle child. The call went to a voicemail that had never been set up as Marianne was a woman of a certain age. It only rang twice which meant it had been declined. Sam, worried and distracted, had to scrap several of the edits she was making on an upcoming commercial spot. Eventually, Lady sent her home.

Elinor, who was still working in the library, was supposed to be shelf reading, one of her favorite activities. It essentially involved wandering the shelves and making sure things were where they belonged. There is never a time when someone shelf reads and finds everything is where it is supposed to be. Even people who love the library do the wrong thing and put items back on the shelves after they are done looking at them instead of putting them on the reshelving cart where they belong. We saw Maggie do it early on. After an hour of finding no mistakes, Elinor swapped with someone on a desk where she could do less damage. She instructed the person to go back over the area she had just covered. She may be distracted, but she wasn't irresponsible. Let's not get crazy here.

Maggie, who was doing much lower-stakes work shoveling goat waste, still lost her focus and got butted in the ribs by an antagonistic goat she'd named Gruber. Normally, he would make a run at her, and she'd skip out of the way. If goat-dodging ever became a replacement for bullfighting, and regardless of what Hemingway said, bullfighting is barbaric and should absolutely be replaced by goat-dodging, Maggie could have been the first champion of the sport. Sometimes, though, a champion is off her game, and when it is woman versus beast, the beast wins and that day, thanks to Willoughby, the beast was victorious, and Maggie needed to wear an ice pack for a few hours.

At the appointed hour for dinner, the beleaguered Dashwoods gathered at the big house. Brandon, who'd been working in the horse barn all day, and who never took his phone with him when doing fieldwork with the big animals because a distraction for him could mean much worse than just a butt in the ribs, was brought up to speed. Jealousy is a green-eyed monster, and luckily, Brandon had deep, brown eyes and was, as we may know by now, almost always the best person in any room he entered. He was concerned but not jealous as Marianne would have certainly been if the situations were reversed, but of course, when the situations were reversed, Brandon simply removed himself from the picture and didn't show up to cause a scene.

Gran and the younger two boys spent most of the day wandering the property trying to find Marianne. It was old school, but not only was Gran old school, but the modern-day options were turning up nothing. Walking through the woods shouting someone's name does give the person, if she is hiding, heads up, but it also allows the seeker an opportunity to find clues, which is just what happened. Marianne had been spotted on more than one occasion walking as fast as her gimpy legs could take her away from them. Gran, armed with two young boys with strong and fast legs, opted not to have them chase her for two reasons. The first was that she didn't want Marianne to try to run away and hurt herself. The second was that she knew that sometimes, young people just need time alone to cry in nature. The Brontë sisters made a career out of it, not a well-paying career, of course. They were women in the 19th century, after all.

The other boys worked all day, but they, too, were concerned when they first arrived in the kitchen to see everyone gathered there, looking worried and murmuring, but when Gran explained that she had a general idea of where Marianne was and that she'd be fine if not a bit sore with a wet bum from sitting on the ground, the boys laughed because Gran said bum, and they were two boys who'd worked all day, and while they loved Marianne, they were starving. So, following their lead, dinner that night was a build-your-own sandwich situation with crisps and veggies, thus nothing was wasted, and should Marianne appear at just that moment, it would've looked like it was; a bunch of nervous eaters unsure of what to do next.

After dinner, Sam, Brandon, Elinor, and Edward went back to The Cottage to see if Marianne had returned, and if she hadn't, they would wait her out there. None of them really wanted to see Willoughby, of course, but being at The Cottage ensured that they wouldn't have to see him at all. Maggie stayed at the big house to help clean up and to spend some time with Gran, who was the only one not acting worried, and she needed that. Middy, who was a two-sandwich man on a good day, was a nervous eater and had three sandwiches and a bag of crisps all to himself.

Shortly after the four of them left, but with enough time for them to reach The Cottage safely, the rain, which had come and gone and come and gone for weeks, finally arrived with a cold front that dropped the temperature precipitously. It parked itself seemingly over Barton Park and the surrounding villages and decided to stay in the way that a good English rain does from time to time. One might describe it as a driving rain, and others might describe it as torrential while people of Gran's generation would say it came down in buckets, which is just what Gran said that day, and everyone would be correct.

It is hard to imagine that staring out of windows watching rain pour down as a worthwhile pastime, but that is just what Middy, Lady, Gran, and Maggie did. The elder two tractor boys retired to their rooms, to do whatever it is teenage and pre-teen boys do. Nothing we wish to discuss in this tale, that is for sure. The younger two headed for the playroom where they played "lost in the woods." It involved a lot of shouting, running from each other, and tussling about as one of them tried to drag the other to safety, which was, of course, what they wished Gran had let them do. While they were boys and Marianne was a woman, they still felt that with their combined strength and her bad leg, they could have gotten her back to the big house.

Maggie and Gran sat shoulder to shoulder on a couch in Gran's room and watched the rain and the sun set behind the rain or seem to. There are some rain clouds that are so thick and dark that they make it feel as though an eclipse is occurring. They sat in anxious silence. Gran held one of Maggie's hands in hers while Maggie held her phone in a death grip with the other. Her phone signal in the big house was just fine, and her battery was strong enough to vibrate her phone with gusto should any message come through, but it didn't stop Maggie from turning it on as loud as possible while flipping it over every 30 seconds just in case, in the painful silence, she and Gran, whose hearing was just fine for a woman half her age, thank you very much, had missed the sound of a message from or about Marianne. Sisters. Like them or despise them, loving them is inevitable.

Maggie turned to Gran, tears in her eyes, and asked the question that she dared not ask. "Is she okay?"

"She's fine, dear."

"Yeah?"

"Yes. She's confused and hurt and longing for something that isn't real. She's likely soaked-to-the-bone and possibly feels a bit of physical pain in her leg that she thinks is the manifestation of the broken heart she felt last year and never had the chance to deal with, no matter how great Brandon is, but..."

"He really is great, isn't he?"

"A catch, no doubt. If I were 40 years younger."

"You're a catch now."

"Thank you, dear. This isn't about me."

"I know, but I wasn't liking where it was going with the pain and the soaked-to-the-bone stuff, so, you gave me an opening."

"I know." Gran turned to face Maggie, who turned to face her. They sat looking at each other on the couch. While fear filled Maggie's eyes, Gran's held calm assurance. "She's going to be fine. Not today. Maybe not tomorrow, but she will be fine. One can't die from a…"

The doorbell rang. It hadn't rung since that day when Charlie showed up. They both leapt to their feet, allowing their hearts to circumvent their brains and think for just a second that it would be Marianne. She wouldn't ring the bell. She knew that the side door was always open. Still, hearts win over brains all the time. Considering that, at that moment, Marianne was outside in the rain pining over a dumb boy whom she knew had never really loved her, they lost their reason for a moment, and they ran to the door.

They skittered into the front hall, one out of breath from the sprint and one out of breath from the fact that she'd sprinted the whole way while holding her breath. Lady and Middy were both there, each standing on either side of a drenched Willoughby. His trousers had mud splattered on them up to the knees, and he was actively dripping everywhere. The phrase *drowned rat* is often used incorrectly to describe a loved one who has been caught in a storm. In this case, the phrase ran through Maggie's mind, and it was the correct usage. Willoughby was a rat, and he looked like he just survived a drowning. Nearly drowned rat is perhaps the most accurate description.

Maggie and Gran stood at the end of the hallway, not far enough that they couldn't hear everything, but not close enough for a casual conversation. Maggie's jaw and fists were clenched. She could have made diamonds if some coal had been handy. Gran kept her hand on Maggie's shoulder trying to reassure her and keep her rooted in place, just in case her rage got the better of her.

While Lady would have happily let him stand there until he dripped dry, she needed him to sign the papers and get out. She demanded he not move from where he stood while she went to get the papers from her office and while Middy went to get some towels so he could dry off just enough not to ruin the legal documents.

Willoughby watched them both walk away, and as they passed Maggie and Gran, he made eye contact with Maggie. Seeing the emotions waft off her, knowing he'd caused it, and knowing one more thing that he knew she'd do anything to discover but knowing there was no way he'd ever tell, he smirked. To one who didn't know him, the smirk was charming. It was an invitation to lean closer to his angelic face and let him share a secret. He used it most days on most people, and it almost always worked.

As soon as she saw the smirk, Gran dropped her hand from Maggie's shoulder and grabbed a handful of the back of Maggie's shirt. Maggie saw it for what it was. Her eyes filled with tears. She ground her teeth, and she felt her legs moving before her brain knew what was happening. Her shirt was pulled tight and jerked her back. Gran grabbed on with her other hand and used Maggie's momentum to spin her away. She let go of her shirt and gave her a loving push in the back. Before Maggie knew what was happening, she was facing the opposite direction and was face-to-face with Middy who was reentering with the towels. He dropped the towels, opened his arms, collected her in them, and held on tight while she howled.

She couldn't hear the chuckle that came from Willoughby's mouth, nor did she hear or see the slap across his face delivered by Gran who had picked up the towels and delivered them and the blow that they all wished they'd delivered. Gran was already a legend, but since Middy was the only one to witness the event, when he told it in the coming years, he embellished it and made her more heroic than she already was.

Being slapped for being a cad by a young woman can build a young rapscallion's mythology, but being slapped by a woman in her late 60s for laughing at a teenage girl after breaking her older sister's heart proves that one isn't a rapscallion at all and that one is a monster.

Lady arrived with a clipboard and papers and found her husband holding her sobbing emotionally adoptive niece while her mother was staring daggers into her uninvited guest while he held one hand to his chest clutching a ball of towels and his other hand to his face, looking down at her in complete shock. She didn't have time to process anything. She turned her mother and hip-checked her away. Willoughby's eyes followed Gran as she walked to her son-in-law and emotionally adoptive granddaughter and hugged a still crying Maggie from the back and was wrapped in Middy's big arms as well. Lady grabbed a towel and shoved the pen in Willoughby's hand. Silently, and still in shocked silence, he looked down at Lady who had the same angry look that he had just seen on her mother's face. All the documents had sticky flags on them, and she pointed and said "sign" over and over. He did so without comment or argument, without ever taking his hand off his face. She pulled open the door and sent him out into the rain hoping the drowning took.

Gran removed herself from the group hug and went and gave one to Lady who seemed to need one too. Sometimes hugs work better than bandages.

Maggie cried the rage out and was sniffling and apologizing to Middy for the mess she'd made on his shirt.

"You've met the boys." He wiped his cheeks. The sympathy cry was his forte. "There is not a mess you could possibly make that is anything like they've done."

She laughed. "Don't make me laugh."

"Promise." He kissed her on top of the head and let her go. "Ice cream?"

"Whiskey now. Ice cream when we find her," Lady said into her mother's shoulder. She stepped away from Gran and pulled her phone out of her back pocket. She tapped a few things. "Told Sam he's gone." Her phone buzzed back in seconds. Lady nodded at the phone. The message had been received. "So," she looked up at her family, "whiskey?"

No one raised any objections, and so the four of them moved in that general direction when Maggie froze. She turned and looked back at the spot where Willoughby was standing. She looked back at the three of them who were silently watching her, waiting to see what she was going to do. She looked back at the mat and back to them. She walked over and saw the mud prints. She squatted down just to make sure she was seeing the right thing.

"Mud," Maggie said as she looked up at the three of them.

"He was covered it in," Lady said.

"Like he walked here." Maggie let her own words bang around in her head. She made eye contact with Gran who nodded. She'd likely always known where she was, but she confirmed Maggie's suspicions. Maggie pulled open the door and was off like a shot.

While Maggie ran through the rain for the spot on the property line where she and Marianne had first met Willoughby, down at The Cottage, Brandon was up in Maggie's room looking out her attic window trying to see out as best he could. He noticed that one of the motion lights on the path between the big house and The Cottage was flickering on and off. He knew Middy well enough to know that he replaced those bulbs every six months if they needed it or not because he didn't want anyone to get hurt on the walk between the houses.

As Maggie approached the spot in the woods, she started screaming her sister's name. Her hair was stuck to her face, and her clothes were stuck to her body. She should have been shivering, but the adrenaline was still coursing through her body. "Marianne!" she shouted and shouted. She sat down on the ground near the hole that started this entire part of the tale and, as is the way with the Dashwoods, found she had more tears. This time, not from rage, but from fear and panic.

Brandon, who put on his work boots and mac, was cautiously walking up the hill and the uneven path toward the flickering light. As he got closer, he heard the sound that reminded him of the times he would visit the military base as a child. Governments are notorious for taking longer to modernize than they should even though they often invent the newest technologies. If he didn't know better, he would have thought someone was sitting in the rain banging away on an old typewriter.

Maggie, feeling the cold seep in as her body started to regulate itself, picked herself up, feebly wiped her face of the tears as it stung with cold rain, and headed toward The Cottage. She felt the heaviness of her clothes and her defeat. She was so sure Marianne would be there. Gran thought it too. Gran was never wrong. She felt as though she failed them all and was sure they would all blame her. Of course, no one would do such a thing, but as we've mentioned, she wouldn't find all of her clarity with her family until adulthood.

Brandon, of course, didn't find a phantom typist, but a very cold, very hurt Marianne Dashwood, who after having her final words with Willoughby in the very spot where she met him, let him walk away before she started for home. The recently re-injured leg, the overuse for the day, and the sudden cold, as she was dressed for the brutal heat, and the lack of food or water all day made her weak. Still, she'd made it almost all the way, and if she'd been thinking clearly, she wouldn't have tried to go down the hill in the dark and the rain. She would have gone to the big house, where she was always welcome. Of course, she wasn't in her right mind at all so she tried to go down the hill, slipped, twisted her already weakened knee, and landed in such a way that she actually, finally, broke her leg. Brandon put her in his mac and used his belt to put a tourniquet just above the protruding bone and carried her slowly and safely down the hill.

When Maggie finally arrived at The Cottage, wet, cold, exhausted, and miserable, she dripped and tracked mud into the kitchen where she found Gran making tea.

Maggie looked at her, confused. She looked back at the door to make sure she was in the right place. She looked back at Gran who had pulled Maggie's chair out and was standing with a big towel waiting for her to sit down so she could cover her with it and tell her everything.

44

THE FUTURE

$\mathcal{De}$ ar Reader, we know this may come as a shock, but this is the penultimate chapter. It may seem sudden as Maggie just turned 17, and so far, she's had pretty eventful summers. Well, the fact is, her 17th summer kicked off with a bang as we've seen, but the rest of it was pretty mundane. The fact is, as we all know, like birthdays, not all summers are magic. As we age, summers are just days when the weather is different than other times of the year; depending on where we live, it might be just the same all year round. She worked. She kissed a few people who made her laugh, but none of them were memorable enough that they are worthy of our time here. This was never a romantic story for our hero. That wasn't her journey as those who've seen her in a previous story already know. She's grown so much, and she still has some growing to do and not much of that growing has to do with romance. Not yet anyway.

That will come to her much later in life, and it will be worth the wait. We've all learned that not all love stories end with kisses. Maggie learned that love and like are not the same thing and that applies to romantic partners as well as those who are actually blood family or found family.

So, we'll catch up with the rest of the cast briefly, and things will get a bit timey-wimey as we look into their futures. Forgive us as we will jump in and out of time, but we promise that we will truly spend the final pages on Maggie as she finished up her 17th year. We've always known it was her story, but as we also know, sometimes our stories are so mixed up with others that we can't tell our own without telling theirs as well. Forward! And then backward.

Marianne made a full but slow recovery. The A&E doctor said that if Brandon hadn't found her when she did, there was a good chance that she could have gone into shock. If she had laid out in the cold and bleeding, the doctors feared that she might not have made it through the night. They kept her in the hospital for three days. When she returned home, Brandon moved down from the big house. Everyone liked having him around, and no one ever said what's his name's name ever again, so we shall not either.

Years later, they would marry and have an adorable girl who also happened to be fearless and brilliant. They named her Henrietta. She wanted to be a pilot like her grandmother. Her father, the large animal behavioralist and her mother, the award-winning actor, told little Henry she could be anything she wanted to be and so she did.

Elinor and Edwards's twins came at Christmastime. They were called Ezra and Emmerson. Edward finally finished his doctorate and began teaching. Elinor finished up her library degree and spent the rest of her life reminding people that working in a library and being a librarian were not the same thing. While she could shush people like the best of them, as her boys could attest, she also reminded people that libraries in the movies and libraries in real life were not the same thing just as she suspected all those years ago when she took her first job at the library in Leeds.

Sam, who had switched to Gran mode halfway through singing "Edge of Seventeen" with Maggie that morning, never came out of it. Of course, because they all had a Gran in their lives, neither she nor Brandon's mother felt comfortable being called Gran out of respect. Still, they both learned a lot about how to gran, if we can use that word as a verb for a moment, from Gran. The twins went on to buy the Just Down the Road village bookshop near Barton Park, where they'd spent all their summers and had the best childhood memories.

Lady, Sam, and Middy turned Barton Park into one of southern England's most visited tourist attractions. The newly added inn was a huge success. While her agent didn't want her to, Marianne Dashwood became the unpaid commercial spokesperson for Barton Park. That didn't hurt in raising awareness. Lady and Middy lived happily ever after all. They spent the majority of their days on the property they loved so much. Sam never moved from The Cottage. She did find love much later with a childless man who had a big heart and a work-from-home job. All the kids and grandkids took to calling him Granddad Marvin as he didn't arrive until after Sam was already a grandmum. He moved into The Cottage and spent a lot of his free time working on the Wi-Fi at the twin's bookshop and drinking tea.

Two of the tractor quartet eventually took over the park. One of them found his true love and moved to Japan. The other, after a brief attempt at becoming a professional wrestler, because the odds were that one of them would try it, moved into stunt work. He and Marianne worked on several films together when she decided to try her hand as an action star. She could hide her leg brace inside cargo trousers. There was one scene where Marianne and he shared the screen when she kicked him through a window as he was on screen as "Henchman #2."

There we have it. Not bad lives for all of them. Now, let's get back to Maggie's 17th year, shall we? We can still do part of it as a montage if that is pleasing, with two final songs. It would be fitting then, to fade into Broken Social Scene's "Anthems for a Seventeen-Year-Old Girl" as we watch her final year at art college. Instead of Maggie remaining in focus while things change around her, the ethereal song would be better paired with fade-ins and fade-outs of Maggie and Gran watching movies, Maggie winning an art contest with only Gran there to see, Maggie dancing in a cow costume, Maggie earning her black belt, Maggie drawing in a field, in the sheep pen, in the horse pen, in the tractor barn, Maggie drawing at a table in the big house while the boys all do their homework, Gran and Lady wash dishes, and Sam sweeps the front porch. She filled her portfolio that year with everything she could think to draw so that not only did she have the pictures when she was done, she had the memories of making the pictures.

Since we are cutting summer short, we can play a song about summer as this book is all about summers, and if this book didn't have the title it did, it could have easily been named for Matt Nathanson's "Gold in the Summertime." It starts with a big 70's disco-pop-inspired hook with Matt and the backup singers singing "Summertime" over and over. Later, he sings about Prince, so this is a great song for our final summer images. We can envision Maggie riding around on her Prince even though, as we know, she does get her driver's license, and she carts the boys around because she loves them, not because she has to. Mundane doesn't mean that there wasn't any fun, but not all fun things are worth documenting.

As the song comes to an end, picture Maggie and Marianne holding one of the twins on each side of Elinor's hospital bed while Sam takes four million pictures that no one will remember her taking. Maggie will sit silently in the corner and draw each of them in their bassinette. Those pictures will hang on Elinor's walls for years and years.

Shortly after the twins were born, Maggie received an email from Anne Steele with a subject line that read "It's Time!" It must be serious for Anne Steele was never found guilty of overusing exclamation points. There was a link in the email, but fear not, it was not spam. Anne would never. Lucy would accidentally, but Anne would never. The link was to an application for The Mansfield Gift.

The body of the email read, "Dear Maggie, the application opens today. Now is the time. Get writing. Love, Anne."

Maggie forwarded the email to Gran and asked if she would be willing to help, and she wanted to know if Gran would keep it a secret. She didn't want to tell her mum or her sisters about this plan. This is not a sudden right turn into a bad YA trope, Dear Reader. Don't fear. We wouldn't do that at this late stage or at all. It was all about expectations. She knew it was a long shot, and if she didn't get in, she didn't want them to know that she'd failed because to her not winning would be a failure when, in fact, plenty of success stories came in sixth out of five places when applying for the Mansfield Gift. She asked because, as we established, while she might drink more whiskey than most girls her age, she rarely got drunk, she almost never drank alone, and she never drove even after just a sip; she was a good, good girl who would never assume that she could demand Gran's help or silence or anything from her even though she knew Gran would say yes as long as Maggie promised to tell Sam about it regardless of the outcome. Maggie agreed to that and to the second promise that Gran asked her to make. More on that in a moment.

So it was that she took Anne's advice, and she started writing. She wrote and wrote and wrote. The essay was, according to the application, the most important thing. If Maggie Dashwood were Ponyboy Curtis, she could simply submit these pages. There are two problems with that. First, that book is written in first person, and, second, the word limit was one hundred thousand fewer words than we've shared here.

She submitted her scores, her letters of recommendation from three of her teachers, and her personal letters of recommendation from Anne and Gran. She used one of Gran's digital cameras to create a digital portfolio of her artwork. She did three interviews. One with a faculty member, a history teacher and Gift Advisor called Dr. Allen. One with the director of admissions. One with a former gift winner who'd gone on to win a MacArthur Genius Grant.

The whole process was arduous, but the waiting after the final interview was the worst part. She waited and tried to focus on school. In America, school ends much sooner than it does in the UK, so she had to spend several more weeks in class, finishing up her course work and having already received conditional offers from several schools around the UK, while she waited for her answer from America. Until she'd gone through the arduous process, she didn't know that she wanted to go to America and attend Mansfield College. It was abstract at first, but after she started to look into it, she wanted it so badly. If she won, she couldn't actually study art right away, but she would have to spend two years taking a rigorous and rigid schedule of liberal arts classes before she could finally, if she wished, major in art. It was the path she wanted to follow.

Two hundred and six years after the awarding of the first Mansfield Gift, five letters embossed with gold lettering are sent out to five addresses across the globe. One to a young woman in Seoul, South Korea. One letter is sent to a young man in Tacoma, Washington. Somewhere in Texarkana, Arkansas, a young man gets a letter. All of these recipients will accept the offer immediately and prepare to matriculate to Mansfield College in the fall, having sufficient funds for room and board already procured.

One letter is sent to a girl, not a young woman, who lives in an unincorporated area in the American Deep South. Her journey to Mansfield College will be tumultuous, but she will get there. She will be very important to Maggie and to all of us. Of course, the final letter, as we've known all along, is sent to Gran's address in Exeter where Maggie said she lived.

It read thusly;

Dear Ms. Dashwood,

On behalf of Mansfield College, it is my honor to present to you one of the five annual Mansfield Gifts. As you know, this gift is the most prestigious honor that can be bestowed on any student at Mansfield College. Every year, thousands of applicants from all around the world compete for one of these five spots. Clearly, your hard work and dedication have been rewarded.

Enclosed are the documents you will need to send back to accept The Gift and begin your registration for Fall Classes.

Congratulations.
Welcome to the Mansfield Family,
Dr. M. Bennet, President

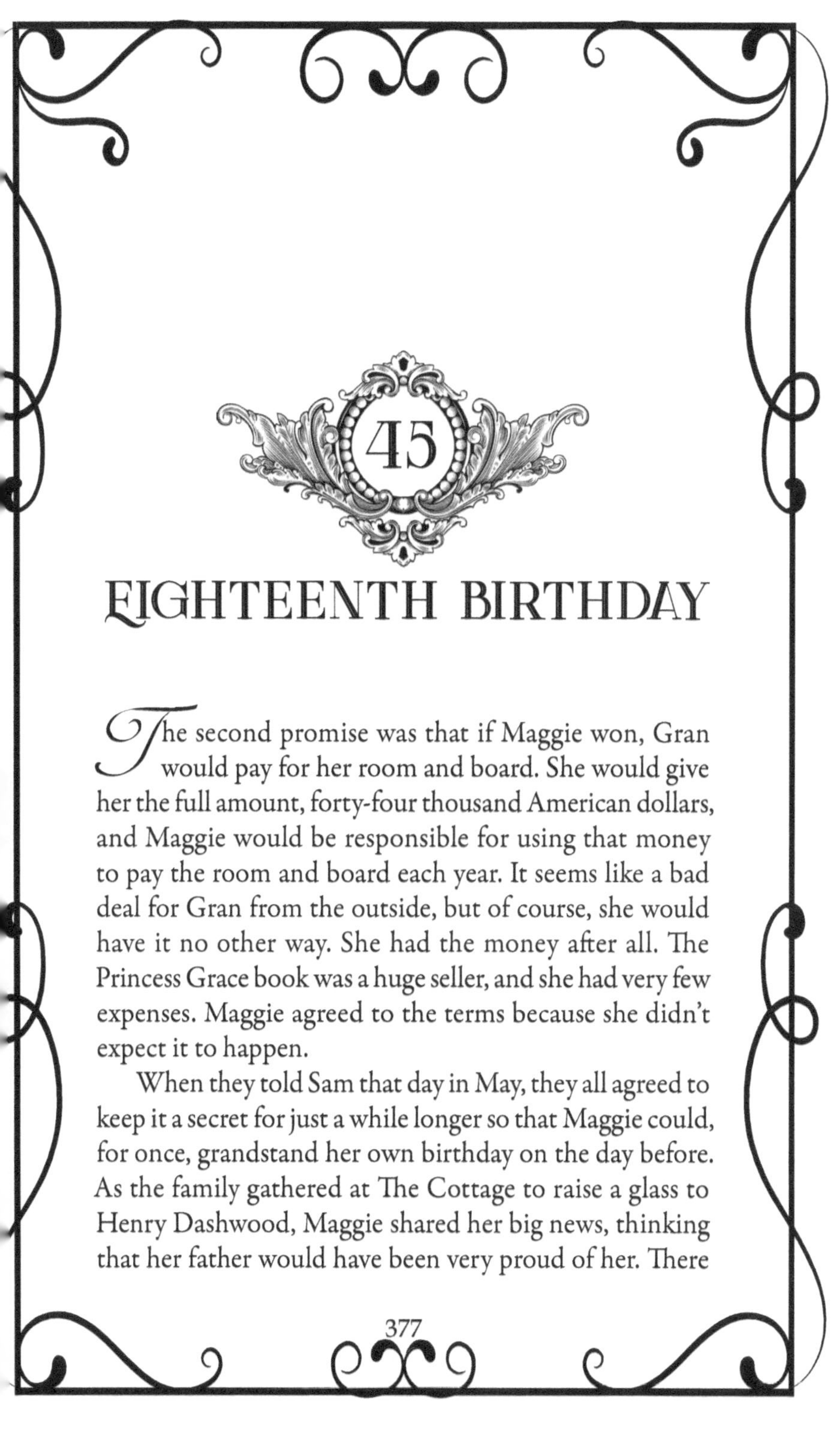

45

EIGHTEENTH BIRTHDAY

The second promise was that if Maggie won, Gran would pay for her room and board. She would give her the full amount, forty-four thousand American dollars, and Maggie would be responsible for using that money to pay the room and board each year. It seems like a bad deal for Gran from the outside, but of course, she would have it no other way. She had the money after all. The Princess Grace book was a huge seller, and she had very few expenses. Maggie agreed to the terms because she didn't expect it to happen.

When they told Sam that day in May, they all agreed to keep it a secret for just a while longer so that Maggie could, for once, grandstand her own birthday on the day before. As the family gathered at The Cottage to raise a glass to Henry Dashwood, Maggie shared her big news, thinking that her father would have been very proud of her. There were tears and elation, and anger and fear, and more tears. We shall leave it to you to decide who did what.

Buzzed and happy, Maggie climbed the stairs to her attic room with enough time for her plan to be enacted without interruptions. She rummaged under her bed and found the folder she knew was there somewhere. She pulled out the picture she started when she was 12. The one she started when she thought her life would be Norland and balls and boring independent schools. She looked at the back of that young girl's head with a messy bun and pencils sticking out like antennae calling to the future. She put her hair down to frame her face, just as she remembered doing five years prior. She didn't remember why she wanted it down like that, but she had, so she paid homage to her wishes.

She couldn't fit into her 12-year-old Frida shirt, so she'd recently ordered a new one as a present for just this occasion. She set her mirror up at the end of her bed and climbed on top of her covers in the best approximation of the picture. She pulled out the small bottle of whiskey she'd brought up, for we said she rarely drank alone, but we didn't say never.

She pressed play and "Birthday Girl" began when the clock struck midnight. She looked at her face in the mirror and raised the bottle to herself. She thought about what was hidden outside the window of that attic room in Norland just outside the drawing and contemplated what she knew was beyond her horizon in a different attic room in a different life. She took another swig, and said a silent word to her father, to her sisters, to her mum, to the Middletons and Steeles, and of course, Gran. She wiped her face as the tears were coming and coming, but she wasn't wracked with sobs. They were cleansing tears. They cleaned out her childhood and prepared her for her future. She set her bottle down. She sketched her young woman's face in the reflection looking back at that 12-year-old.

It didn't take long, and she looked down at the picture of herself and that other Dashwood girl and said what Gran, who was always right, told her all along, "It'll be okay, dear."

NOTES FROM THE AUTHOR

*T*here were so many words I used incorrectly in the early drafts of this book. Many of the words I knew because I read a lot of books. Again, anything that made it through that is wrong is on me, the dumb American.

A&E stands for Accident and Emergency. People go to hospital not the hospital, likely because there isn't just one hospital so the article "the" isn't necessary. The NHS is the National Health Service that is available to anyone in the country at no charge.

In America, pants are long pants. They have adjectives. Outdoor pants. Dress pants. Things like that. In the UK, pants are underwear. At one point, I had Maggie in a blazer and pants, and in another instance, Juliet wiped her hands on her pants. Yikes. Hence, trousers. Also, when asked if "slacks" would be suitable, I was asked what "slacks" were, so… No. Shirts mean shirts that button down. They wear lots of shirts in this book, but if it pulls over, it would just be called a top. A Macintosh, often called a mac, is a raincoat that looks sort of like a trench coat. Like Kleenex or Qtips, the brand has become the generic name.

Snakes and Ladders is Chutes and Ladders. Same game, different names. Words are fun.

Chips are french fries and crisps are potato chips. I knew this, but screwed it up anyway, and thus, they eat crisps the whole time. It is a much easier fix. Fizzy drink is soda or pop or soda pop. Interestingly enough, fizzy pop is also acceptable. There is a whole conversation between Maggie and Junior about the use of "soda" as a word in *Welcome to Mansfield*. I wanted to use this at least once here so that it made a fun connection.

I originally called the front hall a foyer, which it turns out isn't all that common in the UK. Bathrooms are also called the "loo" but not restrooms. I did that at least once in one of the drafts. Duvet is the top blanket on a bed, not just a cover for a comforter, which isn't a word that is used there at all. I had Juliet clean up with a rag. In the UK, they say tea towel or kitchen towel.

So, I did my best to explain the difference in the school system throughout the book generally and more specifically in the conversation with Anne. However, I messed up at first by having Maggie apply for university at the same time she was applying for Mansfield College. Turns out, she would have done that way earlier in the year, and they get conditional acceptances with the idea they still have to do well during at the end of their final year. Kids are not on break from school in the UK. They are on holiday.

I made an allusion to being hungry like a lacrosse player, but that isn't really played much in the UK, and since I already made the reference to rugby because of Middy, I changed it to that.

A lift is an elevator. It makes sense really. We should all call it that. Petrol means gas. Americans sometimes say "fuel," but for the most part, we say "we need gas."

10 Downing Street is where the Prime Minister lives.

Maths vs math. Sport vs sports. This is clarified in the book. Words are fun, huh?

A two-fingered salute in the UK is the same as a one-fingered gesture in the US. We won't get more detailed as this isn't that kind of book.

The Austen Chronicles will return with Universal Truth.

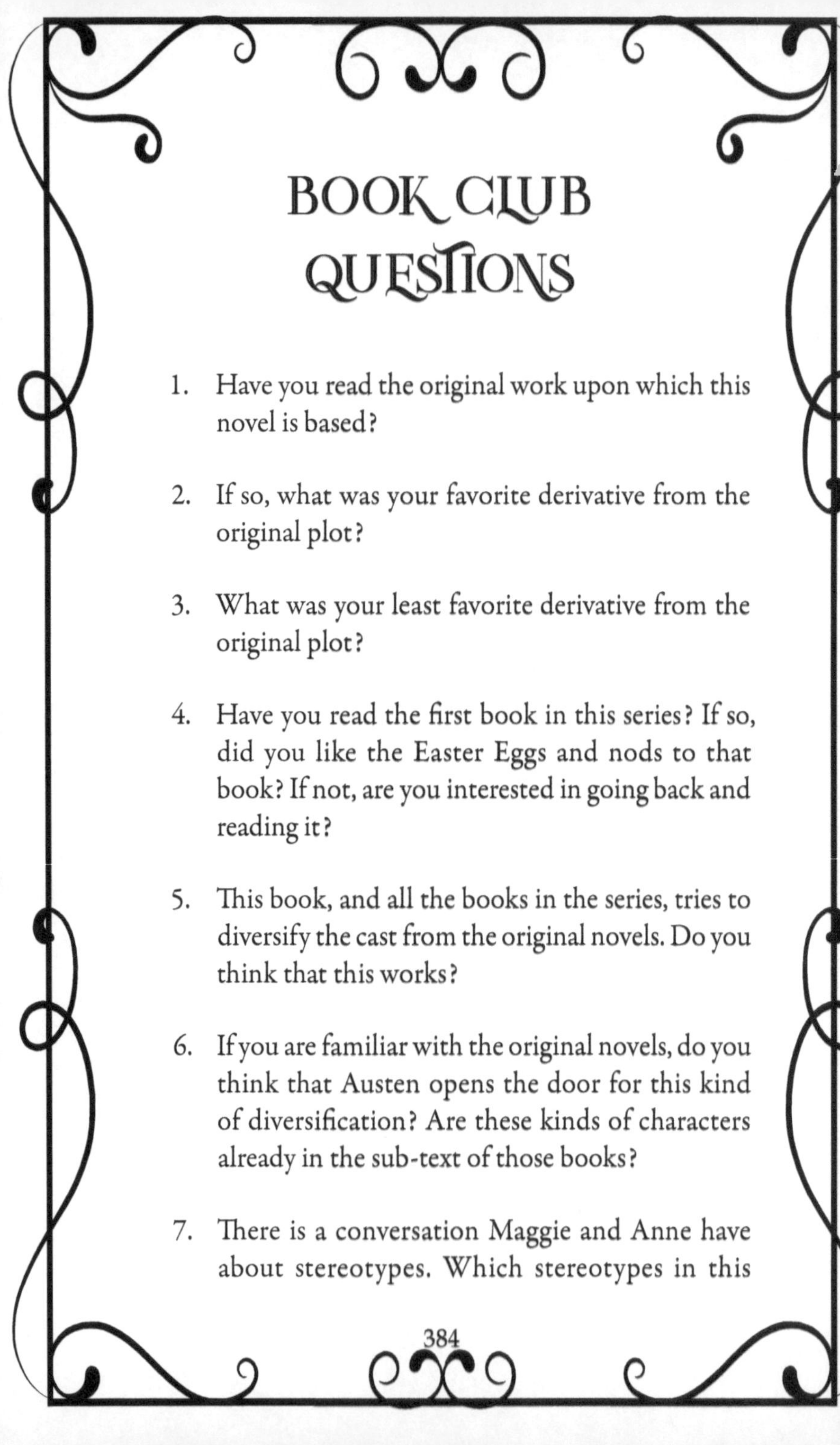

BOOK CLUB QUESTIONS

1. Have you read the original work upon which this novel is based?

2. If so, what was your favorite derivative from the original plot?

3. What was your least favorite derivative from the original plot?

4. Have you read the first book in this series? If so, did you like the Easter Eggs and nods to that book? If not, are you interested in going back and reading it?

5. This book, and all the books in the series, tries to diversify the cast from the original novels. Do you think that this works?

6. If you are familiar with the original novels, do you think that Austen opens the door for this kind of diversification? Are these kinds of characters already in the sub-text of those books?

7. There is a conversation Maggie and Anne have about stereotypes. Which stereotypes in this

book do you think worked? Which ones were subverted?

8. There is a running soundtrack through this book. Did you listen along to the playlist? Did you like the music? Was there something there you never heard before but wished to explore?

9. Who do you think the narrator is?

10. Do you like having the narrator jump in and speak directly to the reader? Why or why not?

11. Maggie and Marianne have an often antagonistic relationship, but there is still love underneath it all. Does this ring true for what you expect out of teenage siblings?

12. Why do you think Maggie didn't ask her mum for clarification after she said, "What will we tell your sisters" instead of "When will we tell your sisters"?

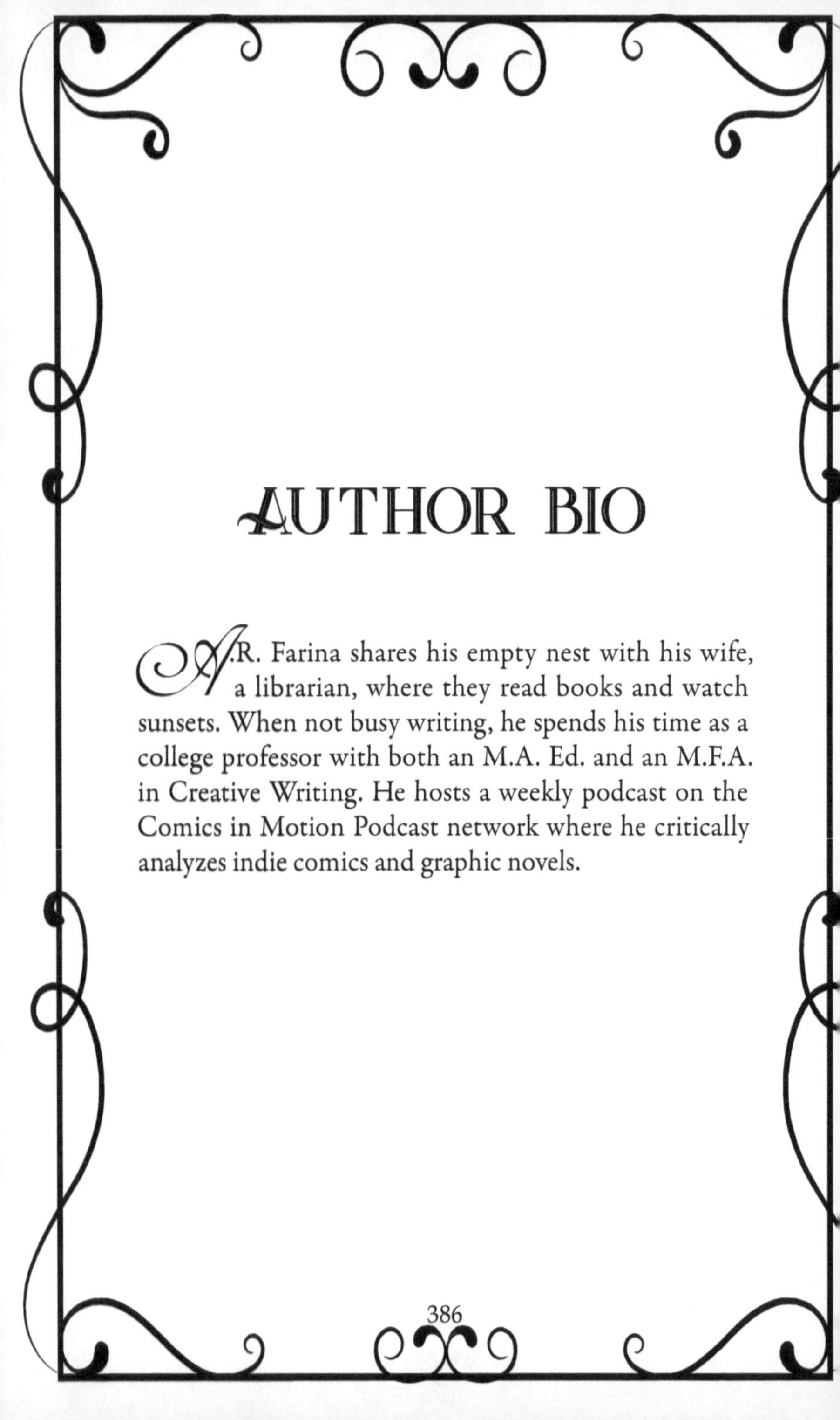

AUTHOR BIO

A.R. Farina shares his empty nest with his wife, a librarian, where they read books and watch sunsets. When not busy writing, he spends his time as a college professor with both an M.A. Ed. and an M.F.A. in Creative Writing. He hosts a weekly podcast on the Comics in Motion Podcast network where he critically analyzes indie comics and graphic novels.

www.ingramcontent.com/pod-product-compliance
Lightning Source LLC
Chambersburg PA
CBHW031834310726

48972CB00005B/1271